Olken Ridge

Bethany Witte-Krantz

Contents

VALDIS
CAPITAL
CITY OF CANN
CANN FOREST
THE INN
HAVN
LLEAVAN

OLKEN RIDGE
FORGARD MOUNTAIN
ISOLD RISHO
SALD FOREST
ARDOUR
HELLOW
CAPITAL
EBBON CITY
EZRIN/JAZ HOUSE
NYRIM
IDAN

God's and Goddess's

Here are all the titles and names of all the Gods and Goddesses. Not all of these beings will appear in this book. It is just a way for you to get a taste of what is to come.

Niamh- Goddess of the Sun

Esmersey- Goddess of the Moon

Their three Children

Athren-God of Seasons

Darach-Goddess of the Nymphs

Darach's and Riand's Children

- Arclavian (First ever Forest Nymph)

- Easian (First ever Water Nymph)

- Gairen (First ever Siren)

Hesper-Goddess of night

Hesper's Children

- Endri God of Vision/Dreaming (Non-binary)

- Runen God of Death

Mabilia- God of the Fated.

Pavati- Goddess of Rivers

Riand- God of the Sea

Arlo- God of the Earth

Translations and History

I used Vulgarlang for all the languages in my book.

Gani is the language of the Brawn'n people. They are the dwarf like creatures that live underground in the root systems of the great Mud Tree. They are adept at masonry. Unfortunately, they have fallen on hard times, forced by the mistreatment of the Ardourians to steal to survive.

"Beme"- nm. threat

"Bepfob"-nf. stay

"Ber"- Help

"Bo"-nf. child (young human being), child (son or daughter of any age): num. one

"Bofwo"- v. can

"Bondo"-adv. why

"Bor"-v. say, tell, confess, mention, instruct, interpret, translate, express

"Bosfe"-v. heal, cure

"Cogco"-adv. tonight

"Cor"-adj. sick, ill, unwell

"Cospen"-Name

"Cot"-prep. of

"De"- v. want, require, lack, choose: pron. you, yours: det. your

"Dedeod" - Leader

"Deo"- the

"Dob"-v. create, invent: det. this: pron. you all, yours (pl): pron. this

"Dognos"- v. let, allow (let), tolerate, enable

"Ef"- The

"Ef"-v. be (exist), be (permanent state): nf. wife

"Efen"- Who

"Ejen De"- Who are you?

"En"- To

"Es"- No

"Ev"-v. get, obtain, possess, acquire

"Fe"-det. any: conj. but

"Fo"- conj. and: det. what: pron. what

"Fob" - Of

"Fon"-det. many

"Jel"- adv. else, otherwise

"Jem"- Father

"Jen"-nf. mother

"Jo"-conj. or, either: det. more

"Joces"- meaning

"Jome"- prep. over

"Le"-num. nine

"Loz"-v. know (a fact), know (be acquainted with)

"Nepfeode"- nf. visitor

"Ner"- Is

"Pegte"-v. insure, assure, guarantee, secure, convince, promise

"Pessel" - Attack

"Rel"-v. should

"Ren"-det. few

"Rowe"- v. rest, relax, nap

"Thojta" - Hello

"Thozle"-adj. only

"Vec"- They, them, theirs (feminine)

"Vel" adv. about

"Vowbe"-nm. dinner

"Vowgoz"-adj. nice

"We"- my

"Websol"-nnt. hour, time

"Wo"- v. be (age): prep. through: pron. we, us, ours: det. our

"wotnon"- v. must, have to

"Ze"-prep. for (in favor of): v. take, receive, arrest, grab, accept, adopt, gain, gather, accumulate: pron. she, her, hers

"Zoc"- adv. not: nm. prison, jail

"Zol"- has

"Zos"- Have

Olken Ridge

Tyanran is the language of the Olken Ridge inhabitants. The Olken residents have used isolation as the driving force for advancements in their society.

"Twa"- *n.* moment, *pron.* I, me, mine

"Twaru"- *v.* am (he,she i am)

"Dyi"- *v.* have, take, bring, arrest, accept, book, drive, must, have to, own, get, possess, lead, fetch, deliver, carry, pardon

"Dawrtu'shtage"- waited

"Ra"-*adv.* so, very, really, therefore, thus

"Dyakfe"- *adj.* long

"Di"-*prep.* for (a period of time or length of distance)

"Thikoflamtu"- *n.* scholars

"Tyokego"- Old Sod

"Te"- *pron.* they, them, theirs, *det.* no

"Twe"- *v.* do

"Fu"- *adv.* not

"Dyaw"- *v.* say, tell, speak, state, mention

"Flotwihaw"- Papa

"twaru"- *v.* am (he,she i am)

"Dniwo"- *n.* home

To you my love, my fated. The stars will always bring me back to you and you outshine them all.

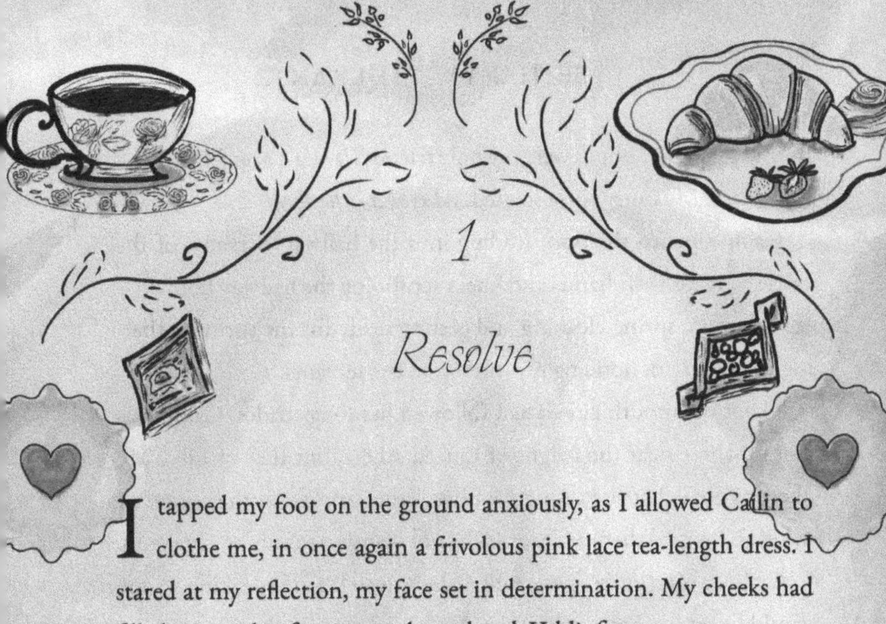

1

Resolve

I tapped my foot on the ground anxiously, as I allowed Cailin to clothe me, in once again a frivolous pink lace tea-length dress. I stared at my reflection, my face set in determination. My cheeks had filled out weeks after my resolve to break Valdis free.

The stone floor felt cold underneath my feet as the chill of the outside seeped into the castle walls.

"You seem to be in a hurry for your weekly brunch with the queen," Cailin noted as she pulled my hair up into a tight, curled-up do.

The reflection of the niceties of my bedroom chamber made my skin crawl, my stomach churn at the idea of lavishing in it, while the outside world reveled in destruction.

Pausing, my foot tapping long enough to answer her. "I am. I want to ask her something." Grimacing as she yanked at my baby hairs, she nodded, content with the vague answer. I have her. Lying would get me nowhere with Cailin. After two months, lying was useless. She always knew when I did.

"After brunch, the queen has instructed me to allow you to walk the garden. With me as an escort," she said, finishing the last touches on my hair.

I beamed at her, thoughts running rampant in my head as Cailin laced the string to my flat onto my calf. *It would give me another chance to mentally map out the terrace.* There were no drawing utensils in my room, nor paper. Books were my only friends. *It was a wonder I hadn't gone crazy.* My inner voice scoffed. *Maybe a little mad.*

Cailin opened the door leading into the hallway. Servants of the castle were on their hands and knees scrubbing the hallway floor.

"They are spring cleaning and getting ready for the spring gathering," Cailin said, noticing my interest in the servants.

I kept my mouth closed as I followed her long strides. Cailin was tall, nowhere near the height of Queen Alieta, but that of Lilja. My chest tightened at the thought of her. Tears pricked in the corner of my eyes. I wiped them away quickly, not wanting to ruin my makeup.

Cailin would only speak when she wanted, as if speaking to me would lower her brain cell count. My blood pressure hummed in my ears as we walked to the greenhouse.

It took everything in me not to bolt past Cailin to ask Queen Alieta my question. Two nameless servants pushed carts in front of us, each one piled with food for the Queen's and I's brunch.

A waste if you ask me, my inner voice sneered. *Most of it gets thrown away, anyway.* As they pushed open the doors to the greenhouse, I welcomed the scent of humid earth coming from the rush of hot air escaping.

The scent brings me back to my cottage, a quiet respite away from the human realm. The sounds of the quiet nature, a rustle of leaves or the footsteps of wild animals. No humans nor elves to bother me. A time that already felt like a lifetime away.

Greenery lined the walls of the glass, set in large built-in planters in the ground, a stark contrast to the chilly weather outside.

She stood by the large tree, planted by her grandfather. Her beauty was undeniable, her long hair cascaded down past her shoulders, and the soft sharpness of her defined muscles. If not for the predicament

I met her in, we could've easily become friends. Her likeness to Lilja and Belle was nearly startling. Unlike them, she was evil.

"Good morning, your highness," I said, curtsying.

"Well, hello, Elowen. It is such a joy to see you. A welcome distraction from my copious amounts of paperwork I have to go through." Alieta spoke with such smoothness as she walked up to me. She reached for my hand, giving it a small peck.

I fought the urge to recoil and the urge to wipe my palm on my dress as we sat down.

"The pleasure is all mine, your highness. I'm glad to give you such a distraction from your daily life." I gathered fruit and a Danish onto my plate, taking care to avoid eye contact with her.

"Your highness," I announced, pushing at the berry on my platter. "I have a question." I looked up at her through my lashes. She paused, her hand mid-air with a piece of food.

Setting the fork down, she crossed her arms in front of her. "Which is?"

"I've been thinking ever since you have been so gracious to house me and protect me from Queen Lilja of Valdis." Shivering as if a memory of her made me flinch. "I don't want to need someone to defend me. I realize I'll never be as strong as an elf. I desire the opportunity to train. I-I want to be stronger." My heart pounded in my throat as I awaited her response.

I had resigned myself to waiting when I was first captured.

To wait for Lilja and the team, if they were alive, to save me.

I no longer wished to be the damsel.

"I see." Her eyes analyzed me sitting across from her, as if able to read the exact reasoning from my body language.

"I don't want to be anyone's pet."

The queen put her hand to her chin, as if in contemplation. "Okay, you can train under one condition."

I grinned at her, a genuine grin for the first time. "Oh! Thank you, your highness!" I clapped my hands excitedly, not realizing her statement.

"My condition is you must attend a date with me once a week, as well as our weekly brunch. My military personnel will not take it easy on you, nor do I expect them to. They will train you so no one can treat you like a pet again."

I nodded solemnly. Was *lying truly the best thing? What if Alieta is good? Wait! A date?!*

"Your highness, a date? You couldn't possibly be serious?" I looked at her, dumbfounded, while she seemed rather pleased with herself.

"Well, of course, I'm serious. I do not say things I don't mean. I want to go on a date with you. Multiple, in fact." She gazed at me plainly, as if her response made complete sense.

I fought the urge to stare at her, mouth agape, like a fish out of water.

"I understand they have hurt you," she said, gesturing to the brand on my right forearm.

"I want you to understand something, Elowen," she spoke as she pushed herself up from the spot she was sitting at.

"I would never hurt you like Queen Lilja has."

I gulped as her tall, muscular form stood over me, her hand resting on the back of my chair. *She's never hurt me like your uncle,* my inner voice shouted at me. Fighting the urge to turn my face away, as she leaned in, kissing me on my forehead.

My skin burned with repulsion as her lips contacted my skin. Without being able to control my mouth, I gasped, making her recoil.

"My apologies, Elowen, I seem to have forgotten myself. Cailin, take her on her walk in the garden. I will notify Fian about your interest in training. If I know Fian well, she will want you to start tomorrow." Her highness wouldn't meet my eyes as she spoke, looking up at the tall branches reaching over the greenhouse instead. Her cheeks tinged pink.

I followed Cailin silently as we walked outside. The snow crunched underfoot as we trailed into the sleeping garden. My mind raced. *Does Alieta like me?* My stomach churned at the idea of going on a date with her. *What would Lilja think?* Another voice whispered from the back of my head: *She's dead.*

She has left you here, alone.

Dead, like Belle.

It's all my fault.

Tears pricked at my eyes as I fought back the emotions threatening to push past my facade. Looking around, I tried to memorize the layout. *I needed to remember the grounds if I wanted to escape.*

2

Failing but Determined

The sun had barely risen from its nap as we made ourselves outside. Snow crunched under our shoes, making it the only noise to pierce through the cold late winter morning. My eyes tried to memorize the path, every bush and tree. Alternating spruce and dogwood trees, the cold bit at my nose, freezing my snot to my nostrils. "Why did you insist on our walking today?" I asked, my teeth chattering as I spoke.

"I was hoping to discourage you, after seeing how far away the training building was," Cailin said, her breath heavy as the road began to incline.

"This is so far from the castle," I gasped out, looking around. Snow-covered bushes lined the walkway. My heart sank a bit; the snow would make it nearly impossible for me to escape undetected.

I wouldn't be able to survive the escape in my current condition. Untrained, no muscle, no real skills to survive the wilderness. An unattainable dream. No knowledge of how to get to Valdis. My inner voice sneered at me. A stray tear ran down my cheek. I quickly swiped it away.

"Long enough for you to realize it's a foolish dream. I don't see a need for a human to learn to fight."

"I want to protect myself. I don't want to be taken advantage of," I said, rubbing the scar on my arm, a reminder of the past.

"I wouldn't have agreed to this sort of thing if I were queen. A human learning to train like an elf is preposterous," Cailin said as she laced the boots up onto my foot. I bit my lip to keep myself from saying a nasty retort. *Some people would never understand.*

My lungs burned as the cold air fueled my body. The large training building loomed in the distance. Smoke billowed out of chimneys, each poking out the opposite sides of the building. A short elf stood in the open doorway.

They took one lazy drag of their cigarette before snuffing it against the door frame. The mysterious figure walked back inside, leaving the large door open. I peered over at Cailin, who seemed unsurprised by the retreating figure. I yanked on the door's metal handle. It was cold to the touch, and I pulled it shut behind me.

"Good morning," I said, my teeth chattering. I eyed the large-mouthed fireplace hungrily.

"Morning, Ms. Elowen. I'm Fian Lorn. I hear you wish to train under me." Fian's voice was low, lower than expected. Their frame was compact, yet muscular. Nearly the same height as me. Their body was virtually all muscle. Sculpted muscles appeared, showing under their tunic that cut off at the shoulders, revealing chiseled biceps.

I nodded mutely as I continued to look at the fire.

"What time do you think you and Ms. Elowen will finish with training? I need to collect her, as she is unpermitted to walk back to the main building unaccompanied." Cailin's voice ricocheted in the large room.

Each wall carried a weapon, methodically hung up. "She will finish at seven-"

"At seven! Why did we need to get up so early?" Cailin's voice was an octave higher than normal, her hands on her hips as she spoke.

"I didn't say in the morning, now did I? Elowen will finish in the afternoon. You may leave Cailin. I find your voice highly irritating this early in the morning." Fian's face was void of any emotion other than slightly thinned out lips.

I raised my eyebrow at Cailin's outburst. Surprised at her incivility towards the Queen's friend. We both watched as Cailin left. I breathed a sigh of relief as the door shut. Fian rolled her shoulders, cracking her neck. She stared at me for a second, critiquing me internally.

"So you wish to train like us, human." Fian's voice was rough from years of smoking.

I jutted my chin out in response, "Yes." Fian's eyes were silver, striking compared to her dark skin.

Fian crossed her arms. "Why?"

I paused for a second, trying to think of a good reason. Would *she believe what I told the Queen?* "I want to protect myself. I'm tired of being someone's pet." My chest swelled as I thought of Lilja out there without me, my voice cracking at the end. *If she were out there, she would've saved me by now.*

"Okay," Fian said as she stepped onto one of the thick mats that lay in the room. "Are you going to get in, or are you hoping to absorb learning to fight by looking at me?"

I gaped at her response as I watched her put her long, straight black hair into a quick braid. I sped to the mat, stepping onto it with confidence. *Kallan taught me some things on the mountain.*

Before they forgot about me and left me for dead. I thought cynically.

As soon as I stepped onto the red-lined circle on the mat, I found myself on my back, gasping for breath. "What was that?" I wheezed, trying to inflate my lungs.

"If you wish to train with me. You must be able to take me by surprise. You might be in the Queen's interest, but I don't play favorites.

Now get up." Fian held her hand out to me, pulling me up quickly. I nodded in her direction, changing my stance.

Fian lunged at me, grabbing my arm, twisting it behind me. I screeched, unsuccessfully reaching for her, as she pinned me to the ground with my arm to my back. I wheezed, rolling onto my stomach, pushing myself up. "Again! This time, don't be so easy to grab."

I stood at the edge of the ring, my closed-toed shoes coasting the edge of the red circle. Fian stood on the balls of her feet on the opposite end, staring at me like a primal animal ready to attack. "How is this teaching me anything?" Spitting to the side, my blood spattered on the ground like abstract art.

"It takes years to take an opponent head-on. A feeble human like you doesn't have thirty years to master a skill like this." Fian rushed me again. Her leg kicked behind my knee, sending me to the ground.

"Do you understand-" Fian said.

"All I'm understanding is that you're teaching me to get knocked on my ass," I panted, glaring at her from the mat.

"Incorrect, I am trying to show you how to not get knocked on your ass. So far, you are failing." Fian held out her hand. I gave her a look, grabbing it.

"I cannot teach you the way Ardourians fight. I'll teach you how to get from their grasp and what to do after. Now. Again." Fian prowled the mat as she spoke; confidence radiated out of her. Her steps were precise. How she moved her mouth as she spoke was with a precision and calculation I had never seen before. To find the cure and survive, *I needed to be like her. I refused to be a damsel in distress. It was time to save myself.*

3

No Risk-No Reward

Lilja POV- After the Attack on Sald Forest.

The world jumbled around my vision. Trees bobbed uncomfortably in my peripheral vision. The sky was dark, save for a few stars. Smoke covered my tongue and the back of my throat. A cough worked its way out of me.

I furrowed my eyebrows at the pain radiating from my head.

"Lilja, are you awake?" Kallan said, his voice barely above the sound of the owl calling out in the distance.

Snow crunched under his feet as we shuffled up the hill. Stars glittered overhead. My heart hammered in my ears.

"Yes," I croaked.

Someone stumbled behind us.

"Elowen," I said, calling to her. Silence hushed over the rest of the group as I waited for her to respond.

"Elowen." Pain radiated from my neck as I moved in Kallan's arms. My pulse throbbed behind my eyes.

"Don't turn. You've suffered a serious head injury," Cassia said. I could hear her rustling in her bag, no doubt looking for something to numb the ever-growing pain building behind my eyes.

"Elle," I said again with a little more urgency. My heartbeat in my throat, fear, climbing its way up.

"Lilja," Armand said, his form just behind me. His voice was low, hollow of all emotions. Something soldiers did to compartmentalize.

"Where is Elowen!" My voice at a normal volume, shouts sounded in the distance.

"Fuck, they found us," Aidan said, his voice gruff. Pain lanced through my head as Kallan moved with urgency.

I bit the side of my cheek to stop myself from crying out as the darkness overtook me.

I teetered to the mantel. My balance had been off since the attack. The glass in my hand sloshed around dangerously close to spilling over. My head pounded as I paced the small one-room cabin. I gulped the bitter liquid in my tumbler, throwing the small remaining amount into the fire, where the glass and alcohol splattered. The flame flared to life, matching the anger burning in the pit of my stomach. I glared at the people sitting at the table, watching me like a caged animal. Kallan flinched as the flame licked up the sides of the fireplace.

"Has anyone heard word of anything affiliated with Elowen?" My voice was loud enough in my ears that I flinched. Keres, Armand, Aidan, Cassia, and Kallan all looked at me, eyes wide. It was rare that my self-control bubbled out of control. But here we sat, with it held together by a taut string.

"I can't contact her! Where is my fiancée?" My voice cracked at the end as my emotions tumbled over the well wall of my self-control. The ground underneath the cabin rumbled.

"We'll find her. Something's preventing her from being able to contact you via the fated link. Perhaps a spell? Once she's out of the perimeter of the spell, you'll communicate with each other." Keres stared at her bandaged hands, the burns from the incident still angry-looking.

"If there's a spell," Kallan said, his voice low as he spoke into his glass.

The door to the cabin banged open, making me jump. A young man burst through the door. Ice clung to his facial hair and hat, as if it wanted to consume him totally. He bowed slightly toward me, bee-lining for Aidan, his boss. He scrambled for the flap of his messenger bag, handing Aidan a book and rushing back out of the door and into the freezing weather.

Aidan frantically flipped through the book, his eyes reading lines of the book with incomprehensible speed.

"Here!" He stood up from his chair, knocking it to the floor. His voice trailed off as he spoke. "A binding spell can link the fated more extensively." He looked up at me. Pity swam in them.

"What does it say? Aidan spit it out!" I looked at the fire longingly, saddened that I threw the cup in it. It had at least one sip left in it, and I wasted it.

"If we do it, there's a possibility it would go awry. Communication could still be impossible. It omits what would happen if communication were unsuccessful." Aidan's newfound information hushed the group. Silence permeated every inch of the cabin.

"We can't take that risk, your highness." Kallan gripped the arms of his chair. I raised an eyebrow at the title usage.

"RISK, you want to talk to me about risk? The enemy has kidnapped my future wife, your future queen, with no way to contact and you want to talk to me about what's right to risk!? She *is* my equal. Aidan set up the binding ritual. We will do it tonight. That's final."

The flames from the fireplace danced on Aidan's glasses as he nodded. *Elowen was his friend and my future wife. I'd be damned if I didn't try.*

Aidan moved in a flurry of motion, gathering items and paper. He finished the sigil on the table as he spoke. "We have to use your elemental power to put a sigil around the cabin. It has to be this exact design. It's what will amplify the spell to Elowen." I gave him a nod, my face grim.

The attack had left me battered and bruised, unable to help Elowen when she was being dragged away by the Queen's men. I gritted my teeth as the cold air bit at my exposed skin. The head wound pulsed at dissatisfaction. Aidan clasped my hand, our energy combining into our intertwined hands. Closing my eyes. I called for the frozen earth beneath the snow, feeling for the movement deep in the earth's crust. With the picture of the sigil in my mind, I gave a slight tug on the movement.

Nothing happened. I groaned, running my hand through my hair. Frozen earth was so much harder to manipulate.

"Hey, take a breath. Let's try again." Aidan squeezed my hand, closing his eyes once again.

Elowen's face flashed before my eyes. Anguish and anger simmered underneath my skin as I listened and felt for the movement under the snow. Yanking on the slight motion, *you will bend to my will, earth. I need this to work. I need to know where she is.*

The ground groaned in response, moving to my will. Aidan staggered. My heart pounded in my chest as I fell to my knees. Exhaustion threatening to take over, a ringing filled my ears, blood dribbling out of my nose.

Aidan hauled me up, pulling me inside. The snow soaking into the clothes covering the bottom half of my body sent a chill up my spine. Kallan pulled out a chair, essentially throwing me down into it. I murmured a thanks as he pushed the chair in front of the now graffiti-covered table.

Aidan flipped through the book again, reading the instructions, his fingers tracing the sentence. Snow clung to his pants, soaking the floor. "We need an item of Elowen's and your blood." He looked up at me, gulping.

"What? What else?! Spit it out, Aidan!" I barked the order from the chair, shivering. Nausea rolled through me, my stomach very much wishing to throw up the alcohol I had just drunk.

"A memory. It says here, a sacrifice of a memory needs to be made.-"

"You didn't mention this before," Cassia said, looking up from her spot by the fireplace.

Aidan shrugged, struggling to unstick the page from the others. "The pages were stuck together. Do you still wish to follow through with the spell? Like I said before, it could very well not work."

Pressure pushed on the inside of my head, making it feel like it would burst with every sound. I merely nodded in response, grimacing at the movement.

"You can't possibly be serious, you can't risk it. What happens if you forget something important?" Keres scoffed, looking at Armand for agreement.

A memory was a small price to pay. Elowen was to be my queen, the love of my life. The time we had been together was not nearly long enough. What was her favorite food? What was her favorite memory of her mother? So many things I didn't know. So many things I yearned to know.

"How in the hell is she supposed to give up a memory?" Armand crossed his arms, his eyebrow raised.

"We have already shaved who knows how many years off of our lives from the spell with Darach? As a species that lives more years than some would care to admit, it might feel like child's play. But a memory? Taking the wrong memory could cause you to lose your sense of self. Your personality-gone," Keres said, her arms waving.

"Aidan, do the damn spell," I said, pinching the bridge of my nose. His vast knowledge of the mystical world coming into use. All the times escaping from our childhood training, becoming worth it. The fire roared to life. His muscles flexed, the shadows of the fire reflecting on them.

Cassia scrambled back from the fire as if it suddenly became aware and wanted to consume everything in its wake.

Keres let out a yelp, stumbling back.

A small figure formed from the flame, not much taller than Elowen, unusual for the Elven community. "You called?" The lean figure asked as they walked out into the small cabin.

They tilted their head to the side, awaiting an answer to their question.

I must have hit my head harder than I thought. "Uh, who are you?"

"You called me, yet you do not know who I am? Elves, quite the crew, aren't they?" The small stature person asked the long-haired black cat that appeared into thin air. The cat meowed back in response, rubbing its body against their master's leg.

"I am Endri-"

"The god of Vision and Dream, of course! It would only make sense!" Aidan's mouth moved fast, as if the words begged to fly out of his mouth, his brain working overtime.

I pushed myself up from the chair, bowing towards Endri. The cabin seemed to tilt in response. "It is an honor to meet you. However, I must admit I am in the dark about how we contacted you."

They gestured back to the chair, gratefully I sat back down with a grunt. "The sigil used to complete the spell of intensifying the Fated bond calls on me. Like our dear muscled friend pointed out, how else are you supposed to get rid of a memory?" They paused, waiting for a response, reminding me of one of my old tutors.

They bent down, picking up their cat, gently scratching underneath its chin, holding it like a baby. "Now let's get to work, Queen Lilja, so you can get your dear Elowen back." Endri pushed the cat onto their shoulder. It meowed in response, its yellow eyes gazing at me intently as if into my soul.

With a flick of their hands, any unlit candles lit up, lighting the room with a mysterious glow. They stepped away from the shadow of the fireplace, striking me with how pale the god before me appeared to be. *I had never met another god, except for Darach. In all my years of life, I had never expected to meet any. Mysterious beings, fueled with rumors and stories of past Elven heroes.*

"Join hands. We don't have all day. We don't want my siblings, or worst of all, my mothers, to realize I am helping you all." They shuddered at the thought as they grabbed my hand, their skin cold. They pricked it with a small dagger, dripping the blood into the middle of the table.

"Why wouldn't the other gods wish to help us rescue Elowen, your excellency?" Cassia said, clasping my hand, giving it a tight squeeze of reassurance. Her dark skin seemed to glow with the light of the candles lit around us.

"They prefer if we limit our interactions with Elves and humans as much as possible. Meddling with the balance of powers is a fickle thing, really. One wrong helping hand and the wrong person could end up in power. Now quiet, I need to concentrate. Glasses, put something of Elowen's onto the table." Their voice was clear and melodic, bordering on otherworldly.

Aidan scrambled to the bed I slept in last night, snatching Elowen's discarded cloak I used as a blanket, placing it into the center of the table. They bowed their head, closing their eyes, chanting. It started off as an indistinct murmur, an ancient language I didn't understand.

I eyed the table sigil as it glowed, shaking, lifting off the ground. Their voice got louder. The blood on the table began to simmer, then to a boil. Elowen's green cloak smoked, smoldering.

Endri's voice grew louder, shouting as the smoke from the cloak and blood went into the air. It swirled purposefully, and Kallan let out a small gasp as it flew towards me. The force knocked me to the ground, forcing the gray smoke into my lungs. Coughs wrecked my body. Endri stooped down to me, grabbing onto the back of the chair, hauling me back up before anyone else moved.

They looked into my eyes, their cat jumping off their shoulder and onto my lap, curling into a ball, purring contently. Endri grabbed onto my face, inhaling deeply, just as the smoke fully entered me, they coaxed it out. They pulled away, looking dazed, their eyes reflecting whatever memory they just pulled from me.

I choked back a sob, clutching my chest. It beat uncomfortably hard. Whatever memory pulled from my brain left no inkling of what it may be. Forever gone.

A tear formed in their eyes, slipping down their cheek as they scooped up the cat from my lap, depositing it onto the floor by their feet. "That was a beautiful memory, Queen Lilja of Valdis. Very moving. If you survive the next few years, I might let you relive it in a dream sometime. Now, when you awake, you may communicate with Elowen."

"May?" I raised a tired eyebrow.

"While I can complete the spell with you, I cannot guarantee that it will work. Unfortunately, that is just up to fate, and I am not the god that controls that. If it doesn't work, you'll feel some minor side effects." They made a small symbol with their fingers before walking over to the fireplace. It roared in response to Endri's nearness.

Endri clicked their tongue. "Syrius, let's get going."

The cat meowed in response, hopping onto the other table in the room, knocking off the nearly empty water basin on purpose.

"Syrius, now that was impolite. Apologize."

The cat meowed back to Endri. "Well, I know it was ugly, Syrius. But you can't go breaking things that aren't yours." Endri bent over, picking up Syrius like a baby.

"Yes, I know they need to redecorate, castles aren't what they used to be." Endri's voice faded as they turned and walked back into the fire.

4

Torture

Lilja POV- Aftermath of the attack on Sald Forest

I peaked an eye open, the warmth of the fire basking over me. Soft snores filled the air. Lazily, I turned my head to see sleeping forms littering the crowded hidden cabin. I held my breath, closing my eyes. *Elowen,* I reached out over our bond. *Please answer me, my love.* I projected blinking away the stray tears threatening to streak down my cheeks.

"Anything, yet?" Kallan said from the chair close to my bed. Dark circles hung under his eyes like a permanent fixture. No doubt staying up to watch over all of us throughout the night. I sat up, cracking my neck, sighing. I closed my eyes, reaching for Elowen. A brick wall stood erect at the edge of my subconscious, hairline cracks littered the entirety. Slow breathing sounded from the other side.

I opened my eyes, facing Kallan. "I don't know. The wall is still there, but there are cracks in it. I can hear, no feel, her sleeping." I sighed, leaning back on the bed, looking up at the ragged ceiling.

"Hey, don't worry. We've got this far. We won't stop now. Nobody has given up. We won't. Now let's get this cabin packed up and form a plan." Kallan placed his hand on my shoulder.

Cassia sat up from sleeping on the floor, her hair stuck up into a bonnet.

"Leave my patient alone. You can pack up, Kallan. I need to check her wounds." She groaned as she stood up, stretching, grumbling about being old. Her gold earring glittered in the sun as she moved about.

Cassia shooed Kallan from the chair where he presumably sat the whole night. She plopped down, reaching down to pull up her bag of medical supplies.

"Your head looks better. The bruise has already changed colors. How's the concussion?"

I cracked my neck. "I still feel weird, but it's better. The pounding is gone."

Cassia nodded in response, noting it in a small journal that she threw back into her bag. I sucked in a breath, wincing as a pain cut across my cheek. Cassia's eyes widened. I brought my hand to my face, pulling it away to reveal blood.

"What the fuck is that?!" Armand said as he stared at me from across the room, gaping. Sleep, still written all over his features, his eyes wide.

"I-I don't know. Ow!" I looked down as blood bloomed on my thigh. I closed my eyes, focusing on Elowen again, going back to the brick wall at the edge of my consciousness. It rumbled as if an earthquake hit it. Screams echoed from the other side of the wall.

"No, please don't. I am! I can't let him know the truth. Lilja is my Fated. I have to protect her."

Pain radiated from my fingertip. I looked down as blood pooled from the bed of my finger, as if someone had ripped my fingernail off. Cassia quickly wiped the blood on my fingernail bed away, leaving an unaffected but tender pink skin underneath.

I hit the wall with my mind, begging for it to break. *Elowen, hold on. I'm coming for you.*

The wall stood unmoving, the cracks the only evidence that the spell had happened. My heart sank as I put the pieces together.

"She's being tortured." My voice wavered as pain radiated from my ears. Aidan threw a chair across the room, anger rolling off him in waves.

The world swayed as I fell back onto the bed. "No," I whimpered. My anger dissipated from my body, leaving only pain and fear in its wake. All my queenly training, my diplomatic training, physical training compared to nothing of the feeling of Elowen's life slipping away. *My love, my life, please no.*

"What is it?" Cassia's face was above mine in a second. I gasped numbness spread across my body.

"She's dying," I screamed, closing my eyes again, pushing against the wall, using every ounce of my strength. It crumbled. I pushed my subconscious past. Unable to voice anything, I pulled the invisible tether that held us both to the world.

"No, not yet! Please don't leave yet, you must live!" I screamed, pulling on the tether. The string felt warm, a life held in its grasp. A life I intended to hold on to.

"The gods can't have her yet!" I shouted, my voice cracking. My heart felt like it was being cleaved in two. Heat radiated from her side of the bond.

I gasped, leaning off the side of the bed vomiting the little food I had in my stomach. "Your highness!" Cassia pulled back the short hair on my head, smoothing it so it wasn't getting in my face.

The room swirled uncomfortably, hazing in and out of focus. I grasped my chest, my heart painfully beating as I stared at the concerned faces before me. Tears streamed freely down my cheeks.

"Emotions in times like this are useless," my teacher's voice echoed in my head.

"Is she?" Cassia said, her voice dying in her throat as she searched my eyes for the unspoken word. It hung uncomfortably in the air.

I closed my eyes again, meeting the wall. The side effects of the amplified, fated bond were clear. The pain she felt would be my own. A simple stretch of the mind could know her emotion.

"She's alive. Someone healed her from the brink of death." Their faces sagged with relief. Kallan placed his hands behind his back, clasped together, pacing the room.

"That's good. You'd most likely be dead if she were," he added. Kallan looked outside the small window in the cabin, speaking the unspoken words we were all thinking.

"We still have a chance to get her back." Kallan's voice was strained with thought as he planned in his head.

"They're just going to torture her for information. Who knows what they've already gotten out of her? She's compromised us." Keres glared at the burn on her arm, her voice full of malice.

"She hasn't compromised us. We haven't kept the old plans since the attack two days ago. Not since I couldn't do my job well enough!" Aidan said, throwing his hands in the air.

"Even if Elowen gives out any information via torture, it'll be old information. Torture is torture, it's nearly impossible to not give out information when pain is the motivation, Keres. You'll do well to remember. I've experienced tortured and you have not. So why don't you shut your trap and be a productive member of this team," Aidan said painfully loud. He pointed his finger in her face before storming out of the cabin, slamming the door so hard the wall vibrated in complaint.

For a moment, no one said anything. Anger rolled off of me in waves as I glared at Keres. She stared at the door where Aidan just exited, and sighed, slumping her shoulders. *Why was she like this?*

I stood, the world swaying, grabbing Cassia for support. "Let's go get my fiancée."

We packed our measly supplies quickly. The world still swayed uncomfortably with every head bobble, leaving me useless. I simmered in my seat, unhappy to watch my team work without me.

"I propose we travel together. We faulted earlier this year by being separated from each other for so long. With the fear of being exposed as Valdisians, we became unaware of our movements. To win this war, we need to act as a united front." Kallan pulled himself onto his horse as he spoke, confidence rolling off him. The sunset filtered through the tall spruce trees shining down onto his dark brown hair, making it appear almost golden, and his scar barely noticeable.

We nodded silently, agreeing, the mood somber. My arm was slung around Cassia for support. I was healing, but the explosion had hurt more than I cared to admit. It had knocked me out cold. I awoke to Kallan carrying me to the cabin without *my* Elowen.

I looked for my horse, only to find it piled with the supplies tied to the back of it. "You guys better not be planning to leave me in this forsaken cabin."

"Of course not, your highness, but we don't exactly trust you being able to ride for yourself," Aidan said as he unexpectedly grabbed me by my waist, hefting me onto the front of Kallan's saddle. I grimaced at the wording, as if he was trying not to set me off

I felt incredibly tiny being snuggled in front of Kallan as we traveled. Like a small child, just learning how to ride. We spaced the plan out, using the information Aidan's runner supplied us. Alieta would not kill Elowen, but the torture would've revealed something about our relationship. I shivered as pain pricked at my ears, as if a small needle was threading the skin together. *They're helping her ears heal? Why?*

My face scrunched at the feeling.

"What?" Kallan asked, as he must have felt me stiffen against him.

"It feels as if someone is sewing Elowen's ear back together." My heart ached at Elowen being in so much pain. I winced as another prick went through.

"We can rest easy. They want her alive. There would be no point in healing her if they were just going to kill her. Alieta must want her for something. See if you can contact her," Kallan said, his voice tight with restraint, as he forced calm words out of his mouth.

I sighed, closing my eyes, going back to the wall that was built between our two minds. The cracks I had made earlier were gone. Slow breaths came from the other side as if they had drugged her to sleep. I hit the wall with my hand, not even making a scuff mark.

"No, they have put her under with something. There are only deep breaths coming from the other side." I held back the groan of frustration, *showing them would do nothing.*

The day stretched by slowly, as we rode back to the City of Ebbon, which was only a few days' ride from our location.

Every fiber in my body seemed to pull back to Elowen. The fated bond between us, becoming taut as we furthered our distance. It felt wrong to go far away, wrong to leave my Elowen in the hands of the enemy. But I had to. We had to figure out the Blight. Our kingdom relied on us to figure it out. *I only hoped Elowen could hold out until then.*

Aidan held up his hand, halting us. "Let's stop here for the morning."

"What?! No, we only just started," I said, lifting my tired head from the neck of the horse.

"With all due respect, we've been riding all night and the only reason you've been able to stay on this horse is because I've been holding you up," Kallan said his voice just below a whisper, only so I could hear.

I craned my neck, peering up at the now early morning sky. *Where did the night go?* The ache in my body seemed to catch up to me as we halted. Pain radiated in my head, making it swim. I struggled to stay on the horse, leaning on to Kallan.

"It'll do Elowen no good if we push ourselves to death. Tomorrow we'll be in Ebbon. From there, we can talk with Queen Zahra and find out what her spies have heard. With Elowen being a human, there are bound to be rumors swirling around," Aidan said as he dismounted, grabbing the large packs of supplies from my horse. His voice was sharp, leaving little to no room for argument. Even as the Queen of Valdis.

The attack changed him. Anger simmered right beneath his skin. Aidan, my longtime childhood friend, felt like Ardour had bested him, and he was going to stop at nothing to get her back.

5

A Little Taste of Freedom

"**A**gain," Fian said as she knocked me on my ass again.

I growled with anger, wiping the sweat beading on my forehead, pulling myself back up. Fian stalked around the circle again, her eyes focused on my every movement.

She reached out her hand toward me as if in slow motion. I moved my arm out of her reach.

Fian pulled back, looking at me; a slight smirk grew on her face. "Finally," her head cocked to the side, "here I thought you were completely impossible to train. Finally, some potential."

I heaved a sigh of relief, staggering back as I retreated away from her. "Watch the enemy in a fight; anticipate what they're going to do." Fian took a swig of her water before handing the glass to me.

"How am I supposed to notice that?" I said before taking a drink.

"Don't you see what you did? You foresaw what I was going to do and dodged it. Now let's go again," Fian said.

The rest of the day blurred by. It comprised Fian berating me, with me landing a few successful dodges.

Sweat ran down my brow as I ran laps around the training room, dodging large pieces of furniture that jutted out from the side of the wall awkwardly. "Faster, Elowen, we need to burn that extra weight right off of you." Fian's voice boomed out as she took a drag.

Extra weight? This is all necessary, I'll have you know. I thought, huffing around the room for another lap. The water I drank previously sloshed in my otherwise empty stomach.

"Alright, enough. You're making me depressed by how slow you're going." Fian's face was serious as she pulled the cigarette back into her mouth.

I slowed, grateful for the break as Cailin slipped into the room. Snowflakes billowed as she shut the door.

"Is she finished?" Cailin said, attempting to rub warmth into her body.

"Yes, you shall take her away. I'm tiring of watching her poor performance. Bring her back tomorrow. Hopefully, by then, she will have absorbed some things I tried to teach her." Fian coughed as she spoke, smoke trickling from her mouth.

"The storm is getting worse. You should head home as well," Cailin commented as she handed me my coat.

I gave my thanks for the lesson to Fian before I slipped out the door. The wind bit at me, the moisture from my sweat chilling to my bone. "Let's hurry before you catch a cold. The Queen will have my head if you do." Cailin hurried in front of me, the snow crunching underneath her feet.

The wind howled as we made it into the castle. A maid behind us wiped up the melted snow from our footprints inside. Our footsteps echoed into the otherwise quiet castle. I raised my eyebrow, peering around for the usual staff members that maintained the castle. "Where is everyone?"

"The Spring Gathering starts next week. It's customary to give most employees a few afternoons off for preparations. There are a handful on call, but not all of them so they can also clean and purge their own homes, to be who they genuinely are," she says like a child reciting lines in a book, her voice ricocheting in the unstaffed castle.

I listened to her explain the holiday with interest, wondering if Ardour and Valdis holidays were the same.

Counting the doors as we walked back to my room, I made a mental note of the layout. The lock on my door knocked into place as I rushed to my desk to draw the map.

What am I supposed to write with?

I looked around the room, zeroing in on the burned wood in the fireplace. I held my breath, staring down at it, as if waiting for someone to tell me no. The flames licked the sides of the wood placed inside as I crouched down, a few wheezing as the water sizzled out.

The heat bloomed on my hand as I reached for an outer piece of charcoal. *Maybe I wasn't so useless after all.* I clutched the charcoal like a child first learning to write, furiously drawing the map.

This would be my way out.

The next few days were a blur. Fian's training was the extent of my days, her knocking me on my ass and telling me to do better each time she picked me up.

My body ached with bruises as I sank into the tub brought into my room by Cailin, it's hot water soaked every inch of my body. I closed my eyes, breathing in a sigh of relief as the tension left my body as a rustling sound filled the air. Curious, I peered over at my closed window. The outside appeared calm.

Where did that sound come from?

An ornate letter settled onto the floor with my name scrawled on the front of it. Sealed with Ardour's stamp. I ripped the letter open, my wet pruned fingers leaving a trail of wet streaks on the paper.

Dear Elowen,

> *I cordially invite you to town in two days. Ardour is pre-celebrating for the Spring Gathering. The weather is still cold, so please dress accordingly. I am canceling the next few days of training so you may enjoy our date.*

Eagerly awaiting,

Queen Alieta,

I rolled my eyes, throwing it on the desk, sinking back into the tub. My mind wandered as I soaked. Alieta's and Lilja's faces swirled in my head like a spinning top. Tears ran down my face as my skin wrinkled like an old woman.

I closed my eyes, picturing Lilja. Her smile, and the calm yet sassy demeanor that drew me in. She tried so hard to be enough for a dying kingdom, and here I sit in a deep tub. *Useless.*

Lilja would know how to fix this. She could solve any problem. Even when I first showed up in the Elven Realm, she took me in. She had a cloak for me every time I misplaced mine. A hug every time I needed it. The knowledge of an unfamiliar realm.

Lilja, I reached out, pausing for a response. The silence stretched. My heart aching, *I have to do something I'm going to regret.* I dunked my head, trying to wash the thoughts out of my head, trying to silence my mind. Resurfacing, I gasped, gulping in air, meeting the painful quietness of my empty, lonely bedroom chamber.

I stepped out of the tub, water dripping down and onto the floor. Puddles forming behind me as I threw myself on the mattress, hating myself for how comfortable it felt. *You should be ashamed of yourself, enjoying these luxuries, while Lilja may be dead. She's left you to be Alieta's plaything.*

A sob bubbled out as the guilty thoughts flowed through me. I rolled over, crying myself to sleep in one of the feather pillows. Where the memory of the explosion played over and over again in my head.

Cailin's knuckles rapped on the door, entering before I could give a reply. I sat up in bed, annoyed to be awake. I groaned, laying back down, pulling the blanket up over me. Leaving my head exposed enough to watch her stomp around my room. "Get up. The queen has instructed me to take you on a walk in the castle."

Cailin moved towards the large cabinet containing the clothes Queen Alieta allowed me to wear. Pulling out a yellow dress, "begin getting ready. How her highness likes you to look, not how you like to look." Cailin gestured to my crumpled half awake form.

"I'll retrieve a small breakfast before we start our day." She laid the dress on the chair, leaving. I waited to hear her footsteps rescind from the door before bounding out of bed.

This is perfect. I get to map the Castle! Lilja needs- I paused looking up at the ceiling, blinking past the tears threatening to spill over my eyelids, clutching my chest, angry at myself. *If she were alive, she would've already contacted you.*

I pulled my secret map from where it laid hidden. The drawing was crude but effective. I kept it pinned between the underside of the desk, trying to memorize every single doorway. Gingerly, I refolded the paper, placing it in the folds of my skirt. I'd add to it when I had a respite from Cailin.

"Not that I am not appreciative of being allowed out of my room, but why does the Queen allow it?" I raised an eyebrow at Cailin as she closed the door behind us, locking it.

"The Queen has asked me to make sure you get out and about as much as possible. She's rather worried about your declining mental health." Cailin sped up. Her thin figure hurried down the hall.

"My mental health?"

"Yes, she was quite-" Cailin stopped talking for a moment, mulling over the response in her head before continuing.

"We quite displeased her highness with the state you were in on the first brunch you had together." She cleared her throat, slowing to open a door, revealing a music room.

It was ornate, as was everything else here. The castle seemed to be built to perfection, and nothing appeared out of place. If under better circumstances I could see myself enjoying my stay here exploring, one large window was against the wall. Detailed wallpaper canvassed the room's walls, and a large rug covered the floor.

"This is the music room. You may request to come here to play. Do you play?" Cailin strode to the harp sitting in the room's corner, strumming a few of the cords.

"I play a little piano. My mother taught me before she passed." I shrugged at the thought of playing again. *That was in the past.*

Cailin stumbled the cords on the harp for a second before straightening back up, "I see."

I glanced over at the various instruments sporadically placed in the room. *This room was useless, nowhere closer to finding an escape. Or finding a cure for the blight.*

She moved out of the room, walking further down the hallway. I pulled out the map, adding the outline to the music room. Listening to her footsteps clattering on the stones.

"Come along Elowen, no dallying." I sucked in a breath of surprise, refolding the paper. My fingers tinged black by the wood. I stuck them in my mouth, grimacing the soot coating my tongue.

My legs ached from yesterday. Fian is going to have field day when she realizes the state I am in. Internally, I groaned. *She's going to have a field day when I get to go back to training.*

1,2,3,4,5

I mentally counted the unopened and unexplored doors. Nearly running into Cailin as she walked down the grand staircase leading down to the great hall. I gaped at the massive size of it. The fireplace was the size of ten men; the only thing filling it was long tables and chairs.

We moved on. The new hallway we passed through had lines of painted portraits, the previous Queens and Kings of Ardour.

An enormous set of wooden doors sat closed, guarded by two stone statues of an elephant on either side.

"Her highness thought this room might interest you the most."
Cailin opened the door to reveal a library.

Now this is going to help.

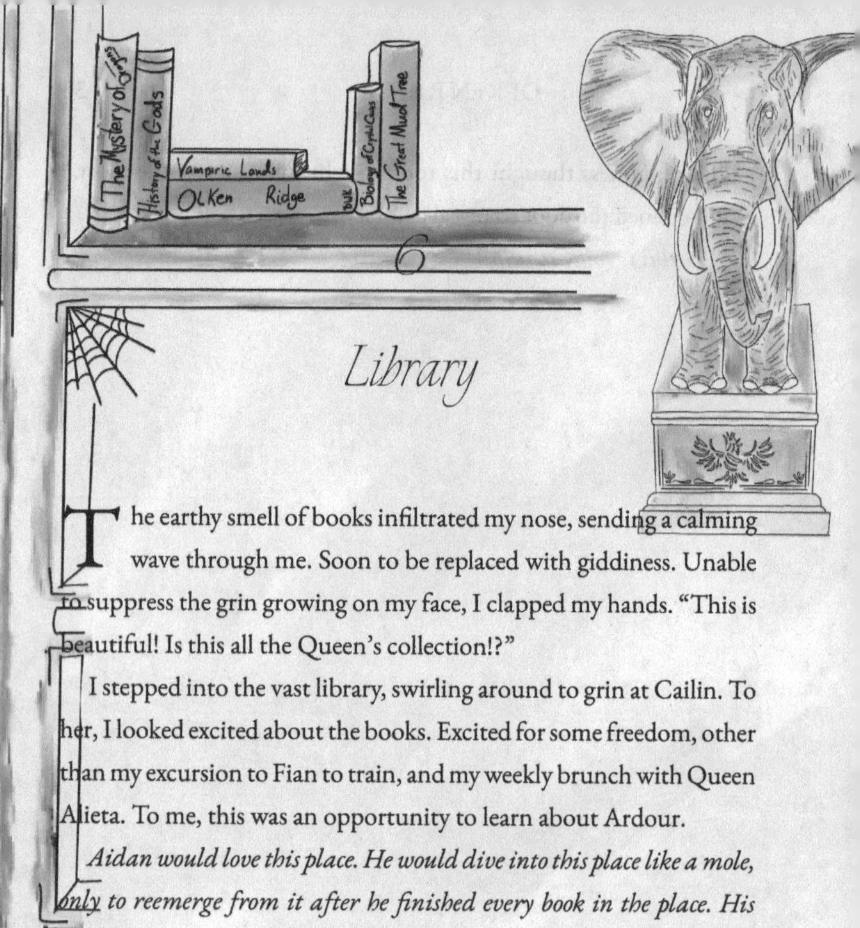

Library

The earthy smell of books infiltrated my nose, sending a calming wave through me. Soon to be replaced with giddiness. Unable to suppress the grin growing on my face, I clapped my hands. "This is beautiful! Is this all the Queen's collection!?"

I stepped into the vast library, swirling around to grin at Cailin. To her, I looked excited about the books. Excited for some freedom, other than my excursion to Fian to train, and my weekly brunch with Queen Alieta. To me, this was an opportunity to learn about Ardour.

Aidan would love this place. He would dive into this place like a mole, only to reemerge from it after he finished every book in the place. His journal would be even fuller of random facts after picking through the knowledge here.

"I'll tell the Queen you appreciate the added rooms to travel to. Do you wish to stay, or would you like to go back to the music room?" Cailin said, clasping her hands in front of her, appearing pleased to leave me alone to my own devices.

"The library!" I said, my heart pounding, feeling like a child alone in a pantry with a sweet jar. "Please," I said a bit more calmly, giving a shy grin, trying my best to appear demure. Books lined all three walls in the library. One wall was nearly completely stained glass, giving the library a haunting glow of a myriad of colors.

Cailin raised an eyebrow at my response. "I'll check on you in a few hours. If you like, I could serve lunch here?"

"I would love that. Thank you, Cailin." She looked taken aback by my appreciation, speechless, she turned leaving. A brief flutter of hope swelled in my chest. I ignored the sound of the lock turning into place as I faced my attention at the library before me. With further exploration, the library comprised three rooms; the larger room branched off into two smaller rooms.

My hands shook as I pulled the map out, I looked around scanning the room for someone who might see it. The charcoal coating my fingers as I made the path to the library. *I would find a way out of here,* I told myself determinedly. As quickly as I took it out, I placed the map back into the safety of my skirt, finally allowing myself to take stock of the environment around me.

Hundreds of books lay haphazardly around the three rooms, forgotten to be read piles. I cringed at the spiderwebs on the bookshelves, a few in disrepair and covered in dust. *Alieta must not read much.*

"What do I even read first?" The pages of the books muffled my voice.

I began scanning the spines of the books, hoping for something to call out to me. They all seemed perfectly ordinary. My eyes ran over an un-embellished book *Olken Elves.* I pulled it from the shelf, curling up into the large armchair by the unlit fireplace.

The memory of Lilja and I having the conversation about Olken Elves resurfaces, causing a jab of pain in my heart. Lilja's face was so distraught when I mentioned the black feathered bird man. The book's spine crackles to life as I open it, begging to be read.

My eyes brimmed with tears as I began tackling the words printed on the pages.

"Olken Elves are an ancient species of Elves. Usually living in pairs in their household. It is unusual for a large group of Olkens being seen together. It is unclear if fighting causes this or their dwindling numbers."

"What are you reading?" The voice rang out in the otherwise silent library. I gasped, looking up, startled. The book fumbled closed in my hands.

"A history book. I thought I should become more knowledgeable about the things that could hurt me during my stay." I peered at Queen Alieta before me, unaware she had snuck into the library.

"I apologize for startling you, Miss Alwyn. You seemed so enthralled in the literature. I've read every book in this library. I assure you I would allow nothing to hurt you when you are in my protection, unlike that blasted Valdis Queen."

I bit back the retort threatening to spill out, opting for an ambiguous one. "Of course, your highness, I thought I should learn more about this world, since I don't know how long I'll be here for."

Queen Alieta raised an eyebrow, glancing around. As if uncomfortable by my response. Cailin opened the door, her face alarmed as she laid eyes on the Queen. "Your highness! How nice of you to grace us with your presence. I was about to serve Elowen her lunch. May I fetch something for you as well?" She rolled in her cart, the content clanking together.

"Is joining you for lunch okay, or would it impede your delve into history? Someone should enjoy these books as much as me. I do not allow anyone else to come in here. Only an occasional maid, when it needs to be tidied up."

I eyed the spider covered shelves. *She should invite a maid back more often.*

"If it pleases you, your highness, the company wouldn't bother me." I gestured to the seat across from me, her nearness unnerving. Cailin scuttled away with the cart, leaving us alone.

She looked at me expectantly, crossing her legs, poised for the conversation she wished to happen. "What are you reading, Elowen?"

"A book of Olken Elves-"

"Olken Elves are extinct. No one has laid an eye on them in centuries. Died out, murdered for being different. They had feathers, a distinct difference from us. Their powers were more complex. Some could turn into birds."

I raised my eyebrow, surprised. "I thought they used dark magic, your highness."

"They might have, although, as I've stated before, I have read these books. Olken Elves frequently come up as evil beings. We know little about them, but it sounds like ignorance on our part. A few texts state that Olken Elves would attack other cities from the sky, stealing and pillaging. The actions of a few cannot lump all of those beings together." The Queen looked off to the side, her eyes had a dreamy gaze like she was staring into the past.

I sat back, taken aback by her answer. That *would make sense. Are they as dangerous as everyone says? Is Queen Alieta ignorant? Is she just a puppet?* She took a breath, sending a shot of flames over to the unlit fireplace filling the room instantly with warmth.

I gasped, sitting straighter in my chair. Queen Alieta looked up at me, surprised by my reaction. Her eyebrow raised as she spoke. "Fire is the magic I hold, Elowen. As did my forbearers, I'm taken aback that you did not know."

"I had assumptions, your highness." My face reddens at my reaction; *I can't tell you the real reason I thought you had firepower.* I thought back to the vision of the phoenix the oracle gave me.

Queen Alieta opened her mouth to say something until Cailin burst through the door. Struggling to hold trays in one hand and push the cart with the other.

"Food is here your highness, I deeply apologize for the wait." Cailin bowed as she set out trays in front of each of us. Undoubtedly, more than what she would've done for me. Queen Alieta said nothing, shooing her away with a flick of her hand until Cailin reached the double doors leading to the rest of the castle.

"Cailin, make sure the fire is lit next time you leave Elowen in the castle somewhere. She's human. The chill will get to her quicker."

We ate in silence, snacking on the small finger foods as we read, as close to comfortable silence as we could muster. The earlier conversation, forgotten.

Queen Alieta grabbed a small sandwich, taking a small nibble before pushing herself up, striding to an overfilled shelf. She bent over, pulling a book from a spider's home. "This book is also about Olken Elves. The author was not an Elf, like myself." She went to hand me the book, burning the spider web tendrils off of it. Holding it mere inches away from me.

"But an Olken Elf wrote this, you may read it, but be wary. Some books in the Elven Realm can be dangerous."

"What do you mean? How can a book be dangerous?"

"Powerful people can cast a spell on it after being written. Reading the pages can set spells off. Manifesting is a powerful thing. By reading the pages, the reader recognizes the worth of the words scrawled on them," Queen Alieta said, her voice light as she looked at my facial expression.

"Do not be so alarmed, the owner or writer has spelled books only for specific people. A human will not be that person. You are in the

Elven Realm by mistake. A mere tickle in the history," Alieta said, as she opened a book.

I gaped at her alarmed, *why was I allowed in the library?*

"What spells do people place on books?" I closed the book I had grabbed earlier, placing it on the tray before me, precariously.

"I've heard the spells can guide the new reader, give advice, or even kill the reader," Queen Alieta said, her voice light as if she were joking.

"Kill!? Should I even be touching these?" I gestured to the rest of the books.

"Oh, don't worry. You'd be able to tell. A ringing would fill your ears and when you touched the book, a spark would happen. Like this," she said, snapping her fingers together, creating a small spark. She grinned at me wildly, like a child telling a bedtime story.

Queen Alieta nodded to herself, satisfied with her explanation. "I will see you tomorrow on our date. I must take my leave. A multitude of royal duties still require my attention." She bowed her head, turning to leave me alone with my books once again.

Date?

Alieta's half eaten food laid discarded on her tray. A chill descended my bones as the books seemed ominously whispered to me. I sucked in a breath, picking up the book the Queen recommended, *The History. My* eyes flitted over the cover of the book. It appeared to be made of tree bark, its corners crumbling as I handled it. Gingerly, I opened the cover and began reading.

The silence stretched in the library; the fire crackled warmth into the corners of the room, invading every breath.

I got up, stretching my legs. The wooden floor creaked underneath me. I meandered down the bookshelves. Dust layered thickly around the forgotten space. It was apparent Alieta had read none of these books in quite some time. *If she read them at all,* a snide inner voice said in my head.

A desk stood in the corner of one of the smaller rooms. The contents sprawled across the top haphazardly. The bust of a man stared at me as I surveyed the contents.

A quill and a capped ink sat at the edge. I looked around the room, as if a person lay in wait watching me. The portrait of a man gazed at me disapprovingly. I held my breath as I snagged it, depositing it into my dress pocket, scurrying back to my seat. My heart racing.

I rushed back to sit down in the oversized chair again, pulling the fragile book into my lap. Where I sat until Cailin retrieved me.

The quill and ink a hopeful lump in my dress as I lay in wait. An infinitely better choice of writing utensil than the lump of charcoal.

The clock chimed, noting it was time for dinner. I shut the book softly, unlike the emotional turmoil inside of me. All of this knowledge of the Olken Elves, with nothing to show of it. The information on the desert they lived in, the life they had before their magic sucked the life out of the land, and yet I'm no closer than I was earlier. Cailin opened the door, looking at me expectantly. The tray of food from lunch lay untouched, forgotten as I delved into the book the Queen gave me. She gave a disappointed look in my direction.

"Could I possibly take a book with me?" Cailin paused, mulling the answer over.

"Yes, just bring it back." She gestured to the ever-growing stack of books I created.

I bit back my smile, afraid my joy would cause her to change her mind. Without looking at the title, I snagged a book in the stack I created, following Cailin out into the hallway.

The castle felt ominous, the air heavy with secrets, begging to be unearthed. "Tomorrow is your excursion with the Queen. Get a good night's rest." I nodded, staring at the book in my hand. I read the title as I heard the lock click into place, leaving me in the darkness of my bedroom.

Olken Ridge

The title seemed to glint excitedly, begging to be opened. The cover tingled under my finger, as if breathing. I lit the lamp on my nightstand, its flame had no movement and cast no dancing shadows as it lit up the room. I raised an eyebrow at it. Waving my hand by it, causing no movement of the flame. My eyes widened, shrinking away from the flame.

The memory of Lilja contacting her while we were in Sald Forest resurfaced. *Could the flame be her trying to contact me?*

Her black hair and disproving smirk flashed before my eyes.

How is that possible? My room was silent except for my quickened breathing, a thought running through my head. A hopeless one. *Keres. Could I summon her? Is she alive?*

I twirled around, searching for paper, trying to remember the sigil I watched Lilja draw countless times. I scrambled for the desk, grabbing a quill. Satisfied with my drawing, I stood in front of the flame, one hand on the nightstand to support my shaking hand. I held the small sigil over the flame. My hands shook as I spoke the words, "Seek the one I wish. With darkness comes light. Keres Genteen, answer the call of the flame."

I sucked in a breath as the sigil burned the paper. The flames almost licking my fingers. For a second, nothing happened. The world seemed to pause itself, snuffing out the flame. Tears streamed down my face as I cried in silent frustration, clenching my fists at my side.

What did I do so wrong? Did I draw the sigil wrong? Did I say the wrong word in the spell? Why does everything have to be difficult? Is she dead too?

I relit the candle, snatching the discarded book up, sliding under the covers of the bed. The flame flickered normally now. Whatever afflicted it earlier was gone.

Olken Ridge was a prominent city, located past the mountain ridge. Its people worshiped the land they built it on, a plateau. The inside of the plateau has miles of tunnels networking through it, effectively making the city secretive.

Once known for the life teeming around the plateau, now a desert. Desolate, thus making the journey to Olken Ridge perilous. A fog permeates the land below the plateau, causing low visibility. The magic use from the residents had siphoned the naturally occurring magic from the land, leaving the land unlivable. Leaving the plateau abandoned.

Cailin nocked on the door, entering without waiting for a reply. She spoke as she went to the desk, where her tools of torture lay in wait. "The celebrations will start in a few hours. The Queen will have to be present for the ceremony. You'll be leaving with her."

I sat in the chair in front of the makeup desk and Cailin immediately went to work. Pulling my hair into a large puffy braid, my hair had gotten incredibly long in the past months I had been in the Elven Realm. The hair that had once tickled the bottom of my shoulder blades now brushed the bottom dimples of my back. Satisfied with the hair, she helped me tie myself into a corset.

"Why do I have to wear one of these?" I said, breathless, as she finished the last rung. "This is a special occasion. You need to look your best. Stop complaining and stop wheezing. It's not that tight."

She buttoned the dress in the back. It clung to me, exaggerating my curves and breasts into supple fullness. The bottom of the dress puffed out, hiding the shapes of my legs. The bottom of the skirt was the darkest color, giving an ombre effect to the rest of the gown. I looked in the mirror and the once overweight girl was gone.

The reflection of a porcelain doll stared back at me, someone I didn't recognize. For the first time in my life, my face was thin. My body no longer seemed to hold the extra softness it used to. I could hear my father's voice in my ears even now, a whole realm away. *You finally look respectable,* is what I was sure he would say. *Like your mother.*

My ears had healed nicely in terms of wounds. Only a faint pink line, the only sign I had any type of 'surgery' to alter my ears. The scar donning my cheek, barely noticeable, as if it was a forgotten moment of my trauma. But the pain Daveed carved into me was not so easily left behind.

I glanced away at my reflection. *I seemed to have wasted away, my beautiful body gone.* "Let's go. We should not keep the Queen waiting for you, a mere human."

I followed her through the twists and turns of the hallways. My heart, numb with the failure of last night. Before I knew it, we stood at the main entrance of the castle. Pine filled my nose as I took in the decorations for the holiday. Dried sliced fruit hung as a garland, decorating the main entrance. Green arches adorned the doors, herbs stuck out along the edges of the greenery.

"You look breathtaking, Elowen." I whirled around, taking in the Queen of Ardour. She adorned a white dress. A long jacket hung on her shoulders, clasped in the front with a gold chain.

I bowed low. "You do as well, your highness."

Do I have to put up this charade? Her fingers grabbed my chin, sending shivers down my spine. *The response of your body is your body, not of the mind,* I thought.

"You do not need to bow to me, Elowen, especially if today goes well." *If what goes well today?* The urge to gag, pushing up through my throat from her response.

I needed to find the cause of the blight.

I need to get to Valdis. I need to find out the truth.

Is Lilja alive?

If she is alive why hasn't she tried to save me?

I shied away from her touch, looking away, trying my best to look unsure of her touch.

"Cailin, you may leave us. My guards will accompany us," she said as the entrance door opened, where two large men stood in the doorway. Chilly air flowed into the room from behind them. The smell of spring hit my nose, a small smile growing on my lips.

Queen Alieta must've noticed the look of surprise on my face as she smiled, motioning for me to step outside.

I fought the urge to run out of the door, to escape. To finally be free. Instead, I sucked in a breath, squaring my shoulders, trying to make myself seem confident. I stepped out into the cold air, stepping into the carriage waiting outside. The Queen was short behind me, pulling herself in behind me.

I raised my eyebrow, as I half expected her to need the footmen to bring her a step stool. So she did not have to exert herself. Yet here she was, sitting thigh to thigh with me. The earthy scent of her perfume filling the small space between us.

Her two guards choose to sit on the outside of the carriage. The world zipped by in a blur; the horses pulling us. I gaped outside, trying to take in all the scenes passing us by, gathering information.

Queen Alieta's eyes burned into me. It would be impossible to draw out the city on my map, but I tried to burn it in my memory anyway. I needed to escape her kingdom and find the reason for the blight.

"Have you been in a carriage before, Elowen? You have spent months staying at my castle, and I feel like we know nothing about each other." The Queen's voice sliced through the sound of clobbering hooves on the road.

I glanced down at my hands, twiddling my fingers together. Reciting my terrible origin story, attempting to keep my voice void of emotion. "My father was a merchant. He traded goods far and wide down the coast."

Memories of the past whispered in my ears, the visions replaying in my eyes as if it had happened yesterday. I found myself willing to answer her questions, truthfully. "Carriage rides were fun when I was a child. Something about zooming around in one was once a way for me to pretend. To pretend to be someone else. But now I realize, fantasies can only get you so far, to ride on a horse is the way to tackle problems head on. It's the way I prefer."

"If it were proper, I too would prefer to ride on the horse versus being pulled by one. It's not the way. Carriage rides as a royal is the practical way." Queen Alieta gazed out the window. There was a certain amount of loneliness oozing out of her words.

I turned away, ashamed at the sympathy pinging my heart; I was all too aware of the feeling of loneliness. In the human realm, people seemed to always be around me. Always present to fetch me anything I wished, but trinkets never brought forth the feeling I had so desperately craved. The feeling of being wanted: loved. Belle had done that for me in Mallert and then Lilja.

This is all my fault; they're dead because of me.

"My mother used to say it was not always best to be proper but to find happiness in one's soul," I said.

"Your mother sounds like a smart woman," Alieta said, her eyes roaming my face, searching for the same feelings she felt.

"She was a brilliant woman," I said, fighting to keep my voice calm.

Alieta gave a small nod in understanding.

"If you don't mind me asking, where did you get the scar?" She all but whispered my direction, as if scared to set me off.

"Which one?" I asked, swiping my hand around my body, referencing the still fresh feeling scars littering my body from her uncle.

She sucked in a breath. "I was referencing the scar on your arm."

A look flickered over her eyes. If I had met her in any other circumstance, I would have thought it to be shame.

"My father did most of it. He was a little disapproving of my first love." Belle's face flashed before my eyes. Her colorless, lifeless body, laying on the ground. Blood pooling on top of her nightdress. Belle's mouth was open to a scream, her expression frozen in time.

"Did he not approve of the man?"

I scoffed, looking at her, my jaw clenched. "No, he disapproved of my attraction to a person. I didn't want to marry the man he chose. Because I wanted to be with a person I loved. She was a woman."

8

Proving a point

Her mouth fell open. To her credit, she quickly closed it, retracing her mental steps before responding. "I had read that same-sex couples were not as respected in the human realm. I hadn't realized to what extent my apologies for bringing up the topic. Let's restart. I don't want to begin this date on the wrong note. Look, we arrived."

She looked out the window, avoiding eye contact with me as I tried to blink away the memory of Belle.

The sounds of life happening outside the carriage drowned out Belle's guttural last breaths replaying in my ears.

Crowds cheered outside. Queen Alietas' subjects had lined the road, excited for the glimpse of her. I shrunk back in my seat as flight or fight coursed through my body. Adrenaline roaring in my ears. *People are going to see me. Many people are going to see me.* My inner voice whispered. Inside the walls of the castle, I was safe, so to speak. Safe from curious eyes ogling at the human 'prisoner'.

Would they think of me as a prisoner? Or simply a toy of the Queens.

I wonder if there would be any of Aidan's spies at the event. What would they tell him? Was he, like Lilja, presumed dead? My stomach churned at the idea, all the elves I had called family, who took me in, dead?

"Come on, Elowen, once I finish, we can explore the market. The Gods and Goddess's are the ones who built our world into what it is today. Today, our people celebrate the new form of the Earth. For spring comes near."

She exited the carriage, holding out her hand to me.

Ours, the word slipped out, with ease. I almost hadn't caught it. She thought I was hers.

I would never be hers.

Begrudgingly, I took it, my thoughts only furthering my soured mood. Knowing if I didn't, I'd more than likely face plant into the trampled snow before me, retracting my hand back as quickly as I could. I blinked, staring at the courtyard. The Ardourians had decorated the market similarly to the decorations hung at the castle. Greenery woven together to make a garland hung between the buildings. Children ran around the square with streamers. A few in the shape of dragons, gold colored paper shimmering out of its mouth as the children ran. An enormous statue of a paper mache man stood erect in the middle, on a stone stage.

Unconsciously, I shivered. The air had yet to turn warm into the spring air. Snow still littered the ground, dirt and melted sludge had covered it. "Are you cold? I forget our species are as different as we are similar. You catch the chill quicker than an elf. Here," she extended her hand out to me again. Her nails were clean, unlike the dirty plans Ardour cast to Valdis.

"I'll use my power to keep you warm. You'll just have to hold my hand for it to work." She straightened her posture, gazing into my eyes as if pleading with me. A smile played on her lips like she has been planning this all along.

I reached out, touching her hand. Once intertwined, heat spread from my hand, traveling to the rest of my body until my body halted its shivers. Queen Alieta grinned at me, pulling me forward to the festivities. People gawked at us, our intertwined hands causing unwanted attention. I fought the itch to pull away, the warmth too tempting to want to keep.

An elderly man shuffled to us, a large decorated staff in hand. "Your highness, a lively blessed day to you and your acquaintance." His eyes flicked down to our conjoined hands and quickly back to her face. So fast, if you weren't looking for it, you would swear it never happened.

Queen Alieta nodded her head in response to the man, grinning. "Hello Sir Victor, the celebration looks magical so far. Let's get this speech on with so we can continue with the festivities, shall we?" With the wave of her hand, the elderly man scrambled forward, using his staff to part the sea of people before us. The smell of roasted nuts wafted in the air, along with smoked meat.

Queen Alieta leaned into me, her lips just barely brushing against my ear. I bit the inside of my cheek, resisting the urge to pull away. "I am going to let go of your hand. You must stay in the spot I leave you. Don't cause a scene. Be good, little mouse." She gave my hand a tight squeeze before pulling away, the chill quickly setting in again.

The ice firmed itself to my toes once again. I took a step back at her reaction. One guard stood his ground, grunting at my movement. The other followed Queen Alieta to the small set up temporary stage, like a dog.

The crowd cheered, whooping as Queen Alieta waved with a smile adorning her lips. "The people of Ardour. I am pleased to see so many of you enjoying the festivities of this season! The sickness on the other side of the mountain ravages Valdis residents. We are fortunate to not only be untouched, but to thrive midst this crisis. Ardourians are the bricks to the foundation of this great time. Attacks have ceased on the shores of Nyrim and Llidan. We are truly prosperous. In the words of Athren, we must purge unnecessary things to be who we are truly meant to be."

As Queen Alieta finished her speech, the crowd went wild. My stomach flipped, threatening to spill whatever weighed on my stomach. She has to be responsible for the blight. The annihilation of Valdis allows growth for Ardour. Kallan and Armand tortured the general and received all the confirmation I needed. Alieta had to be involved in the Blight.

My thoughts were interrupted as she shot out a flame of fire from her fingers to the pyre below the paper machete stature. Sending the statue up in flames, I looked back at the Queen. Fire flashed in her eyes. The paper machete casing fell away, burning up revealing a beautiful woman. Her features a mirror of the paper casing.

I shivered at the small blast of heat; it doing nothing to warm the chill plunging into my bones. Queen Alieta descended from the stage, looping her fingers around mine. "Let's go buy something to eat. I'm famished."

Her heat spread through me once again, pausing the shivers that wracked through me.

"Does Ardour have anything to do with the blight?" I said, anger simmering inside of me. My free hand gripped into a fist, my nails cutting into my palm.

Perhaps it was insane to ask so forthrightly. But people were dying. Fate entwined Lilja and I's lives together. To love and to hold. Although fate brought us together, the feelings we had for each other were real. It felt like my duty to protect Valdis like she would. Even if she no longer stood on the earthy plane.

Queen Alieta raised her eyebrow, pulling me closer; squeezing my hand tighter to an almost painful grip. "Why would you ask such a thing?" She sounded horrified as she glanced around, looking for anyone eavesdropping on our conversation, the heat from her hand becoming increasingly uncomfortable.

"You make it sound like Ardour is thriving so well because of the blight, as if without it you'd be less well off." My heart beat fast in my chest. I shrank away from her as far as our clenched hands would allow.

"I can assure you the crown has nothing to do with the blight. It is merely a coincidence. It is true Ardour has never been so well off. My parents' time was tough. Thousands of elves suffered. A number of them perished under the fights against Valdis. It is high time prosperity reigns over us. My uncle and my parents have created structure for my people," Alieta replied, her voice monotonous as if just regurgitating information fed to her on a silver spoon.

"Structure? You mean reigning over all. It's not right." My eyes were wide as if she would be able to read the truth written in them.

She looked away from me gathering her thoughts. "Quit this banter and enjoy the festivities, please, my little mouse. This isn't how I envisioned today to go. I have never wanted to reign over all elves. Ardour is enough for me; I only want my people to thrive." She ran her thumb over the back of my hand as she used her magic to warm me.

How was she able to utilize it so well without overexerting herself? My inner voice wondered.

The heat that was just a moment earlier was too warm had turned into a soft warmth. The smile that played on her face gone, replaced with a thin lipped expression.

The day pulled by. The Queen ignored my outburst earlier. Either from annoyance or truthfulness, *I didn't know.* Ardourians laughed around us as we explored the market. A puppet show played for the small children. One child ignored the show, running around in the melting snow, caking themselves in mud.

We stood there for a moment, taking in the scene before us. Even with the earlier instance, this one was peaceful as we watched the kids laugh at the puppet show.

It wasn't long before it was disrupted. The child's uncoordinated feet caused them to face plant into the slush on the ground. She sat up, her almost white blond hair stuck plastered to her face as she tried to wipe it away. She opened her mouth, wailing. I unloosed my fingers from Alieta's, running to the child. My urge to help the child, overwhelming. No child should be let to suffer if I had the ability to lend aid. She looked up at me, her eyes almost comically large as they brimmed with tears.

"I want my mama!" She said, using her fists to wipe the tears away. Her hand went to her hair, twirling it as she wailed.

"Shh, it's okay, little one. What's your name?" I patted her head, shivering.

"My name is Marci," she hiccuped.

"What a pretty name, Marci. My name is Elowen. Can I help you find your mama?" I held out my hand to her, giving her a smile.

"I miss her!" Marci said as she launched herself into my arms.

I looked back towards Alieta, my eyes wide as I stood up. "What do we do?"

"Like you said, we find this little one's mama." She eyed the kid and then me, lingering on my lips. Red flushed my cheeks as I looked around. Everyone seemed to be having a great time, no one appeared to frantically looking for a child.

"Marci, do you know what your mama's name is?" Alieta asked.

"Her name is mama." Marci gripped my neck, hiding her face as her tears soaked the corner of my dress. My hands purple with cold as I twirled her around, trying to keep her spirits high.

"MARCI!" a gruff feminine voice called out. I whipped my head around toward the sound. A short plump woman appeared from behind the stall selling soup. She had on a food covered apron on, her hair white like Marci's.

"There you are! You're in so much trouble, young lady. Look at you all soiled. Today is meant to be a celebration and here you are getting carried around by some stranger." She looked up at me finally, scrutinizing me. Her eyes focusing in on my scar on my cheek and then on my ears, before looking at Alieta next to me.

If I weren't so cold, I would have laughed at the complete 360 her facial expression did. She immediately dropped to her knees, her eyes on the ground.

"Oh, your highness, thank you so much for finding my dear Marci. I was up to my neck in worry. I couldn't even keep up with the rush at my stall."

"Do not worry yourself, madam. Marci didn't cause any trouble. My companion immediately went to aid Marci when we saw her fall," Alieta said, her voice full of pride.

The vision in my eyes started to darken as the cold wind cut through me.

"Are you alright, my lady?" Marci's mom asked as I went limp, falling into the mud.

"Elowen!" Alieta said, reaching for me. She grabbed me, her hand touching my cheek. I leaned into it, the heat intoxicating. My teeth chattered as her eyes searched mine.

"Shit, you are freezing. Why didn't you say anything?" Alieta scooped me up.

"Do you have somewhere she can warm up for a second? She is nearly ice," Alieta asked the woman.

"Yes, your highness behind my stall is the door to my home. It's nothing special, but it's warm." She hurried in front of us, Marci in tow. The smell of the soup wafted to my nose as the door flung open. Her house was dark, even with the fire that roared in the fireplace. The windows shuttered, only allowing slivers of natural light in.

"I'm so cold," I said, my teeth chattering together, even with Alieta's heat glowing throughout me, a shiver wracked my body. The women plopped, sniffling Marci by the door and yanked a blanket to the ground, directly in front of the fire.

My self-respect left my body as I cuddled closer into Alieta whom dropped down in front of the fireplace. "Shh, little mouse. Let me help." Her hand cupped my cheek and heat flooded into me. My teeth were chattering so hard I fear they would break.

Alieta's arms wrapped around me, placing me in her lap, her arms wrapped around me, pulling me impossibly close. My instinct screamed at me to get closer, to wrap myself in her warm embrace. It was as if it screamed for me to be inside her skin.

The logical side of me was itching to be away. Far enough away that I couldn't feel her breath on my neck. Far enough away that I couldn't feel the soft skin of her hands on my face.

Marci's mom busied around the room frantically, grabbing another blanket. Putting it on top of Alieta's shoulders. "Here you go, your highness, my apologies for the mess. Children make it mighty difficult to keep the place clean."

"Thank you for your help, madam, truly." Alieta held out one of her hands, grabbing onto the ladies, kissing it lightly.

"Oh, your highness," the older women squealed, her cheeks flushing pink.

"Please give us a moment to recuperate. If that's okay?" Alieta looked up at her, her doe eyes doing the work of persuasion.

"Of course, your highness. Anything for you. Marci, let us give the Queen and her friend some privacy." She pulled away from Alieta, scooping up her child shutting the door with a slam so hard it shook the frame.

"Come closer, little mouse, let me warm you." She pulled my chin closer, her lips and mine close. Warning bells in my ears went off and I scrambled off her.

"Your highness," I said, my blood roared in my ears. "Thank you for your help. I feel guilty for making such a scene. We should get back to the festivities." The fire warmed my back as I inched closer to it. Welcoming the flames instead of the arms of the enemy.

Alieta paused, her hands up in the air, accepting my refusal. She looked toward the door, listening to the quiet before speaking. "It sounds like the festivities of the day are over. Now, while I am sure someone is having a party somewhere. I do not think you are equipped to party the night away in your current condition. Her smile shone on her face, as if she was laughing at my reaction.

I tried to play it off, giving her a small smile. *Stay cute, demure. Don't let her sense your discomfort,* my inner voice chanted as we left Marci's house. I tried to ignore how my heart swelled as Alieta dropped coins into the woman's hands. *She's nice to her subjects. Can she really be that cruel to Valdis's subjects?* Be the cause of thousands of souls, while she could hold me so tenderly.

The walk to the carriage was short, her hand seeming to be permanently looped with mine. *The only reason I allowed this was to keep warm,* I told myself.

She had to be responsible; I thought to myself as the horses pulled us back to the castle. My heart constricted as we got closer and closer to my overly comfortable imprisonment.

"Thank you for spending the day with me, Elowen. My apologies for allowing you to get so cold. It was quite enamoring to watch you save the child, Marci. I forget how sensitive humans are to the chill."

Queen Alieta clambered out of the carriage, holding her hand out to me.

"I want you to know, I have nothing to do with the blight that ravages the Valdis community. I'm not a bad person. While my kingdom might reap the benefits of Valdis' demise, we did not cause this." I avoided her eyes as I got out. *Alieta had to be responsible.*

The guards opened the door, as the Queen walked me inside and up to my room. Silence was prevalent on the way up. Alieta opened the door to the bedroom, my cage. I went to walk inside, but she pulled me back. We were impossibly close, a few mere inches away from each other. "I wanted today to be special, Elowen. I-I-I'm sorry things got muddled. Please forgive me." Queen Alieta grabbed the back of my neck, pulling me toward her, kissing me. Her teeth grazed my bottom lip, capturing it.

I gasped, grappling for her waist, pushing myself away from her. *No, this can't happen!* Petrified, I leaned against the door, my chest rising fast. Her face reddened before dissipating. "What was that?" I fought the urge to rub the feeling of her lips off of my own.

"That is how I wanted today to go, Elowen. This could be your life. You are an enigma, my little mouse. Your eyes show such emotion, yet you never speak of them. I want to provide for you. I feel drawn to your person. As if Mabilia has brought you to the Elven Realm for me." She waved her hand around, gesturing to the castle. My eyes flicked to the guards, their expressions blank, unreadable.

"To prove to you I am not a bad person, I will meet you halfway. I will not lock you room tonight. You may be free to roam around the castle as you please. These two men will be the detail to follow you around, to make sure you don't wander where you are not supposed to go. Their names are Lucas and Wallace." Her jaw was clenched, as if it angered her to have to prove herself to me. Without waiting for my reply, she turned walking back down the hall, her footsteps the only sound echoing in the hallway.

I closed the door to my room while my new babysitters gratefully stayed on the outside of the hallway. Bile climbed its way up my throat as disgust ran through me.

The Queen kissed me.

No Matter What

I swallowed the sickness that threatened to climb out of my mouth as I paced my room. My thoughts running wild as if at the front of a herd of untamed horses. *I need to find out what's causing the blight. Queen Alieta seems to be innocent, or at the very least, playing the innocent queen. Could she really be innocent? Lilja would want me to find the cause.*

A few stray tears welled in my eyes as I thought of her, a flash of the attack flashed before my eyes, Kallan holding her body. She died for this. I have to do anything. Right? That's what she would want? Me to succeed? No matter what. Right?

Queen Alieta wants me. Maybe she holds the key to the blight. Whoever was in the vision Sylp showed me is the guilty one. A man, he appeared to be my father's age. He looked important. What did the Olken elf call him? Commander? He would be old now.

I thought of the vision: the man pouring the poison into the water. His maniacal smile grew on his lips as he signed the death certificate for thousands of people. *The vision dates back 400 years. How long do Elves live? He could be dead?* My stomach dropped. "The man who was responsible could be dead," I said to myself. I stopped pacing long enough to change out of the festival clothes. Slipping back out into the hallway, the guards eyed me curiously as I yanked the door closed.

"Would you gentlemen, show me the paintings of the past leaders of Ardour?"

They shared a glance, nodding. Without a reply, they turned and walked down the hallway. I suppressed a grin. If this went as planned, I could find the person to blame.

The guards soon confused me with the twists and turns. I quickly lost my bearings. Each hallway looked the same to me as I noticed a pattern. Most hallways comprised the same number of entryways. Until we ventured deeper into the west wing, the hallways had fewer doorways, as if the rooms were larger. The light in the hallway was dimming as the sun turned toward the moon.

"Why does this place look different from the rest of the castle?" I asked both of the guards.

"When Ardour was first created as a kingdom. The existing castle was in disrepair. The king at the time wanted to show his strength within the architecture, so he built around the old castle building it out. We're venturing closer to the Queen's rooms. From this point forward, these rooms are almost entirely the Queen's private rooms." I nodded a thanks to him, my mind whirling. *So many rooms? For one person?* With my mind wandering, I barely noticed my new babysitter stopping. I stopped just in time for me to avoid propelling myself into him. Paintings covered the hallway walls, nearly every inch of the wall hidden.

I marveled at the details of them. The painters had captured the essence of the person they painted. I paid close attention to the men. They all appeared almost angry. Their eyes were vacant of emotion, while their partners appeared almost bubbly. *Opposites must attract,* I thought to myself as we neared the end of the hallway.

The paintings appeared to become more modern as we meandered through the hall. Each painting in the line appeared less muddy yellow as time seeped into it. I looked up at the second-to-last painting. The central person in the painting seemed to be Alieta's father, his face young-looking. A pretty blond-haired woman sat next to him, holding a baby, presumably Alieta herself. My breath caught as I looked at the man behind Alieta's father. My eyes were drawn to his uniform, the design the same as on the man in the vision. The same type of pins and buttons decorated the front. In fact, they appeared identical.

I squinted at the face, perhaps a few years older in this painting. His facial features were virtually identical. He was the man who, all those years ago, had decapitated Sylp's father. The man who locked the nymphs up. He was responsible for the blight, the assumption fueled my anger since my capture finally illuminated in proof. The crown of Ardour was responsible for the pain and suffering of Valdis.

I gestured to the man. "Who is the man behind the king?"

"That Ms. Alwyn is Daveed, the uncle to the Queen. It's getting late now. Would you like to return to your room?" Wallace said, his voice low.

Her uncle must have been working under the command of her parents, and since they are gone, he's working for her, a puppet for a larger monster.

I mulled the question over in my mind. My heart thumped in my chest as I made my resolve. "No, take me to the Queen, please. I'd like to talk to her." Lucas sucked in his breath, but didn't argue with me.

"It's just through that door." One of them tapped on the door I stood next to. *What was I planning?* My palms grew sweaty as I heard a faint voice on the other side. I slipped in the door, leaving the guards in the hallway. *Lilja would want me to do anything to save Valdis, right? Even if it meant sleeping with the enemy?*

Queen Alieta wanted me; she thought Mabilia sent me to her, that I was her fated, a little mouse, brought here for her.

I could use the emotions she had for me for more freedom. To make her trust me. For more opportunities outside the castle. No doubt with her in tow, but I could slip away. Take a free opportunity and run away. My inner thoughts chanted the reasoning to the rest of my brain, trying to calm the rest of it. I wiped my sweaty hands on my clothes. My heart beat behind my eyes as I set them on her.

She sat in her enormous bed, her long hair cascading down the front of her. A small book was in one of her hands, the other hand occupied with a flask.

"Elowen, what a pleasant surprise. What do I owe the pleasure?" Her voice held no hint of surprise. Quite the opposite. As if she expected me to come knocking on her door in the night.

"Queen Alieta-"

"Call me Alieta, darling. Like I told you before." The Queen corrected me as she took another swig of whatever was in her flask. Her lips set into a smile.

"Alieta," I breathed, trying to wipe the sweat off my hands and onto my dress. "I was thinking about what you said earlier, a-and I agree. I want to be together like this," I said, gesturing to myself in her chambers, the opulence overwhelming. Cloth wallpaper covered the walls. Gold embellishments shone proudly on the corners of her bed frame. Books lined the wall to the right.

In most ways, Alieta seemed like a perfectly normal adult. Someone I could grow close to. Her mood, her temperament, all so similar to Belle. But her family was causing such destruction.

Shakily, I walked up to her bed; her eyebrow rose at my movement. Trying my best to act like an animal ready to pounce on its prey. She closed her book as I got to the side of her bed. *Lilja, please forgive me,* I thought as I pulled Alieta's face closer to mine. Capturing her lip, I sucked on it. Earning a grunt of pleasure from her.

I needed her trust, with her happiness as a guise.

"Alieta, please," I said, pulling away, pressing our foreheads together.

"Please, what?" Alieta said, a grin growing on her face. *Smug bastard. I'm giving her exactly what she wants, me wanting her.*

"Before, I was an unwilling pet, but now I want to be your pet. Please make me yours," I said, a little breathy moan at the end of my words. That was all it took for Alieta to pull me onto the bed.

She rolled on top of me, pulling the shift I had put on earlier up far enough to reveal my bare skin.

I tucked myself into the darkest part of my brain, compartmentalizing as Alieta had her way with me. My body reacted to her, only furthering her actions.

My inner voice chided me. "Don't feel. Don't see."

The mantra was repeated over and over again until the deed was done. *I was doing this for Lilja. Getting close to Alieta would allow me the freedom to explore, learn, and escape.*

"Hm, I knew you would come to me, little mouse. I just didn't realize you would be so submissive to me. I love it when my women squirm under me," she mumbled into my mouth, pulling away to kiss down to my breasts. I pictured Lilja's face on hers. Her voice swapped out for Lilja's.

I pushed my feelings aside for the moment, deep down. My heart hammered into a little steel box as we completed the act.

We lay there panting as we caught our breaths in silence; the guilt threatening to break the fake facial expression donning my face. *I betrayed her. I didn't deserve her.*

"Oh my darling, I have waited so long for that moment to come. To lie here like this has been my dream since I first laid eyes on you. The moment we created just now cements it. Only Mabilia could have sent someone as beautiful and kind to me." She leaned over, kissing the top of my head that was on her arm. Her breath smelled like the alcohol in the flask that lay beside her bed.

I gasped, choking on my air, coughing.

"Alieta, this-this was a mistake. I have to go." My voice cracked as my resolve chipped away, like an old plaster wall. I rolled out of the bed quickly, smoothing down my mussed hair. My eyes darted from the bed to the door, wanting to run away. Rub my skin raw. Forget this ever happened. *Not worth it.*

But it was worth it. Valdis needed to be saved. Even though I had yet to set foot in the kingdom. Lilja had fought so hard to keep her people alive. Some hated her for her 'disappearance.' If she were dead, it was my responsibility to keep her goal alive.

"We share a connection, darling. Can't you see? Now we are together forever. Forever entwined." Her thin yet muscular hand stretched out from the bed, as if reaching for me. Alieta twisted two of her fingers together to symbolize us holding them up.

Forever?

"Sleep on it, little one, you will see. The fates bring us together," she said as I reached the door.

I yanked them open, looking back at her grinning face and then back at the men. The guards looked at me, their eyes in slits as they eyed me up and down as if knowing exactly what I had just done with their queen. *They probably heard us,* my face red.

"Would you like to go back to your chambers now?" One of them said as I leaned against the door, my eyes on the ceiling, as I debated throwing myself out a window.

"What? Oh. Yes, please, I-I have training with Fian in the morning." I took one last glance at Daveed before following the two guards into the labyrinth of hallways and bringing me to my room.

I shivered as I closed the door, trying my best to ignore the wetness between my legs, the love bite on my breasts. The fireplace was dead; no flames protruded from the coals that lay there. *I deserved to shiver.*

Leaning against the door, I slid to the ground, tears staining their way down my cheeks. A silent sob stifled up as I used the collar of my shift to wipe the snot off my nose.

Why?

Why?

WHY!?

The gods had a sick sense of humor. I pounded my fists against the floor, leaving bruises for the morrow. A silent scream came out of my mouth, the shame of the encounter leaving me silent. Snot and tears mixed on my face like a deranged artist's palette. The world was dark, darker than ever before.

Lilja, Lilja, Lilja. How could you? How could you leave me in this world by myself? With this responsibility.

On my hands and knees still, I crawled over to my bed, clambering up.

I had to do it. I have to do this. Valdis needs me. I repeated the mantra as I calmed my racing heart. The kingdom will fall if I don't complete what Lilja started. All those elves will die if I don't help find the cure for the blight.

With the blankets pulled over my shivering frame, I snatched Olken Ridge from the nightstand. Flicking it open to where I left off, shame coursing through my veins.

Because of the network of tunnels under the plateau, the naturally occurring rooms were ideal meeting rooms for secret organizations to thrive in. Others say the religion on the plateau used the rooms for sacrifices to enhance their powers and control over non-magical elves.

The River God Pavati's shrine is there. It is said that the rivers of the world flow through the plateau, becoming purified on their route.

I raised an eyebrow at the last sentence in the book, my heart thrumming. *Could that be the key to the blight?* My mind went back to the vision. The man poured the contents of the vials into the water. Could the River Goddess purify the poison away?

I flipped through the book, scanning the pages for more information about the shrine, finding nothing. My bare feet pattered on the cold stone floor as I scrambled to the door, ignoring the questions from the guards that followed behind me.

The statues guarding the library stared at me ominously as I entered it. My eyes scanned the titles that glittered in the candlelight. "What are you doing? Another round with the Queen?" Lucas asked, earning a smack from the other.

There had to be something else. In another book, I need more information. "What? No! I-I finished this book, and it ended so well. I *need* to find the second book."

"Can't it wait till the morrow? Don't you have training in the morning?" Wallace said, trying to reason with me.

"No!" I paused, pulling myself away from the shelf long enough to glance at the guards.

"I mean, no. It's too enticing to not finish reading it tonight. I must get the book if I wish to sleep a wink."

"You'd think she'd be tired enough after tonight," Lucas mumbled under his breath.

I turned back to the shelf as I swallowed the lump in my throat. I held the candle up, the titles of the book becoming legible. *Pavati,* the title gleamed as if it were a peacock trying to find a mate. It took everything in me not to let out a shriek. I shivered as the bound book came into contact with my skin, sending a tingle down my spine. *This was it,* I thought back to myself. I turned back to the guard.

Despite the experience from earlier, I felt a small smile play on my lips.

"Can we please just go back to your chambers, miss? It's late, and I cannot speak for the Queen's wants, but I very much doubt she gave you this freedom to go wandering the castle in the dark alone." He crossed his arms, his biceps rippling under his shirt.

"I'm not alone. After all, you're here with me." I gave him a long look, as if trying to prove that I was right. He grunted, turning away from me as he led me back to my cage. *Not for long.*

I tossed and turned throughout the night. Unable to crack open the book on Pavati, not wanting to risk the guards furthering suspicions. The birds' call alerted me to my sleepless night. My brain wandered as I readied myself for Fian's day of training. My eyes fixated on the book as I braided my hair, almost as if it called to me.

The guard, who was absent the night before, knocked on the open door. "It's time for training, Miss Alwyn. Are you feeling okay? You appear out of sorts."

I raised an eyebrow at him. "Yes, I am well. Just feeling a bit tired." I yawned. The bed seemed to call to me as we walked away from it. My face flushed as I thought about the night before.

He gave me a sympathetic look as we traveled through the castle, nearing the back door. Lucas snickered, elbowing Wallace.

"Elowen, good morning. I have something for you," the queen's voice sang, echoing in the quiet castle. She held a pink box, and a large ribbon hung off the side.

"I'd hate for you to be cold on your walk to the training building." Her head was high. If I embarrassed her by my exit yesterday, it didn't show. I took the box, feigning a grateful smile. My hands shook as I undid the ribbon to reveal a golden cloak. Red and green threads adorned the hood and the edges. It was disgustingly expensive-looking. The Queen grabbed it from the box, unraveling it, laying it across my shoulders, and pinning the phoenix brooch in the front.

Bowing, I smiled at her, pushing down my annoyance. *She keeps trying, trying to get past my barriers. It won't work,* I thought miserably, fighting another yawn.

I needed to gain her trust so I could find a moment to escape. The Queen grabbed my chin, pulling me up from my bow, planting a small kiss on my lips.

"Train well, little pet." She didn't notice or didn't bother to mention the bags under my eyes.

Without another word, she turned, striding away from me and the ever-cycling babysitters. He motioned me forward, toward Fian.

"Elowen! Took your sweet time today, I see. Three minutes late! If this were an attack, I'd be dead because YOU didn't have my back. Now take that pretty cloak off and give me twenty laps around the room."

I gaped at her, looking back for my babysitter, who had mysteriously disappeared. *Lucky bastard.* My lungs burned. However, what had once felt impossible had now felt like a mere annoyance. The training from Fian had worked after a few mere weeks. I was now in the best shape I had ever been in my entire life, at least physically.

I all but swayed, walking back to the castle. Exhaustion weighed on me heavily. The excitement of reading the book was the only thing keeping me on my feet. I trudged through my room's door, allowing the guard to shut the door before leaping over to the book. My fingertips tingled as they came into contact with the cover.

Pavati's shrine is located inside Olken Ridge, rumored to have a large body of water at the site of the shrine. The water has magical properties. It's said to heal any sickness for the price of three ingredients.

The pages' words seemed to swirl and glow as I tried to read them, becoming illegible. I gaped as the words floated off the page, flying up into the room. My mouth hung open as the words formed into a transparent silhouette. There stood a woman. She appeared to have long, black double-braided hair. Beaded hairpins secured her hair tightly in place. She held her head high as she spoke, her eyes staring dead ahead. Unfocused, as if she could not see me.

"To the one who will save me-"

10

Pavati

"To the one who will save me, Olken Ridge is not all that it seems. The land surrounding the plateau is perilous. Dark magic users have sucked it dry. They have trapped me here. I can undo it. I can cleanse the water once again. For three hundred years, I kept it away. Bring me the supplies I need. The heretics keep me locked away. They are dangerous-" the person's eyes shift around the room as if looking for someone to stop her from talking.

"I have on good authority that this book will find you. How ironic, a book about me, Pavati, the goddess of rivers. Fate is a fickle thing, Leland has assured me. It will reach you." Pavati jolts away from the focus of the spell, clawing her way back into the frame, blood streaking her face. Her calmness shattered.

"Please! You must get me out! The land needs my help to survive! Bring me the blood of a water nymph! A claw of a water dragon! A human who-."

Pavati's form blinked out of existence, filling the room with silence and darkness. The stars that had formed her dissipated, flickering to the ground like little sparks of flame.

A human- she needed a human. I swallowed the lump in my throat. Human blood, *no*, a human sacrifice. I felt sick, bile climbed its way up my throat.

I had to, Lilja's people were on the line, Elbio. If I didn't step up, who would?

My mind swirled with thoughts as I scrambled out of bed. My bare feet pattered on the cold stone floor. With my body full of newfound energy, I left my room heading toward the library, with one of my ever-rotating guards behind me.

I needed more, more information. A water dragon? How was I supposed to find one of those? A mere three ingredients and the blight will be over.

As I approached the library, the door was wide open. The queen stood in front of a shelf, grabbing a book. "Your highness," I said, sweat beading on my forehead. My eyes shifted around the room, landing on her.

"I did not expect you to be in the library at this hour." I glance at the clock. Fians' training session took the better half of the day. The clock neared the seventh hour, almost time for dinner.

"I could say the same for you, Ms. Alwyn. You were coming in here with a fire underneath your feet, looking for something in particular. Perhaps I can help. Like I said before, I've read every book in this room."

I mulled over her reply. *Tell her the truth. Her uncle is behind this.*

"I was reading about a goddess, and the book mentions a water dragon. Quite honestly, I thought dragons were fables, tales you told your children to behave. I wanted to read about them." *There is no reason to lie about this. She won't know what it's for.* She put her hand on her chin, as if in deep thought.

"Dragons are real, at least in this realm. I am a bit ill-informed about the existence of dragons in the human realm. There are four different species of dragons, much like the four elements. They are very ancient beings, older than elves. Elves believe dragons are the original creators of magic. With their claws, they carved the lands, and with their fire, they breathed power into a select few of us. If you could believe that. Unfortunately, there are very few alive now. In the past, they were hunted to near extinction. The rumor of the time was if you killed a dragon, their power would go to you. As you could imagine, that much power was very tantalizing."

Queen Alieta walked to the smaller room off to the side before leaning down on the very bottom shelf. She pulled a spotless book from the shelf, holding it out to me. I outstretched my hand, ready to grab it and retreat to my room.

Queen Alieta pulled it away and behind her. "I will give this book to you. But you have to go on a picnic with me and read it to me."

I pulled back my hand. "But I have training tomorrow with Fian." My heart jumped in my throat. *What was she planning? The night we shared was a mistake. I thought I could take the stress of betraying Lilja.*

My chest heaved up as I struggled to keep my breath. My heart beat behind my eyes as I fought to control my breathing.

Queen Alieta looked down at me, her eyebrows raised. "Your guard tells me you appeared exhausted this morning. Perhaps one day off, to rest and relax, will do you some good."

"Besides, I'd like to see why this book is truly so interesting to you. You may have it only then, so decide now." She had a lopsided grin on her face; her eyes held no emotion. I nodded, doing my best to look timid.

Elowen, Darach's voice seemed to say in my ear. "Of course, your highness," I did my best not to react.

Bells began tolling, Alieta's eyes went wide, turning to the guards.

"I would love to go on a picnic with you," I said before bidding her good night, I gave a curtsey.

Can anyone else hear her?

"One of you stay with Elowen, the other figure out what the bell is tolling for," Alieta said, her lips in a forced smile. I paused for a second, taking in her body language. Her hands twitched toward a phantom sword on her hip.

Wallace gripped my arm, tight enough to warn me not to fight against him.

The bell was the least of my concerns. Darach was nearby. I held my breath as every instinct in me told me to run back to my bedroom. Instead, I balled my fist, forcing myself to walk.

Elowen, her voice called out in my ear again. I looked at the guard's face in my peripheral vision. He showed no sign of hearing Darach speak to me.

"Good night, Ms. Alwyn. Ms. Cailin will be by in the morning to help you get ready for your date tomorrow," the guard said as he opened the door, shutting me inside.

My room was dark, save for the almost full moon streaming through the window. Its glow enveloped the room in an eerie glow. "Darach, are you here?" I whispered into the darkness.

For a second, nothing happened. My hopes fell until Darach, the mother of all water and forest nymphs, emerged from the shadows.

"Honestly, I don't know how my sister Hesper and her kids do this every night." She shivered. "The darkness is just terrible. It gets rid of my tan. No wonder they are so dreadfully pale."

"Darach, why are you here?" I said, trying to keep my mouth from gaping at her.

"Pushy thing, aren't you? I've come here today to tell you, fate is in motion. Bring Pavati's book with you tomorrow for your date." She claps her hands silently. "For your date. I have to say you have more gusto than I thought. Never did I think I'd see two queens pining after the same human. I can't say I see what they see." Darach looks down at me past her nose.

"Tomorrow is the day you will escape, because I'm going to help you."

For the rest of the night, we went over the plan. It was simple. I drug the tea the Queen drinks, wait until she passes out, and run to the north.

I tried to suppress the trepidatious feeling of excitement that coursed through my veins. *Freedom, one thing that has constantly felt out of reach since my captivity in Ardour. Finally, within my grasp because of a little tea mixture.*

"How am I supposed to drug the tea without her noticing?" I ask Darach as she hands me a small dried-out flower.

"That is for you to find out, Elowen. I can't give you all the answers now, can I?"

"Is it going to kill her?" I asked, my voice barely audible. A slash of fear ran up my spine, followed by shame.

Darach paused, stepping back. "Why does it matter? But since you ask, no, death will not befall her. She will simply fall into a deep sleep. Long enough for you to get far enough away. Now, my small human acquaintance, go to bed. I can't have you exhausted for what is to come."

"For what's to come? What's coming?" I asked the space she had once occupied seconds before.

11
Present Day

Lilja POV-Present Day

Kallan and I poised ourselves on our horses, with Esmersey as our only guide. Ardour was quiet; the darkness of night blanketed the kingdom. A majority of its subjects were asleep, unbeknownst to them, the queen of the enemy kingdom and her right-hand man rode toward it.

While Queen Zahra had welcomed my team with open arms, I couldn't help but feel antsy. Every day away from Elowen was like a stab to the heart. My subjects thought of me as a failure. A queen who didn't deserve a crown. Perhaps they were right. The loss of Elowen and the attack on Sald Forest weighed heavily on my chest as I gazed at the walls of the enemy.

"What is your plan, your highness? We cannot exactly ride right up to the castle, knock on the door, and demand Alieta hand over Elowen," he said, his voice low. His tan skin masked by a large scarf.

"I don't have one." My heart hammered behind my eyes. The sword I donned bounced on my leg with the movement of the horse.

"What do you want to do?" He asked, the sense of urgency heightening in his voice.

I mulled over the answer as we made it to the last row of trees before the massive outer wall. I dismounted, tying the fateful horse to a tree limb. Perhaps it *was* insane that I had no plan. If I wasn't worried about Kallan, I would happily march right to the castle door and cut down everyone who got in my way. My eye twitched at the thought. Nobody else could get hurt because of me.

"Get inside, find information. If we can, we get Elowen out. We have to make sure Alieta is treating her well." My voice wavered over her name. The image of her flashed before my eyes, a distant memory of my fated.

I refused for it to be only a memory. I had to get her back. Guilt ate at me as of late. I had promised to protect her. To keep her safe. Not only did I fail, but she fell into the arms of Alieta, enemy number one.

"Let's go then." He rubbed his cold hands together. Steam rushed out of his mouth as he spoke.

The rest of the team had stayed in Ebbon City awaiting command. I had deemed it too dangerous to bring all of them on this mission, much to their dismay. Aidan had looked as if he wanted to pummel me when I told him he was staying. If Kallan and I did not return, the rest of the team had to keep to the mission of finding a cure for Valdis.

Kallan and I clambered over the wall, years of training finally paying off. I crouched down on the walkway, and Kallan followed me shortly behind.

For a moment, neither of us moved, waiting for a guard or a commoner to set the alarm. I breathed a sigh of relief, running up toward the upper circle section. My heart hammered as we passed the area where Elowen and I stayed. Our own place, *if only it wasn't a facade.*

A drunkard cackled as he swaggered into the alley near us to piss. Kallan and I hit the deck, flattening ourselves on the cobblestone floor. I held my breath, waiting for him to leave our area. Even though we were a story above him, I didn't want to risk being seen. Two figures dressed in black did not instill faith into onlookers.

"We need to keep moving, your highness," Kallan said. I cringed at the title; no doubt, only a ploy to keep me from snapping at him. I took a calming breath, and the earth seemed to beg me to manipulate it. For me to use it to crush the obstacles in my way.

He peered over the wall like a cat. The drunkard had crumpled to the ground, passed out. We dropped down to the ground, and I grimaced at the smell in the alley, overwhelming.

I tugged my tunic over my nose, bee lining out. Shops lined the streets, a stark difference from the alley. We danced shadow to shadow. *It would be so nice to turn invisible. Is that even a power?*

The festival for the change of seasons occurred a few days before, banners still hung proudly from building to building. Paper strips were still strewn in random spots of the street, yet to be picked up.

"There is something below us, networks of tunnels," I said thoughtfully as my shoes slapped the cobblestone path.

Kallan only grunted in response, pointing to a child. She slept in a corner of the face of a shop, her bag overfilled with newspapers. A small, filthy dragon stuffy sat next to her, dropped in her slumber. She had a tattered cloak, the only defense against the still cold weather. My heart tugged for the child, all alone in a world that would try to crush them.

Kallan walked over to the child silently, plucking a paper, and I placed a coin in their sleeping hand; her grubby hand closed over it like a clam. Even in her sleep, she was trying her best to survive.

We continued moving, hiding in the shadows to avoid the guards that patrolled the grounds. Kallan folded the paper in his satchel.

Before long, the castle, where Elowen lay, stood before us. My heart hammered in my chest, the earth seemed to siren call for me to use it to my will.

"Elowen, my love. Please call back to me," I projected through the fated bond. I closed my eyes, feeling for the tug. The brick wall between us stood proudly, staring me down as if laughing at my attempt.

I stomped my foot, the map of the land imprinting itself in my head as I did so. The ground grumbled in protest, and nearby buildings groaned in protest, shaking.

"Your highness, Lilja. Calm yourself. It will do us no good to be taken into custody by the Ardourians," Kallan said as he peered around the dark street. He pressed his back against the wall. I followed him.

I peeked out into the courtyard, shivering, as the cold cut through the streets. Various plants lined the winding walkways, our path to success. Oddly enough, no guards patrolled the inside.

"So much for guards. Not that I'm complaining, but damn, does Ardour think they are invincible?" Kallan whispered as he stepped out of the shadows and into the courtyard, his hands on his hips.

Ardour does think they are invincible against Valdis; years of growing had done their Kingdom a wonder. An abundance of plants filled the courtyard. Ardour had someone upkeep the maintenance of the streets and buildings. Besides the child, the people we had passed in the streets, appeared well to do. None bone thin, from the lack of food.

I followed Kallan, not trusting my own judgement of marking the way. The fated bond pulled at me; she was so close. My heart fluttered at the thought.

"Can you feel her?" Kallan whispered as he ran up to the castle. "Anything that could lead us to her?"

"She's close by." I focused on the tug, the feeling of unconditional love. I held my breath as if it would allow me to pinpoint her location. I moved toward the back of the castle. Plants seemed to be poised in every corner possible against the walls.

Branches snagged on my skin and clothes as I inched closer to the balcony that jutted from the wall. Guards spoke lowly somewhere on the other side of the garden. My heart hammered in my chest as I felt their footsteps reverberate on the frozen ground. Kallan and I quickly crouched down, trying to seem as small as possible.

"Careful, Lilja. We can't afford to be caught," Kallan said, stating the obvious. I rolled my eyes, fighting the devil on my shoulder that said to smack the shit out of him.

Huh, really, I didn't think of that, I thought cynically.

My hands brushed the side of the rough balcony stone. I grunted as I pulled myself up. Food from Ebbon City had reinvigorated my body. Valdis had always struggled with enough food for everyone. Oftentimes, I left dinner without food when I still lived in the castle. With the knowledge that the 'leftover' food would go to the servants and their families.

Queen Zahra had been smart enough to shut down her city from the outside world. Even going as far as blocking the use of water from rivers running through Valdis. No doubt saving them from Valdis' fate.

I pulled myself up, turning to help reach for Kallan's hand. "Damn you need to lay off the food stall. You weigh enough to put an ox to shame."

"Shut it and pull me up." Kallan grinned at me. We had scaled to the first level.

I peered in through the glass-paneled balcony door. Darkness seemed to ooze from the walls, preventing me from getting a good look.

"Up or through?" Kallan asked. I bit my lip, mulling over the answer.

"Up." I reached up at the next stone that jutted out enough for my hand and foot to grab onto.

"Any guards?" I asked Kallan, not turning around. With my feet in the air, scaling a castle, I was essentially blind to the earth. I wouldn't be able to sense the footsteps of anyone approaching.

"We're good. I can barely see anyone at this time of night," Kallan said, his hands pushing up my foot.

"Did you feel that earthquake earlier?" Someone's voice spoke out.

"Yes, Arlo must be mad," a feminine voice answered.

My eyes bulged out of my head as I flattened myself to the wall. Praying to be invisible, freezing in place.

The other scoffed. "The earth god has better things to do than have a tantrum. Odds are it was a fluke."

The balcony above the one we were on was so close. My hand inched up, my legs shaking with the exertion of staying half stretched onto the wall.

Elowen, I have to do this for Elowen.

"What the-" The man spoke. They had seen us.

I stretched to look. Their mouths stood agape before the woman sent a flare of flame up with her palm. I dropped to the ground, crouching like an animal ready to pounce.

"Move!" I shouted to Kallan. Kallan and I launched ourselves at the guards, each of us fighting one. He fought the woman. I punched the man's face, knocking him to the ground. Power hummed under my skin as I pulled the earth around his body.

"Blake!" The woman shouted; somewhere, bells tolled.

The flare of fire had alerted others. Flames erupted around her as her anger got the best of her; she threw a ball of flame towards us. I twisted the ball, singeing nothing but a bit of my clothes.

"We have to go," Kallan said as guards began swarming the yard in front of us. An arrow sang by my ear.

"Damn it." The earth swallowed the woman; she had seen too much. My stomach churned at the death.

"Halt!"

"Stop in the name of the queen!" Another guard yelled.

Kallan and I bolted for the front, dodging guards as we ran for the horses. The bell tolling to the beats of my heart as it ached at the newest failure of my reign. For I couldn't even save my fated from the enemy.

12

Sleep Tight

I paced my room many times before Cailin arrived. My heart racing, my breathing erratic as I tried to calm the nightmare that still ran through my bloodstream. Lilja had been running for her life with Kallan. I swallowed the bile that threatened to come up, moving to look out the window, pressing my forehead against the glass. The snow had finally disappeared from the landscape, the land finally catching up to the change of season. Bright green grass had pluckily peeked through the snow, emerging from its long slumber.

A whole season had passed since Lilja and I had laid eyes on each other. Held one another, I swallowed back the tears that rimmed my eyes. The thoughts were nearly overwhelming.

Calmer, I surveyed the room. The one I had stayed in for months, my cage. It looked incredibly ordinary, in only the way a castle could look. The room was bare, bare of anything that screamed 'me'. Anything that could identify what type of person I was. In here, I was just "my pet," a plaything, a possession. The outside seemed to call for me, an existence where I could be me, my own possession.

Carefully, I placed Pavati's book in the satchel I found in the closet. I inspected the dried flower ball in my hand, and an almost fern-like leaf wrapped around it like armor.

How was I to hide this, to bring it with? I opened the closet that held all the dresses that Queen Alieta deemed respectable for me to wear.

Each of them was like a costume, a facade, one ornate item of cloth to turn me into something else. Someone else.

My hands went over each dress searching for ones with pockets, pulling them to one side of the closet, trying to narrow down which one would make the most sense in the long run. It wasn't as if I could bring any supplies. Darach had only given me a route out, not a first-class ticket of luxury.

After all, the opulence that was in my life right now was exhausting. The room was too much, too stifling.

I opted for the blue one. I had yet to wear it. It was the longest dress in the closet, ideal for warmth at night. Delicately, I wrapped the dried ball in a napkin, slipping it into the pocket of the gown, just as Cailin knocked on the door. "Eager to start the day, I see. Up and already picking out a gown to wear. A perfect choice, I might add. The length will keep your legs warm on the journey."

"Journey? We aren't eating in the garden?" *My plan is already falling apart,* my inner voice replied. *It's not like I had a plan,* I thought sarcastically.

She let out a laugh. "Gods no, the Queen wishes to show you her favorite spot." Cailin grinned. Her smile fell short of reaching her eyes. Fake.

"Oh, I see. Of course, it would be lovely to go somewhere. These months have felt rather stuffy." I said, trying to recover from my disappointment.

"Where does the Queen plan on taking me for our picnic?"

"It's a surprise." Cailin refused to say anything else as she helped me get ready for the day. As calmly as I could, I grabbed my satchel, pulling on the obnoxious-looking cloak. I grinned at Cailin nervously. Hoping my nervousness wasn't translating into my smile.

She led me out and into the hallway, down to Queen Alieta. The days had finally warmed, although the nights were still frigid.

"Good Morning, Ms. Alwyn. As always, you look ravishing. I hope being without your book for one night was okay for you." She held the book in the air as I descended the steps to her.

"Perhaps, if I were under duress. It was only because I was excited to read it for you, your highness." I gave a small bow before reaching up to take the book out of her hands. She pulled away at the last second before grabbing my arm to pull me in. Using our closeness as an excuse, her lips found mine. I froze for a second, repulsed, before coming to my senses. *Distract her,* my inner voice seemed to chide.

Even though every cell in my body wanted to pull away, I kissed back. She captured my lip, sucking on it. Queen Alieta pulled away first, appearing pleasantly surprised at my reaction. I bit my lip, trying to look demure. I was red with anger, which only added to my new plan.

Cailin cleared her throat, getting our attention. "I'm sorry to interrupt, but it appears the carriage has arrived."

"Thank you, Cailin. You may go. This trip will just be us and the driver. We should be back by morrow." I stiffened beside her, praying we were going to go north. Queen Alieta helped me into the carriage as they loaded supplies onto the back. With the crack of the whip, we were off. I did my best to avoid her eyes for the rest of the trip.

The sound of the wheels hitting the stone road filled the carriage. My eyes scanned the landscape as we took off. Buildings seemed to be jammed together in the Kingdom, tightly built for its citizens, as if running out of space.

"Ardour has been expanding a lot in these past years. Growth is happening at an exponential rate, as is the birth rate. The population is booming, as is the economy. My people are running out of places to build." Alieta said as we got farther from the capital. Houses thinned out as we left the comfort of the giant walls separating the inner kingdom from the countryside. With the gates far behind us, I scanned the horizon, looking for any sign of what direction we were going.

Queen Alieta must have noticed what I was doing as she said, "If you were wondering where we're going. We're going to my favorite place, it's a small little waterfall up north. It takes a half-day's ride to get there, but the view is worth it. Don't worry yourself about the cold either. If you get cold, I am sure we could find other ways to get you warm." She placed her hand on my thigh, rubbing circles with her thumb. Heat from her magic passed through my body from her hand.

A shiver ran up my spine.

"See, warm. Imagine what I could do with more contact."

I fought the urge to roll my eyes. However I used them to roam her face with my eyes. Allowing them to drink in her features, before turning to look back out the window. I shut my eyes, leaning against the wall, allowing the carriage's motion to lull me to sleep.

After all, when would be the next time I'd find time to rest?

"Elowen, wake up. We've arrived." Queen Alieta's hand cupped my face. Instinctually, I gasped, jerking away from her touch. At some point, I had turned in my sleep and had leaned on Alieta. She narrowed her eyes into slits as I steadied myself.

"I'm sorry. You startled me. I thought you were her," I said, holding my hand to my heart for an extra effect.

Queen Alieta didn't reply before she climbed out of the carriage. Coldness oozed out of her pores as she rigidly held out her hand to me, helping me out. The driver scrambled to pull out the supplies for the picnic off the back of the carriage. I twirled around to see the view.

A waterfall was in full view. Water fell off the cliff, spraying small droplets into the air. Sunlight turned them into tiny rays of light as they cascaded down to the earth. It fed into a river rushing down south. Large rocks jutted out to the sides of the water. The grass surrounding the area had already emerged from the clutches of the snow. Little flowers sprinkled around the exposed land like sprinkles atop frosting.

"It's beautiful, isn't it?" Queen Alieta said, looping her arms around, squeezing me.

I fought against my instinct to shy away from her touch.

"Let's sit and enjoy the view." She gestured to the ground where the driver had already laid out the blanket and small cushions. I glanced over at the driver who was bent over in another chest, pulling out baskets of food items.

As gracefully as I could, I sat on one cushion, pulling out dishes from the chest next to me. Queen Alieta watched as I did so, making me feel undeniably mundane.

As if back in the Human Realm, preparing for visitors to my father's mansion.

She left her eyes on me as the driver placed the baskets next to us. Anxiety itched through me like crazy. *How was I supposed to do this? What was she planning to do? Darach says she wants you. Use that.* My inner voice said, pulling me into my resolve.

I pushed back my shoulders, trying to make me seem more confident than actuality.

"Driver," I said as he went to pull out more food. Queen Alieta and the Driver gazed at me. "Would you mind pulling a bit aways out of view? I-I just mean- the Queen and I would like some privacy for our lunch." Queen Alieta raised her eyebrows as she leaned back, her hands on the green grass.

"That is, if you are alright with that, my Queen?" I cocked my head to the side so I could see her from my peripheral vision.

"Yes, of course, Elowen. What a wonderful idea to keep our trip a bit more intimate. Fin, please do. Take a nap so you feel well enough to drive us back later on tonight."

With Fin now out of the way, I stared at Queen Alieta, unsure of what to do next. "Well, with Fin gone, would you like to prepare the food? Then perhaps after we could read that book you wanted or find some other way to entertain ourselves?" She gestured to the half-unpacked lunch.

"Oh yes, of course." My hands were already moving, grabbing various items from the baskets that consisted of small sandwiches and similarly sized pastries. *I could crush it on her food.* Mentally, I shook my head. *She'd obviously see that.*

The next basket held a teapot and herbs. Queen Alieta sat up, grabbing the pot from my hands. "Here, I'll fill this up for us while you organize the food." She was already halfway standing up when I grabbed her hand.

"No, it's okay. Why don't you relax? You work hard all day, maintaining the castle and the paperwork. It's my turn to return the favor. Sit, sit." I grabbed the teapot from her hand, getting up, walking up to the edge of the water.

I could feel her eyes on me as I stooped down to the water. *How was I supposed to slip it into the pot without her noticing?* My thoughts swirled in my head like an oncoming tornado. The water rippled around me. A pair of familiar eyes looked up at me.

Sylp! I called out to her in my head! How are you here?! I thought excitedly.

"*Accident it was. Me too surprised. Different, you look. Land explore I. Been here not before. Coincidence not. Fate is.*" Her eyes were wide in surprise as her body bobbed in the water.

The water nymphs had spent years caged in Sald Forest. It was unsurprising that she was out exploring the world.

Had she seen Lilja? Did she know what had happened? That Ardour locked me away? I pushed down the overwhelming thoughts that threatened to boil over my resolve.

"I have a flower to drug the Queen so I can run away. Do you have any idea if she is staring at me?"

Sylp swam away up to the rushing waterfall, nearly invisible to the naked eye. She sat up fully, peaking through the water towards the Queen's direction. Sylp nodded, her blue skin blending in with the water. *"Eyes on you, she has. Do will you what?"*

I had no time; her eyes burned into my back. *Time was not on my side.* I grimaced at the thought as it entered my mind.

You have little choice, my inner self said as I slipped into the freezing cold water. Sylp slipped out of sight. "Alieta!" I gasped as the frigid water shocked my system. Frantically, I kicked my legs, trying my best to stay afloat. I reached down into my pocket, pulling out the flower ball, shakily stuffing it into the pot. "Your highness," I wheezed, my inability to swim slowly catching up to foil my plan.

Just as I was about to give up hope, Alieta's hand shot into the water, hauling me out. "You know, when you offered to get water for the tea, I didn't realize you meant you wanted to take a swim." Our bodies pressed up against each other. Her magic radiated from every part of her body.

She furrowed her eyebrows in confusion as she held me painfully close. Regardless of the heat, I still felt the chill of the water seeping into my bones. I shivered, my body's failed attempt to warm me.

"I-I-I can't swim." My teeth chattered together. "I slipped, at least I got the water for the tea," I said weakly, holding up the teapot.

"Hold on, let me dry you off before you get sick." She grabbed the pot from me, heating it with her hands before walking it back over to the blanket. Queen Alieta turned back, walking toward me like I was prey.

I shivered, frozen to the spot as she cupped my face, kissing me. The warmth was instant, washing over me. The heat spread through me, starting at my lips. So hot it was almost painful. She pulled away, breathless. My dress and cloak were now miraculously dry.

We sat down, and I quickly added more herbs to the teapot. "Here," she unclipped her cloak, throwing it over my already dry one. Her hands moved quickly, clipping it back into place and grabbing a pastry for me to hold.

"Thank you," my voice sounded meek, unsure. I took a small nibble of the pastry, trying to keep my face passive. "How did you find this place?"

"My dad used to bring me here when he had a free minute. This is where he taught me how to swim. How to hold my first sword." Her voice sounded wistful, her tone plucking at my heartstrings. Doubt grew in the back of my mind as my strangely steady hands poured the tea into her eager hands.

"I'm jealous," I said, not wanting to take away from the memory that played before her eyes. "All my father ever did was make me hate myself. I can almost hear his voice, reprimanding me for not being like everyone else, for not being the prettiest girl in town, or the thinnest. He's the one who branded me, you know. Usually, the family is distraught when the clergy brands and throws out their loved ones. The clergy members are the ones who have to brand them, but no, not my father. He seemed all too ready to throw me away and pretend like he never had a lesbian daughter to begin with."

The thoughts welled out of me, words I had never spoken to even my fated. Words I had never once uttered in my life flowed through my mouth like the water I was just in. She was the enemy, yet not. Her ignorance was so frustratingly confusing. Did she know or did she not? I bit the pastry bitterly, looking down into my lap, as a stray traitorous tear ran down my face.

She looked at me with pity written over her face, wiping away the tear. She took a large drink of her tea, looking down at it, her eyebrow raised. "This tastes great. I wonder what herbs the kitchen packed for us?" She said before taking another large swig of it before pouring another cup full.

Hopefully she doesn't overdose on it, I thought worriedly.

"So, what did you have planned for today?" *Keep her occupied until the herb takes effect.* Darachs' voice played in my head, so clear I wondered if it was actually her.

"Well, as you know, Elowen. We started off on bad terms. My Uncle, while his intentions are always good, this time they went awry. He saved you from that dreadful Queen Lilja, but tortured you for information. You survived, of course, but at a cost-"

"He scarred me for life." I stuck out my chin, turning to the side so she could look at my 'Elven' ears.

"He was wrong, Elowen. I know that, but we had to be sure. Uncle is the best torturer in the Kingdom. If you were with them, he would have known then. Can't you understand it was for the greater good-"

"The greater good? You call an old man torturing me, the greater good!?" I scoffed, the anger in my body spilling out like an overheated tea kettle. The doubt was now gone.

"Alieta, I'm scarred of life. Your uncle did this to me!" As if the world sensed my anger, the animals stopped communicating. Even the sound of the waterfall seemed to fizzle to a dull roar. He might have been a faceless man as he tortured me, but now stood revealed on a podium.

"Your uncle caused all of this pain in Valdis! I saw him poison the water in the Sald forest 400 years ago, in a vision. He conversed with an Olken Elf as they helped poison the water going to Valdis. I don't know what sick plan you're plotting with him, but I will stop at nothing to stop him from ruining my home." I pulled away from her now standing looking down at her seated form.

"Your home? Elowen, Valdis is not your home. Your home is here, by my side. My uncle can't have caused this. He has been nothing but kind to me my whole life. Fate brings us together."

"Kind? He tortured me to death! He would have killed me if not for that water mage you made save me. Your uncle is many things but not kind. Why don't you ask him about his ploy? Maybe then you can see what he truly is." I scrambled toward the dragon book, my satchel in my hand. Queen Alieta clasped my wrist, surely leaving a bruise.

The heat from her skin was gone as the tea had taken effect. With her Elven strength, she pulled me down, my body on top of hers.

"What you say about my uncle may be true, but I'll be damned if I let you walk away from me. I've been nice thus far. Hell, I bought all those pretty little dresses in your closet just so I could watch you walk around in them. I fed you, I clothed you, and I even let you train with Fian. Just so you could satisfy yourself with doing something. I've been patient this far, waiting for you to get over whatever Lilja has done to mess with your head. I've waited for you to come to your senses and realize I am all you need. Now you are going to marry me when we get back to the castle, whether you like it or not."

She rolled us over, her grip tight, but not as tight as it used to be. I laughed as the anger subsided in my body, replaced with disbelief.

"Marriage? Marriage? You want to marry me? You barely know me. The joke's on you. I'm leaving."

With all my strength, I pushed Queen Alieta's tall frame off of me. Her form crumpled next to me as I got up. Brushing myself off before grabbing the dragon's book. Queen Alieta's chest heaving up and down.

"What-what did you do?" Her tone was breathy, as if she had trouble forming the words in her mouth.

"Oh, you're finally feeling that? That would be the tea you liked so much. Thanks, by the way, for drinking so much. I thought we were going to have to lay together again before it worked." I flipped the book over, reading the index. *Water Dragons pg 29.*

The paper was stiff as I leafed to the right page. *They have rumored water dragons to live in the mountains to the north. Preferring the lakes that exist in the mountain range.* I shut the book with a thud. "That's all I need to know for now. Goodbye, Alieta. I wish I could say it was nice to stay with you. But it wasn't"

She struggled to sit up as the flower finally took over her. A groan escaped her mouth as her eyes slipped shut for what would hopefully be a while.

13

Break Out

Lilja POV

"**M**aybe it's a spell. Valdis has wards against certain types of mental communications. Ardour's castle may have a similar spell. It would make sense," Cassia said. Her hood was still on, forgotten as she looked down at the dagger on her lap, the sharpening stone ground down the imperfect edges.

Kallan and I had arrived in Ebbon City the night before. We hadn't stopped moving since.

I poured myself over the newspaper we had bought from the child. A salacious title took up half the page: *Queen Alieta and her new mystery woman.*

The Spring Gathering was four days ago, long enough for a multitude of bad things to occur.

"Apparently, they appeared quite close. Other than the speech Queen Alieta gave, holding hands the whole time." Queen Zahra took another sip of her tea, taking a deep breath in.

"It would be freezing for a human!" I slammed my fist on the table. The implication between the lines made my blood boil. Elowen wouldn't be like that unless she had to. Queen Zahra lifted an eyebrow but didn't respond.

"A hiccup occurred toward the end of the ceremony. The Queen and Elowen both disappeared for several hours. Only to reappear at the end, with Elowen appearing disheveled," Queen Zahra said as she set down her teacup, it clinked onto the saucer.

Kallan raised his eyebrow, saying nothing. He leaned back in his chair. Legs crossed, pushing the chair up and down as he listened.

Cassia spoke up first. "She has to be working some sort of angle. It's still unclear what they forced her to tell Queen Alieta. They've compromised none of our previous assets." She took a bite of the small sandwiches on the table, picking at the rest of her food.

"We never gave her a chance to give out sensitive information. We readjusted our plans right after the attack," Keres said as she looked down at her food, pushing around each vegetable with a fork. Her burned hands had since healed, angry scars covered the tender skin. She had refused Cassia's scar healing balm.

"True, but no military mass has moved to any of the secret locations we visited together. No one has infiltrated Sald or this city. So unless they haven't acted on the information gathered that she may or may not have given. We're probably safe," Aidan said, never looking up from the book he had opened, hiding a majority of his face.

"Probably isn't very comforting," Armand admitted as he bit off a chunk of meat from the turkey leg in his hands. Like a child, the fat and grime of the food before him coated his hands.

"There's the option of her not saying anything. Unlike the rest of us, Elowen has not trained since childhood. But one thing is clear: she has a pure heart. She would not give out information if it would hurt us," I said, my jaw clenched. I hit the table with my fist again. At this point a knuckle shaped dent will be ingrained in the wood.

She would die before that happened. We took her in. From the sounds of it, the Human Realm sounds like a terrible place to be. My inner voice whispered at me.

A young man in military clothes interrupted our lunch by scurrying over to Zahra. His tan face was red from exertion. He leaned down to her, hand covering his mouth in our direction, his voice indiscernible over Armand's lips smacking. I gritted my teeth, my eye twitching, as I tried to control the urge to throw my fork at him or a sizable rock from the smooth polished wall. Queen Zahra's eyes went wide, looking up at me.

"What? What is he saying?" I asked, even before the boy had finished whispering into her ear. He looked up at me, giving a slight bow before running out of the room.

"She has escaped-" Zahra said, her face full of shock.

"Elowen escaped!?" Aidan shouted first. He stood up, knocking his chair to the ground. His glasses fumbling down to his lips, falling off the tip of his nose. The book that once was in his hands thudded to the floor.

She escaped where I had failed, finding the piece of the puzzle I was lacking. My heart soared.

"Yes, the boy just said she was spotted heading toward the Forgard Mountain. She's moving by foot," Zahra said, standing up. The charms on her hair clinked together. I pulled my hair up, standing up. It just got long again.

"Team, pack your bags. We leave tomorrow night. If Elowen has gotten out of Alieta's measly hands, she will need our help. Where we failed, she succeeded. It's time we act. Queen Zahra, I thank you for the hospitality of these past months. Thanks to you, I am fully healed and we finally have contingency plans in place. We will keep you updated on the movements. Once the attack becomes imminent, we will send a notice."

The wooden chairs scraped against the red stone floor. Aidan and Kallan were the first one up and out the door, yelling orders to nearby servants to pack provisions.

The last few months were long. I've felt useless, like a child unable to help a struggling kingdom. Zahra's healers said I was lucky to be alive.

Leaving me to heal slowly, as my fiancée struggled to stay alive behind enemy lines. I sent scouts out across the country, keeping track of movements and talk of Ardour's military. So far, nothing has changed in their movements. Other than a few lone riders, heading north to an unknown location. Each rider with the same emblem.

Elowen POV

The cloak Alieta had gifted to me tugged at the branches as I ran through the dense trees and undergrowth, and I cursed under my breath. Once I felt comfortable enough, I had to cover it with mud. The golden cloak would give me away when I got to the town. The sun had set low into the earth, bringing forth the night sky. Esmersey's large form shone bright, guiding me on the way.

I felt an odd connection to the Gods of these lands. Their existence ingrained themselves into my head, as if it were the only gods I had ever known.

Had Alieta awakened yet? Was the carriage driver back from his nap? Does she know I am gone yet? Would the team find me? Was I alone? Was Lilja dead?

Tears sprang to my eyes as I gripped my bag, not willing to risk losing the two books on my escape. I surveyed the sun, making sure I was heading in the right direction. *North, I just had to keep heading north.* I thought to myself as I slowed to a walk, exhaustion taking over me, the adrenaline leaving as I saw a large tree with a small enough hole in it for me to fit.

Tiredly, I wiped out the debris, using my frozen hands to pull out the dead leaves. My hands were purple as the cold seeped in. I sat in the small enclosed space, covering myself with the cloak and the fallen leaves from last season, allowing myself to wait, hidden, for the next day.

"Elowen, come here," Lilja called. She stood in front of Sald Lake. Her short hair was slicked back from water, waving me to her and grinning. "Lilja!" I shouted, running to her, the wind tearing at my clothes and hair as I launched myself into her arms.

Tears ran down my face as I nuzzled my head into her chest. "I thought you were dead. I love you."

I breathed in her scent, expecting her to respond right away, but she didn't. I pulled away a bit to look up at her, to see Alieta looking down at me.

"Aw, little mouse, I love you too," Alieta responded, swooping down for a kiss.

My heart raced; the nightmare was over, but not the effects of it. I shivered as I stood up, my body achy from the position I slept in. Leaves crunched under my movement.

The sun glowed in the sky, telling me it was sometime near noon. *Shit, I fell asleep. Alieta is probably close on my heels.*

My brain ran wild as I moved north, attempting to stay as quiet as possible. Shouts rang out in the distance as a dog barked. "Men, the dogs have a scent. Keep your eyes peeled. She can't be far!" A man's voice shouted.

I crouched, my body still moving as I lengthened the distance between me and the people chasing me. The trees widened, revealing a creek. Silently, I thanked the gods as I clambered in. *This would hide my scent.*

I gasped as the cold water shocked my system, gritting my teeth as I kept going. The smell of cold earth filled my nostrils, and I kept on. Water crept up my clothes, climbing me as I sloshed forward. *I had to keep moving.*

14

Death

The dogs barked behind me as I trudged through the still freezing water. The algae-covered rocks under my feet, causing me to teeter. My heart raced, looking around. As long as I could keep my pace up, the dogs were the least of my problems. The chill had set into my bones. Even though spring had awakened from the grips of winter, the water was still frigid.

"We lost the scent! Men spread out. She's here somewhere. Come back with her or be prepared to give your hide to Daveed and the Queen!" A man shouted, his voice farther away than last time, jumbled by the forest.

Each step sloshed up, soaking me further. Desperately, my eyes scanned the forest in front of me. My teeth chattered together as my fingertips were turning into an unnatural purple tint. Trees seemed to cover every inch, densely growing together as if they were one organism.

My feet slipped on the rocks submerged in the river. I gasped as I fell in the water, splashing all up my chest and arms. The dog barks echoed in my ears. Shaking, I crossed my arms across my breasts, attempting to keep my body heat in.

A sob passed my lips as I stared past a dead tree. Its limbs stood bare, its life cut short by the brutal winter. Behind that stood a small village where the elves had yet to wake from their slumber. I stumbled out of the creek, my body shaking as I walked toward a house.

I had to hide. I had to get warm. It would do me no good to get hypothermia. The smell of animals infiltrated my nose, pigs rutted around in a small pen. Chickens in another, one rooster, perched himself on top of the village's perimeter fence. The sounds of the dogs were gone now, but I still moved with urgency. Elves were faster than humans. The only reason I could get so far was because I was ahead. I couldn't hide inside a house, putting the lives of these villagers in danger. It's doubtful the men chasing me were going to be polite to anyone they thought was hiding me.

I stumbled into the coop, shutting the door behind me. The chickens looked at me sleepily. A few ruffled their feathers at me before turning back around. Fresh hay laid in the corner. Silently, I thanked the gods for the clean pen before diving into it. Shivers racked my body, my teeth chattered hard enough that I prayed they wouldn't break.

I shut my eyes, willing myself to be invisible in the hay, wishing I had some sort of power, like an elf. I clutched my satchel between my hands.

Screams called out into the air. The guards had arrived. I sucked in a breath.

In, out. In, out. My brain shouted. I sucked in a breath, choking on the air entering my body. The sounds of death covering my hack.

I was hyperventilating. My brain tried to reason with me as I struggled to slow my breathing.

Stop!

Stop!

STOP! Just breathe, my brain begged me. My vision skewed the world, pulsing in and out. The weight of my head seemed unmanageable as it nodded down. The world going black.

Smoke wafted through the cracks by the door. The shivers had stopped racking my body, but my joints groaned in protest as I vaulted myself up. The smoke was thick, making my eyes water. Hay poked out of my clothes and hair, scratching me. Anxiety rolled through me, mixed with adrenaline. *I had to get out.*

I peeked through a slot in the wall. A chicken stepped onto my foot, clucking uneasily. My breath caught in my throat as smoke billowing from the house across from the chicken coop. Its thatched roof decimated as fire ate away the dry bits of roof.

A tall thin figure stood in the middle of the road, their body features distorted by the smoke that hung heavy in the air. They held a staff with a large gnarled piece of wood. Like claws on a bird, the unfinished wood clutched a black stone on the top.

The person stood turned, as if they could sense my stare. Their head whipped toward me. Instinctually, I ducked down.

My stomach flopping as a male voice infiltrated my mind, "I can see you. Death seems to follow you, young Alwyn. I sense an odd path for you."

Every fiber of my being seemed to pause. My hair on my neck was the first to respond, sticking straight up. Silence permeated the countryside, as if afraid of the man who stood before me. Not even the cocky rooster next to me had the gall to crow.

"Do not worry, the only souls here are the ones passed. The soldiers have long since left. Your feeble mind saved you." The male voice projected.

Feeble? The hairs on the back of my neck stood to attention. *I was weak. My mind could so easily overtake me.*

How could he possibly know that?

My eyes flitted around my surroundings, my back straightening as a calmness seeped into me. It was as if this figure was imbuing me with trust.

"Who are you?" I thought to him as I rubbed my hands up and down my arms in a failed attempt to warm my still damp body.

"Runen the God of death-"

I let out an audible gasp, my hand trembling at the doorknob. "Are you here for me?" I fought the urge to glance back at the hay where I once was.

He let out a hollow laugh. "Do not fear, if you had not passed out in the hay. I would have guided you to the other side. As you know, fate is temperamental. You traded your life for these souls. You and I shall meet again, soon." His thin pale hand swept to the side, glowing blue balls bounced in the air.

Seven of them, tears well in my eyes as realization hit me. Dead because of me.

"How did I exchange my life for theirs? My life is not valuable. I am a human in a realm I do not belong. A mere bump in the fickle line of fate." A stray tear ran down my cheek as I thought of what Alieta had said to me.

"Indeed, not by your hand, of course. Your life is more valuable than you believe. Perhaps the future will reveal that to you soon." The souls danced around him, hovering unsteady as if unsure where to turn, looking for their bodies.

The death god held up a hand. A blue orb swirled around his pale fingertips. He looked up at them, his eyes surprisingly emotive. Sadness carried in them as the orb reached down and rubbed the tip of his nose. A kiss.

"Those soldiers have gone west toward the mountains. That is all the knowledge I can give. My sibling Endri has already helped your friends to the west. I figured I should come and help. Good luck, Alwyn. Should you continue, you will soon reunite with your newfound family." The blue souls disappeared, a black hole opened beneath Runen, and with that he was gone, leaving me alone in the now empty ghost town.

I stumbled out onto the main road of the village. The tang of blood filled my nose as my body moved autonomously. Grief clouded my thoughts as I walked through the shambles of the village. *It was my fault. People were dead because of me.*

How did I not awake to this chaos? How could I not hear their screams as the queen's guards cut their live short?

I sucked in a shaky breath, as I gazed at a small shrine. One built for the creators of the realm. As if a mocking substitute to the ingredient Pavati needed me to procure, a lone dragon stood, his mouth open in a menacing snarl. His palms carved upward for an offering to sit caged between his claws. I gave it a bow before continuing.

Tears streamed down my face silently as the path grew more uneven as I trudged on. Smoke still hung in the air, making it harder to see, a bird crowed in the distance. The last house in the village lay to my right, its door ajar. My hands shook as I approached. *I needed supplies.*

"Hello," my voice called out into the empty air. My footsteps creaking on the porch were the only sound. Timidly, I peaked my head in. The one room farmhouse lay disheveled, fire still crackled in the hearth dying.

I rounded the flipped table, gasping as a young woman's body lay in her own blood. She couldn't have been much older than me, *a soul I killed today.* Her brown hair matted to her face, her throat cut.

Her eyes were open, lifeless, her mouth left open as if she were still screaming.

A sob ripped through me as I shakily closed her eyes, murmuring a prayer. Her skin was already cold. A worn scrap of a kitchen towel lay next to her hand, as if she had dropped it in the scuffle. An embroidered 'W' on the corner of it was now dingy off white with slivers of blue showing through. My shaking hand grabbed at it.

"I'm so sorry," I murmured into it as I laid the wrinkled cloth over her face, unable to gaze at any longer. Tearing my eyes off of her long enough to take stock of her kitchen from the long winter. With my bag in hand, I snagged the few vegetables that would fit in it next to the books.

A piece of wax paper folded around a small stack of cured meat. I gave one last look at the body on the ground, my fingers gripping onto the tacky wax paper. Eyeing a small change purse on her body, I bent over, pulling it from her waistband. *She doesn't need it;* I told myself. But I couldn't help but feel a pang of guilt as I stuffed it in my bag, grabbing the sword she never had time to use before heading outside.

The trees surrounding the village were quiet once again. At the beginning of my journey, a quiet forest would have seemed beautiful to my naïve soul. But now all the hairs on my neck stood up, ready. Ready for whatever danger could pounce out onto me.

The W ladies' horse neighed uncertainly. His nose flared as I jumped off the porch. I gave it a sad smile as I approached, giving it a carrot I had snagged from inside before saddling him up. He stomped a few times as I finished the last buckle, giving him a gentle pat, I jumped on. *She won't need him anymore,* my inner voice chided me as I guided him out of the town.

We followed the road, keeping up a good pace. Trees blurred past as I urged the black horse forward, leaving the carnage of the town behind us. With the moon high above us, I slowed him to a trot. He neighed appreciatively as I dismounted.

Nobody appeared to be around us. The absence of firelight in the dark forest suggested that no one was close by. "It'll be a cold one tonight, boy," I said to the horse's blank stare. I pulled the cloak Alieta gifted me around my shivering form. My inner voice screamed at me, wanting me to throw it away, bury it like the past I wanted to bury. But its heavy material kept me from the cold.

Exhaustion creeped up on me. My cloak reeked of ammonia and smoke, the only indication of my day. A strangled laugh escaped my mouth as the euphoria of being free finally hit me. The last two days seemed to fly by. I was so close to finding my friends.

Sylp! She had to be the answer to how to find them. She had to be in contact with them. *Who was alive? My* inner voice seemed to whisper. *Who remained after the explosion? Was Lilja dead? Was Keres dead? Why did she not answer my summon?*

Lilja, are you still there?

Silence met me on the other side of my brain. Another small defeated sob broke through the night air as I tried to conserve my body heat. The euphoria I had just felt gone as the loneliness infiltrated me. The horse sat down beside me, trying to comfort me.

Shakily, I pulled out the book about the water dragon book out, straining to read under the moonlight Esmersey provided.

Ancient creatures, older than the gods themselves. Long ago, they ruled over the skies, causing havoc. Rumored to have stores of gold and wealth in their lair. Resulting in many dragons to be killed by bandits and merchants, who wanted to get rich. The Brawn'n are the only known creature to pray to such beast. The creators of all under the old age magic, dragons. In Isold, the Brawn'ns city is the largest known shrine to the Dragons.

IF there are any surviving dragons, they are bound to be cruel and distrustful. Known to kill the elves that come too close to their lair. They are the definition of a heartless killer.

15
Easy Picking

Lilja POV

A caravan was our first hit. We needed to make a name for ourselves. Even then, we needed clothes as a disguise. The caravan meandered slowly. The load they traveled with teetered as the wheels hit small rocks on the road.

I glanced back at my friends. Kallan's eyes were calculating as he assessed the group. One man rode on the covered wagon, steering the two horses. Two men rode atop small horses, their packs overflowing with supplies. Supplies we needed.

The group all looked up at me with undeniable trust and respect, yet I couldn't help but feel anger. They should have left me. They should have abandoned me in Ebbon City and got my future wife out of Alieta's hands.

"I'll cause a distraction. Men always love a damsel in distress." Cassia unpinned her hair, letting flow down, her tight red curls bouncing. She handed her horse's reigns to Keres before bounding down the small hill we perched on. Her dress tore at the branches and dense underbrush, adding to her 'distress'.

"Help please, my friend, she fell into a poachers' trap. I can't get her out, please you have to help me," Cassia sobbed. She fell on her knees in front of their horses, causing them to pound their hooves nervously on the ground. Mud splashed up her trousers, adding to the dramatics.

Kallan raised his eyebrow. "I can't say I'm surprised. Cassia always did like the theater."

"Remind me to have her try out for the next play when we get back to Valdis," Armand mused as he twirled his sword around in his hand.

The men looked around before getting off the horses. "Now!" My voice carried through my group like wildfire. Everyone rushed down the hill. Our trust in one another flowed between us. We had encountered many terrifying foes together; pirates, bandits, witches. *This fight is no different,* I thought.

Cassia had a crazed grin on her face. She jumped back, grabbing her reins back from Keres. I pointed my sword at the man I assumed was the leader. He swallowed, visibly shaken.

"Don't kill us, please! We have nothing. This is all we have! What do you want money? We have no money. We are just trying to get to our families." He shook with fear and adrenaline.

"Gentlemen, I do not wish to kill you. The opposite, in fact. You can stay alive as long as you behave. Kallan check there pockets. Armand, monitor the wagon driver. We don't want him to take off." Dismounting, I went to the back of the wagon, climbing inside. In the back, chests neared the roof of the wagon. Mostly, food and clothes as its contents.

"Shit, I was hoping you had at least something of interest." My hands grabbed the bag of dried jerky, biting a piece off of it. I threw down one of the barrels in the back of the cart. The contents spilled across the ground, getting soiled. Guilt pulsed through me, I grimaced. *That was a bit much.*

Armand stood next to the driver, grinning like an idiot. He twirled his sword in his hand, swinging it around. I half hoped he'd nick his finger, so he'd do his job more than horsing around.

"They only have a few gold coins each, Lil. What do you want to do?" Kallan leaned close to me, speaking low.

"Which one of you is the leader?" I shouted, my head pounding. *Elowen needs me.* The men looked at each other, their eyes wide. For a minute, no one answered, and I thought I was going to have to resort to less scrupulous methods to get the answer I needed.

"Gentlemen, I do not have time for this. Answer, or I'll start breaking fingers." With my words of encouragement, one of them lifted a hand, pointing at the man who I assumed earlier was the leader.

"Now, I'm only going to ask this once. I have places to be. Do you have any more gold?" I chewed on the jerky stubbornly, trying to get it soft enough to not choke on.

Keres still looked in their packs, moving around items the only way she knew how, aggressively. "I don't know what you're talking about. I told you already, I-we don't have nothing!" He all but wailed, sweat beaded on his forehead. His eyes darted back and forth to my men.

Dissatisfied with the answer, Keres unclipped the pack from the horse, sending the contents sprawling on the muddy ground before starting it on fire. Fire flickered on her face, giving her a haunting glow. Spooked, the leader's horse reared back, sending the leader on to the ground with a thud. He coughed, the air knocked out of his lungs.

"Please, we don't have nothing!" The caravan driver sighed. Armand's sword, dangerously close to getting rid of his five o'clock shadow.

"Don't. Say. Anything. George," the leader spit, wiping the mud off of his face.

"Hetic, my sister will kill me if I don't bring you back home like I promised," George said, his voice shaking. Despite his tone, he sat high on the caravan, doing his best to ooze confidence and control over the situation.

George's eyes lasered in on me, not once glancing at him. "You promise to mean us no harm if I reveal where it is?"

"I swear to the Gods George, don't," Hetic said, his hair disheveled. With the butt of my sword, I sent him sprawling into the mud, unconscious.

"I'm just trying to get back to my friend." A bitter taste spread as the word *friend* left my mouth. We needed to keep up pretenses, stay unidentifiable. We couldn't let anyone know I was the Queen of Valdis trying to find her Fated.

"This must be an important *friend* indeed." George stroked his beard. He was much older than me. Closer to my parents' age, grey speckled his beard.

"The money is in a hidden compartment in the wagon. Right before that last nail." George gestured to the right.

"How do we open it?" Kallan said, already moving towards the spot he pointed at.

"Push the nail head. It's loaded on a spring."

Aidan grunted as he beat Kallan to the button. A box dropped from the carriage's underside. He turned to me, holding the box open. Gold glittered as he grinned with childlike glee.

"Good job gentlemen. George, thank you for your cooperation. Unfortunately, I do not trust you enough to just let you go as we depart." I dismounted. George and his other non-unconscious friend took a step back. Armand threw a rope at me from his pack. Already sensing what I wanted to do. He was always ready to subdue people.

"Don't be afraid, gentlemen. We won't kill you, just merely make it incapable for you to follow us." I worked quickly. Wrapping the rope around both men, Kallan slipped off their shoes and threw them in opposite directions. My final touch was shoving a rag into each of their mouths.

Cassia and Keres worked equally fast, grabbing enough supplies for us for a few days. Aidan flipped through their books, looking for anything pertinent or interesting. "Find anything that could help us?" My head swam with pain as another headache washed over me.

"Nothing but a more updated map. What's this place?" He showed George, who just grumbled. The cloth in his mouth inhibiting his ability to answer. Aidan gave him a sympathetic look before pulling it out of his mouth.

"It's the path to the Forgard Mountain. Most maps don't show it, people around these parts say it's haunted. Nearby villages hear screams from under the mountain. People who enter the path don't come out. The Brawn'n live there. Nasty creatures, if you ask me. Pests, always stealing from the villagers. That's why so many of us are on the move. Steal worst then you lot, they do. Steal our sheep and vegetables straight from the ground." George carried on talking, his mustache going up and down as he continued. I tuned him out as I tried to push myself inside Elowen's head again.

The brick wall had deteriorated, as if fading into nothingness. My heart swelled at the thought of hearing Elle thoughts again. In the short time I had known Elowen, her presence had filled the hole in my person. I had always thought of myself as a well-rounded person. Knowledgeable about the world and also sensitive to its problems. I ruled with an iron fist. My kingdom needed saving, and my parents made me to fix it. Yet the emotional aspect, I lacked. I've never had a partner in that way. Men and women lined my bed, kept me warm at night. But never had I had a person who I could bare my soul with.

Elowen was an enigma. A secret missing piece of myself. The last puzzle piece to my soul.

Can you hear me, Elle? Which way are you going?

His voice drowned out any hope that I'd be able to hear her reply. If she replied. Hope spurred through me, the headache plaguing me dissipated.

"Are you listening to me?!" He gruffed. "It's the least you could do for stealing my stuff. I'm a rather nice person to steal from, don't ya' think? The simpleton of a brother-in-law is the only reason I'm being so nice. My sister, you see, is something fierce, mean as a bobcat-" He couldn't finish his response as I nodded to Aidan to stuff the gag back into his mouth, his prater annoying me. We mounted our horses, riding closer to the mountain, closer to my beloved.

His wife must not listen to a word he says.

"Aidan, set course for that direction. Elowen would most likely set that path as it's the less traveled." He nodded, his nose deep in the new book he 'acquired,' from the caravan and its three occupants.

"Have any of you had encounters with a Brawn'n?" I called out to the group as I bounded closer to the mountain. The land sprawled by us, uncultured, ripe for farms and villages to spread to.

"No, they mostly keep within their own kind. They rarely mingle with the rest of the fae folk," Aidan said, as he continued to read his book. It was a wonder he even got anywhere. His reins sat limply on his lap, his horse trained to follow the one next to it.

"Quite, possibly, because people prosecute and treat them unfair-ly." Cassia looked off to the west as she spoke. The words hitting closer to home with her. Orphans always had an unconscious bias toward them.

The land before us changed gradually, beginning to slope from soft green cushions of grass to rocky terrain, unlike the land I grew up playing on. I thought back to my childhood, constant lectures and hands on learning. Thinking back to the constant barrage of coun-terattacks and drill with Aidan. His father Sterk'n watching over us like the great sun god Niamh watching over her children; careful and calculating.

"What will we do when we find Elowen?" Kallan rubbed his chin thoughtfully. The hair on his upper lip had grown out into a horrendous mustache.

The playful chatter between the group had stalled, intrigued by the question. My eyes upturned to the cloudy sky. Not a single silver of the usual pale blue sky shone through, the clouds densely packed together as if a storm planned to roll in. I sighed, the day's events catching up on me seemingly all at once. The weight settled on my shoulders as if set under a stack of rocks. "We see what she knows, something must have triggered her escape. Some type of motivation to keep moving. She must think we abandoned her."

My voice cracked as an unusual show of emotion surfaced through my words. "Who knows what Alieta has done to her? What horrors she has had to live with as we-I sat underneath a mountain-"

"You can't blame yourself. You were unconscious, Lilja. It was I who was at fault. I led them right to us. I-I thought I got rid of them all. That it was safe." Aidan's eyes rimmed with tears as he closed his book to speak.

His glasses teetered on the tip of his nose, dangerously close to slipping off. Aidan's lip trembled as the guilt weighed on him. On one hand, I was angrily happy that he felt the full impact that moment had on us. But on the flip side, my heart ached with him. Ardour would have attacked us, eventually. Regardless, if someone had led them to us.

"It doesn't matter who's to blame, it still happened. What's important is that we get Elowen back. Cure this damn blight and get the fuck home. I'm tired of all of this running around, and I'd like to sleep in my own comfy bed." Keres snapped her reins, pulling up to lead the group. She gave me a look as she finished talking before taking off into a gallop.

The wind whipped at her hair, making it look as if black flames burned on her head. We all followed suit, spurred by the energy of regret. Night laid on us quickly, as if Hesper, the Goddess of Night, had placed a blanket on us. The green grass had fully given away to the rocky terrain. Hills covered the foreseeable path before us, rolling through the land like small waves.

"Let's call it a night and give the horses a rest. We'll start again in the morning," Kallan said as he stretched on his horse. I gave him a slight nod. We couldn't run the horses into the ground.

"Once we hit the next town, we'll buy supplies to continue on this travel expedition. Who knows what Elowen has planned? It's our responsibility to help her in any way possible. We have already let her down once. Let's not do it again," I said as I swung off my horse, preparing to sleep on the cold ground. I would do anything if it meant getting Elowen back. Even if I had to kill anyone who got in my way.

"No! Leave me alone!" I shouted at the faceless man. My engagement ring was in his outstretched hand. Black smoke swirled around his face, obscuring any identifiable facial features.

"Who are you to, Lilja, the Queen of Valdis!?" He grabbed onto my wrist, forcing the ring onto my finger. Blue swirls spread up my arm like an infection, pain spread in my chest as I breathed through the pain.

"She's my- my Fated!" I gasped, tears running down my face. The darkness creeped on the edges of my vision, the pain becoming too much to bear. *No, I told him! He's going to hurt her, and it's all my fault.*

Daveed laughed, still gripping my wrist. "If she is your Fated, then where is she?!" He stressed the word Fated, stretching it out from emphasis.

"I-I-I DON'T KNOW!"

My hand flew to my chest as I launched forward from my uncomfortable sleeping position. A sob of relief broke through me. "It was just a dream. Just a dream," I said, trying to reassure myself. I rubbed my leg to self soothe. The sun had barely peeked past the horizon. Chep, my newly named horse, neighed anxiously at me, startling him.

I picked up the discarded book I had fallen asleep to, carefully tucking it back into my satchel. Chep munched on an apple as I saddled him up. The sound of a branch snapped in the trees behind me. I paused at the sound, listening for anything else.

My stomach gurgled angrily, empty save for stomach acid. I sighed, moving again. It must have been an animal. I flipped through the contents of my bag and grabbing out a stale piece of bread.

Chep trotted down the path, purely out of instinct. Freeing my hands to eat my breakfast.

It was hours before I spotted another soul. Her hunched form gathered herbs from the side of the path, her small basket almost full.

"Good morning," I said, giving her a small nod. "Do you think you could point me toward the closest town going this direction?" My finger pointed further up the path. She jumped, turning to me, giving me a toothless grin.

"Aye, I can do you one better. I'll guide you there myself, if you'd be willing to give this old bag of bones a ride back. I'm too old to be doing this type of work." She had a pale purple handkerchief to tie her hair back.

The old lady held out her hand, her fingers knobby as arthritis attacked her joints.

"Alright." I took in my surroundings, looking for a hint of a trap.

"Can you get up on here?" I said, as I patted the space behind me.

With a yank and a few curse words from her, she sat happily behind me, her head pressed against my back contently, as if she decided the best course of action was to take a nap. Sure enough, small snores filled the air. I tried to ignore the growing wet spot on my tunic as I followed the vague instructions of the women.

I could very well be walking into a trap. Shaking my head, I focused on the path ahead. *Would she question my ears?* The scar tissue had faded considerably since the incident happened. What once was angry red scars were now faint pink lines.

My worries quickly left me as fields popped up on either side of the path. Houses dotted between them and soon an entire village in full swing sat in front of me. "My lady," I coughed, wiggling my back to rouse her. "Where do you live?"

A big yawn sounded behind me. "Oh, we're here already? You must have rode like the wind, such a nice day for a nap. Apologies for the spit on your shirt, it's not everyday I can take a break. My shop is right over there, the finest store in town. Anyone whose someone shops there while passing through town. Anyone dumb enough." The old woman peered up at me as she dismounted, grumbling something about people being dumb.

"Well, are you going to get off that big, dumb horse or just stare longingly from the outside?" She put her hands on her hips. The horse gave a stomp, as if it knew she was calling him dumb.

"Um, yes," I stammered anxiously. I dismounted, wiping my sweaty hands on my pants. The one room shop smelled of dust. A myriad of random items were strewn around the place. Ropes strung up against the wall, climbing materials hung on large nails.

"Now, where were you going? I got a grandson here who could guide you wherever you need to be getting," she said as she picked at her yellow rotten teeth with a small knife. The climbing gear seemed to glare at me. *The climb to Forgard Mountain was going to be difficult.* I bit my lip. *Did I need a guide? A man guide? I wish Lilja was here.*

"I'll be alright going by myself. There's no need for a guide. I appreciate the offer, but I'd never forgive myself if something happened to him." I slung the rope over my shoulder, the weight awkward on my short frame.

I swallowed the weight of my heart. Lilja should be my goal. My fated. The truth deterred me, what could be the truth would be too hard to handle. Besides, the cure was more important. She would want me to save her people first and Forgard Mountain was the first stop.

"Don't you worry about him getting hurt. I got so many grand babies. Like cockroaches they are. Can't kill them if you wanted to," she cackled, throwing dried fruit and meats into a bag for me, as if she knew what I was trying to attempt.

"I don't offer refunds if you lose your nerve. The Brawn'n people have been extra alarming as of late. They've been stealing all kinds of our produce, damn bastards. All of them are thieves!"

My eyes perked up at the word Brawn'n. "Oh, I'm just heading north. I have no intention of running into the Brawn'n people." I kept my head down, still looking at the random trinkets in the glass display case.

"You best be careful being a lone rider and all. I've been hearing news of a group of bandits roaming through the area. Just as bad as the Brawn'n people, if you ask me. Oddly enough, they ain't killed nobody yet. You don't want to be the first one they do kill."

I nodded. *I, in fact, did not want to be the first one they decided to kill.* "How much for all of this?"

"Two gold coins."

I balked at her. "Two gold coins?!"

"Aye, that's what it cost. Them Brawn'n people be eating all my produce, snatching it right out of the ground. Inflation, like it or don't. Pay or leave. It's your choice." She placed her hand on her hip, tapping her foot.

"The Brawn'n are dirty folk, living in the dirt and are lazy. That is why they steal, lazy. As the gods as my witness, it's the truth." She stared me down as she spoke, eyeing my purse.

I gave a slight pout, begrudgingly reaching into the W lady's purse, pulling out two of the three gold coins. *No doubt they were that lady's life savings.* She bit at the gold coin, holding it up to the light, and then grinned at me. "Thank you for doing business with me!" Her arthritic fingers quickly stuffed the coins in her apron pocket before shooing me out the door.

After loading up the horse, I saddled up, leaving the town feeling robbed and a bit more anxious. The sun was high in the sky, but I didn't stop for lunch. Anxiety riddled my stomach. The ground got more and more uneven on the path. Off the path was even worse, with gnarled roots jutted out of nearly every inch of ground.

Dismounting, I led the horse by hand. I couldn't afford to have him lame. The day passed by quietly. No fellow travelers passed me. Enormous mountains loomed over the horizon, much like Ebbon mountain. They were huge snow-capped mountains, the beyond space behind them was indiscernible. Olken Ridge had to lay beyond the mountain range, riddled with mystery.

I clenched the hilt of the sword, my knuckles white. My heart beat fast in my chest as I thought of the bandits roaming the countryside. As night befell me, the temperature dropped, my now dirty cloak doing nothing to protect me from the wind that howled through the rocky ground. The wind howled as it passed through the rocks, making it sound like they were screaming.

A large boulder sat on the side of the road, a discarded half burned wood sat in front of it. My hands shook as I stared at it, my body shivering with the want of warm fire.

I dismounted, the boulder giving a welcome reprieve to the wind. I blew warmth into my hands, looking around. The hairs on the back of my neck stood on end. I was being watched.

Lilja POV

Night reached us as we pulled into the town. It had been a day since we started the story of bandits roaming the countryside. A mercantile sat across the street from a bar. "Have you heard anything else from Elle?" Kallan inquired as he gazed longingly at the bar.

I guided the horse towards the shop, a candle lit in the window. "No, nothing since her nightmare bled through the wall. If the trend continues, I think I should be able to contact her soon. I don't know why I wasn't able to before."

Aidan dismounted, walking up to the paint chipped door, peering inside. "There could have been a mental block, either from your end or hers. Could be from trauma, drugs, or a spell. Who knows? Hello!" He knocked on the door, the glass shaking in the door frame rattling.

For a second, it was looking as if we would have to stay the night in the town. A bar patron stumbled out of the bar, shutting the door so loud the side of the building shook with might. He stumbled to the alleyway to piss. "Whose being so loud out here? I'm too old for this." An old lady opened the door with a small lantern in her hand. She wore a nightgown and slippers, shivering.

"Oh well, hello handsome," she said, tucking her gray hair behind her ear. Kallan sniggered, attempting to cover it with a cough.

As if noticing the rest of us for the first time. "Are you guys going to cause me trouble?" She held up her lantern higher, attempting to look menacing. Her face weathered with age, wrinkles creased almost every inch of it.

"No, ma'am, we were only hoping to buy some supplies off of you before heading on our way to the north." Kallan dismounted from his horse, walking over to the elder elf, kissing her on the hand.

"Well now, bless ye' on yer journey. Just a few hours ago, I had a good-looking young person going that way as well. Those bandits are thick this year and I tried to warn her out of it. Maybe you could check on her. She bought quite of a few things from my shop." The lady's cheeks were pink from Kallan's flirtations as she spoke. My mind was going a mile a minute.

"What did she look like?" Cassia blurted out before I could ask in a more tactical way.

She placed her free hand on her chin as if in deep thought. "Well, she had the daintiest little ears, pretty quiet."

A young lady? Could it be Elowen? Small ears? Maybe she made her own.

"Her eyes?" I asked, my voice low. Close to breaking as I thought of Elowen alone on the road.

"Why does it matter what color her eyes were? She is just a random traveler-"

I cut her off, my anger bubbling to the surface all at once. "WHAT COLOR WERE HER EYES. Answer me!" My shoulders were tense. My hands closed into a fist, aching to punch something. She took a step back, startled by my outburst. Like she was worried I was going to have my horse rear back and trample her.

"What my friend is trying to say?" Aidan gave me a dark look.

"We think our friend is the person you were describing. She is new to the area and might need our help. Do you think you could remember anything else about her? Weight? Height? Her eye color?"

Aidan looked at her in faux adoringly, eager to hear what she had to say.

She placed a hand on his biceps, giving it a squeeze. "She was thin, yet muscular. Her eyes were blue. Maybe up to your chest in height."

My heart sunk, *thin?* Elowen was so curvy and beautiful it would be hard to describe her as thin. I closed my eyes, collecting my thoughts. *Queen Zahra mentioned Elowen had lost weight. Maybe it was her.*

"Thank you for the information, madam. Could you open your shop so we can purchase supplies for our journey?"

She eyed me up and down; the lantern covering a majority of her face. "I guess, but hurry, my old bones need to lie down for the night. Come inside before I freeze to death."

The shop was a meager one. Fruits and vegetables lay dried in large baskets off to one side, reminding of the large shops down to the south in Lleaven before Ardours men destroyed it. On the other side of a display case, ropes lined the wall.

"We will take the ropes enough for all of us and dried meats and vegetables. Enough for several days of hard travel. We'll pay you extra if you hurry," Kallan spoke firmly, enunciating each word quickly. He gave me the side eye, holding out a small bag of gold. Plenty enough for twice that amount of supplies. She reached out her hand, holding it out like a small child eager for sweets.

"Cheenip, get your sorry ass down here and help me package these fine people's order. NOW!" I cringed, her voice obnoxiously loud. We needed to get back on the road and get to Elowen.

A ragged-looking boy bounded down the steps, his eyes still half asleep as he threw items into a sack. His grandma did the same. They had the order packed in a matter of minutes. The gold coins chinked happily in the old lady's hand as we pulled out of the town.

"Why did you pay them that much? We could have saved the extra gold coins for something else." Keres rode next to me and right in front of Armand, her hair blending right into the night laying before us.

"She was going to swindle us, anyway. That town appeared as dead as the dinner we had three nights ago. The Brawn'n steal from them. I'm surprised they haven't just moved on," Aidan grumbled, his jacket wrapped around him like a blanket. He looked about as cold as a popsicle.

The farther we got from the town, the rougher the road got, forcing us to follow on foot.

"This is going to take forever-" Keres complained as a loud sound cut out through the air.

"What was that?" Armand said, leaning straighter on his horse.

"I'm not sure," I said as the sound of metal scraping interrupted me.

"It must be bandits, or a Brawn'n. Quick! Whoever it is might need help." Kallan scrambled onto his horse, clicking his tongue, urging it to push forward into the unknown.

17

Reunited

Elowen POV

I brushed off the feeling. *No one is there.* My inner voice said, trying to reassure me.

My hands shook as I lit the discarded wood. *Warmth, I need warmth.*

"If you try to fight back, I will kill you," a woman said. I scrambled away from the small fire. Reaching for my sword, but a black boot stood on it. I locked eyes with a man as I followed the leg up. A beard covered half of his face. An eye patch covered one of his eyes.

The woman who spoke held a sword toward me, the tip pointing dangerously close to between my breasts. Just a hair thickness away from touching me. Her accomplice grabbed my sword off the ground, looking through Chep's pack. "Where the fuck is all of your gold? All you have in here is food?" He bared his teeth at me. The black spots of rot covered a majority of them.

His grubby hands grabbed my forearms, hauling me up, pushing me against the boulder. I let out a yelp, struggling against him. Kicking my leg up, meeting the soft spot between his legs. He howled, letting me go, dropping my sword.

"Fuck," his accomplice said as she moved toward me. My training kicked in as I grabbed the sword, hitting the crumpled form of a man in the head, sending him sprawling onto the uneven ground. The wind howled as the woman and I stared at each other. A dark shadow covered half of her face, emphasizing her sunken cheekbones. Her head was full of matted pieces, the only wispy part in a small ponytail.

"Leave me be or I kill your friend." I pointed the sword at the crumpled man before me. My heart beat in my chest. Every insignificant detail, I absorbed. Her breathing was even, her body lean, not an ounce of fat covering her. She shook in the wind, the cold biting through her.

She took a step back; her face completely enveloped in the night's blackness. The small fire I had built a mere moment before was only a candle flame.

"How would you like to do this, lady? We won't leave until we have the gold you have on yer person." Her sword switched hands, a mindless tick. With her sword switching hands, I lunged, the training from Fian and Kallan rushing through me, like instinct. A sixth sense. Our swords clanged together.

"The only way you're leaving here is if Runen takes you to the other side." I gritted my teeth at the clash of our blades connecting, sending a jolt of pain up to my shoulder.

She let out a crazed laugh, pulling back to lunge at me again. I swung wildly; the blade nicking her on her arm. Blood immediately welled to the surface, soaking her shirt.

"You bitch!" a man's voice called out from behind me. I swung around. The man who I had knocked out now grappled with me. He loomed over me, a dagger in hand.

I needed to end this soon. Otherwise, I was going to be in trouble. I rushed him, the length of my sword being the largest disadvantage at close combat. He swiped at me. Heat spread from my side. *Fuck, that hurt.* He grinned, stepping back as if he thought I was going to stop my attack.

I was to die soon, I doubt Runen and I would meet again for tea. I thought back to his words. *Pavati needed a human death to make the spell. I was a ingredient,* so I could not die tonight.

'Fight through your pain,' Fian's voice echoed through my head as I slid the blade between his ribs. He coughed, blood sputtering out of his mouth, splattering me on the cheek. His partner screamed, a heart wrenching scream. I twisted the blade in his torso, feeling a wet crunch as I pulled it out.

"May the air carry your spirit far and may the earth find happiness with your absence," I said, as I turned to the woman. She was on her knees clutching her chest, tears streaming down her face as she glared at me.

"Ven, you stupid bastard." Her hands shook as she stood, her blade in hand.

"You killed him. You killed my fated, you will find the same fate he did," she screamed as our swords met. It was as if his strength and hers coursed through her veins. His death invigorating her to have me meet my end by her blade.

Shit, I'm coming, my love. Hold on. My eyes widened, my movements faltering as the voice of my fated ricocheted in my head.

Hoofbeats thundered in the distance, approaching us with vigor. Was that Lilja?

My attacker took the opportunity to swipe across my side. A whimper slipped past my lips, her leg swiped mine sending me sprawling onto my back. The rocks dug into my skin.

Her crazed eyes gazed on me, her mouth wide as if preparing to bite into me. The ground grumbled answering the call of someone blessed with magic.

A shadow connected with the woman, sending her flying off of me. She struggled against my savior, kicking, a desperate, silent whimper escaping her mouth, as defeat washed over her. Even in the dark, I could recognize the outline of her face.

"Lilja," I sobbed. "You're alive." I wheezed, coughing, half sobbing as the air returned to my lungs.

Lilja leaned down to my attackers ear. "if you lay a finger on my Fated again, I will make sure you beg for your end."

The women stilled, the fight or flight leaving her body. She gave a small nod, as if she was worried any bigger of a motion would send Lilja's dagger into her neck. Lilja eased her body weight off of hers, letting her scamper away to whatever hellhole she came from.

"What are you doing here? How did you know where I was?" I demanded, the relief from seeing her beautiful, handsome face gone, now replaced with anger.

Lilja looked good, her face and body still as filled out as the last time I saw her. She had been eating well in our time apart. The weight looked good on her. No longer was she the dangerously thin queen. She was muscular. Power radiated throughout her, yet she stood anxiously. Her hand absentmindedly scratched at the back of her head.

"Elle, I got injured. I needed to heal-" Lilja said. It was the first time I had noticed the scar. A thin line barely discernible in the dark on the right side of her head. The woman who attacked me whimpered, her sobs becoming louder from around the rock.

Lilja and I shared a glance as a scream rang out. The women had returned, charging back at Lilja.

"You killed my fated and I'm going to kill yours!" Her dagger gleamed dangerously. Lilja turned around, surprised. I lurched forward, pulling her behind me, tipping my sword upward and thrusted. Her eyes went wide, glancing down at the sword now sticking out of her abdomen. I didn't think I just acted.

My stomach churned as I pulled the sword out. Her blood rushed down the blade, sending a sickly wetness over my hands. She took a step back, staggering before crumpling to the ground, gasping. My body seemed to shake as the light left her eyes. It could have been minutes or hours, I didn't know. The rest of the crew stood silently, as if knowing the gravity of the situation. *I had just killed two people. I had just snuffed out two lives prematurely taken.*

Runen's shadowed face danced before my eyes.

Lilja gently unclasped my fingers from the sword, my hand aching, handing it over to Aidan. Her stiff, now bloody fingers grabbed my face, sending the ever familiar sparks up my body.

"You had to, Elle. Do you understand? She was going to kill me. You did what you had to do." Absent-mindedly, she wiped the tears falling down my cheeks, giving me a small kiss on my forehead, snapping me out of whatever trance I seemed to be in.

"How did you guys find me?" I said, finally looking at the rest of the group. My rag tag team grinned at me as they worked, grabbing supplies from the two bodies. Aidan scooped me up in a hug, squeezing me. The pain in my side was present, but not overbearing. I pushed it down. Not allowing it to ruin the moment, I squealed in childlike excitement. *They found me.*

"Put her down, you giant oaf. Let her catch her bearings first." Armand gently punched Aidan in the arm. Even as he scolded Aidan, Armand bounced on his feet, ready for a hug.

"Aidan's spies have been checking in with you. You have been quite the busy bee, little human." Kallan dismounted from his horse, coming up to a forearm handshake. Our foreheads touching.

"We had no way to rescue you," Cassia said.

"What are you even doing out here?" Keres crossed her arms, still on her horse.

I straightened my stance, not bothering to look at Keres. "Pavati contacted me via-."

Lilja grabbed my arm. "Not here. Let's set up camp and speak over a fire. It feels too open here."

"Pavati? You mean the Goddess of Rivers? How in the world did you manage that?" Kallan asked, leaning toward me. The fire crackled, sending popping coals outward, keeping the chill away.

I scooted closer to Lilja, the anger still palpable in my mouth. *We needed to talk in private. I was angry, but also relieved to be back together again. Being alone on the road was hard, even harder when you have highly trained military men coming after you. How would she react to me sleeping with Alieta?*

I gave a nod. "Yes, Pavati. Once I made Alieta trust me, she allowed me access to the library. From there, I combed through any book I had time to read. That last book I picked up was this one." I began pulling out the book from my bag. The cool cover sent a shiver down my spine. Much like it had done before, as if she was calling to me again. Begging for me to come save her.

"Her image showed up floating out of the page."

"This book was a Niphes book?! Can I see it?" Aidan held out his hands in a grabby motion. His excitement nearly made his journal fall on the ground..

"Aidan, for God's sake. Hold on. Let Elowen finish." Lilja pinched the bridge of her nose, as if a headache was coming on.

"Pavati said she was the reason the blight had not affected you for 300 years. She kept it at bay, but now she's being held hostage somewhere. Pavati asked me to bring ingredients for her. A water dragon claw and water nymph blood. If we bring her those, she said she could reverse the blight." I squirmed in my seat uncomfortably, nodding as I carefully omitted the last ingredient.

She probably only needed human blood, like the water nymph. My brain rationalized, *There's no point in concerning them. It was my choice.*

"Just two ingredients," Armand said in disbelief. He lounged on the ground, his elbow propping up his head. "That's all we've needed this whole time?" I winced, trying to not let my face slip to reveal my true feelings.

I hated to lie to them.

"That's why you are heading to Forgard Mountain?" Lilja asked next to me.

"Yes, once I found the solution in Alieta's library. I saw no reason to wait on being rescued. I realized no one was coming for me, or so I thought." Lilja grabbed my hand, giving it a squeeze.

"Everyone, let's head to bed. Tomorrow morning we head for the mountain." Lilja announced, mouthing for me to wait. The rest of the group took this as their cue to pretend not to hear us. Unrolling their blankets, preparing for the night's slumber.

Her arms enveloped me as we stood together, finally in the same space. I breathed in her scent, my head fitting perfectly into our hug. As if two once lost puzzle pieces joined together again.

"Elle, I'm so sorry it took us so long to be reunited. I tried," Lilja said in a small voice.

A tear ran down my eyes as I listened, the pain still reverberated in my heart like a prick of a thorn. Too small of an effort, to small of an explanation.

"I promise, darling. I tried. Even though I am the Queen of Valdis, I was powerless. I couldn't safely get to you. Alieta's guards do a constant rotation. Nearly impenetrable. We wouldn't have been able to extract you without sacrificing someone. So there I sat in Ebbon, healing so slowly. Waiting for you to contact me via the bond, waiting for the message that never came."

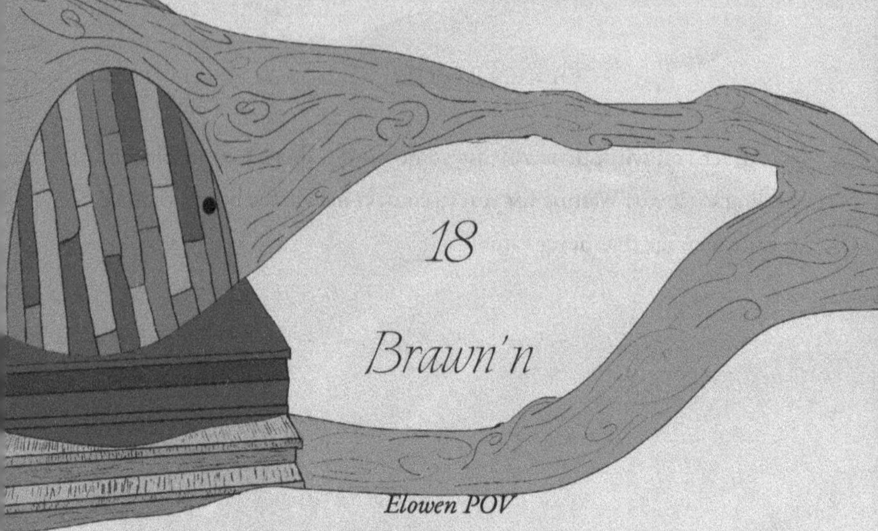

18

Brawn'n

Elowen POV

I leaned in, kissing Lilja. Her lips tasted of the salty tears running down her face. "Let's talk about this later. Emotions are high. When the sun comes up, we'll talk about this again. I won't lie. It hurt me deeply to feel forgotten." With the cloak Alieta gave me, I tightly wrapped myself as the fire crackled next to me, sending off waves of warmth. My side burned uncomfortably as I wiggled to find a comfortable spot. *I'll have to tend to that later*, I thought to myself.

"Can we sleep next to each other?" Lilja whispered. Her voice sounded unbelievably small. For the first time, she sounded unsure.

My heart ached in my chest as I shook my head. I wasn't ready to forgive her.

She left you.

She abandoned you.

She let Alieta have you.

Lilja said nothing, turning away from me. The cold creeped up on me, as the sounds of the night were the only thing to fill the air. Bugs chirped a soulful, longing song as the night dragged.

"Wake up, wake up, wake up!" I sat up groggily, sleep still attempting to pull me under.

"What?" The room was dark, the bed soft under my touch. My heart clamored in my chest.

"Who's there?" I called out into the darkness again.

"Me!" a feminine voice called out, following a large fireball rushing towards me.

I launched myself up, gasping for breath. The sun peaked over the horizon. Lilja sat up beside me, sweat covered her brow. She scrambled toward me, closing the space I had left last night. Lilja grabbed my face, her hands clammy.

"Are you okay?" She pulled me into her chest. Her own heart beat fast as she held me.

"Yes." My breathing came in short. I pushed her away, standing up. The scab that had formed over the night pulled uncomfortably at my skin as I walked the few paces away to Chep. He stomped his hoof as I leaned into him, startling him awake, burying my head into his neck, counting my erratic breaths. "I'm fine Lilja, don't worry. I just need to catch my breath." My voice tremored as I spoke the lie, a tear falling down my cheek.

The rest of the team's sleeping forms sprinkled around our temporary camp. *Thank the gods.* Lilja gave me a long look before looking away, whistling hard, waking everyone one up.

Kallan shot up, his hair sticking out in multiple directions. "Who? What?" His hand scrambling for his bow, ready to fight.

Lilja bent over, picking up her blanket. Her voice was hard, leaving no room for discussion. "Let's go. We will hit the mountain before sundown if we hurry."

Aidan was the first to move, already sensing Lilja's mood. "Of course."

My heart still pounded in my chest, like a blacksmith's hammer. With every pound of that imaginary hammer, sharp pains pinged into my chest. Without saying a word, I grabbed my discarded cloak, mounting Chep.

"Do you want to talk about it?" Aidan said as we rode out of our camp and back onto the road.

"Talk about what?" I asked, playing dumb. *He should say it. I wanted him, No I wanted them all, to ask what they had abandoned me to experience. Alone.*

"What she did to you. What Alieta did," Aidan said, looking away from his book and at me. His eyes were wide, sympathy and love written in them.

"Alieta is completely in the dark about the horrors her uncle is accomplishing or deranged. That much is clear. He tortured me. He stole my ring. Daveed cut my ears, saying 'if I wanted to pretend to be an elf so bad, I might as well look like one.' Alieta convinced herself she saved me, that she saved me from Lilja." I spoke loudly so the group could hear me over the pounding of the hooves from our horses.

I thought back to when I blatantly asked her, the confusion the shock of the question was enough to show she was either an impeccable actress or ignorant to the evils Daveed was completing.

"Why was she under the impression you needed to be saved from Lilja?" Keres raised her eyebrow, glancing at me.

"I wouldn't give into Daveed's torture, he wanted to know everything. I told him I knew nothing, but that answer did not satiate him. My answer just further convinced Daveed I knew something, so I played it like Lilja was just keeping me to use as her plaything. He kept the ring because I told him it was my mothers." My heart beat uncomfortably hard in my chest as I continued. I bit the inside of my lip to stop it from trembling. The tears from earlier were gone as I sat back in my saddle. I refused to allow my hurt to show through the pain the memories brought me.

"Unconvinced that I knew nothing, he kept hurting me, pushing me to the brink of death. At the last minute, Alieta had someone save me, and let her healer fix me up. There was no way to fix my ears." I shrugged, forcing myself to look ahead, trying to seem un-bothered by it. Sweat covered my brow, as I forced my breathing to remain normal, ignoring the pain in my side and the feeling of my heart ache for Lilja.

The group was silent for a few moments. Cassia steered her horse near me, getting as close as possible. Lilja led at the front, not once looking back at me. "When you were tortured, Lilja felt everything. The spell she did had side effects, connecting you both closer than before. We still don't quite understand how the spell didn't work." She paused, taking in a breath.

"Is there anything you needed me to look at that you felt they healed incorrectly?" Cassia said, her voice full of concern.

"She felt everything? Every cut?" Unable to control my facial expression, my mouth gaped open. *Can she feel everything?*

Cassia gave a terse nod. Without waiting for a verbal response, I nudged Chep up to Lilja. "Are you okay?" I waited for an answer. Lilja kept looking ahead, without so much as a glance in my direction.

"Define okay?" Lilja glanced at me, her eyes that normally shown with so much warmth towards me brimmed with tears.

"Lilja, I have to be honest with you. I felt like I had to connect with Alieta in more physical ways for her to trust me." My voice broke at the thoughts running through my head.

I had to tell her. I had to be honest. She'll understand.

There was a long pause as we rode, long enough for me to question if she had heard me or not. Forgard Mountain loomed over us. We were nearly at the base.

"Are you?" She asked, before the ground gave away.

A scream echoed in the chaos. I thought it was mine, but I couldn't be too sure.

"Bandits!" Kallan yelled through the dust.

"PESSEL!" Shouts rang out, people barely shorter than I emerged. They rode oversized gophers, most of them men. They had large beards, their faces dirty with mud and dust.

The uneven ground dug underneath my back as I pulled myself up. "No! It's the Brawn'n," I wheezed, the pain in my side worsening. *That's not good.*

"As if there's a difference." Keres pulled herself up and over a large slab of rock. Pulling out horses with us, as we tried to huddle closer to each other.

"Now is not the time for petty corrections, Ker," Armand coughed, clambering up from the spot he fell to. Dust swirled around us as if we stood in an artist's painting as they created their next masterpiece.

"Lilja! Where are you?" I squinted through the dust, pulling myself over the debris to her form. Her hair was a completely different shade, covered in a thick layer of dirt. "Are you okay?"

"Are you?" I gave a small nod, trying to ignore the ever-growing pain in my side. *I can take care of myself.* Sweat ran down my temple as I helped her up.

Our attackers stood motionless, their spears and bows held at the ready, as if eager to kill us and get on with their day.

"EJEN DE?" a voice emanated from the back, the sound coming closer. Heavy footsteps echoed the hollowed out earth. *Stomp. Stomp. Stomp.* Lilja grabbed me, pulling me close to her, as if ready to push herself in front of me.

I must have hit my head. They make no sense. The Brawn'n who spoke last turned to the woman to his right, murmuring something. "Who you?" her voice was hoarse as if she was used to yelling. My head throbbed and I welcomed Lilja's hands. The dirt floor felt unsteady under my feet, as if it wanted to swallow me.

"We need to get to the mountain, and unless these people are just going to let us pass with all our supplies. We need to barter with them," I whispered to Lilja. The Brawn'n seemed to have to steal to survive. Perhaps we could barter with them. Pavati was clear enough, we needed to get to the dragon.

The rest of the group stood tensely. Armand and Kallan stood with swords in hand. Keres with a ball of fire, graciously illuminating the darkness of the pit. Cassia, with her bow, trained at the man who spoke last.

"I am Lilja, the Queen of Valdis, the leader of this group." She gestured her free hand to the team.

Do they understand us? I projected my thoughts to Lilja.

How am I supposed to know? I would have much rather an above ground approach. Not in some dug out trap. I have to admit, though, it's pretty clever. Can't run away down here. Her ever pleasant voice rang in my head, her face was neutral. Not portraying any sort of emotion other than a hint of a smirk, as if pleased.

The woman presumably translated what Lilja said to the man. He grunted before speaking in the unknown language. A sizable hat adorned his head, its design meant to look like a dragon, the man's head meant to be the mouth. "Thojta, we cospen ner Zed. We deo dedeod fob Isold."

"He says hello. My name is Zed. He is the leader of Isold. I am his daughter. Where are you traveling to? We do not wish to be at war with Valdis. I added the last bit." She clasped her hands in front of her.

"We're heading to Forgard Mountain. The River Goddess Pavati has guided us. She told us to get a claw from the water dragon, rumored to live at the top of the mountain." The scene before me seemed to tilt as I spoke.

With my words, the Brawn'n people seemed to come alive with my sentence. As a brief understanding of my words, went through them.

"Es." The man spoke again. I didn't need a translation to know he said no. His daughter looked up at him in surprise.

"Es? Jem, zos en ber."

Lilja and I looked at each other, our eyebrows raised. He sighed loudly with disdain, waving us in before turning around and walking back into the tunnel. His daughter clapped loudly out of excitement. "Follow us!"

Keres gathered the horses, checking them over for injuries from the fall. Kallan and Lilja murmured to each other about who knows what. Probably talking about the Brawn'n's fighting technique and tunnels. Kallan looked tense as we walked into the cramped tunnel, the ceiling nearly brushing the top of his head. It forced the horses to walk with their heads down, as if bowing to Zed.

I trailed behind the group, letting them pass, holding out my hand, letting it follow the rough dugout tunnel. Sending a welcoming chill to my overheating skin. Unlike the city of Ebbons' tunnels, these were jagged, as if unfinished, forgotten with time.

The animals the Brawn'n rode squealed as the cavern widened, revealing the city of Isold. Ancient giant gnarled roots curled their way through the city, separating it into sections. An image of the Oracle flashed through my memory as I trailed my finger over a small root near the road we now walked on. Moist air filled my nose, mixed with the scents of sandalwood. Large fires set sanctioned at each side of the entrance, drying the air. They built their houses into the thickened roots of the ancient forgotten tree. Small children ran through the streets giggling and laughing. I gave them a weak smile.

"We are almost to the council building, my father would like to speak with you and your team," the Brawn'n woman spoke, turning to face us. She instantly frowned as we made eye contact. She skipped toward me, stopping a few paces in front of me. "Are you okay?"

My clothes clung to me, glued with sweat. I faltered, the world swaying as I tried to nod.

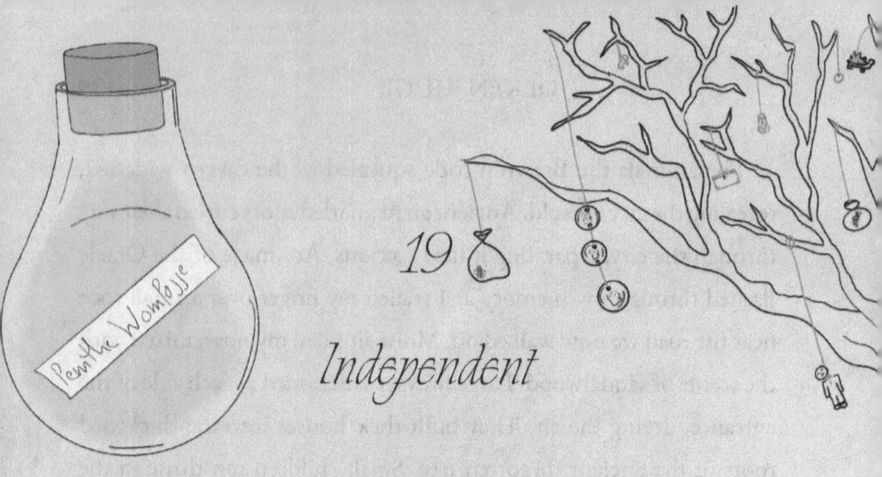

19

Independent

Lilja POV

The ground shifted as I turned, looking for Elle. An unbecoming gray sheen replaced her usual rosy cheeks. Her feet shuffled beneath her, swaying. The leader's daughter was in front of her first. I willed the earth to curl around her body, cocooning her. Aidan was close behind me, running to her. I touched her forehead, wincing. She was burning up.

"What's wrong with her?" Aidan was already down at her side next to me, his books strewn on the ground around us like macabre confetti.

I twisted her arms around, looking for cuts, bruises, for something I could have missed earlier.

"You must have felt it when she got hurt, think." Kallan's voice came from behind me. I didn't justify his statement with a look. The leader's daughter cradled her head. *That should be me.*

"I'm thinking," I grumbled. We had garnered a crowd. The children who had once been playing in the street now stood gawking at us. Their mothers shielded their eyes, hiding them from the scary sight.

I thought back to the pain I had felt days previously.

"Her side!" I pulled up her tunic, gingerly, hissing in shame as it revealed an angry-looking cut. It couldn't have been more than a few inches in length. Dry blood circled around it, the skin inflamed. Angry red streaks emanated from the wound.

"Infection ravages your friend's wound. Pick her up and bring her to capital. I will have a healer come," the leader's daughter spoke, looking up at me.

Looping my arms under her, I stood up from my crouched position. Anger rolled through me like a wave that had crashed into a cliff. Panic gripped me as the thought of infection burned through Elowen's fragile human body.

I ignored the rest of the city, my eyes trained on the capitol building and the heat emanating from my fiancée's skin. The Brawn'n had built the capitol building into the largest root of all. It resembled trees from back home. As if an ancient mud tree had sunk down beneath this mountain.

"How could I let this happen? This stubborn girl is going to be the death of me," I said to no one in particular. The metal door opened, revealing a spacious room, iron made benches filled the area.

"Lay her on the floor. Lelset should be here soon." No sooner did the words leave her mouth, did a back door bust open. A small lady emerged, small even to the standard of Brawn'n. She used a staff to steady herself, the grooves of the wood painted with earthy tones. Charms shook on it as she walked toward us.

The floor? She wants me to lay my future wife on the floor?

"Bondo rel we bosfe dob bo? Ejen ef ze," Lelset grumbled, her voice crackly with age.

"Lelset, we have no time to be disgruntled. Please heal her." She clicked her tongue, looking over Elowen with her eyebrows pursed together. I balled my fist, willing the thought of forcing the healer to heal my fiancée to pass. My hand twitched as my feelings welled inside me. I gripped Elle's hand, disturbed at the lack of warmth.

How could I not notice her discomfort? A wound that would be nothing to an elf was so deadly to a human. I just got her back.

Lelset chanted, her staff chinking together as the charms connected with each other. With her free hand, she pulled a small jar from her apron. I could only describe the contents of which as brown murky water. I made a face, giving a small nod to her. As if to say, 'Yes, heal my fiancée.'

With her teeth, she pulled the cork off of the bottle, and smoke billowed out of it, a foul smell emanating from it. Keres gagged behind me

"She has to drink that?" Cassia asked behind me. She sounded half disgusted and half intrigued.

"Don't be ridiculous. It only has to be poured on your friend's wound. Nobody wants to drink that stuff, it's vile," the Brawn'n woman spoke with her nose curled up as Lelset poured the murky potion onto Elowen's wound. Elle winced as it dissolved into her pale gray skin, seeping into her wound like the ground of a desert. Elowen jolted upright, gasping, her chest heaving up and down. Her eyes were frantic as she took in her new surroundings.

"Awake, now leave me alone," Lelset said. I raised my eyebrow at the language switch. Lelset took the leftover liquid in the bottle and swished it around before drinking it in one swig, before teetering away. The sound of her charms fading away as she left.

Elowen POV

I groaned, holding up my head with my hand as the pain subsided in my side. The cold stone ground sent shivers up my spine as Lilja cupped my face. Her brown eyes pierced into my soul, trying to read every thought I ever had.

"Are you okay? I'm sorry I didn't think to ask if your side was okay. I forget humans heal slower," she said, her voice jittery as she rambled, grabbing my hand, helping me up.

"I had it. I didn't want to bother you with something I planned to handle." The bite to my words was hollow as tiredness washed over me.

She left me.

Lilja kissed me on the forehead, looking back at Zed, the leader of the Isold. As if she was realizing where we were again. "Can we have a room for the night? My fated is unwell. We'd like to rest before we continue on our journey."

A vein popped out on the middle of his forehead, creased with silent frustration. "Jem dognos vec bepfob, wo we zoc ev fon intifada. Jel we ze bor Jen."

"Recwes," Zed said in a warning tone.

Recwes must be his daughter's name, I thought to Lilja. My body sagged against hers. Exhaustion threatened to take over with each breath.

There was a long pause. I felt Lilja shift her hand closer to her sword. Ready to pounce. "We mean no harm to the Brawn'n community. We only wish to seek refuge with the dragon. The team and I must complete the task Pavati has asked of me. The balance of the world hangs on us." My voice came out firm, considering how I felt at that moment. Lilja's hand was around my waist, pulling me close to her, holding me up.

Recwes translated, her face grim. Zed's facial expression switched, before making his face neutral again. *Ah, the art of looking like you don't give a shit,* Lilja's voiced chuckled in my head. "De bofwo bepfob fe we wotnon loz jo vel deo beme cogco jome vowbe. Deo cor bo thozle zol a ren websol en rowe."

Recwes beamed. "I shall show you a room to rest. My father has requested your presence for dinner to discuss the threat." Without another response, two men flanked her. She beckoned us to follow. Lilja picked me up, bridal style, earning a squeal from me and a smirk from Kallan.

"Is this necessary, your Highness?" I murmured into her neck. I rolled my eyes, but a small smile grew on my lips as the fated bond sparked between us.

"Quite, can't have you passing out again." *Plus gives me an excuse to be close to you,* Lilja projected to me.

My cheeks flushed as her voice echoed in my head, giving in. Recwes exited the building we were in, immersing us into the city. They heavily integrated dragons into their buildings. Dragons stood as support pillars for some of their buildings. Their light posts had them twirling onto the poles, making it look like the light was the fire from the dragon's mouth. Brightly painted murals adorned a majority of the flat surfaces.

Though the murals seemed to give the underground city of Isold a breath of life, another issue seemed to weigh heavily on the city, poverty. My heart ached as I took in the sight of Isold's people. They were thinner than normal, much like Lilja when I first laid eyes on her.

Children ran in the streets unaccompanied and appearing knobby and malnourished. Trash piled in alley ways and at the edge of the streets. The acrid air coated the back of my throat, causing me to cough. The hot trash and Elven waste wafted through the air.

The Brawn'n carved a majority of the buildings into the roots. Others were out of mud and bricks. Fires roared in each, giving off a warm glow amid the stench. I walked close to Aidan, Lilja right beside me. I felt at ease with him, no pretenses or a fated desire to pull me in. A friendship where I felt no obligation to be a certain way.

I wonder how deep in the ground we are. The cold does not touch this city.

"Another city in the ground. Can't we find hospitable cities above ground?" Kallan whined as we rounded another corner. A large pillared area stood in the middle of a courtyard. Unlike the disrepair of the rest of the city this part was clean. The stones washed white, swirling dragons painted around the support beams as if dancing toward the top of the mountain. Beside it, a gnarled rooted house. They had rubbed the wood smooth, showcasing the grains beautifully.

Recwes noticed my gaze. "The building of the dragons. It is a great honor for our people to house and feed the dragon Gichimanidoo. In our language," she pointed to the temple. "It is called, Dobjette Cot Woso Ocle. Creators of land Temple," she translated automatically, ushering us to the house.

"The great Gichimanidoo is fed by the priest once a month. Our people prepare the food for him throughout the month. Often times sacrificing a meal to appease him."

"Why would your people do so much for him?" Aidan asked, his fingers stained with ink. One hand holding his journal the other with a quill in hand.

She paused turning back to us. "The dragons are creators of all, we do not wish to be punished. A great flood could happen again if we do not keep him happy." Recwes patted her chest. She brought two fingers to her mouth, kissing them and pointing them towards the temple.

"We are the watchers," Recwes said it like a prayer.

"A flood! Fascinating! Could you and I perchance speak more on the matter and why your people believe the flood was caused by the dragon?!" Aidan's mouth moved a mile a minute.

Recwes sighed opening the door to the home. "The height of everything down here is for Brawn'n, including my house. Topsiders do not come down here much. This is the only room I have for visitors. This will have to work," she said carefully trying to avoid looking into Aidan's direction.

We all peaked inside. Cassia was the first to enter. Everything in the house reflected the height of the Brawn'n people, including the beds. An intricate ornate hearth stood on the far wall; it appeared the expertise of the Brawn'n was stone and clay. Enough beds lined either sides of the wall, minus one.

"This is fine, thank you." Kallan bowed.

"I'll be back in four hours. Be ready for dinner." The door shut with a thud.

Lilja laid me on the nearest bed, smoothing out my hair. "How are you feeling?" She looked over to Cassia, who already was on her way over, a canteen of water in her hand.

I yawned. "Tired. The pain in my side has lessened. I would have told you if I thought it was infected. I'm efficient at taking care of myself. In this realm and the human realm. I've been taking care of myself for too long."

Hurt flashed before her eyes.

"I don't need anyone else," I said, turning on my side facing away from her.

"Elle, please understand. I tried, Kallan and I went to Ardour, to try and reach you. We were seen and were forced to retreat," Lilja pleaded with me.

The rest of the team seemed to try and melt into the walls, to avoid the conversation Lilja and I spoke of so openly.

I bit the inside of my lip turning back to look at her. "You tried to save me?"

Her eyes softened. "Yes, my darling. I failed. Again. Once as the Queen of Valdis but also as your Fated."

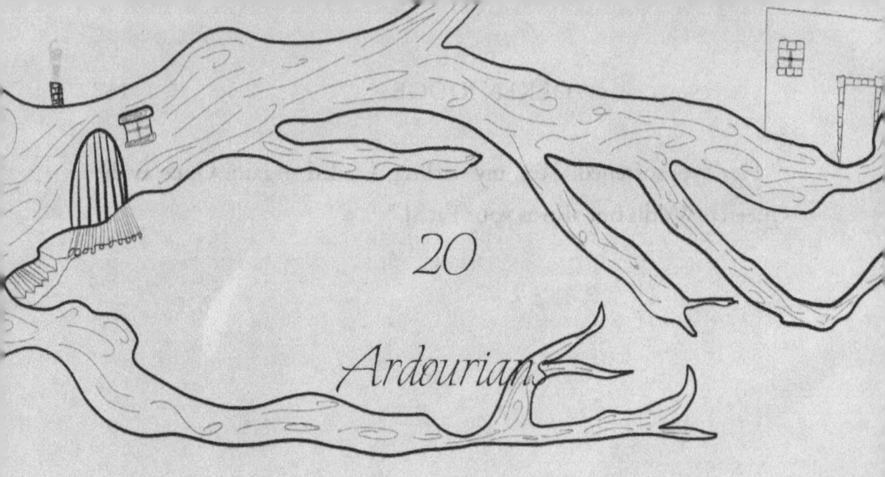

20

Ardourians

Lilja POV

My heart ached as I watched Elowen sleep, her face peaceful. But beneath that beautiful facade was turmoil; her emotions ran free in her brain. I turned away, back to the team. My shoulders sagged, sleep urging me, the bed soft underneath me.

"She'll get better. Her color is already coming back." Kallan clasped my shoulder, pulling me into his chest. An infrequent response, one I gladly accepted. My childhood friend smelled like dirt and the cold air.

"It's not her physical health I'm worried about, I can feel it." I sniffled into his shirt, attempting to pull myself together before I pulled away. I was never much for showing my emotions in front of anyone, even the Elves before me. They were my closest friends, my one true family. Even with all the love they imbued toward me, I was ashamed of the feelings I could not contain. I am a queen and should act like one. I thought about the words of my parents' advisors. *To show feeling was to show weakness.*

"Feel what?" Cassia asked. She had pulled her bow off her back, setting it next to the bed she had claimed.

I gulped air, pushing out of Kallan's embrace. "Her feelings, her emotions, are in turmoil. She put a brave face on earlier when I had asked, but she's lying to herself and to me. Elowen feels like we abandoned her. She feels like she can only rely on herself."

Emotions were one thing I wasn't efficient at. Years of pushing down my emotions to show nothing. After years of this, outwardly showing emotions didn't come easy, nor did understanding them. Even for someone with a Fated connection.

"All we can do is show her we're there for her, that we're still on her team. Even if she doesn't want to believe it. She survived Ardour because she wanted to help you, Lilja. Not because she has an emotional attachment to Valdis. Elowen has a good heart; she wants to help her people." Aidan pushed up his glasses, pulling his journal from his pack and going directly to writing after he finished speaking.

My heart tugged at the jealousy in the pit of my stomach. Elowen seemed so close to him now she was back. Aidan always had a way with people; his soft demeanor made people willing to pour their truths out. Elle wasn't immune to it. One question and she bared her soul to him. Her anger was pushing her away from me. Little did she know, I was willing to let the world burn for her.

Perhaps it was my fault. I was scared. Scared of how our relationship would change, I was ready to accept her back fully. I was willing to push past the events that occurred in Ardour. But I *didn't* live them, the horrors followed her like ghosts. A haunting that possibly replayed behind her eyes when she slept.

I straightened my shoulders, like the earth, my divine power. I would do everything to make her feel loved and secure.

We unpacked the necessities only; our time spent in the Brawn'n's village was uncertain. Armand checked the room over for any traps or hidden doors. He grunted, clasping his hands behind his head, satisfied with the lack thereof.

"Sit down, brother. Your pacing is making me anxious." Keres flipped her hair off to the side, poised on the last bed as if waiting for someone to paint her likeness.

Cassia flopped on the child-sized bed with a sigh. "Why do you think they are being cordial?"

I smoothed Elowen's stray hairs down; she leaned into my touch. It caused a small smile to play on my lips. "I'm not sure what their angle is. They helped Elowen. They could have let her suffer."

Kallan paced the room, in the somber light, his scar seemed to flicker in and out of existence. "That Lelset lady sure didn't seem too happy to heal her."

"Recwes, seems excited to help us. Her father is more of a cause for concern." Aidan leaned against the fireplace, casting a shadow in the room.

"He seems to want nothing more than to steal our stuff and kick us out," Kallan said.

"That's the uncultured bias swimming around in your head. Something has obviously pushed these people to live in these conditions." Cassia put her arm over her eyes, shielding her from the light of the fire.

"They were planning to steal from us before you and Elowen convinced them not to," Aidan countered, flipping through pages of his book.

"I have no other information on the Brawn'n besides the location and observations. My immediate reaction is the Brawn'n have immense knowledge of the earth, yet none of them seem to have magical properties," Aidan said, his voice switching into the old Aidan, a man who could break bones with one hand. His voice was monotonous, like giving a run-through during a lull in fighting.

"However, inside and outside the house, the stonework is impeccable. We have to assume the Brawn'n have hidden places and passages in the entire mountain," Kallan said, adding to the mix. He peered out the window, watching for anything suspicious.

"It's clear they revere the Dragon and treat it as a deity," Keres added in.

"Right now, as it stands, if the Brawn'n people continue to treat us with respect, we extend that notion. If they don't allow us to pass to get to the top of Forgard Mountain, we will fight our way through. For whatever reason, Pavati needs the claw and the blood of a nymph. The blood should be easy to obtain; the claw is less likely." I stood up from the bed. Elowen's arm shifted as if searching for my body heat again. I gave the guys a smirk, running my hand through my hair.

Maybe I had a chance.

"How can the blood of a water nymph be easier? Sylp made Elowen a deal last time. She has the mark on her wrist to prove it," Keres said, pointing towards her sleeping form.

I rolled my eyes, not saying the retort that settled on my tongue. *She wasn't wrong. She says it as if I were not there when it occurred.*

The last few hours passed slowly. I fought the urge to slip into the blankets with Elowen. Cassia and Armand snored quietly in their beds, seemingly without a care in the world. Their feet hanging off the too-short beds. Armand's arm covered his eyes, his mouth gaping open as he slept. Aidan perched himself in the chair closest to the fire, writing in his journal.

Kallan paced the room, Keres dejected herself to look out the window, people watching.

A small knock on the door rustled the group as Recwes entered. Her previous clothing changed to an airy tunic. "Rest over, dinner is now. Wake the sick one."

I opened my mouth to reply, but Aidan beat me to it. "Her name is Elowen, not 'sick one'." He crossed his arms, glancing at me.

Elowen POV

We exited Recwes's house; the air filled with nervousness. My body ached less than before, but exhaustion still held me with an iron grip. Lilja held out her hand toward me as I walked behind her, making a grabby motion with her fingers. I pretended not to notice as a dark house loomed over us.

"This is Zed's house, my father."

Dark shadows appeared to move from building to building. I squeezed Lilja's hand to signal her.

I know my love. Keep an eye on them.

"What does your father wish to speak about, Recwes?" Lilja squared her shoulders. She cracked her fingers as she spoke. A shiver ran up my spine at the unknown. By Lilja's dejected tone, I knew she was attempting to appear threatening.

No guards loomed in the shadows of the homes.

"He shall speak about the threat, and how we will both benefit." Lilja and I exchanged looks as we entered the pitch black house.

Our footsteps clattering on the stone floor were the only sound. "Where is everyone?" I asked, murmuring. Fires flared to life on either side of the large room. In the middle was a sunken pit, and bars stood erect around the pit. Stadium-style seats lined the sides of the room.

Lilja's hand found mine, giving my palm a squeeze. At the end of the room was a large, cushioned seating area. Recwes pushed on ahead as the guards who flanked the inside of the house stood behind us. Their unspoken message was obvious: we were prisoners.

"What's the meaning of this?!" Kallan said, his hand dangerously close to the dagger that was fixed on his hip.

"I told you my father wanted to talk to you about the threat." Recwes pushed her long hair back.

"I mean this with no ill intent, but the guards at our back are not relaying the message of peace." The words flew out of my mouth with such speed it surprised even me.

Recwes looked back at me, her usual light skin paler than moments before. Lilja gripped my hand tighter, her lips tightly shut. The energy in the room had shifted, static-charged with anger and an unspoken threat.

Zed sat on a large, worn cushion. He had not bothered to clean his body before the meeting; dirt from the surprise attack still slathered his body. He twirled his spear in his lap, the sharpened metal glinting dangerously in the firelight.

"Jem fo is deo joces cot dob," Recwes said, voice wavering. "De le pegte wo vowgoz."

"That was before, daughter. Before I realized something," he said, switching languages, his accent nearly undetectable.

"What did you realize?" Lilja spoke first, her voice hard with anger.

"That you're more valuable to us as soon as you told me your identity. I had scouts verify you are who you say you are. Fascinating to learn that the Queen of Ardour has a price on your head." His hand stroked his facial hair, his eyes shining with opportunity. He extended the spear; the metal gleamed as it pointed at me.

"Alieta is insane. She has no knowledge of the world behind the castle walls." I pushed my shoulders back, taking a step forward. *He can't do this.*

"Please remind your friend it's better to be seen and not heard when the elves are present. Even with the ears of an elf, a human is still a human." Lilja squeezed my hand, forcing me to stagger back, now standing shoulder to shoulder.

Please be quiet, darling. We are unfortunately overpowered. Don't worry, I'll find a way out of this. I'll make him pay for the comment later.

It's not the comment I'm worried about. This greedy man will sell us out and hand us over to Alieta. Or worse, her Uncle Daveed.

Tightness gripped my chest as panic threatened to take over. The dagger belted onto my thigh suddenly felt heavy with the gravity of the situation.

Zed pointed the spear at me. "Queen Alieta has a hefty price on both of you, but you especially, human. You don't look like much. Must provide a good fuck."

Lilja visibly stiffened, my hand grounding her in place. A rumble moved over the ground, so quick it was barely discernible.

"No one speaks of my future queen like that," Aidan growled, stepping forward, his usually abandoned sword in his hand. Poised and ready to kill. His movement started a chain reaction, causing the pandemonium. Zed's guards stepped forward, their weapons already in hand.

Armand and Kallan moved together as if they had already planned to be crossed by Zed. I gaped at Aidan, surprised at the sudden anger that slipped out of his mouth.

Lilja's hand slipped out of mine, going toward Recwes, who had now moved to the sidelines. Her dagger was on Recwes's throat in a second; she didn't even let out a squeak. In an instant, the fight had stopped. With Zed's hand forced, if he wanted to keep his daughter alive, he had to cooperate.

"Now, since we seem to communicate freely. Let's get down to business. What did you tell Ardour? Before you think about answering, if I even sense you are being untruthful, I will slit your daughter's throat." The blade twitched in Lilja's hand, excited for the opportunity to erase this moment from the map. Her poise was perfect. Not even a hair out of place.

"I've already sent word." Zed clasped his hand in his lap, the spear he had handled earlier now in the hands of Keres. Cassia stood behind him dangerously, holding her bow.

"To whom? The Queen or to Daveed?" I asked, forcing my voice to be strong. My palms screamed for relief as my nail beds threatened to pierce the soft skin.

"Who do you think, human? The Brawn'n have experienced discrimination because of their difference in appearance and living conditions. It's high time we get treated like topsiders and not like second-class citizens. Long ago, the military came through here. A few brazen citizens, including myself, grouped together, attempting to make a better life for ourselves. We were just hoping to talk to him, so he could see our side of things. That way, our family wouldn't have to live in this squalor. Daveed was the leader of that group. He massacred the rest of my crew, my closest circle, leaving only me. At the time the late queen and king still reigned, Daveed was their closest confidant-"

"If he killed your inner circle, then why are you helping him?" I balked at the man in front of me.

The saddened, cornered man paused, his face slowly tilting up from the ground to look at me. His eyes hardened with rage as he stared up at me. "The best way to rise from the bottom isn't by playing nice, human. Sometimes you have to join the wrong side for the right things. Befriending him will aid in the rise of Isold. The reward money is enough to feed my citizens for weeks. Kill me if you want, but let my daughter go. The Ardourian army should be here by the end of the day tomorrow."

The atmosphere in the room stilled, as if Zed had siphoned out the sound with his words. A dull roar filled my ears as anger coursed through me.

This fucking close to saving Pavati, and things are going wrong.

"Let us leave. Daveed doesn't need to know that you helped us escape. Say we overpowered your defenses. If we fail, Valdis is in jeopardy, including Isold." I stepped forward, ignoring Lilja's protests in my head.

"If you escape, Daveed will stop at nothing to get you. There won't be anything stopping him from slaughtering the whole of Isold." He jumped up, his hands reaching for my neck. Instinctually, my hands went to my thigh, where I had strapped a dagger a mere hour before. The sharp blade met his leg with a hungry bite, making a clean cut. He crumpled to the ground. His daughter screamed, struggling free from my surprised, soon-to-be wife.

She pushed past me, cradling her father. "Get away from him!" Zed's face was ashen with surprise. The food in my stomach swirled uncomfortably. Lilja's warm hands caught me as I staggered back from Recwes's push.

Cassia crouched down, putting her hand on his wound. Her bow lay discarded by her feet. "We have to leave. We can't let Daveed win." My voice was shaky as vomit climbed its way up my throat. I swallowed it, refusing to show weakness in front of them.

"We can't abandon these people to die." Armand slashed a guard, rotating the weapon in his hand.

"I'm not suggesting that." I retorted, pacing the room back and forth. Recwes and Zed's eyes followed me.

I turned, pointing my knife toward them. I paused, mulling over the words in my mouth before saying.

"Two people need to stay and devise a plan. A distraction. Something to convince Daveed and Alieta that we escaped. You and Kallan are probably the best bet."

Kallan's head popped up from the guard's body as he pick-pocketed the corpse. His black hair nearly covered the scar that went down the top half of his face. "What?!" His mouth gaped open.

"Listen, you two are probably the most mischievous bastards out there. If anyone can trick Alieta and Daveed that we escaped on our own, it would be you two. 'Escape' then hang out in the town somewhere to make sure they don't retaliate. The rest of us will head up the mountain to the dragon. Once the Ardourians leave, come find us."

Keres and Armand stepped out, guarding the room as we settled the plan.

"Why would you help us? We tried to imprison you and your team." Zed looked up at us, and a sheen of sweat coated his forehead. Blood soaked the cloth Cassia had placed over the wound I inflicted.

"He will kill us. You have to understand, I don't do this because I wish you ill will. I'm doing this so my people may have a better future," Zed said, wincing. His eyes were brimming with tears.

"Fatther zoc roc de." Recwes smoothed out his hair.

I mulled over the answer that sat on my tongue, looking over to Lilja. She had joined Kallan, clearing the rest of the room, making sure Zed had no hidden guards ready to pounce on us.

"Even though you wanted to hand me over, you were trying to do it for the good of your people. I can't let the Brawn'n fall for me. Not when I'm so desperately trying to save the Kingdom of my fated."

Zed knew he had been beaten; he no longer had the upper hand.

"We will try to diminish the terror Ardour could inflict. I swear it." I banged my fist on my chest, nodding to him.

"Valdis will not retaliate for your action, Zed. However, if you try again and speak to my Fated the same way-" Lilja paused as if contemplating the next words about to come out of her mouth.

"I'll end you. Isold won't stand a chance." He visibly gulped, the threat clear.

Cassia stayed with Zed for the rest of the afternoon, the rest of the day went by in a blur. Armand and Aidan flurried in busy movements, combing through the city for convenient places to put our plan into play. Kallan and Lilja spoke at length, solidifying the plan of splitting up

My heart ached at the idea, but I could see no other way to leave the Brawn'n intact and allow our getaway. I wandered my way back to Recwes's house as I readied to escape the town of Isold in a game of pretend.

21

Little Mouse

Alieta POV

My leg jumped up and down underneath my desk.

Tap, tap, tap.

My quill scribbled furiously on the paper, as if the thoughts were about to disappear.

"UNCLE!" My voice traveled far, earning a satisfying, urgent shuffle as the servants on the other side of my office ran to notify him of my demand.

I pushed myself off my chair with such force the large, oversized wooden chair teetered anxiously behind me. I glanced back at it, rolling my eyes. *So dramatic.*

"Your highness?" He said, giving a small knock.

"Come in, Uncle. No need to stand like a peeping teen. Come, come."

With him now fully in the room, I sized him up. The scent of him hit me first. The musk of sweat and a hint of a cigar wafted in. His once dark hair was now the silvery gray color you only get with age. Wrinkles sprouted from his face every day like weeds in a walking path. He bowed slowly, his age finally catching up with him. "You requested me?"

"Yes, are we any closer to finding my future fiancée? Have your men made progress? I knew I should have sent my own," I rambled, as I wore a path into the gold-laden rug covering my office floor.

"Your highness, the men I dispatched have sent word. They lost her in the forest to the north of here. Don't fret. I feel as if a breakthrough is coming. Perhaps we may even find out who is helping her. I do not say this to pry, but what was the story behind her escape?" Uncle smiled, the ends of his lips not quite reaching his eyes. His eyes were nearly devoid of any emotion other than curiosity.

I paused my assault against the carpet to glare out the window, not willing to face the man who had been helping me run Ardour my whole childhood. "She drugged me and escaped. What a humorous girl. My little mouse tried to convince me of something curious."

"Oh? Do you perhaps want to share this information with me? Lessen the pressure on your shoulders. You already take on so much, your highness." Even though I stared out the window, I knew he leaned toward me. Like a little bird spying on a worm in the grass, ready to strike.

I took a steadying breath. *He should not know how much his presence as of late bothered me. Conceal, do not show him.* I pushed my shoulders back. *I would not pace in front of this man or anyone. The Queen of Ardour is calm and collected, not fraying at the seams of sanity.*

My eyes were trained on the training house, no doubt where Fian was. Most likely, training new recruits into hating their lives, breaking them down only to build them into the perfect soldiers to stand behind me. Soldiers void of emotions, perfected to do everything I tell them to do. A long pause stretched between us, wanting him to wait for my answer.

"No, I will hold this burden alone. Don't worry about it. Is the banquet prepared for the celebration of the trade agreement between Ardour and Chaikamen?"

"Yes. The Chef thoroughly planned all the food. The Chaikamen prince arrived on the continent a few days ago. Fear not, your assistant has thoroughly welcomed them to the great kingdom of Ardour." I held up my hand, still facing the window, effectively silencing him.

"I care not if Esmersey and Niahm welcomed them. They signed the papers already, and I paid a hefty price to exchange produce with them. Leave me, notify me immediately if they found word of Elowen." I watched his reflection as I spoke.

He nodded, leaving the room, his jaw clenched. I crossed my arms as he left, huffing in discomfort. *Could he be behind this blight? Did I care if he was?*

Ardour had become one of the most successful kingdoms in the whole Elven World. Fatalities had skyrocketed to an unprecedented amount.

Is Ardour reigning over everything truly necessary?

The day dragged on without Elowen as a comfort. Even though we had only shared the sheets once. I yearned to have her scent envelop me once more. I missed the way she sat in the oversized chairs in the library. How her hair cascaded over her shoulders as she hunched over a book, putting the prettiest waterfalls to shame. I shook myself out of the melancholy memory lane, forcing myself to be present.

The sun had set behind the oversized Ebbon mountains as I looked over at the large table my servants had laid out in the banquet hall. Silverware lined the seating chart, placed as a perfect mirror. Someone of importance had taken every seat. The royals from Chaikamen and their companions. My inner circle, including Fian, sat around the table.

I raised my glass, standing holding the glass up high as I looked around the room, as my childhood instructors drilled into me.

"Make sure you look around the room as you speak," my rickety tutor would say as he smacked a ruler in his hand. *"Body language is the key to connecting with the entire room. This makes for a cohesive speech."*

"While I have not had the pleasure of welcoming you myself, Chaikamen leaders, I hope the Ardourian culture has thoroughly welcomed you. While we both benefit from the arrangement, I have to truly thank you from the bottom of every Ardourian citizen's heart. Please enjoy the food and festivities tonight."

The seat occupants erupted in painfully polite claps as I sat, placing my glass to my lips. I took a customary sip of the mead inside.

Uncle slipped through the large double doors, his face red as he stomped over to me. His cane hit the stone floor with a much younger tenacity than I was used to seeing displayed by the older elf.

"Uncle, what is it?" I asked as I hid my lips with my goblet. I couldn't have the entire table reading my lips. Nosy bastards, they all are. The news would spread around the room like wildfire. The field mice would know.

"I've received word the Queen of Valdis and Elowen have been spotted north of the capital in a grimy hole in the ground called Isold."

"Where the carver folk live?"

"Yes, I've visited in the past. They live in squalor, thieves they are-"

I held up my hand. His voice was grating on my brain. "Enough, I care not how the carver folk live, nor a tangent from you. Gather some horses and tell Fian to gather men. We leave in an hour." I took a large gulp of the mead in my goblet, the liquid warming me as it went down my throat, settling in my stomach.

"Ladies, gentlemen, and everyone else. I bid you an apology. I must depart immediately. Please stay as planned. Enjoy the many pleasures of Ardour." I gave a polite bow before storming out of the room, my hands balled into fists.

"Lilja is the cause, a weak queen from a weak kingdom. Elowen is mine and will continue to be mine," I said to myself as I stormed to my room. Even with the many servants I had, I still preferred to grab my personal items when I traveled. *It gives me a sense of mundaneness,* I thought as I stuffed clothes into a chest.

With my knife strapped to my hip, I was ready. Ready to get back my little mouse.

Kallan POV

I grunted as small rocks dug into my abdomen, surely leaving bruises as I peered through the telescope to the main entrance of Isold.

Aidan's position was barely visible to me, and invisible to anyone who didn't know where to look. He took a spot on top of a large root close to the entrance, his large, burly form, comically covered in brown paint; a true hide in plain sight moment.

A flicker from a mirror was the only signal necessary to notify me of their entrance. Pushing myself off the ground, I ran, crouched down to the other side of the roof's building, and jumped down to ground level. I ignored the pain in my joints as my body rolled to a stop.

"They're coming!" My voice is barely above a whisper. The guards under my command sprang to motion. The jail cells had been expertly upturned. Furniture flipped, a chair broken, the body of one of the guards from yesterday lay in front of a cell door. A bell rang, its loud tolls signaling to Aidan to play out the next part of the plan- explosion time.

A day had passed since the confrontation with Zed, with his attempt of offering us up on a silver platter to Daveed. Since then, Lilja and the rest of us had tried our best to mitigate the impact Ardour's men would have on Isold.

The younger Brawn'n had evacuated to a deeper part of the city, a safer place than one I stood in. An explosion vibrated the ground, the contents on the floor rumbled with excitement. Screams shot into the air as fear ran through the city. Out of instinct, I held out my arms for balance, looking down at the guard next to me, his near toothless smile widely displayed.

"We must move topsider, the Ardourians are here." He grabbed my arm, pulling me out of the jail cell, as planned. His grip dug into my arm, leaving a bruise, feeling a little too real. Smoke puffed up at the entrance where Ardourian soldiers approached, walking through the smoke like wraiths.

"Where are the prisoners? What's the meaning of this?! We must have the prisoners in our grasp tonight! The general demands it!" The lead of the group shouted, his voice carrying over the near-deadly quiet city. I glanced up at the ceiling of the underground city. Sweat prickled up on my skin as I pictured the heavy rocks falling on us. I moved my head in vain, attempting to cast out the thought, and my eyes met with the approaching Ardourian scum. *I need to have my wits about me.*

"I have this one! He killed the guard guarding his cell. The other bastards disappeared into the city." He launched my body toward the Ardourians. I yelped in surprise as the ground scraped my arms. The leader reached for me as I scrambled away like a sick game of tag.

I struggled to keep my face full of feigned fear as I brushed myself off, running into the twists and turns of the rooted city.

The Brawn'n streets were empty, hiding from the potential attack from the Ardourians. Shouts filled the air as I rounded another corner. "Find him. Get that damn human too!"

Elowen. They wanted Elowen. Fat fucking chance of that.

An explosion rocked the ground again, sending a small rumble to me. A diversion long enough for Armand to arrive at the secret exit used for the Brawn'n leaders.

"Leader Zed's house fire." A thick Ardourian accented man spoke, his tall form nearly upon me. I needed to lose him in the city if I had any hopes of not being followed.

"Othdo! Ber! Othdo!"

A bell tolled in the distance as the fire grew in size. An invitation to return *doesn't* seem to be in the cards. A tight smirk crossed my face as I threw down some barrels into the street.

"Fuck, get back here, you bastard. I'll put your head on a spike, yet." The accented man spoke as he sprawled himself over the barrels. I turned back around, grabbed the blade from my thigh strap, and threw it at him. It hit with a heavy thud as it met the squishy target of his right eye. He screamed, clutching his face. I turned back around, into the rooted mess of streets.

Armand POV

I grinned, watching the fuse catch before tossing the bomb toward the window of Zed's house. It should only cause a big bang and a bit of smoke, *bang*. I watched for a mere second longer as smoke began billowing out of the once posh house, frowning as greedy red flames began licking the wooden window frame. *Oops.*

I turned, shrugging. That's what he gets. "Othdo! Ber! Othdo!"

Kallan should be halfway across the city. I booked it toward the exit that led up to the dragon's lair. *This dragon better be worth all this huff.*

Recwes popped up from one of the side buildings. She waved me over, not waiting for me to fully catch up with her short form, making it halfway down the street before my longer legs made it to her. "You must hurry. The Valdis Queen must keep her word; Isold needs to be protected. The guards must not catch you. My father is talking to the leader of the Ardourian party."

The edge of the town approached quickly. The Ardourians had not discovered us. However, the shouts were a clear sign they had been following Kallan. I prayed to the gods that he had outsmarted them. Rocks jutted out against the wall, boulders lay soundly where they had fallen. Any path that had once marked the entrance was gone.

"Where is this exit?"

"Shut it. We don't know where the guards have dispersed. There's no evidence that they bought the deception. Follow me." Recwes clambered over the boulder, her short form disappearing behind it. Once over, she stood close to the never-ending wall of earth holding up the mountain above our heads. Her small fingers pointed to a black hole.

I balked at her. "Down there? Aren't we supposed to be going up?" Gods Kallan will hate this.

"Once down, go away from the city. There will be a tunnel heading up. At some point, it will lead to the mouth of the great Gichi-manidoo's cave." She crossed her arms.

"Gods, this was way too much running." Small pebbles flew as Kallan's feet kicked them up. He stumbled to a stop, doubling over, catching his breath. Covered in dirt and a couple of splatters of blood. Otherwise, he was in one piece.

"Were you followed?" Recwes asked before an arrow flew past her.

I turned toward the direction of the arrow, and the Ardourian grinned at me. Her blond hair was nearly stark white, an obvious target. With a breath, the arrow that was meant to kill us sent flying back to her as I summoned the surrounding air. She dodged it the last second before sending another shot in our direction, nicking my arm.

"Damn," I gritted my teeth, clutching my arm. Sucking in air, the air surrounding us spun, propelling the white-haired Ardourian flying.

Her body fell awkwardly. She lay there, stunned. The air knocked from her lungs. Recwes ran to her, a blade in hand, slitting her throat. Blood splattering across her face, she turned to us, not bothering to wipe it off.

"Go now, before more show up. I would say come back and visit us sometime, but don't. You have brought my family misfortune." She turned, disappearing behind boulders.

"In hindsight, we deserve that. Let's go." Kallan cracked his neck, shaking out his nerves before jumping into the pit.

For a moment, light was nonexistent. A blue light illuminated from Kallan's bag as he pulled out a small blue crystal. "Where did you get something like that?" The light scarcely illuminated his face.

"I bought it from a seller in Ebbon City on our first night. Figured it could be useful." He held up the light just bright enough to light up a few feet in front of us.

"She said to head away from the city. There should be a tunnel going up," I said, traipsing over the larger rocks that littered the ground. Kallan nodded, heading further into the darkness.

"Gods, it's dark. Why can't we ever find ourselves on a sunny beach surrounded by beautiful men and women?" Kallan said, stumbling over a rock.

I snorted, grabbing the rock from his hand, pushing past him.

"If only it were that easy. Come on, we can't have got much farther." The crystal was cool to the touch, the stone shining at least twice as brightly in my possession.

"Magic users get all the fun tricks," Kallan grumbled as he followed behind me. With the tunnel better illuminated, the slope of the path was obvious. It twisted around and around as if it were a spiral staircase. The sides of the walls were smooth; clearly, this was dug out purposely.

"Why do you think they need this tunnel, anyway? There isn't evidence of this path being used often. No modern-looking lamps. There are more spiders than people down here." As I spoke, a large cave spider darted across the tunnel floor. It was the size of a small cat. I clenched my jaw. Running away from that monster was not an option.

"Do I look like Aidan? I don't know everything. Let's hurry. I need a breath of fresh air, above ground." Kallan followed close behind me. I rolled my eyes at his tone. My usually fearless friend stood behind me like a child, ready to grab my arm for protection.

"I'm curious, that's all."

"Curiosity killed the cat, Armand."

I fought the urge to trip him, but decided against it. Not wanting to put us further behind the others. "Whatever, Kal."

22

Mr. Grumpy Dragon

Alieta POV

"What do you mean they escaped!?" My uncle's usual frail voice was gone, replaced by what seemed like a younger man's voice.

I cringed inwardly, gripping the hilt of my sword. Roots jutted everywhere as if the city was being consumed with them. The Brawn'n people had built their entire city around the roots of an ancient giant tree. Houses seemed to grow inside and on top of different-sized ones. They lined the sides of the streets, making steps into buildings not built into them. The citizens of Isold had disappeared. Not a soul ran the streets. I raised an eyebrow, turning to look at the injured leader.

"My uncle apologizes for using such a tone, Zed. However, I can't help but wonder. How could you allow this to happen? Do you not employ guards? Or are you perhaps incompetent?" My arms crossed against my chest, flexing my muscles for the shorter leader to see. Zed appeared tiny, sitting on a large, oversized throne. The chair was too large, a show of ineptness.

He shrank down in his seat before sitting up, trying to appear bigger. His confidence grew as he spoke. "They killed two of my guards by escaping. If I am not mistaken, my captain Denjos threw the bastard at your men's feet. They could not capture one without them all getting away. One of them torched my home." Zed threw his hands in the air.

Daveed turned around his hands both on the top of his cane, his knuckles white. "Which one of you lost him?" A blond-haired man walked forward, his eyes trained on Uncle's feet. His head bowed in shame, kneeling before us, ashamed.

"I apologize, your highness. We chased them as far as the edge of town and lost him. We lost one of our own, and another soldier lost his eye and may still succumb to his injuries."

My fingers curled into a fist, my fingernails becoming dangerously close to cutting into my palms. Uncle walked toward the bowed soldier, his cane barely clicking on the ground. With a blur of movement, he struck with the handle of his cane.

"Did you imbeciles have sight of Elowen or the Queen of Valdis at all? Or am I supposed to go on a whim and assume they escaped this cesspool?"

The soldier's head whipped to the side, clutching his jaw. Blood and a few teeth splattered to the ground.

"Find them. Burn it down if you have to." His voice caused a murmur to strike through the grouped soldiers. A few grinned, eager with delight. Other hesitant guards shifted their weight from side to side. They looked at me for approval.

An emotion I didn't recognize ticked into place as I looked at Uncle. His anger was ruining him. I looked around the city. Trash littered parts of the street, and buildings sat in disrepair. *This is all they have,* my inner voice spoke. I straightened my back, glaring down at Uncle and then at the guards.

They will listen to my orders.

"Search the city, kill anyone who resists. Don't burn this damn place down; otherwise, we'll end up going up with it. The Gods surely would be upset if we burned the roots of the ancient trees these people call their home." I flicked my hand, dismissing them.

Zed mumbled a thanks, his head turned down. "Uncle, follow me, now." My personal guards lingered behind me as I strode to a more secluded spot. I held my hand, halting them where they stood.

Uncle followed dutifully, his cane making hard whacks on the ground as he did so. "Your highness?"

"What is the meaning of your character today? I know it will benefit me to find Elowen, my future bride. But why do you seem none the more eager to find them?" Without waiting for his response, I plowed on.

"Striking a member of the royal guards? We need their support more than any. Isold is a sacred place. The roots are from the noble trees that once covered this land. Why wish to burn them down for a puny, weak queen?" My heart beat a mile a minute on the inside. My body language was the exact opposite, and I spoke, showing no emotion on my face, my voice steady. He could not know how much his presence had bothered me. Nor should my guards see the unrest of the royal family.

After all, Ardour was the best in the world and would remain so.

Elowen POV

The steps seemed never-ending as we made our way to Gichimanidoo's Shrine. The sounds of our feet clambering up were the only hint we were here. We carried no lights as we followed the directions Zed and his daughter had given us. How long would it take to reach the lair? My thoughts ran rampant in my head. I knew little about Gichimanidoo. *Was he sentient? A mindless beast held on a pedestal?*

Stop thinking so hard, Elle. Let's focus on getting up there. Long hair strands stuck to my face, glued by sweat. My body seemed unfazed by the copious amounts of steps that we had climbed. I pushed myself hard, forcing myself to the front. Darkness clung to us; no light illuminated our path. Cold, damp air burned my lungs as I took another breath, a welcome change from the warm, damp air in Isold.

"We must be getting close," Cassia said. She took in a large breath, coughing a little, her breathing labored.

Lilja slowed down. Her full-out run had turned to a slow pace. "I concur. The earth feels different up here. Less compact. I can feel the Dragon move around. It must be a considerable size."

I balked at her. "Less compact? What does that even mean?"

She loomed over me, brushing a strand of hair out of my face, sending the dormant butterflies in my stomach to erupt into a frenzy. I could smell her, her earthy warmth mixed with sweat from the climb. "It means, darling, that the ground up here is less stable. Likely to tumble down like an avalanche.-" As if on cue, the ground rumbled. A roar tore through the otherwise quiet air.

"I guess that answers that, if one wrong rock breaks, this whole mountain cap will fall off," Aidan said, attempting to keep his voice as calm as possible. I could hear him fumbling around, his sword humming as he pulled it from his hip.

"It would be great if my glasses would stop trying to escape my face. I swear they're always trying to fall off," he said, groaning.

I laughed a little, patting him on the shoulder. "When we get to the castle, I'll have Lilja help you find someone to get them fixed."

"How will we know if we've reached the top?" Cassia said, her bow in hand.

"We'll have to keep climbing," Lilja and I said simultaneously. I glanced over in her direction, her silhouette barely discernible. I sent her a small smile before looking back up the seemingly never-ending dark stairs. *Don't, Elle, she left you. Rely on yourself and only yourself.*

Hours passed. Our once eager run was now a slow-paced walk. My legs burned with exertion, my muscles taunt with use and strain.

Aidan walked beside me, his sword back on his hip, as the rumbles had stopped more than an hour ago. We no longer heard the roar of Gichimanidoo.

"Is it possible to take a wrong turn in the mountains?" Keres asked, her voice feeling almost impossibly loud in the enclosed space. "It's so dark in here. It is unlikely the Ardourians followed us. We've been walking for half a day, at least. Here, let me add some light to the situation."

She snapped her fingers, illuminating the stairwell with a dancing flame, as if the light called to the stones at the wall and steps. Small stones reflected the flame, bringing the stairwell to light, similar to early morning.

"Nice work." Aidan clapped her on the shoulder before walking forward, inspecting the wall. The stones were unseen in the earlier darkness. Now they glinted with the small flame Keres had provided, the use of it clear, guiding us.

"They look like some sort of crystal. Almost like the stones at Ebbon City. Fascinating!" He struggled to grab onto his bag, pulling free his notebook and something to write with.

"Let's go, library boy. We need to keep moving if we have any hope of reaching the dragon." Lilja grabbed him by the back of his shirt, yanking him away from the wall. "Keres, can you keep that up for a bit?" Sweat clung to her forehead, and little strands of her hair stuck to her skin.

"Lilja, this is barely using any elemental power. I could do this all day if I wanted to." Keres gave Lilja a rare grin before leading the way. The light seemed to reinvigorate us, pushing us farther up the mountain.

Before long, the rumbles had started again as if Gichimanidoo had awoken from a great nap. The lambency of the stone grew closer together, giving the stairwell a glow comparable to the afternoon sun. However, it provided no warmth. Our breath frosted out of our mouths, as if dragons ourselves.

A dark black hole stood at the top of the stairs, past the power of Keres's flame.

"That must be a room." Aidan bounded up the stairs like a true researcher, eager to uncover the secrets of the old, forgotten dragons of the past. His pack jumped on his back with him, things inside clattering around.

The fatigue we all felt soon was forgotten as we giddily followed. The darkness fed into a large, ceremonial-like room. Keres followed Aidan as his shadow, using her magic to light the room. Oil lights circled the room, illuminating it in a ghoulish glow as Keres lit them. Carved statues of various dragons stood erect on the farthest edges, each one representing an elemental power: earth, fire, air, and water. Shadows danced on the furthest wall where two large metal double doors stood closed. The water dragon drawn upon it, his mouth open in a blood-curdling snarl.

We stood for a second in awe of the craftsmanship of the room. The Brawn'n people had truly magnificent skill.

I clutched my satchel to myself, breathing a sigh of relief.

One step closer.

One step closer to curing the blight.

One step closer to helping Lilja with the pressure of being a queen.

"Let's stay here for a few hours. Long enough to get some rest while we wait for Armand and Kallan. I'll watch for the first few hours," Lilja said, dropping her bag on the ground, the contents echoing throughout the room.

"But we're so close." I eyed the doors before looking back at her.

She filled the space between us, cupping my face. For a split second, I welcomed it, reveling in the heat from her palm. Her scent enveloped me in an embrace. Before my brain caught up with me, I turned my head away from her, taking a step back.

She left me.

Hurt flashed before her eyes before continuing.

"The dragon can wait a few more hours. It's been alive since the beginning of the universe. We need to wait for Kallan and Armand. End of discussion, Keres dim the lights. Unroll your packs and go to bed." Her voice was strained as she turned around, swiping her sword off the ground before stalking back to the steps.

Awkward silence filled the room as Lilja and I's lovers' quarrel poisoned the air. I set my stuff on the ground near Aidan, with my back against the wall. I pulled the book from my bag. It felt warm to the touch as I flipped it open, straining to read under such low light. My brain had other ideas as sleep overtook me easily, my body exhausted by the ordeals of the last few days.

"Alwyn, you must listen to me." A voice called to me in the darkness. I peeked an eye open, looking around at the sleeping forms of my friends, everyone but Lilja.

I shifted Pavati's book, touching me; I hissed as the book was hot to the touch, burning me. As I flinched away, the book flipped open. The stars that once formed Pavati did so again. Her body seemed the same physically, but her eyes revealed a much older soul.

"Alwyn, you must listen. The Dragon Gichimanidoo will try to trick you so he can undoubtedly eat you and your friends. Before you reach the plateau, you must get both the blood from the Water Nymph and the claw from Gichimanidoo. The fight will start there. Be wary."

"Wait! How do I get the claw from him? We don't exactly have an entire army at our disposal. Something as ancient as a Gichimanidoo will be impossible to kill." I leaned off the wall so close to Pavati I could nearly touch the vision of her.

"Kill? Gods, no. You only need a claw. Humans are so violent. Something as ancient as a dragon would be impossible to kill. They brought life to the land long before elves existed." She shuddered.

Lilja peeked her head out of the stairwell. "Who are you talking to?"

I looked back at Pavati, who shrugged her shoulders. "Once the book has found the fated being, it's spelled so only that person may communicate through it."

Lilja looked at me with curiosity and awe as I answered her. "Pavati." She balked at me.

"If you're in life or death peril, Alwyn, and fear death is near. Pour your blood on my book, and I will come and aid you. Do so knowing the spell will weaken us both greatly. Do it only if you must say the words as follows. 'My body is the host, the host for you. Please use my blood and my bones as a willing host.' Say this while holding the blood to the pages. I will come."

The stars that formed her body dissipated, falling back into the book. With the blue light gone, I turned to Lilja, who stood with her arms crossed. Her forehead creased with worry as if she was worried I had gone insane.

"Pavati warned me the dragon would try to trick us and eat us-"

"Eat us? Who's going to eat us? Can't these adventures ever be safe?" Kallan huffed, his body bent over as he crawled out of the stairwell. A thick layer of dust covered him. He ran his hand through his hair, and puffs of smoky dust floated off.

"Finally, a room, something not so closed in. I can breathe." He lifted his head, his skin pale from the anxiety running through his body. Kallan plopped onto his back, nearly tripping Armand.

"For fuck's sakes, Kal, at least get out of my way before you flop like a fish." Armand grinned at us, putting his hands on his hips like a proud farmer looking at his garden.

"Now what did I miss?" Brown paint covered him. I opted not to ask.

Keres rolled out of her makeshift bed, patting him on the shoulder. Besides me, the others groaned. "Way too much, brother. Catch up later. Why in the world are you painted like horse poop?"

Aidan laughed, making a crude joke.

"I'll have you know I'm a hero!" Armand said, using his shirt as a rag for his face, wiping off the brown paint that covered his already dark skin.

Kallan scoffed. "A hero banned from ever returning to Isold. Remember, you sent the leaders home up in flames."

"Armand!" Lilja gasped, mouth open.

"I thought we would not drop that bit of lore, Kal," Armand growled, flipping him off.

"You said it, yes, but I never agreed," Kallan said in a singsong-y voice, still on the floor, his hands in the air in mock surrender.

"Lilja, it was an accident. I swear on Esmersey and Niahm. I only meant to create a bit of smoke, but the curtains caught on fire, and poof. There went the mansion." He made a little explosion sign with his hands, looking sheepish.

I began gathering my things, putting the book in my bag, and throwing it over my shoulder. "Let's go. No time like the present to meet Mr. Grumpy Dragon himself."

Lilja looked at the giant doors across the room warily before unsheathing her sword. "Elowen, we're not finished talking about the Pavati thing. Kallan, get off the floor." She leans down, grabbing the back of his shirt and heaving him up to a standing position. He moved like a puppet on strings.

"Pavati says we won't need to kill him to get the claw-"

Keres crossed her arms, her dagger looking dangerously sharp in her grasp. "Gods, did you get any more information out of her? Like maybe how to get the claw off the dragon that's older than time?"

I sputtered, not having an answer, before Armand came to the rescue. He threw his arm around me, leaving whatever brown he used to paint himself on my tunic.

"My dear sister, that would take away the fun. Alright, let's get this over with." With his arm still around me, he pulls me over to the large, oversized doors. The dragon-sized door pull gleamed with excitement. It was a large golden ring, big enough to dwarf the size of Armand's hand as he unlooped himself from me to grab it.

23

Fashionable Entrance = Eventful Exit

Lilja gave us a forced grin, her grip nearly white on her sword. "We don't know what will happen, so be aware, be smart, and don't die. I don't feel like making new friends this late in life." She gave a nod to Armand to yank the door open. A damp smog rolled out, filling the large circular room with the reek of mold. Every instinct yelled at me to run away and never return. I swallowed the lump in my throat, pushing down the fear.

I pulled my shirt over my nose, my stomach rolling uncomfortably. The room was dark, water dripped from the ceiling. The floor was so smooth it was slippery. Years of water eating away at it, creating a sloping edge into the room.

Lilja flicked her hand toward the right and left, splitting us up. Armand snuck over to the right. I grabbed the edge of his sleeve, pulling him back toward Lilja, Cassia, and Keres. Switching sides with him. He grunted in surprise, but went with it. I turned toward Kallan and Aidan, not looking Lilja in the eyes.

Kallan bent down, dipping his finger in a dint on the floor, inspecting it. *Oil,* he mouthed, wordlessly, Keres flicked her hand, sending a tiny spark along the way of the reservoir. It roared like a wave, and it spread throughout the room, illuminating the room in a warm glow.

"WHO dares to visit me at this hour?" A loud voice grumbled, sending stalactites crashing onto the floor. He elongated the s in each word, sounding almost snake-like.

I stepped forward, gripping my satchel tightly, pushing down the anxiety that threatened to reveal itself. *I have to do this. I have to save Valdis. This is my Fate,* I thought as I took a deep breath. "Gichi-manidoo, we have come to you for a Quest-."

The oil light circled the room, giving light to everything but the center of the room. Water sloshed, "BAH, a quest, how boring. I've had enough quests for a lifetime. A problem I have to fix, always. Quests are the only reason I get visited by you elves and-." He took a deep breath in, "Oh, and a human. The only ones that visit are the Brawn'n people, just to bring those damned sacrifices."

More water sloshed from the center of the room. A shadow seemed to grow from the floor, taller and taller until the top of his head nearly brushed the ceiling of the cap of the mountain. Fear ticked in my heart, the shadow reminding me of the monster that stirred in my dreams as a child.

"We have come for an item, for a spell for the goddess of rivers-" I spoke up again, my voice firm, swallowing my fear. Everyone's eyes stared holes into my back.

I had to do this for Valdis, no for me.

I needed to prove it to myself.

I was strong. I was enough.

I could finish this quest by myself.

"For my dear Pavati? Humph, she has not visited me for nearly 300 years. Pavati could have just come and visited. But no, she sent her lackeys. HOW disrespectful. Oh well, no issue to me. I'll just eat you all, so she has to visit me. See if I let some goddess send her lackeys to me again." He hacked, his cough full of phlegm. Snot flew, covering

Armand in a thick layer. The brown paint that covered him slid off, washed by the snot.

This was supposed to be a dangerous dragon? Perhaps the years of his existence had made him milder, content with age.

Cassia held up her arms in a cross motion, as the dragon stooped to eat her first. "Wait! Do you have a cold? I'm a healer. We could trade for some medicine for your claw!" She crouched down farther away from his mouth, falling to the ground as she scrambled backward.

He paused, rearing back, another coughing fit wracking his body. White strands of hair flowed over his head, flowing with the movements of his cough.

"This? I just have a tickle in my throat. It's so damn damp in here. The Brawn'n people never think to light the oil strip surrounding this room. Fire isn't my specialty; that's my sisters. Gosh, I'm getting too old to eat people. Snotty, grab one of those jars and bring it here." Armand balked, wiping away the snot on his face before trudging over to the small mountain of jars strewn in the corner behind the door.

The pottery was nearly half of Armand's height; he nearly toppled over with the weight of it. Cassia pulled a few vials from her pack, giving them a shake.

"We require a claw, oh great dragon. Pavati is being held against her will in a cave." My heart hammered in my chest as I spoke.

"WHAT!" Another cough interrupted his words. "Against her will?! My, my, you Elven folk are pieces of work. It's always, let's kill, always violent." A cough tore through him violently. He sank a little farther into his pond in the center of his room. His fins on his face fluttered instinctively as they came into contact with the water. The water overflowed, hitting our feet as he continued his tirade, his head exposed.

"Perhaps I have a minor cold. Leave me! I wish to rest."

The book that I read was a little off the mark. Dramatic, maybe. Dangerous? No. I gaped at him, crossing my arms before walking up to the edge of the water. "No offense, your greatness, but if we don't get a claw from you, Pavati may die, and so will most of Valdis." Courage filled me as I stood below him. Liquid beaded on his whiskers, presumably snot. Icicles knotted themselves in his hair, clanking together as he moved. We were nearly eye to eye.

He slipped himself up from the water, towering over me, his snout nearly in my hair, taking a large inhale of breath as if seeing if I smelled good- good enough to eat.

"You- what do you gain from this? You may look like an elf. But you're a mere little human. Why don't you go back to where you belong?" He pointed at me, his clawed finger digging into my shoulder, his head tilted, awaiting an answer.

My mind raced as I forced myself to stay where I was. My heart beat in my throat, the dinner from the night before threatening to come up.

"I'm Elowen Alwyn. I have been repeatedly told that I am fated to the Human and Elven Realm." My heartbeat filled my ears as I spoke, my voice loud, clear, and it seemed to vibrate off the cave walls.

"The gods seem to think I am the tipping point to this war. Pavati has spelled a Niphes book to me. I grow tired of having to prove myself to people who will not even take a moment to listen. She told ME I need to collect these things. SO let me get your claw and be on the way." With a blur of movement, I snagged my dagger from my hip, bringing it down on the tip of his finger with deadly speed. *Thank you, Fian and Kallan, for all the annoying training.*

My patience for the pushback on my quest was waning. I wanted to succeed.

For a second, no one moved, stunned. I crouched down, grabbing the claw tip, running to Cassia. I snatched the medicine vials from her hand, throwing them at the dragon. He roared in anger, spewing icy water in all directions. "You brat! Hold still so I can eat you!" His body slithered out of the pond, and his tail was like the fins of a fish. Water waved off of him, hitting the wall, knocking pots onto the ground. Pickled fish slid onto the ground. A wave of fermented food and salt hit my nose, making me almost gag.

He flicked it toward me, narrowly missing my legs.

Lilja waved her hands, beckoning us to the door. "Let's go!"

"I needed it! Once we save her, I'll have Pavati come and visit! I'm sorry!" My hand gripped the claw, my knuckles white.

A sob slipped from his mouth. "You're all so mean. For years, I've been up here. In the old days, humans and elves sacrificed so many yummy things to me and my siblings. The history books speak of me and my siblings as dominant beings. Fear would run through the elves' veins at the mention of us. Now I'm old and no longer able to leave this place," he broke his tangent in a cough.

"I can't even seem to get rid of this damn cough."

I paused, turning to look at him. He had paused his attack on us, curling into himself, looking pitiful. "Take the medicine. It'll clear the cough. Make a little steam for yourself to breathe in. If I see any Brawn'n people, I'll have them change up the sacrifices a bit." I paused just long enough to give a curtsy before fleeing, Lilja close behind me.

"Aidan, help me create a quick exit, before our dragon friend stops crying in a puddle." Lilja felt along the walls, tapping, trying to feel for a weak spot. I glance back at the dragon's door anxiously, my palms becoming sweaty. Armand summoned the air around him, forcing the large water dragon carving to crumble in front of the door. He coughed with exertion as if the magic used to push the statue to the ground was from his lungs.

"Gichimanidoo won't be pleased with this!" Aidan said, his voice rising.

"Hopefully, the flood was a fluke!" Cassia said.

As if on cue, water pooled from under the door, spilling past the head of the carving, appearing as if it was coming from the statue itself.

"Kallan! Are we pointing north?" Lilja asked, staring me down in disbelief.

Kallan pulled a compass from his bag, twirling it in his hand. "Yes!" A boom rang out from behind the door as Gichimanidoo tried to push the crumbled rocks out of the way. A stalactite from the ceiling came crashing down.

"That is our cue! Alright, this is the spot. It'll be brutally cold. But this will be the fastest way out." Lilja and Aidan stood side by side, Lilja's arms flexed out as she summoned the strength to move the mountain walls away. My heart fluttered at the sight. Her dark hair was swooping over her eyes.

The wall began to crumble, and rocks tumbled around us. Cold air rushed in, biting at my exposed skin like an angry spirit. The water that had splashed my feet, freezing on the outside of my shoes.

Gichimanidoo roared in the other room, his defeat forgotten as the embarrassment of his claw being taken overcame him. The door shuttered open. Water rushed out, pooling around our legs, rushing us to the hole in the wall.

"We must move now, Lilja!" My voice was hoarse. Shakily, I put the claw in my bag, clutching it to my chest. The snow-covered mountain was blindingly bright. Lilja and Aidan grunted; sweat glistened on their foreheads. The ground beneath us moved, sliding us onto the side of the mountain. My stomach lurched. Trees upturned as we dug up their roots. Snow followed us like an arrow reaching its target, bigger and bigger until an avalanche had formed, tearing past us.

"Cassia, can you do anything about the snow?" My teeth chattered as snow pelted me in the face.

"Yes! Just a minute!" She said. Turning her back to me, she crouched down, placing her hands on the rock slab, pulling a shield up made of water until nothing bombarded us.

"What now?" Armand asked, pieces of the snot still hanging from the tips of his hair, glistening in the sun.

As Gichimanidoo poked his head out of the new ventilation we provided to his home. He opened his mouth, spewing a gushing blast of water at us. The ground approached us furiously. Lilja pulled a rock from the ground, knocking the slab on it. The momentum turned us to the left. The land seemed to be cleaved in two by the mountain range. On one side of the land was the lush green, lively Ardour; on the other side was the desolate Olken desert. A canyon formed the entrance to the desert, a land carved by thousands of years of water erosion.

"Turn! Turn! Now!" Lilja shouted as we left the roaring dragon behind and approached a cliff. The slab flew off the edge, plunging us into the rapids below. The waterfall created by the dragon rushed down around us. For a second, we were weightless.

I gasped, water filling my nose and mouth. My head could barely hold itself above the frigid water, and yells filled the air. I kicked my legs furiously, unwilling to let the bag holding the dragon claw go. *I'd rather drown than have to explain how I lost the one thing we needed.*

"I got you, baby, I got you," Lilja repeated in my ear as she put her arm around me, pulling me to the shore as we fought against the current.

Unceremoniously, I flopped onto the frozen rocks, not caring if they bit into my back, my arms still frozen to my chest as I clutched the bag.

Lilja lay next to me silently before laughing. Birds flew away from us because of the noise we had created, jarring them.

"What?" I said in between, catching my breath.

"You were amazing! The skill, the confidence, everything!" She turned over on top of me, facing down, kissing me. I gasped at the contact before melting into it.

She pulled away, too soon, standing. Outstretching her hand to me. "SOUND OFF! You guys better be alive!" Lilja said into the trees.

"I'm alive!" Aidan whooped his hand in a fist around his journal, holding it up like a trophy.

"Me too!" Armand plowed his way through the trees. He patted down his body as if making sure it was all still there.

"Keres and I are okay!" Cassia and Keres popped out together completely dry.

"How are you dry?" I whined. "Where did you land, a tree?"

"Like this." Cassia flicked her hand, coaxing the water that soaked my clothes. She winced for a moment as if it caused her pain.

I opened my bag, checking the contents, grabbing onto the claw, showing it to everyone. "We got it! Now we just need the blood of a water nymph. That should be easy."

"Untrue, water nymph deals always come at a price. Much like using magic," Keres said.

"Let's make a fire and find something to eat for tonight. Tomorrow, we summon Sylp and see if she will aid in our quest," Lilja said.

We're so close; I told myself as I grabbed the dry twigs up. The fire soon crackled loudly as water escaped from the wood we had collected. All of us but Keres sat by the fire, her powers warming her as she slept. Lilja worked on the dragon claw with a wire, fashioning it into a necklace.

"Water nymphs are tricky creatures. My book doesn't have a lot about them. But what it has is that they are not good," Aidan said, his glasses on the tip of his nose as he used the low light from the fire to read through his history book.

"We could just force her to give us her blood. We just need a little," Armand said, as he used a sharpening stone to perfect the blade on his sword.

"That would work theoretically, but I don't exactly enjoy the idea of being afraid of water my entire life. Worrying if a Water Nymph will come out and snatch me to a watery grave, sounds like it will add a few hundred years onto my life," Kallan said, slouching back from the fire. His toes just coasting the danger zone. His shoes and socks hung on sticks next to him, drying.

"Sounds like you're talking about sirens. Nasty creatures. Monsters, their only ambition is to pull as many sailors to their death as possible," Cassia said, her teeth clattering together.

"We could just ask?" I said, staring into the dancing flames.

"Elle, Sylp won't hesitate to make a deal out of the situation," Lilja said, finally looking up from her project.

"She helped me when I escaped from Alieta. She wouldn't just want her family to stay locked up in a cave. Pavati might not be mortal, but she's in mortal danger. As are we, the whole Valdis nation is in danger of being written out of history, because of Ardour. A little goodwill could help us right now. She didn't look good the last time we talked," I said, looking at the rushing water, as if expecting her to pop out of the water.

"Elowen, you are bound to her. She could call on you at any moment, do any type of favor. Sylp could ask you to kill someone, and you'd have to do so unless you wanted to die yourself." Lilja spoke vehemently, anger coating her words.

I stared at the tattoo on my wrist, the little wave marking me. It itched as if it was moving just under the first layer of skin. The image of Sylp clasping my arms as we made the deal in Sald flashed before my eyes, a shiver ran down my spine.

"We needed that deal, Lilja. I might not have the same life experience as you guys, and I might not have grown up here, but this is my life now. This is my home. So we need to make it into a livable situation by any means necessary."

"DO NOT downplay the worth of your life, Elowen Alwyn. You are valuable, your life is worth more than you think. I would watch the world burn if I got to have a lifetime with you. We will exhaust every option to heal my kingdom. This is not a mess that I will allow you to clean up with your life being the mop." Lilja tossed the dragon claw to me.

"Put this on and don't take this off. You got it, you deserve the honor of wearing it. Now go to bed, we have a big day tomorrow. I'm taking first watch." She stood, stalking over to the water's edge.

No one said anything after her outburst and dispersed quickly. They unrolled their packs and fell silent, other than the soft snores of them trying to pretend to be asleep. As if they were small children trying to avoid their parents' fight. I sighed, getting up to sit next to Lilja, grabbing her hand away from prying ears.

A welcome reprieve for us to be ourselves.

"Lilja, this isn't just about one person. We need to save your kingdom. I- I know my life is valuable, but we have to find Pavati. Sylp was and is the only way." My thumb rubbed the back of her hand. I tried to memorize the veins that traveled to her forearm.

"Elle, there's always a safe way, always a way for us to stay together. Before we met, the idea of saving Valdis absorbed me. A failing kingdom- a curse that my parents bestowed on me. All this time, I have had a one-track mind- the present, never thinking about the past and most certainly not thinking about the future. Now that I've met you, found you, after all these years, the future seems so probable. I can see what my life will look like with the blight gone. That future has you. With you by my side, we can mend the land the past has scarred."

My heart seemed to cleave in two. The pain I endured in the castle compounded on itself, and tears rolled down my cheeks freely.

"What is it, my love?" Lilja asked, kissing my forehead, her eyes swimming with concern.

"I don't deserve you. I don't deserve us." A sob bubbled up out of my throat.

"Yes, you do." She pulled me into a hug, her grip tight as if she was worried I was going to disappear, again.

Which only caused me to sob harder as the flashes of Alieta flickered before my eyes. A haunting memory of the mistake, a cause I thought was necessary.

"I tried to tell you. To tell you earlier, before we were taken by surprise by the Brawn'n." I said in between sobs.

I took a steadying breath; the crickets and bugs around us seemed to intensify as the words readied themselves on my tongue.

"I slept with Alieta!" The light from the moon seemed to shine down, shadowing Lilja's reaction.

The bugs and animals ceased their nightly song; the ambiance of the night was gone, leaving only Lilja and I.

"It was a mistake. I thought I needed to do it so she would trust me more. For her to think I was on her side. B-but it only made it worse. She's crazy about me. Alieta wants to keep me as if I were a doll. As if my only existence depended on whether I could wear frilly clothes. Worse yet, the room, the library, and the food. I liked it."

"I know," she said.

My voice was only above a whisper now, as I pushed past her response. Not even bothering to fully comprehend the words coming out of her mouth. "While you struggled to live, I sat in comfort, and I liked it. I thought you left me to rot in an oversized gilded cage. I thought you forgot about me."

She grabbed my face, forcing me to look right into her eyes. "I understood what you were trying to tell me before the Brawn'n tried to rob us. It's okay. You were doing what you thought you had to do. I can tell you didn't make the choice lightly. In terms of the comfy bed, the library, and the food. Of course, you would like those. Everyone in their right mind would love those. It doesn't make you a bad person. Fuck after being on the road so long, I'd love it too."

"Please, my love, do not let those moments define the rest of your life. I tried so hard to get you out, I promise, and I'll continue to make you feel wanted and not forgotten. And even though there are thousands of stars in the sky, Elle, I would search them forever to find you again and again."

Tears streamed down my cheeks as I stared into her eyes, willingly becoming lost in them.

She leaned into me, kissing me under the night sky. The moon goddess, Esmersey, the only witness of our love, of this moment, paused in time. Cherished.

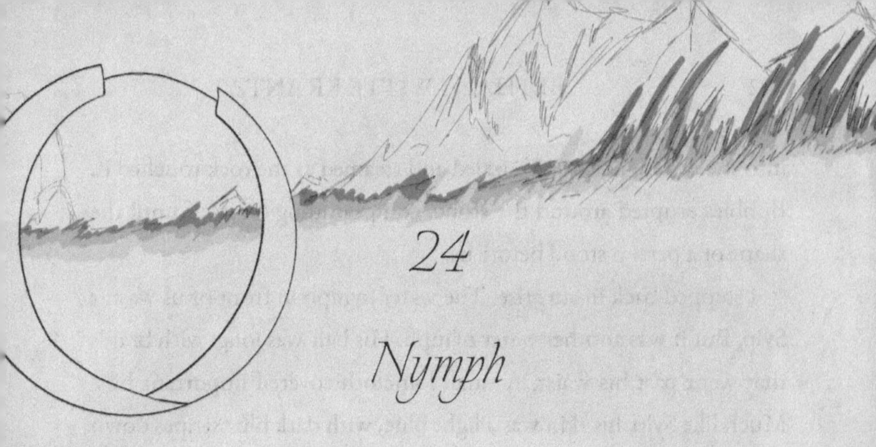

The sun rose slowly as we gathered the supplies from the summoning spell in Aidan's book. I made a mental note to ask him why he seemed to have a whole grimoire in that messy notebook he carried everywhere.

"The last piece we need is a piece of jewelry-" Aidan announced as he pored over his mysterious notes.

"Elowen Alwyn, don't give him your ring for this spell. I am tired of remaking it," Lilja called out as she strapped a large pack to her back. Armand snickered next to her as he smoothed out any impurities on his sword that he couldn't get to in the dark the night before.

Keres extinguished the flame. "I have nothing I'll part with."

Cassia sighed as she took a small hoop from her ear. "Here, use this. But someone owes me a new gold earring. I stole that from some pompous governor." She threw it at Aidan, who nearly dropped it as he put all the ingredients on top of a rock where the years had eroded a dip in it.

"What's next?" I asked as I tried to peer over his shoulder.

"Now we catch this on fire, and throw it in the water," Aidan said as he held out the rock bowl to Keres, who flicked her finger at it. The contents ignited easily. Aidan yelped before composing himself.

"To water, thy enemy of fire. We call upon you, with the hope that you bestow your wisdom on us." He crouched, placing the stone into the water. The liquid sizzled and steamed as the rock touched it. Bubbles erupted around the stone, compounding on itself until the shape of a person stood before us.

I stepped back in surprise. The water nymph in front of us wasn't Sylp. But it was another water nymph. His hair was long, with braids that went past his waist. A small loincloth covered important bits. Much like Sylp, his skin was a light blue, with dark blue stripes down his sides. In his hand, he held a trident, a large staff pronged at the top.

"Surprised you are." He grinned, his pointy teeth almost threatening.

I stepped closer, attempting to bridge the space between us. "Yes, a bit. We were half expecting Sylp."

He gave a hollow laugh. "Busy Sylp is, instead come I. Secondhand man, am I. Valdisians, you require what?"

"We require the help of the water nymphs. Pavati, the Goddess of Rivers, is being held captive. She has asked me to collect ingredients for the spell that frees her. I've already gathered the other ingredients-ingredient," I stammered. "The blood of a Water Nymph is the last ingredient we need. Will you help us?"

"Give you blood if. Get what I?" He grabbed a rock from the water, the end pointed, inspecting it before dropping it once again.

"You get a safe world to live in. The polluted water is worsening, and unless we save Pavati, people will continue to die. Why do you need to benefit from a drop of blood?" I fought the urge to ball my fist.

He raised his eyebrow, banging his trident on a rock peaking above the rushing water. "Spicy, you are." He stalked toward me, holding out his webbed hand to me. His eyes looked me up and down. "Group to warn Sylp me told. Weakened powers flow water through. Soon, no more Pavati, if scale *doesn't* tip for us. Blood, you take mine, human. Quickly, water, I wish to return to."

I grabbed Lilja's dagger from her hip, giving her a small kiss on her shoulder before turning back to the water nymph. His previous mischievous smile now gone, his body tense, as if the gravity of the situation had only just now settled on his shoulders.

"What's your name, sir, second in command?" I asked, the blade hovering over his scaly skin.

"Name is Ogo,-" he sucked in a breath as I sliced into his hand. I worked quickly, closing his hand into a fist, tipping the flow of blood into the vial. His blood was green, unlike my own.

"Thank you, Ogo. Your sacrifice won't go in vain. We will stop Ardour." Lilja grasped his shoulder, nodding at him.

Cassia held out a clean bandage to me. I wrapped his wound silently.

Pavati's voice replayed itself in my voice. "The blood of a water nymph! A claw of a water dragon! A human who-" I yearned to bang my head against the rocks in the river bed if it were to give me clarity of the last sentence she spoke before dissipating out of existence. *If it were only blood from a human, her words would have stayed the same as for the water nymph.*

A human who would be a willing sacrifice. It was the only explanation that made sense. Pavati needed a human to die for the betterment of Valdis.

My heart battered my chest as my thoughts ran rampant in my brain. *The pieces were all together now, only a bit longer.* My chest tightened at the idea of leaving.

This is for the greater good! I have to do this. Pavati needs to be saved, one life over the many saved.

Ogo tilted his head to the side, his facial expression troubled. "Troubles you something?"

Wiping my hands at my sides, finished, I looked up at him, my face grim. "I hope I'm brave enough to do what needs to be done."

"Bravery, nothing is fear without, human." He clasped my forearm before erupting into the water, melting before the current.

Lilja had already made it to her pack. "Let's go, guys, Ogo says Pavati is weakening, so we have to pick up the pace."

The camp we stayed at was easy to pick up and pack away, though some of our belongings were unrecoverable from our slide down the mountain. Cassia tapped out the fire with water, stomping on any still glowing embers.

Birds chirped in the trees as the Goddess raised herself into the sky, and we made our way down the side of the mountain. The greenery subsided as we continued. Appearing as if magic was still seeping away from the earth. A line of dead grass extending out in the desert. It crumbled with our touch as we walked through it, as if frozen in time, and I had just disrupted it.

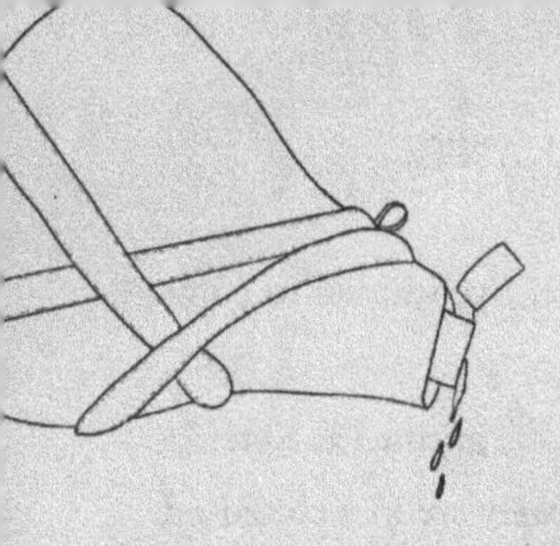

25

Olken Ridge

The petrified grass crunched under our feet as we made our way down to the sand. Nobody spoke as the sun beat down on us unapologetically, its heat burning the top of my head and scarred ears. Sweat rolled down the small of my back.

"We should be able to make it to that rock formation tonight. After that, it shouldn't be more than a day to Olken Ridge. Elves have siphoned this land's magic away as overeager magic users. So, no using the elements unless necessary. The earth has already gone through enough abuse," Aidan spoke as he walked next to me, pointing to a large arched rock in the distance. He wrapped his head in a spare pair of pants he had in his pack. That he somehow saved himself from going down the mountainside.

"If we don't melt first," Armand grumbled. The poor guy was nearly bright red; his black hair reflected the bright sunlight, no doubt making him overheat.

"I, for one, am not suited for these conditions," Cassia groaned. "I miss the sea." She made a smacking sound with her mouth. "I can almost taste the salt."

"I'm almost positive that you're tasting the salt from your sweat," Kallan chuckled.

Keres never added to the group of complaints but was smiling. "It feels great to me. The sun is so bright, it's like it's fueling my powers even more. Ever since I heard about this place, I've wanted to come here."

"At least someone is having a good time." Lilja grinned at Keres.

The air surrounding us seemed stale, as if we were in a closed-off room for the winter. The wind never once stirred the sand we disrupted by our trek. It appeared, truly, to be dead.

Large stones sprinkled through the path, as if we were in the remnants of an old river bed, leading us to the pillar of a rock formed from erosion thousands of years ago. It dwarfed us as we approached, a welcome reprieve from the sun beating down on us. I closed my eyes for a second, trying to think of the land back when it was lush with life. Grass would have grown on the sides of the rock formation, and water ran through the riverbed where kids would play. My heart ached for what once was. The scene settled the need for my sacrifice to Pavati. The scarred land before us needed to be healed.

"I'm not meant for this weather. No wonder Elves don't come up here. It's like Runen lords over this place," Kallan murmured, looking around.

Despite the heat beating down, I shivered. Runen flashed before my eyes. The memory of the seven souls floating next to him. The blue orbs dancing across my eyes, a show only to taunt me.

Aidan nudged my shoulder, his eyes filled with worry. As if asking, *Are you okay?*

"I definitely do *not* want to meet Runen again so soon," I said as I looked around, the hair on my arms sticking up, as I took in my surroundings, as if his ominous shadow would be looming over my shoulder, ready to take me to the underworld.

Aidan's eyes widened as we dismounted, making our camp. "Runen?! What do you mean, see him again?"

"We met when I was escaping into the countryside, and trust me, it wasn't a warm and funny meet and greet." I plopped onto the ground, and a chill settled over me as I thought about the skinny man who attracted spirits. The smell of ammonia passed my nose like a memory resurfacing. Sand infiltrated every nook and cranny of my body, making me squirm.

Lilja stood behind me, stooping down to kiss my sunburned head. "We can't have a fire tonight, so please make yourself comfortable."

"I've read that deserts get cold at night, so our best bets are to sleep close to each other." Aidan looked up from his notebook as he scribbled a drawing of the rock formation.

Cassia took a step away from Armand and stuck her tongue in his direction. "I'm not snuggling with Armand; he's literally dripping with sweat."

Armand's mouth opened in mock hurt. "Hey, you don't smell that great either, pirate," he said as he mussed her curly hair.

Cassia swatted his hand away, but smiled at him. "Get your big, oversized hand off of me. Sleep with Kallan. You guys go on way too many adventures together. It's getting suspicious."

"I'd have you know, Armand would be very lucky to get a piece of this ass. He would also have to smell significantly better," Kallan barked with laughter so hard tears sprang to his eyes as he settled on the ground, his blanket rolled out underneath him.

Armand crossed his arms, not even bothering to pretend to be irritated with a great big smile on his face.

The sun hung low; the day was ending. Esmersey and Niahm were once again together for their brief embrace before the other rose high in the sky. Lilja sat next to me, both of us leaning on a large rock. We passed out dried meat and bread for dinner.

"Tomorrow, we reach Olken Ridge," Lilja spoke between mouth-fuls, *how queenly of her,* my inner thought chided. A small smile played on my lips, sand crusted to the sides, chapping them. I prayed to the rain goddess to bless us with a few random drops of water in the hopes, the rain would revitalize us before Olken.

"We must stay vigilant. We have so many examples of us finding people where they shouldn't exist." Cassia sat cross-legged in front of me, her hair pulled back in braids that Keres had done.

"I agree," Kallan said, sitting next to her. "It better not be fucking underground this time. If it is, I quit!"

"Kallan, you wouldn't," I chuckled, chewing the dried jerky, as I continued to listen.

"Oh, I would," he said, leaning toward me.

"Elves should only view upon my face in the sunlight and not by cave light," Kallan said as he leaned back, his hands digging into the sand.

"What I know is that with us working together, we can do this. Not only are we a team, but we're a family. Secrets don't lie between the bonds we have formed for one another." Lilja held up the flask she carried with her bag, taking a swig before she handed it around in a circle, allowing each of us to take a swig of the fermented liquid inside.

My heart ached. *I'm vigilant. My* thoughts ran rampant in my head. *It's for the greater good. Pavati needs a sacrifice. Perhaps she'll just need the prick of a finger. Just my blood and not my life.*

She would have worded it differently, my inner voice seemed to argue.

Once the bottle made it to me, I took a giant swig; the liquid burn-ing its way down my throat as I fought to forget about my situation. Lilja's eyes burned into me as I gulped before handing it back to her.

It was as if she knew something was wrong with me, as if she knew I was hiding something from her.

I covered up with the cloak, throwing some of it over Lilja, praying she wouldn't ask me about the thoughts taking place in my head.

I love you; I projected into her head before I closed my eyes for the night.

It wasn't quite dawn when I opened my eyes again. Lilja's hot breath blew onto my neck as she slept. Her eyes were still closed. Her face was vacant of the stressors of our lives.

War.

The blight.

The thoughts of her people.

Worst of all, worrying about me. Tears welled in my eyes as I reached up to cup her sleeping face. I leaned in, giving her a small kiss on her lips.

Pavati needed me. Lilja needed me. Valdis needed me.

"Good morning, darling." Her voice was raspy as she brushed the thoughts out of my head.

"Good morning, Lilja," I said, murmuring into her lips as she gave me another passionate kiss.

She pulled away for a second, letting the blissful morning air between us, letting our foreheads touch the skin-on-skin contact, warming me.

"Elowen, my love, my everything. The morning air pauses between us as I stare at you. Your beauty is startling even in front of Niahm."

I smirked. Regardless of everything else happening in this world, Lilja still tried to woo me.

"I love you, Lilja. I'm sorry I don't say it as often as you do. These past months-"

Lilja cut me off, setting a finger on my lips. "Elle, you do not have to reason with me. Our bond." She grabbed my hand, placing it on her chest. "The bond between us is enough. I know the months previous have not been easy." Her voice cracked, tears swimming in her eyes. "You had to do what you had to survive. No one faults you. You're the one who found the answer to a question I have been searching for over a hundred years. Elowen Alwyn, you are a hero. At no point have you disappointed me."

The sun's rays peaked over the land as we stared at one another, marking the start of the new day. The hurt I held in my heart melted as it was my turn to lean in, kissing her.

"You are exquisite," she said as she reciprocated the kiss. Reluctantly, I pulled back before we could deepen the mood, glancing back at the forms of our sleeping friends.

We watched the sun rise lazily out of the horizon as we held hands, her thumb rubbing over the top of mine.

Lilja kissed my forehead. "I love you, Elowen Alwyn. The thread between our two worlds could never have kept us apart." She stood up after what felt like an eternity, extending her hand out to help me up.

"Now, Ellie, let's say we find ourselves a god." I nodded, pulling my hair into a clasp.

The heat that had abandoned us the night previous had returned. Sweat beaded on my forehead from either stress or the heat; I couldn't be sure. We worked quickly, waking the others and gathering our camp back into our packs. By the time we finished, the heat had returned full force. It seemed to simmer on the earth in a hazy glow.

"Are we there yet?" Kallan groaned.

I glanced back at him as I walked an arm's length away from Lilja. As if walking side by side would give the others an idea of what we did before we awoke them. He donned an extra shirt wrapped around the top of his head, protecting him from the sun.

"Not yet, you whiner. Does it seem like we're any closer to the plateau? The same plateau that's currently looming over us," Armand said, his arms crossed. His tan complexion was darker than ever, the sun doing wonders for him.

Keres and Cassia trailed behind him. Each of them had their hair pulled up off their necks. They were grinning at each other, totally immersed in the topic between them.

"I feel as if 'looming' is the wrong descriptive word, my bulky friend." Aidan walked directly behind me; laughter was evident in his voice.

"Bulky!"

"Perhaps the anticipation of this plateau is a better way to say it. The word looming sounds too negative. Yes, I said bulky. I've seen how many muffins you put away in all the towns we've been in. The history book, my journal, will talk about it." Aidan tapped his journal, opening his book, writing something down, before snapping it closed again.

"I'll have you know I'm *not* bulky. I'm muscular. Something you'd be more of if you trained more than reading!" Armand sent a puff of air toward Aidan, scattering a few of Aidan's papers across the sand.

Lilja rubbed her face with her hand, exasperated. Although a small smile played on her lips. "Gentleman! As if I can call you that. Do not make me turn around! I will send you back to Valdis to play the proper generals you are supposed to be."

"Oi! It's not like I wasn't telling the truth. Aidan, don't put that muffin comment in your journal," Armand said with his hands up in the air as if in mock surrender, glaring at him.

"It was *not* like I could help to be voracious about the thought of an abandoned society. This is a historic moment. I- I mean, we'll be the first ones to set foot on Olken Ridge since its downfall, caused by a societal greed so strong it turned this vast place into a wasteland. The books I could write about this will be the first in a long line of theories of how this place transformed into the ruin it is today." Aidan shuffled his papers as he talked, his voice nearly shaking with excitement. Even while walking in a desert, he haphazardly wrote facts into his ever-growing journal. It was a surprise that none of them fell to the ground.

"Armand, stop messing with Aidan! Don't be jealous that he's smarter than you." Keres looked up from her conversation with Cassia.

Cassia piped in. "On the bright side, we're nearly there, my intellectual friends. So soon you won't have to listen to the constant chatter of these three overgrown children."

The stone formations we approached appeared more purposeful in design. Weathered carvings peeked through the broken pieces littering the old pathway. Two large statue guardians stood proudly as we neared the grand staircase. One grasped a spear, and the other held the remains of a broken shield.

We approached the shrine that stood in the middle of what I assume used to be a garden. Bricks made small perimeters around the old, dead flowerbed. Empty and broken pots littered the ground around it.

The weather had worn down the features before me. It was clear that the statue was Pavati. She stood on a pedestal overlooking a basin that once was a fountain. I took my jug of water and poured a few drops onto the head, allowing the water to puddle at her feet.

Kallan flipped a coin into the water, as did Armand.

Lilja poured some of her own water into the water basin, nodding her head at me. "Pavati, the river goddess, please watch over my family on this adventure. May our mission become fruitful." I reached into my bag, holding onto the book. As if it were my lifeline, it thrummed as if with excitement. The energy of it being near its creator.

Carved stone steps led the rest of the path. Some had broken down over time, a few were mere dusty pebbles, a ghost of the land that used to be full of life. I peered back at the desert; I could just barely see the mountains that divided Ardour and Olken's desert. A land void of life stood between us and the enemy, not far enough.

A yell sounded across the desert, freezing us mid-step. I looked at Lilja with alarm. Kallan nocked an arrow, holding it close to him.

"What in the gods' name was that?" Cassia whispered. Sand blew around us as the wind picked up. I squinted up, and a form flitted across the top of the steps.

"Uh, guys. I think we have visitors," Armand said in a low voice as he flipped his blade in his hand.

"Maybe they're friendly," I muttered meekly, clutching the book in my bag.

"Yeah, 'friendly' because everyone we met thus far has been *so* nice," Keres spoke up.

Lilja crouched down, flexing her palm onto the ground, her eyes closed with concentration. Aidan followed suit, his eyes widened in surprise. "Holy Gods! There are so many of them."

"So many of what?!" Kallan and I spoke at the same time. We glanced at each other uneasily.

"Elves, so many elves. Or some kind of animal group has taken up this ruin. Thousands of them," Aidan said in wonder, his historian-like excitement already breaking through his nervousness.

"It's not clear through the stone. Too much interference with the sand. Proceed with caution and go quietly. There is no telling who is up there," Lilja spoke as she stood up, brushing her hands on her trousers to get rid of the sand that clung to her palms.

We neared the top of the steps without interruption. The higher we got, the more the wind became a constant annoyance. It whipped the sand through the air. *One step closer to Pavati's shrine.*

Desperate, we wrapped clothing around our faces, covering our noses and mouths. Even with the protection, sand held onto the sides of my mouth, and my saliva all but dried up. I didn't dare open my water, not wishing for the sand to contaminate my jug.

We stood in silence as the old, forgotten buildings stood before us. I expected a dust-covered city. Ruins of a forgotten way of life. Bones of those who could not escape the world they had been catalysts for. Instead, a few forgotten buildings stood abandoned in front of an immense wall.

"What in the Gods is this?" Aidan marveled at the wall. A giant set of doors stood off to the side.

"Who are you?" A large voice boomed through the air. I whipped my head around to the sound. A strange man stood on top of the wall, holding a large metal and wooden staff. It had a weird glow about it. Bright green light shone through the space where the wood and the metal met.

"Hello, we're Valdisians. We have come far to this place in search of- knowledge," I yelled, my hand at my brow, trying to shield my eyes from the sun, hoping that my voice was loud enough to carry in the wind.

Lilja POV

I stood in awe of my soon-to-be wife. She spoke so clearly to the strange man who was present on top of the wall. If one had not known her, they would have no idea that she nearly stumbled over her words. Her pause was not noticeable; her charm was easily infectious to anyone near her. One could convince oneself it was a spell.

"Of knowledge?" The guard questioned.

"Yes, sir." She bowed her head in a symbol of respect.

"How do you know the knowledge you seek is in such a place as this?" He probed.

"I've heard far-" Elowen spoke as the two doors inched open.

"Oi, Dyantu! Get your decrepit ass back in here. Not everyone is a scholar! We don't know if these people are trustworthy." The guard shouted, his voice slipping into an accent.

A man with a cane hobbled his way out. The many seasons this man had seen had hunched his back, but he still moved with tough determination.

"Twa twaru' Dyantu, twa dyi dawrtu'shtage ra' dyakfe di thikoflam-tu'," he said, smiling a toothless grin.

"Tyokego te twe fu dyaw Tyanru!" The guard said as he sighed loudly. This had clearly not been the first time the older gentleman had done this.

"Oh, my apologies. My name is Dyantu. I've waited so long to meet scholars like yourself. Come all the way from Valdis. Such a long way. Why, I believe I've only read about such a place. Once you come to the great Olken Ridge, you don't tend to leave. Please come in and let me give you the tour. Just know this is a no-magic place. An absolute rule, nothing magical whatsoever." His face was grave as he looked up at us. He was so short in stature that he could have almost passed for one of the Brawn'n people.

"Do you understand?" The guards imposed over us. Almost threateningly, as if our answer determined the well-being of our person. His shadow loomed over us.

"Yes, my kind sir. I have no power. My group won't use any power. You have my honor," Elowen spoke up for us all, my heartbeat in my chest. Worry bloomed through my body, and I fought the urge to look at the rest of the team while trying to keep my face as neutral as possible. We were so close to the end of this mission. Years in the making, the saving of my people is almost within my grasp. I clenched my fists as I nodded along. Magic had its drawbacks, anyway. A few days without would not be impossible.

The old man's eyes narrowed into slits as he scanned my family before grinning again as if we had just become his best friends. "Great! It's time. Now I know all the advancements we have achieved will surprise you. Please wait for questions as I take you around." Dyantu gave a hand signal to the guard, who slammed his spear onto the ground, signaling the staff responsible for the door. The spear was an odd design, and I made a mental note to investigate the weaponry in this environment.

A spell must have locked in the sound and smells into the locked city. *How ironic.* Sounds of life blasted us as we entered, as well as the smells of food and the heat of machines throughout the city.

My eyes widened. I quickly changed back into a more neutral look. Lamps hooked together with a string hung on posts. Each one connected to the other. Tarps connected to lamps hovered over the market before us, protecting it from the blistering heat. Floating carts were being pulled by camels, an animal I had only set eyes upon in books.

"How do the carts float if not by magic?" Aidan asked, causing me to look back at him. The scholar in him peaking through, he didn't bother to school his facial expressions. He might as well be a child in a sweet shop. Aidan had always been inquisitive, sneaking out from his home for hours on end to come to the royal library to read.

"That, my friend, is the power of innovation. Now, silence, look as much as you want, but wait for questions," Dyantu said as he stomped his cane around, and he kept going forward. The elves here were tan, their skin blessed by the constant sun exposure.

Stalls of the market were lit on the inside, similar in design to the lamps on the outside. Everything seemed to hum here. The people looked at us strangely as they walked through the market leisurely. I raised an eyebrow at them. They moved as each of them had some sort of diplomatic training. A training I graciously avoided as a young elf, much to my tutor's dismay.

"Now, as scholars, you must want the library," he spoke as the cane he used smacked the brick that outlined the roads.

"Yes, sir!" Aidan said as he furiously scribbled down notes in his book. Almost frantic to look around before going back to his book, as if he was worried about missing a single detail. I fought the urge to laugh at him as he strutted right behind the older elf.

"When the great awakening occurred and brought about the new reformed Olken Ridge about 1200 years ago."

"The great awakening?" Kallan asked as he trailed behind me, an old habit of his, always watching my back.

"You scholars are not aware of the great awakening?" The old man cast us a look from the corner of his eye.

"Of course, we know! My dear friend only means for the history to be furthered," I piped in, pushing my hair back out of my eyes and off my forehead. Even with the tarp coverings, the heat still beat down on me

.

Why couldn't we go anywhere cold?
I'm a Queen.

I shouldn't have sweat dribbling down my ass cheeks. I thought to Elowen, earning a small smile from her as she tried to appear to be intently listening to Dyantu.

"Ah, yes, I suppose lower beings could not learn about all the greatness of the awakening in textbooks. It's a close-kept secret, hidden. We, the Tyanran people, known by most of the outside world as the Olken people, believe in furthering our mechanical advancements and then dealing with people who would otherwise push back against us.1200 years ago, most people feared our magical powers. The use of magic deformed a multitude of the Olken elves. Feathers sprouted from their skin. Some even took to flight, changed by magic in a way that isn't natural. The result of the people of the time using that much magical power sucked the life force out of the land for what appears to be forever. What used to be a sprawling metropolis is now a near-barren wasteland."

"Do the bird people still exist?" Elowen asked. At some point, she had inched closer to me during the conversation. Her hand clung to mine.

"The Olken Elves, as your people call them? Humph, I hope not. Magic has no place in the Tyanran people. We have evolved, abandoning magic altogether."

Elowen and I looked at each other, the same thought running through our minds. *If he hopes the Olken Elves are gone, then what happened to them?*

"This place is amazing. You have truly molded this into an example the rest of the country should follow," I responded to him, all the while looking at Elowen.

We had to get out of here. These people are insane.

"Ah, here we are, the library." The library stood in the middle of the plateau, looming over the rest of the buildings. Multi colored stones decorated the front of the steps.

"I do believe a seminar is taking place in the lobby, about the great eradication of magic on Olken," Dyantu said as he stood proudly in front of the steps, his hands placed on top of his cane.

The weight of the quest seemed to melt off of me as we stared forward at the building. A building that housed the knowledge of a world thought dead by the rest of the elves of the realm, and we stood in front of it.

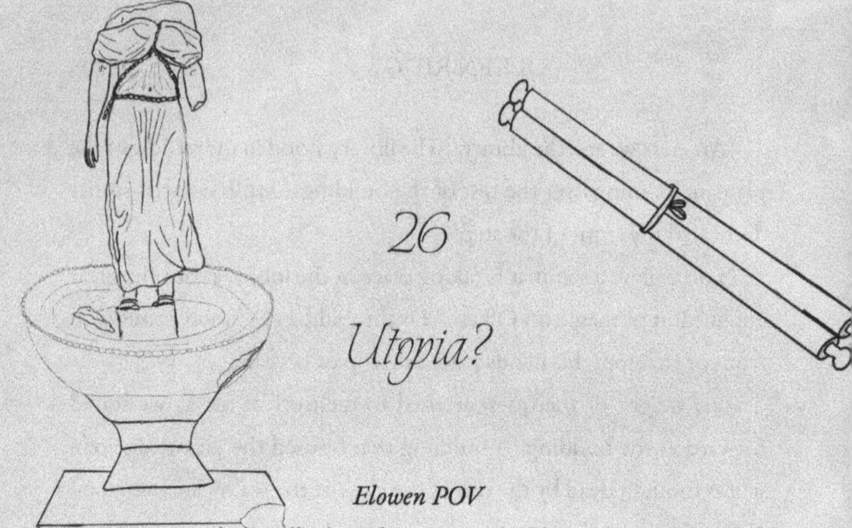

26

Utopia?

Elowen POV

Cautiously, I walked up the steps to the library. Dyantu had left us alone to our own devices.

"I, for the life of me, can't tell if they are incompetent or incredibly smart. That old guy just let us stroll in here and left us," Armand said. He looked up, marveling at the vaulted ceilings as we entered. A lush green landscape fresco decorated the walls, a snapshot of a lifetime ago.

"Shut up, you oaf, obviously, the only dumb one is you right now. Why not tell the whole world what's going on?" Kallan smacked his arm.

"In all honesty, the Olken people probably don't get very many malicious people here. They appear like a well-rounded city. Nearly a utopia." Aidan drew a quick sketch in his journal.

"Nothing is as nice as it seems." Lilja stood back from us, taking in the scene before her. She seemed calm, sure of herself.

"Exactly, just look at our dear neighbor Ardour. They have quite the persona going for them," Keres said, walking further into the hall.

"What's the plan, boss?" Kallan crossed his arms, looking at Lilja.

"I don't know why you are looking at me, Kal. Elowen is the only reason we have gotten this far. Ask her." Lilja looked me up and down, the corner of her lips turning upward, as if she enjoyed making me the center of attention.

"Well, you heard her. What's the plan?" Kallan turned to me, his black hair slicked back with sweat.

I surveyed the room. A few people chattered to each other in the corner near the steps that went to the second floor. Before us stood the lobby and the doors that led into the library. Under normal circumstances, I would be ecstatic to be in the room with such a history tied behind it. My thoughts go back to the times of reading with my mother in town. Us riding our horses and racing to the library. She would always find a way for us to sneak in, a place reserved for men only. We would sneak in around the back, clambering inside a window. Cigar smoke saturated the air. Even the books had smelled.

I smirked at the memory, pulling myself back to the present. Through the large glass panes, books lined the walls, going all the way to the ceiling. A wall of scrolls took up one side of the room.

"We go in there," I jabbed my finger towards the doors separating us from the knowledge we so desperately needed. *Where was Pavati's shrine? How could we find her in a land seemingly barren of water?*

Shrines were a source of power- magic. The Great Awakening would have caused people to shun her-forcing her into hiding.

"Find any knowledge from the Great Awakening. That has to be when Pavati began to have issues. Her fountains and sigils created for her are beyond repair throughout the plateau and broken. It might have occurred when that happened. The elves would have stopped going on pilgrimages to her site, leaving the location of her shrine forgotten with time." I started walking for the door, stopping just before the handle. A chill ran down my back, and I turned around, meeting eyes with someone on the balcony above, before they quickly ducked back, running away from the edge.

"We should also have someone explore the city, looking for any more signs of Pavati shrines. Is there any way you could contact her with the Niphes book?" Cassia asked.

I shrugged my shoulders. "I don't know. Each time she has contacted me, not the other way around," I admitted.

"True. Armand and I are definitely not scholars. We could go scope out the land." Kallan slung his arm over Armand's shoulder, responding to Cassia.

"I could go find a place for us to stay," Keres volunteered.

"I'll come with you, Keres," Cassia said, grinning. Her eyes glinted with eagerness for exploration. The pirate coming out in her.

"Sounds good. Come back before nightfall. The nightlife here is unknown. Plus, it's bound to get pretty cold at night." Aidan said. He opened the door distractedly as he stepped in front of me. Not even bothering to glance at our parting friends as he walked into his heaven.

Everyone dispersed with their part of the plan. The earthy smell of ink and paper filled my nose as I pulled down a book from the shelf. I groaned as I realized the whole book was in the Tyanran language.

"We might be in trouble," Lilja said as I turned to her, the book she grabbed in her hand.

"We'll have to find someone to help translate these," I said, fighting the urge to fall to the floor in despair. *This fucking close and now unable to read the information.*

"We might not need to, guys. Some of these are not in Tyanran. Just keep looking," Aidan said as he pulled out a scroll from the other wall, blowing the dust off of it.

"The older information will probably all be in scrolls, anyway. This history will be fantastic for my journal. Imagine, my journal in the library at the castle!" His eyes shone with the future.

Lilja nodded, humming in response and only half listening. My eyes landed on the large group congregated at one table. All of their eyes focused on one person. I pointed at them. "That must be the lecture Dyantu spoke about. I'm gonna sit in and see if I can learn anything about the great awakening."

I strode over, pulled out a chair, and sat down. The woman who stood before me had glasses on top of her head. Her hair was a brassy red brown pulled behind her; a few strands dangled in her face. She held a book in one hand, squinting as she read.

"The great awakening was the tipping point for Olken Ridge. Magic had rid the land of fertile soil, stripping us of the largest thing, feeding our people. Greedy elves used magic frivolously, not working, living in leisure." She glared down at her book as if wishing to rearrange the council. "They decided it was best to stop the magic use on the plateau. Does anyone know how non-magic users forced the Olken elves to cease their usage?" She looked up from the book, her eyes narrowing on me.

"You girl," she pointed to me with the hand she used to hold the book. "Do you know how they managed such a feat?"

My cheeks heated as she threw me in the spotlight. "No, ma'am."

She looked over the rest of the Elves listening to the lecture, as if unsurprised by my lack of knowledge. "Anyone else?"

"They killed them," a young boy said. He appeared no older than a human child in his early teens.

"Exactly, Mrunma. With magic so prevalent, they recorded down every single person who had the use of magic. With that knowledge, they dispatched a team of highly trained personnel to finish the job. A few failed, yes; however, the massacre was successful. They came during the night, some eradicating whole families."

As she spoke, my heart dropped. Bile climbed my throat in disgust. I fought the urge to tell them it was terrible. The group of eight people sat around me smiling, their faces portraying the opposite of the feelings I felt coursing through my veins. The woman spoke with such a matter-of-fact tone, like she was saying flowers came from seeds. It was jarring.

"With the magic users gone, the last remaining members of the plateau had to keep striving for greatness. With the land being barren, they had to find a solution to food and how to keep people out." The woman set the book down, looking at me, crossing her arms.

"Ms. Outsider, what's the general assumption about Olken Ridge?" The group turned to me, a few looked at me with raised eyebrows, and the others with curiosity.

"Uh, well, I-" I said before taking a breath and restarting. "The main assumption is that Olken Ridge is desolate and abandoned. My friends and I expected to find ruins, trying to learn more about this place."

"That's exactly why so many people don't come here, allowing us to grow undisturbed by the outside world. Food was harder to find. How did we manage that?" She asked the class.

The older gentleman in the front raised his hand quickly, eager to answer. "Yes, Krofke."

"The source," Krofke said, his voice gravely with age.

"Perfect! Yes, the source. Olken Ridge's top supporters, the believers in our cause. A magic-less space for normal Elves to exist. Without the fear of being overpowered by those who want to use their strength against us. No longer will we be servants, no longer will we be the ones to do the work. The source for us." She almost chanted the last part as if she had prayed it.

"The source for us," the rest of them said in unison.

I gaped, quickly remembering to school my features. "Well, class, I think that's all I have time for today. Does anyone have questions?" She asked as she picked up the books around her, placing them into a large bag.

"Yes! I have a question. Um, when did the statues of the River Goddess become so dilapidated?"

She took a step back from her bag, a look of surprise crossing her features. "Ah, yes. Pavati. Tyanran people vandalized her shrines when magic had its great downfall here. Pavati has not visited our great home for many years, and the Olken people at the time and now agree. There's no reason to support a goddess who does nothing for us."

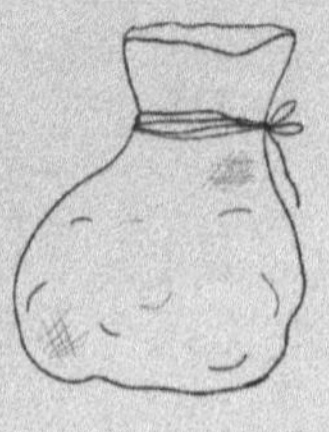
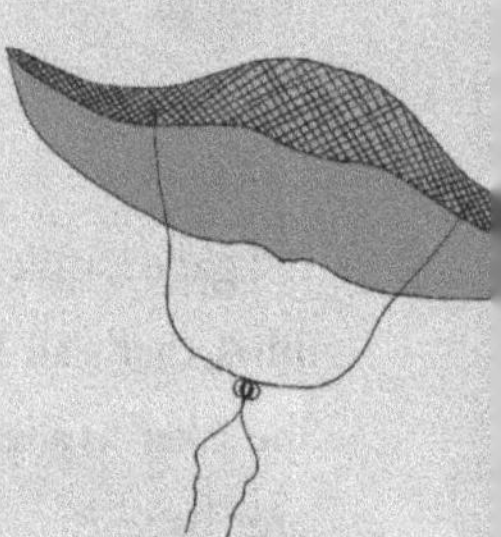

27

Language Barrier

The teacher finished packing up the books she had sprawled out on the table, nodding her head to us before walking up the steps.

As she walked out of earshot, I turned to the kid. "What's the source?"

"The source for us," he said, looking around, and speaking as if it were a blessing. "The source brings us the food we need to survive on the plateau. Without it, the plateau would be lifeless."

"Who are they?" I asked.

"What do you mean, they? The source is the source. It's not people, or one person. The leaders receive the food." He looked at me impatiently, as if he couldn't fathom why I couldn't grasp the information he had given me.

"Who gives it to your leaders?" I sat back in my chair, annoyed at the back and forth.

"Gives it? No, that's wrong. It appears. This is stuff you learn in your first year. Go and ask someone else. I don't have time to explain to a stupid outsider. You might have come to the plateau for knowledge, but we will always be superior." He stood up, pushing himself with his hands on the table before leaving.

I mulled over his response, ignoring his rough reaction to me being an 'outsider.' The hair on my neck was standing up as I felt someone's eyes on me. Brushing it off, I went to Lilja. She had sat herself at a table closest to the scrolls. Various written documents lay strewn over the table.

"Olken Ridge is a terrible place." Despite the heat that beamed down on the land, I shivered. My soul was frozen from the hatred the non-magic user had toward the Olken elves. Lilja looked up at me, her eyebrow raised.

"What are you speaking about?"

I looked around, looking for anyone in our general vicinity. "They killed them." My voice cracked as I spilled the information to Lilja. They were people; they couldn't have all deserved to die.

She sat still for a moment, absorbing the information, nodding her head as if genocide made the most sense. "That must be why they have erased all of the shrines as well. The people on this plateau are trying to sponge their history off of the land."

"They can't do that, though. Olken elves were people, some were bad, but- but they didn't deserve to all die." I was one breath away from a breakdown. The thought of all of them just killed, some in their beds. The children, the innocent, all of them gone. Erased from the world as if they didn't matter, like they didn't exist.

"Elle, hey, there isn't anything we can do about it now. It' is in the past. All we can do now is to make sure they don't become forgotten and to make sure their fate does not befall *our* people." Her voice was firm; the strength of failure was built upon the faults of her parents. I knew she would rather die than let her people die the same fate.

I have to help her, save Valdis, my inner voice chanted to me. I nodded, my resolve hardening.

"I can't discern any of these. They're either in Tyanran or in another language I don't even know. I'm a Queen, I' am well-versed in languages, and I can't even recognize these." She ran her hand through her hair, a few strands falling onto her face.

"I understand how you feel." I plopped down next to her, leaning my head on her shoulder, tentatively, and even though I was honest about the events that occurred in Ardour, my heart still pained in remorse.

Perhaps the pain I felt from my actions would always follow me. Like a dark shadow, something I wouldn't be able to stray away from.

"The lecture I sat in on was unnerving, to say the least. Where *is* Aidan?" Perking my head up, the thoughts in my head became too loud for comfort. I peered around, seeing no sign of my overly excited friend.

"I don't know the location of our well-read friend, but if I don't take a break from these, I'll lose my mind and forever be known as the crazy Queen of Valdis. Let's go find him."

The library was silent as we peeked through it, looking down every aisle. A few Elves had tucked themselves into random corners, reading. It wasn't until the second floor, did we find Aidan. He was sitting cross-legged on the ground, books stacked around him precariously, as if one wrong breath would make them all come crashing down. A book from another shelf fell to the ground as we passed the last one. I squatted down, picked it up, and put it back on the bookshelf. The cover was blackened with soot.

I grimaced, brushing it off my hands. "Did you find anything interesting?" Lilja asked, her hands on her hips as she peered down at him. Like a mother would to a child.

"Yes! Truly, the Olken Ridge people are fantastic. The ingenuity they have to pull the water-." Lilja held up a hand to Aidan.

"I want to hear if you have information on the Pavati Shrine." She leaned onto the bookshelf behind him.

"I uh, got nothing yet. I got rather absorbed, the water pipes going into the center of the plateau."

"Aidan," Lilja said in a warning tone. "We're here for the mission, not history. You-"

"Wait, that's it!" I said, clapping my hands and simultaneously saving Aidan from Lilja's wrath.

"What is?" Lilja pinched the bridge of her nose.

"The water! Pavati is the River Goddess. All we have to do is follow the water system. We should find her shrine!"

Lilja grabbed my face, kissing my forehead, making me blush.

"You are a genius!"

"Now the question is, how do we find the water?" Aidan said, picking himself up from the floor. He brushed the dust off his trousers, his fingers stained with the ink of a thousand dying trees.

"You two and Cassia. Maybe she can sense the water with her magic. With it being so dry, it can't be too difficult. You and Lilja can sense if there are any caves nearby," I said, heading to the steps to go outside, nearly shaking with excitement.

The sun beat on Armand and me as we walked through the twists and turns of the city. Armand, at some point, put on an ridiculously enormous hat. It spanned his shoulder width.

"Where did you even find that thing? You look terrible," I teased, a smile on my lips, weaving through people shopping.

"Hey the shopkeeper said this type of hat is really in style right now. Plus, at least I don't have sweat running down my face, like you," he retorted.

I shrugged my shoulders as I wiped the sweat on my shirt, turning down the alley. I opened my mouth to say a smart remark as someone ran into me, sending me sprawling.

"Hey!" I said. My butt surely bruised.

"Catch him! He's got my change purse!" An old man yelled, his hands on his knees as he caught his breath. The wrinkles on his face showed the age of someone who had seen many seasons.

The man picked himself off the ground, grabbing the purse he had dropped, nodding at me as he took off again. He was short and skinny, probably a young, rebellious elf.

"Don't stand there! Grab him!" The old guy yelled.

With the surprise wearing off, I leapt up as Armand and I booked it after him. He had the advantage. He knew the streets of Olken. The thief was fully using it to give himself an edge against us.

Without pausing to think, we were on the move. A thief deserved to be caught, no matter where we were. Greed was the poison of the world. If this kid wasn't going to give the money to the poor, and if they want to be greedy, they could answer to me.

The kid grabbed a stall of fruit, crashing it to the ground, effectively blocking our way. He scaled the wall of one of the buildings using the gutter as a ladder and climbed it like a monkey.

"Help me up, Armand! You continue on the ground!" I said as I glared at the kid running away.

Armand interlocked his fingers and let me put my foot into his palms before using his shoulders to heave myself onto the roof. The kid jumped buildings, heading toward the west side of the city. "When I get my hands on you, you're gonna regret giving me such a hard time!"

He jumped to another building, sending me a middle finger. I gaped, this fucker. I followed his route, barely gaining any leadway.

Just when I thought he was going to another building. He turned, pausing long enough to wave cheekily before jumping down.

"He's going down to the ground, Armand," I huffed. I was seconds behind him now. I dropped into the small alleyway, with no indication of where he had gone.

I'd lost him.

Armand rounded the corner. His hat had fallen off his head. The string made it hang on the back of his neck.

"Where did the speedy bastard go?" He leaned against the wall, smashing the hat. Armand breathed heavily, gasping for air. *Aidan was right, way too many muffins.*

"How the fuck am I supposed to know? Look around," I said, throwing my hands out toward him. *This is taking up too much time.*

"Finding him is the right thing to do, Kal."

"Don't you think I know that. How can a kid steal from an old man?" I huffed my hands on my head as I tried to breathe air into my lungs.

The alleyway was no wider than my arm's length. Trash and random crates took up the walking space. A dead end. It was the space between two large buildings, never meant to touch. At the end of the alley was another building.

"They would have had to come out the way you came in. If you didn't see them run out, he has to still be in here." I put a finger to my lips as I pointed to the largest of the crates. It was big enough to fit a young, rebellious elf.

Armand got to the crate first, and I pulled my sword from my hip, signaling him to open it.

He yanked it open, looking inside. "It's empty?" Armand said as he looked back up at me, surprised.

"Yes, I can see. Mr. Genteen," I said, rolling my eyes.

Randomly dated newspapers covered the bottom of the crate. With my sword, I pushed them out of the way. My eyes zeroed in on the metal round lid covering presumably a network of tunnels underground.

"You don't think they went down there, do you?" I said, my eyes bugging out of my head.

"The only way to find out is if we go in." Armand clasped my shoulder, grinning.

"Push this damn crate out of the way so we can open it. Why does it always have to be something underground? Couldn't they have a hideout in a broken old tower?" I said as I sheathed my sword, rolling up my sleeves.

"You know, I said I was going to quit if we had to go underground again. This is it. I'm quitting. As soon as I see Lilja, I'm telling her. Mark my words."

"It's your luck, Kal. You must have pissed off some God. Maybe you should do an offering?" He said, laughter in his voice as he pushed the crate. Grunting, I pulled the metal lid up enough to push it off the hole it covered.

The space below was black as night; no light peered out. It smelled moldy, the air almost stale as I took a deep breath, dropping down. It was circular in design, and the floor was barely wet. "Well, on the bright side, there's no wastewater down here," Armand said as he dropped right next to me.

"That would be terrible," I said as I got my bearings. My heart beat in my throat as I fought the thoughts of the walls closing in.

"Let's go this way." Armand pointed to the west. Further to the edge of the city.

"If we can't find this kid in twenty minutes, we call it quits. Lilja and the rest of the crew will look for us soon," he said as he grabbed for my satchel, pulling the crystal I bought from Ebbon City. I squinted as I got used to the light. It illuminated the path enough to see.

"Do you think this counts as using magic? I don't want to listen to Aidan lecturing me tonight," Armand said as he walked in front of me.

"I won't tell him if you don't, because I don't know if it counts. You're the magic user. Lead the way, Mr. Magic Crystal." I gripped onto my sword, fighting the instinct to run away as we ventured deeper into the darkness.

28

Underground River

Kallan POV

We didn't speak as we followed the tunnel. A few rats squeaked, scuttling by our boots and the soft murmur of the market above us.

This is ridiculous, I thought as I stared daggers into Armand's back. He held the glowing rock at chest height, only illuminating the front of the path, leaving me in darkness.

In a flash, all the light was gone as Armand stuffed it in his pocket. He stopped moving, holding his hand up. There was enough light from the forgotten storm drain to make the shape discernible.

A black flying bat flew past our heads, and we scrambled to the floor.

"What the fuck? Let's go. We'll never find him down here." I kicked a broken mug across the room. Hitting the wall, it shattered before falling into a hole in the floor. It was nearly invisible before the mug had fallen into it.

"Owe! You son of a bitch. That hurt." A high-pitched voice said.

"Gotcha," I said, grinning as I grabbed the boy by the back of his shirt.

"Give us the purse, you little gremlin," Armand said, snatching it out of his hands.

"Let's unmask our troublemaker," I said, pulling the mask off the kid, revealing a woman. Feathers sprouted from her face as her emotions got the best of her.

"You're an Olken Elf," I said, almost dropping her. I flipped her, pushing her face into the ground, putting my knee on her back.

"Please! Don't tell the council! I don't want to die!" She screeched, her breathing heavy as I pinned her. Her voice was scraggly, like she hadn't spoken in a while.

"I'll give the money back. Pretend like you never saw me," she said.

"Now wait a minute, nobody is killing anybody. I'm not even inclined to bring you to the Olken Authorities, but you can't go on taking purses from old men," I said, flipping her face up, pulling my knee off of her back. The dark obscured her features.

"Kal, we should get Lilja and Elowen. She's exactly who can help us." Armand held up the crystal again, the blue light exposing her face.

"Help? Help with what? I don't sleep with people anymore. Get your fix from someone else." I grimaced as she spoke, panic rising in her voice.

"No! Girl, you have it all wrong. We actually need your help," Armand said, panic rising in his voice now, too. He stepped away, hands in the air.

"Guys, calm down. Armand, go get Lilja. I'll stay here with her." Grabbing some discarded rope that was musty from lying in a trash heap, I tied it around her feet and her hands. I grimaced at the dirt under her nails and the calluses on her hands. She's had a hard life.

He nodded, tossing the crystal to me. It significantly dimmed as it left his hands. "I'll be back. Don't let her escape."

"Yeah, fat chance," I said as he trudged back the way we came, leaving us in awkward silence. I refuse to be bested by the small Olken elf before me.

It was a while before she spoke. "What do you guys need from me?" She asked, her voice timid. She scooted away, her back against the wall. I didn't move to pull her back.

"I'm not even sure if you can help. Lilja and Elle will be the judges." I sat cross-legged on the floor, peaking around. The crystal was no longer strong enough. Shadows danced around the room as the crystal shifted in my lap.

"You don't have magic?" She asked.

I scoffed. "No, I don't." I kept my eyes trained on anything but her. The Olken Elf before me wasn't a threat, my instincts told me. Her body language almost screamed melancholy. The room in the drains reflected the same emotion. Trash littered the floor, and clothes were piled in the corner.

Scattered on a makeshift desk were papers and maps. The brick walls, while shrouded in darkness, had drawings as if she were creating the outside in this one room.

"Did you draw those?" I asked, signaling to the wall.

"I don't have to tell you anything." She grumbled, looking off to the side to avoid eye contact I was attempting. My heart ached for her. This little elf before me seemed broken, held together with baggy, oversized clothes as a bandage.

"You know, my team—my family- don't plan to hurt you. We need to ask you some questions." I scooted away from her. *I felt a strong pull toward her.* The urge to throw my arm over her shoulder to comfort her was nearly overwhelming. She reminded me of Elowen when we first met. Scared and confused, abused by her previous life.

"Why did you steal the bag from that merchant? Don't you have a family somewhere? How old are you? Do you know where Pavati's shrine is? What's your name?" Questions spewed from my mouth as I found it unable to sit in this room without knowing her. My skin seemed to itch with want. This little elf seemed to weave herself into my good graces by just existing.

"You don't have to answer any of those in a particular order." I stood up, pacing. My ears were ringing. The walls felt like they were shifting, coming closer by the second.

Armand POV

I clambered out of the storm drain, my heart beating in my chest, as I found a newfound resolve. People meandered through the skinny market area. "Please, ladies and gentlemen, I have an emergency. Get out of my way." I fought the urge to push people. My hat banged on my back as I dodged and weaved around people. My anger rose as people meandered in front of me.

I beelined for the closest wall, looking around. Olken Ridge's desert homes were smooth. No way for me to climb up mud-smoothed walls to help reflect the glaring sun. A crate caught my eye from the stall behind me. Yanking it into place, I jumped up onto it, clambering up onto the roof. Pulling myself to my feet, I looked around, searching for the library.

The Tyanran people moved at the pace of a snail, used to their secluded lives of fake utopia. I shook my head in dismay as I searched for the silhouette of the library, the tallest building in the center of town. I took off on a running start, jumping over the gaps in between buildings, relishing the feeling of the wind in my hair. The sun had already reached lower in the sky by the time I reached the library. I doubled over, catching my breath.

My thoughts came rampant as I reached for the door, as Lilja, Elowen, and Aidan were coming out. I tried to grin at them, but it came out more like a grimace. I panted, catching my breath.

I really need to do more running drills when I get back to Valdis. I've had way too many sweets on this latest adventure. Maybe I had put on some weight.

"What is it, Armand? Did you find something interesting?" Elowen's small stature stood before me as she spoke, putting a hand on my shoulder. Concern etched on her face as she stared at me, catching my breath.

"Not something, someone. Quick Kallan has her tied up. Let's move." My eyes met Lilja's as I spoke, straightening my back. Even though Lilja and I essentially grew up together, I couldn't help but feel a sense of gratitude for being one of her trusted advisors. Our liberation from poverty depended on her. Her parents had taken in Keres and me, teaching us how to be functional adults versus the criminal life poverty had thrust on us.

I led the way, weaving through the now dispersed crowd of Tyanran people. The sun had set, leaving the markets nearly deserted as people went back to their homes and to the bars. Music flowed out of them as we passed by, flutes filling the air.

"Is Kallan okay?" Elowen asked as she struggled to keep up with us. Her human body, slower than ours.

"Yes, well, yes, if you disregard that, he's claustrophobic and underground." I rounded the alleyway that held the storm drain, yanking the lid back up.

"Armand, we need to talk about how you give me information." Lilja gave me a warning glare before jumping down the drain, not even bothering to ask for further information. Aidan followed behind her, holding his glasses in his hand as he jumped down. His other hand was in an unbreakable grip on his journal. Its pages holding onto the binding with dear life.

"I'll go down first, Elle, and you can jump down, and I'll catch you." She nodded mutely. If I hadn't met her before her kidnapping, I would have mistook her silence as fear, but whatever had happened in those long few months had changed her. She was quieter, more deliberate in her words, and more resolved. Stronger, her eyes glinted with strength only found by pain. We had only heard small snippets of her time with the Ardourians. It was enough to create nightmares. The other memories she kept close to her chest, not ready to speak them into the air.

A rat stumbled over my foot as I reached the bottom. I looked up, the waning light barely showing the details of Elowen's face. "Okay, Elle. Jump down." I caught her with ease, her form light as a feather.

"Thanks, Armand." Elowen patted my arm in appreciation before falling behind Lilja, looping her fingers with hers.

"Lead the way, quickly." Lilja urged me to the front of our small group.

"We caught this lady because she was trying to steal a purse from a merchant. He needed our help, so Kallan and I ran after her, following her down here. We thought she was a boy, at first. Kallan seemed pretty interested in her. Oh, and I bought this neat hat. It's supposed to be very in style," I rambled as I tried to remember the correct twists and turns needed to get to Kal.

"Armand, is it too much to ask for you to show, not tell me every single thought you've had for today?" Lilja muttered, sighing, and feigning disappointment. A small smile played on her lips to show she wasn't serious. Aidan laughed, trying to stifle it into a cough.

"That hat is very nice," Elowen grinned, her smile from ear to ear.

"See, at least someone can appreciate style." I pulled it on for show, giving a little turn as I rounded the corner.

Elowen POV

"You okay, Kal?" I asked as I took in the room. Even though we were in the desert, the air in the sewers was musty, as if water flowed underneath us. I sent a small prayer to Pavati for the blessing of no wastewater to wade in. Sweat ran down the side of his face; his eyes closed. His black shirt moved up and down as he tried to calm his breathing.

"Yep, just trying to catch my breath." He gave us a weak grin.

"Where's the girl?" Lilja asked.

Kallan kept his eyes closed, pointing a finger at the corner of the room. I turned to look where he pointed. The darkness seemed to shroud the area.

"Keep looking," he panted. I strained my eyes into the darkness. An alcove seemed to sew itself into existence. A girl who appeared to be my age looked back at me. Black feathers stuck out of the sides of her face, smoothing into her hair. I took a step closer to Lilja, keeping my eyes on her. Fear shot through me, my dream replaying behind my eyes.

Lilja's hand rested on my back, her attempt to comfort me. As if to say, *'I'm here.'* "What is your name?" Liljas' voice was strained as if she was trying to keep anger from bubbling to the surface.

Silence stretched for a moment. "She asked you a question." I squared my shoulders, standing up straighter than before. *She has to answer,* I projected to Lilja.

"My name is Kufo." Her voice was meek as she scooted down further into the alcove.

"We're looking for Pavati, the Goddess of Rivers. Do you know where she's being hidden?" I looked at Lilja, surprised she was so blatant with her questions.

Another awkward pause stretched, as if Kufo was mulling over the answer in her head. "Hidden?"

"Yes, hidden." Aidan inched closer to Kufo, eager to have a better look at her. He looked at her quizzically, as if memorizing every strand of hair and feather that popped out of her head. He sketched her face in his journal, attempting to capture her features on paper.

"She's held captive, underneath," Kufo said, her head popping out of the hole farther as she spoke.

When she scrambled out, Kufo couldn't have been much taller than me. She was thin, almost dangerously thin, like Lilja when I had first met her.

"Underneath? What do you mean?" Lilja crossed her arms. I went over to Kallan, grabbing his clammy hand, trying to comfort him.

"They captured her," Kufo repeated, grabbing a bag off the floor, holding it out to Lilja.

"Take this and leave. I don't want any trouble." She shook the bag in front of Lilja as if it was going to entice her to grab it. Lilja made no sign of reaching for the bag. Armand grabbed it, smiling at her, trying not to seem threatening. It failed because instead of looking innocent, it did the opposite. His white teeth shone in the darkness, making him look like a shark ready for a bite to eat.

Kufo scooted back down in her alcove, side-eyeing Armand, her feather bobbing with the movement.

Lilja ran her fingers through her hair, looking up at the small grate. Ignoring Kufo's want for us to leave her alone.

"Did anyone get a hold of Keres or Cassia? Do they know we're down here?"

"No, we should get out so we can meet them. They'll be concerned if they can't find us. Plus, I think Kal could use some fresh air." I untangled my fingers from Kal's, walking over to Lilja.

"What should we do with her? She obviously knows something," I projected to Lilja, using our fated abilities. Lilja stiffened before looking at me. Her eyes searched my face to find the answers plastered on my face.

"We need to take Kufo with us. She appears to be alone here. So no one will miss her-"

"Miss her? We aren't planning on killing her, are we?" I sent back. Lilja raised an eyebrow, the corner of her mouth turning upward in a rueful grin.

"What? No, we aren't. We need her," Lilja said out loud.

"I don't know if you realize this, but we're still here. Do you want to share with the class what you're talking about via mind-link? It's not fair. I want to know all the gossip." Armand rustled through the bag he grabbed from Kufo, grabbing out the coins and handing them to her before throwing the bag behind him and into the trash pile. Kufo grabbed the coins greedily, stuffing them into her change purse. *So generous of him.*

Lilja leaned over to whisper in his ear. "You don't wanna know."

"Well, now I definitely want to know." Armand grinned, his facial expression anything but pious.

I squatted down to Kufo's hidden height, meeting her eye level. "Kufo, you need to come with us. We need your help," Lilja said, finally responding to her.

"No!" she shrieked, dunking farther into the hole she created. "Leave me. You gave it to me. Therefore, I didn't steal. It's mine!" More feathers sprouted from her hair as her voice rose.

"Kufo, it's okay. You can come back once you help. That's it. Nothing bad will happen to you." I held out my hand, hoping she was going to grab it and leave with us. She screamed, flinching away.

"Let me try," Kal said as he pushed himself off the wall. The front of his hair was drenched with sweat. Lilja helped me up as Kallan took my place in front of her. "Come on, little bird. Let's go, I'll keep you safe. You help me and I keep you safe." He repeated the phrase, solidifying it as the true intent.

Her eyes flitted around the room, stopping at Kallan. He wiped his sweaty hand on his trousers before holding it out to Kufo. She sat up a little higher in the dugout, looking at him tentatively. She stuck out her head, biting the tip of his finger, just enough to draw blood. She licked her lips, the small amount of blood coating her teeth.

A fury of movement happened in a moment. Aidan drew his dagger, and Armand grabbed his sword, poking the blade centimeters away from her throat.

"Owe, little bird. That hurt." Kal drew his hand back, inspecting the cut before holding it with his shirt.

She screamed, "Blood good. Good blood means I trust you! It's fine, I'll go. I won't bite again." Kufo held up her hands, and her mouth turned into a grimace.

"Calm down," I squeaked to the boys, pulling Aidan's arm back.

"Let's head back," Kal said as he held out his hand. Blood welled at the tip of his finger.

"Not like I haven't had a cut on my finger before," he said, lightly, trying to calm both parties.

Kufo looked up before snatching Kallan's hand and blushing.

I raised an eyebrow at the touch. Kallan rubbed his thumb over her hand, looking ahead. Aidan led the way out. The night sky was delivering a full show as we emerged from the storm drain. The city was dark, limiting the light pollution to the sky. Stars littered the sky like tiny jewels.

"It's so beautiful here," I said, marveling at the art overcasting us.

"Yes, it is," Lilja agreed, kissing me on the top of my head.

"Finally, fresh air." Kallan took a big inhale before walking forward, still holding Kufo's hand.

The streets were dead as we made it back to the library. Keres and Cassia came into view as we turned onto the main street.

They rushed toward us. "Where have you guys been? We've been waiting here for an hour," Keres said. She gave us all a once-over, landing her sights on Kallan and Kufo. She raised her eyebrow, saying nothing about it.

"Sorry about that. We had a minor detour, but we found our next clue." Kallan finally stepped away from Kufo, allowing her to stand by herself. Her feathers had retracted except for one stray one, which stood straight up in the middle of her head.

"Clue? I don't know a clue." She held her hands together, looking at them as she spoke, her accent heavy. Clearly not getting the figure of speech.

"Before we continue, let's get to the place you found for us to stay. You found one, right?" I yawned, pulling my hair up. Even in the dark, cooler air, my hair was still damp with sweat.

"Cassia and I found a place nearby. It isn't glamorous, but it's enough for us all to fit." Keres looked Kufo up and down as if judging her soul. "Plus our pet."

I cringed at the wording. Alieta's face flashed before my eyes. "Please-"

"Keres, can we please not refer to Kufo as a pet?" Lilja's hand went around my back, rubbing little circles. I hadn't told her all the horrors of staying with Alieta. There hadn't been time. Yet somehow she knew, or at least suspected, some of them.

"Kufo is a person, Ker. She might help us, plus, look at her. Kufo doesn't exactly scream threat." Armand patted his sister's shoulder.

"Can we please show them the place we found? I'm exhausted, and Kallan smells like he's been in a sewer," Cassia whined. She looked to Keres, awaiting her answer. Kallan gave her a strangled laugh, not admitting he was, in fact, in a sewer not an hour before.

"Lead the way, captain. I can't say I want to smell whatever ambiance these guys rolled in either." Keres motioned to her, like a dramatic maid leading us into a mansion.

I couldn't help but smile at the interaction with them. Even though Keres and I were not exactly close, it was nice to see her be close with someone.

"Armand and Aidan, go get our packs and meet us back at our current accommodations. Keres go with so they don't go on any more quests," Lilja said as she followed Cassia.

Aidan lugged his pack into the building Cassia and Keres found. His glasses were on top of his head, pushing his hair back with them, making it stick up in random directions.

"You guys definitely weren't lying about this place, not being glamorous. This place looks terrible," Armand said as he dropped all our packs onto the ground. Keres slammed the door shut behind her as a chunk of plaster fell off the wall and onto the floor. Dust flying everywhere.

"Hey, you guys, try to find a place to stay in an environment that hates outsiders. This place is in disrepair, yes. But it also means other elves don't come here." Cassia had pulled her curly red hair up, a broom in hand. Its handle was broken in half, leaving it half the height it was supposed to be.

"She has a point," I piped in as I pushed the broken furniture out of the way. Cassia followed close behind me, pushing the dust and debris into one corner.

"I mean, Ebbon City had a hotel, and it was a secret city. Want me to blow this dust out of the house? One hand movement and I can get it to go away. It'll take less than a second." Armand grinned as he wiggled his fingers, trying to saturate us with his charm.

"No, because we don't know what spells they've set on Olken. If any of us use any type of magic, it could set off something. Better to be safe rather than sorry," Aidan said as he grabbed the spider-webbed bucket from the corner.

"Well, how can Birdie over there get excited and sprout feathers like flowers in the spring, and nothing happens?" Keres peered out of the crack in the shuttered window.

"All Aidan is saying is that we should be cautious with the magic usage." Lilja grabbed the other bucket lying in the opposite corner. The hair on the back of my neck stood up at the idea of someone or something magical watching over us. My mind flashed back to the shadow that appeared at the library.

"Let's clean up and then ask Kufo questions and go to bed." I yawned. I stretched, my muscles aching, whining for relief only a bath would give.

"Aidan, let's go get water, and I'll let you quiz Kufo once we get back in," Lilja said. She smirked at me as I yawned before turning to leave. As the door shut, I took the free moment to take in my surroundings. The building we chose appeared to be forgotten in time. The furniture lay uncovered, left to rot in the elements. Dishes lay dirty in a pile, waiting to be washed. Sand nearly covered every inch of the place, along with its partner in crime, dust. Pillars lined one side of the wall, opening up to a crumbly, dead garden in the middle of the courtyard. Dehydrated plants stood as memories of their heydays. I walked out into it, the night calming as I looked up. The fossilized plants snapped as I brushed up against them.

"I don't think anyone has been here for a long time," I said as Cassia called to me from the opposite side of the garden.

"I know, it's crazy. I imagine this place is really nice, all cleaned up. Keres and I think we found out why, too. Let me show you." She waved her hand, beckoning me.

A shiver ran through me, my sixth sense. I looked up, as a shadow moved on the roof. I stared at it as it disappeared. Was *someone there?*

"I think someone is on the roof," I said, crouching down, trying to conceal myself in the plants.

Cassia paused, as if trying to listen for any unusual sounds. Her eyes were in slits as she scanned the top of the building. "I don't see anyone, Elle. You're on edge. We've all been pushing ourselves too hard as of late. It's normal for your nerves to be on edge." She paused for a minute, sighing.

"If it makes you feel better, Keres and I walked through the entire building and the roof before we let everyone come here. This place has been empty for a long time. Now come on." She grabbed my elbow gently before guiding me into a room.

"It has been so empty for years. Something bad definitely happened here." She pointed into a lit room. I followed where her finger pointed. A large, deep red stain took up the circumference of a corner. Next to it was a decomposed corpse. Its flesh had rotted and dried. A thick layer of dust covered it, a natural mummy.

30

Kufo

I covered my mouth, my eyebrows raised. "Oh, gods. How long does it take a body to mummify?"

"With the weather, it's hard to tell," Keres said, leaning on the doorway. Her black hair was wet. She had somehow snuck away from the cleaning.

"A matter of months or even years. This hot air is very dry, no humidity, just wind. It dehydrates everything," Cassia spoke as Keres nodded, agreeing.

The rest of the room was empty of a struggle as if it were a surprise killing; an unnoticed murder. The person's personal effects remained untouched; a hairbrush was left on the dresser. Sheets from the bed crumpled off to one side. The only thing that had changed over time, the plaster had chipped off sporadically. What was once ornate tactile wallpaper, peeled off in places. The dust and sand blanketed the room like a shield.

"Where did you find the washroom? I'm dying for one," I said, crossing my arms to comfort myself. The figure from the rooftop flashed before my eyes again, as if Pavati attempted to warn me.

Cassia must have read the look on my face. "Don't worry. Keres and I cased the place before we brought you all here. What kind of people would we be if we didn't?"

"There's a washroom three doors down." Keres jutted her thumb down the dark hallway. Her water footprints lead the way.

I mock, saluted her. "Thank you, madam." Trying to ignore the feeling of panic. *It's anxiety.*

Going back to the main entrance, we had transformed. The dust and broken plaster no longer crumbled into piles on the floor. The ghosts of the past were pushed aside with each cleaning motion. Wooden furniture now stood proudly, dust and cobweb-free. Lilja stood up from washing the floor, her chest heaving, the rag in her hand hung loosely at her side.

"Lilja, you want to call it a night? We could use a bath." I looped my arms around her from behind, leaning my head on her back, giving her a small kiss. As I made contact with her, my heart paused its fluttering beats. I sighed with relief.

"Are you saying I smell?" Lilja teased, her voice light. She turned around in my arms, smelling her armpit, grimacing.

"Okay, I see your point," she chuckled, kissing my forehead.

"At least you can recognize that," Armand said, flicking water onto Liljas' back.

"Did you splash water on me?" She said, her voice loud, feigning being upset. She untangled herself from me to rush to Armand. He yelped, trying to back up. I laughed as he slipped onto the floor, falling straight on his back. Lilja knelt, putting him in a choke hold. Mussing his hair, like young siblings would do in a fight.

His face turned red.

"You dare splash water on your Queen?" Lilja said, pulling him into a headlock. He struggled, trying to get out of her grip. She pushed his face to the ground, her hand on his ear.

"Oh my Queen, you poor stinky thing," he said into the cool tile, smiling.

"Gods, you two be good. We're not children anymore." Keres whipped her towel in their direction, smacking both of them.

Cassia, Aidan, and I all laughed as they yelped. "Come on, my stinky highness," I said as I held out my hand to her, trying to save Armand. I pulled Lilja's hand, leading her to the washroom. Our footsteps pattered on the stone floor. Laughter from the rest of the crew hung in the air.

Kallan and Kufo were nowhere to be found as we opened the door. It was a simple setup. A large clay bowl sat in the corner of the room. A pipe hung over the bowl, and a bench sat over to the side.

Lilja turned on the water, allowing the steaming hot water to fill the basin. She pulled off my shirt, helping me undress. My heart swelled at the intimacy. "Even with the time we've had together, I'm always surprised by the roles you take on as queen," I said, worried about saying the wrong thing.

"Roles?" Lilja tilted her head, awaiting my reply as she began pulling down my trousers.

"I mean, even though you're on top, you never shy away from the work. Like earlier, you were cleaning on your hands and knees just like everyone else," I said, stepping out of the fabric. I crossed my arms as I stood there, exposed. My skin pebbled up from the cold.

"Why wouldn't I? Just because I am the Queen of Valdis does not mean I expect the world to be catered to me. Perhaps it is because Valdis has struggled to survive since my infancy. My– our people expect a lot from the leaders. They have struggled, food was scarce, and family was the same way. My parents were and are sick. They have worked so hard to protect the people in a way they think is best. I was angry for a long time about how the kingdom came to ruin and how my parents reacted. The people think my parents have done nothing to stop or to better the situation. My parents and their advisors were worried about an uprising. Which is partially why when I became of age, they passed it on to me."

Lilja paused as she lowered herself into the water.

"Do the people think the same about you?" I asked as the hot water hit my sore muscles.

She stared at me, a thoughtful expression flashed over her face before she answered. "When my parents and the people appointed me queen, I disappeared off the royal map. I left the castle. There had to be a way to help and better the situation. My team and I left, gathering food and supplies in ways I'm not proud of. But it left food on my subjects' tables and in their stomachs."

"So, by their standards, things are improving?" I asked as I lathered soap in my hand, rubbing her shoulders. The scars on her back were bumpy, a memory of the past. Hopefully, one she'd be able to talk about soon.

"I hope so. The blight, however, has worsened. Our people are suffering. When I was in the mountains recovering, I was helpless. News kept coming in, and I couldn't do anything to help. I will always work if the conditions continue to improve." She rolled her head back and forth, rubbing out any knots.

Lilja rotated in the tub, sloshing the water as she did so. "I will always work for us." She gripped my cheeks, pulling me in for a kiss.

I pulled away, my heart beating in my chest. My eyes searched her face before I leaned back in, capturing her lip. Lilja had taken me, my heart hers as I let her have my body. Lilja has been trying so hard to help the Valdis people. She was always trying to better the people around her. It was my turn to help them. Valdis needed strong people pulling it to the top, and I needed to be one of them.

"Can I ask you something?" I said as I looked at her.

"Of course you can. Nothing is off the table between us," she said, her lips thinning as she waited for me to ask.

"How did you get the scars on your back?" I leaned against the tub, allowing her the room to reply.

"It was from being whipped when I was playing pirate. At the time, we didn't know Cassia, so it was Keres, the boys, and I. We attacked an island called Nyrim. The ocean had been unruly for days. I was so seasick at first, a terrible captain of a ship, if I am being honest," she said, trying to keep her voice light.

"Nyrim was the second place we had hit. The first pillage we did went so well. When we arrived at Nyrim, we got cocky. The water was rocky, so we had thought the supply boats would be easy picking. We were wrong." Her eyes shone with pain, as if transported back in time. I grabbed her hand, grounding her.

"When we attacked, it was the dead of night. No one should have seen us coming. But somehow they did. I was the first to dock, and they surrounded me in seconds. Kallan had pulled the boat back immediately; otherwise, we would have lost our whole ship. Unfortunately, I was stuck on the ship with angry elves. They took their time punishing me." She shivered at the memory, pulling my hand to her lips.

"How long were you stuck on their ship?" I asked in a low voice, afraid that if I spoke louder, my voice would crack with emotion.

"A week. It was a week before the guys came to save me. Armand had pulled the wind away from the ship, leaving them motionless long enough for Kallan to ride right next to it. Aidan had thrown himself onto the ship. Before the Llidan incident, his fighting was at its peak. He cut down half of the ship's men, getting to me. Aidan found me in the brig, at the bottom of the ship. I was sick and my body was broken from the beatings they gave me," she said, her voice even, as if the pain had happened didn't affect her at all.

But I knew better. Her bottom lip trembled slightly. Her eyes were vacant as she relived a moment of the story. I pulled her into an embrace, holding her head to my bare chest.

Kallan POV

I pulled the remaining wallpaper off the wall. The room was small, but enough for Kufo to sleep in here alone and protected.

She sat in the corner, cleaning the floor. Her one feather still stood straight up on her head. I smirked as I moved to brushing the dust off the shelves.

Elowen and Lilja's forms took up the doorway, their hair wet and clean.

"Kufo, can you clarify what you said about Pavati being held?" Elowen bent down, leveling her height with her.

"Goddess and the clean water are together." Kufo kept her head down as she cleaned another dirty patch of floor.

Elle looked up at Lilja. "Clean water?"

"The river water is nasty. My father called it the 'no-touch' water. He claimed one touch of it would cause instant death. I was never bold enough to test the theory. With Pavati, the water is nice, purified," she said dejectedly, her words broken with the knowledge of two languages.

"Nasty how?" Lilja asked, her interest peaking.

"Poison, it's poison water. One step and dead," she said in a singsong-y voice like a nursery rhyme.

Lilja and I exchanged a look, *the blight.*

"Bad little river, for bad little kids. One step in, no step out. Bad little river, no step in," she sang as she scrubbed, her one feather bobbing with the tune. The world was forgotten to her; Kufo's experiences in life left her stunted. Her emotions and actions were more suited for a younger elf.

"Kufo, little bird. Can you show us?" I asked, my hand gripping the rag. *It wasn't right to ask.*

"No! No! No, that water is poison. I won't go," she screeched, scrambling to the corner.

We backed up, all our hands to our lips to quiet her. "Shh, little bird. Be quiet." I held up my hands in surrender.

"How about we give you money for your services?" Lilja said, rummaging through the change purse on her hip.

"Money?" Another feather popped out of her head before quickly popping back in. Clearly, the way to her heart. *She must have lived her entire life in poverty.*

"Yes, we will pay you. Lilja can pay you in exchange for your help," Elowen nodded eagerly. I smirked. Elowen, offering Lilja's coin, was humorous. Her voice had been stronger since we got her back, more assertive.

Lilja pulled out a gold coin and held it out to her. "I will show you how to get to the Pavati, but only if you pay me!" Kufo grabbed it quickly, not wanting Lilja to change her mind and take back the gold coin.

"Do you want another?" Lilja asked, holding out the coin.

"Yes! Give me!" She lunged forward, but not as fast as Lilja, who put the coin in her fist. Kufo talked oddly, as if she were unused to having full conversations with other people.

"Tsk, Tsk. Not yet, Kufo. I will give it to you once you bring us to the nasty water. Okay?" Lilja put the coin back in her coin purse.

Annoyance flickered through my mind as I watched Lilja speak to her before I tamped it down. Kufo needed to give up the information. Lilja was doing what needed to be done. Valdis had suffered immensely thus far, and we were finally within arm's reach of success.

"No, water is scary. I won't go unless you pay me more." She crossed her arms, looking out the slats of the window.

"Okay, Kufo. I guess I will keep all these coins in my purse." Lilja got up, turning around to leave.

"Wait! Okay, okay. I'll take you. Coins, please." She held her empty hand open. A grin plastered on her face, another feather popping up.

Elowen laughed before shaking her head. "Kufo, you can get the rest of the coins tomorrow. When we wake up, we'll head out."

"Kallan, let's get to bed." Lilja leaned into me. "Lock her in here until tomorrow morning. We will leave for this mysterious river after breakfast."

Elowen's face was grave as she stared at us, no doubt already knowing the words passing between us. Kufo was never part of the plan. Arriving at Olken Ridge and finding people there was a surprise. *Plans were meant to be changed; it was an integral part of success to adapt at a moment's notice,* my father's voice echoed in my head.

Overall, Kufo didn't appear to be a danger to anyone. Albeit fast, she nearly outran Armand and I earlier, and would have too if she hadn't hidden.

I gave her a small nod before looking back at Kufo. "Little bird, you're safe here. I'm going to lock you in, but I will let you out tomorrow."

"Safe?" Kufo said in a small voice, tilting her head to the side, watching Lilja and Elowen leave.

"Yes, safe. You sleep in here tonight, okay? Tomorrow we will go on an adventure." I backed toward the door.

"Safe. You'll let me out tomorrow," Kufo said, like she was manifesting the right answer.

"Goodnight, sleep tight," I said as I shut the door, propping a chair against the door handle.

Alieta POV

Uncle teetered his way into the inn room I occupied for the night. My hair pulled at my skin; it lay in a tight pleat from after my bath. Candlelight lit the room, and the shadows of the flames danced. My plate of food lay before me, a steaming pile of mashed potatoes and a meat I cared not to identify, made my mouth water.

"Your highness," he said, giving a curt bow of his head.

"Uncle," I waved my hand at him in a shooing motion. My other hand was already hovering over the fork that sat beside my meal.

"But your highness, I bring news of Elowen." His voice shook with age, a subtle smirk tugging at his lips. So small, someone without training would have missed it.

I folded my hands in my lap. His voice was an act. An act I was tired of.

One moment, he would go from appearing as a feeble old man, his voice frail with age. As if his vocal cords were worn out from repeated use. However, in a moment, his voice would switch to something much firmer. One that demanded attention.

"Go on, Uncle. I am tired and wish to sleep." Throwing out a yawn for good measure, staring at the space above him. Uninterested in looking him in the eye.

"My spies have noted Elowen and the Valdis team made it to Olken Ridge. Years ago, I influenced the leaders of the area. I have quite the connections to the north," he said, collapsing into the chair near the fireplace. My eye twitched as Uncle put his boots on the side table, where my decanter of wine sat.

"Well connected?" I leaned back in my chair, attempting to unravel the half-truths pouring from his mouth. My power thrummed under the surface, as if a volcano close to erupting. The heat spread to my fingertips, dangerously close to lighting.

"Yes, your highness. I was but a young general. I was on a pilgrimage of sorts, reaching Olken at the peak of its growth. The land was still green, albeit drying out, but still green," He rambled on. As older elves liked, my mind wandered before my patience snapped.

"Uncle! You were speaking of Elowen." I grabbed the fork, gripping it, shoveling food into my mouth.

"What? Oh, yes, Elowen. My spies confirmed Elowen has found her way to Olken Ridge. She appears to be with a group of Elves resembling Queen Lilja and her crew." Uncle turned his cane around, staring at the golden handle as it sparkled in the firelight. Though he appeared like a brittle old man, his heart had hardened as his skin sagged with age.

My ears rang as I glared at him. "Uncle, please tell me, instead of coming here first to babble to me about your bygone era, you told my team to ready themselves." I clenched my jaw as we stared at each other, the tension palpable.

"Of course I did, your highness. They'll be ready within the hour," he scoffed, as if the question was even necessary.

I paused for a second, the emotions rushing over me.

"Let them have a night of rest. The men have pushed themselves too hard these last few weeks. Between the failure at Isold and traveling to this town, they could use a few hours of fun and rest." I let the sentence come to a halt, letting the words sink in.

Uncle must not know the extent of my obsession. Elowen was mine; she appeared to be correct about Uncle. The more I thought about it, the more discrepancies appeared in his explanations. He knew a lot more than he wanted to admit.

He *was* more complicated than I wanted to believe, but that understanding made him dangerous. I could no longer put it past him to weaponize something I enjoyed.

I made a small cough before continuing, pushing past the myriad of thoughts exploding in my head. "As do you, Uncle, so please enjoy yourself. Have a drink, find someone to warm your bed for the night. Tomorrow we will head to Olken Ridge."

He made a face, but got up. As he reached the door, he mumbled a goodnight. I breathed a sigh of relief as the door clinked shut. I got up, pacing as my thoughts carried away from me. *What did I remember of Olken Ridge from my childhood classes?* Abandoned, the magic use was too high, and a massacre.

What's Elowen doing there?

I groaned, leaning over the desk, shoveling another forkful of mashed potatoes into my mouth. *I needed a drink.* Pulling on a cloak, I abandoned my food, leaving it behind to join the night.

Uncle wasn't what he seemed, and perhaps Elowen wasn't either. I once thought of Elowen as a timid, abused mouse. But she left me. Worse yet, she wasn't just running away from me, but apparently running toward Lilja. The woman who left her kingdom to rot from the blight. A blight, apparently, Uncle had a hand in orchestrating.

My head ached at the thoughts as I entered the nightlife.

The streets of Risho smelled of piss and alcohol as I meandered my way through it. Drunk shouts sounded off in the distance, and music flowed as I went on a search for a decent bar.

No one bothered me as I prowled. The hood disguised me enough to look like a late-night traveler. A rowdy bar caught my attention, two swinging doors marked the entrance, and a trough sat off to the side. One singular horse slept next to it; the reins were tied tightly to the fence in front of it. Music assaulted my ears as I walked in. Women of the night wiggled their hips in front of me, catching my eye.

One woman was short in stature. Her plumpness reminded me of what Elowen looked like when she first came into my possession. "Oh, hi, honey. Wanna have some fun?" She questioned me as we caught eyes.

"Maybe. You remind me of someone," I mumbled as I walked past her and to the bar that was currently calling my name.

"Oh well, honey, I can be anyone you want me to be. For a price, anyway. As long as you can pay, you can call me anything you want." She stuck out her lip as she talked, pouting.

Once I sat at the bar, I motioned to the bartender. "A beer, please. Also, get one for my friend here." I nodded to the whore.

She clapped her hands excitedly, making her way to the seat next to me. "My name is-" she started, but I held up my hand, stopping her. I dropped a couple of gold coins in her direction, not letting my eyes drift from the bartender pouring our beers.

"Your name is Elowen for the night, doll. Don't forget it." The bartender slid the beer down the line. The mug's contents burned as it slid down my throat, leaving a warm pit in my belly.

Elowen wanted me, the thought rambled in my head as the memory replayed in my head. She crawled into my bed, desperate for my touch.

"Keep them coming, bartender. I could use a night to forget." I swiped the beer meant for the whore, chugging it. I wiped my mouth with the back of my hand, leaning over to Elowen for the night. I pulled her face forward by her chin, kissing her. Her lips were soft against my own.

Another mug flew down the counter, and I caught it right before it ended on the floor. My other hand was already up her skirt.

She is confused and hurt. She doesn't know what she's missing out on. I don't understand what else I could have given her. Elowen could have had the whole kingdom at her disposal if she had stayed with me.

"Oh, honey, I can be her all night and day for as long as you'd like." She grinned as I pulled away, chugging the third glass of the night.

Tonight was going to be a long one.

"Damn, you reek. What did you do? Sleep with the pigs?" Fian said as she rammed through the door, a cigarette in her mouth unlit.

I groaned, nuzzling into my pillow, my arm around a soft body. *Elowen?* I thought as I opened one of my eyes to a slit. The bed sheet was draped over soft skin. My heart sank as I set upon her face, before anger replaced the feeling.

"Hey, you," I said as Fian poured me a glass of water.

The whore smiled sleepily at me. "Yes?"

"Get out," I said, my face neutral.

"What?" She whimpered, batting her eyelashes.

I rolled my eyes, gritting my teeth, shame washing through me. "I *said,* get out. Do you not understand the words coming out of my mouth? Leave."

"Come, pretty. You heard the lady, let's go." Fian grabbed the woman's elbow, pulling her up gentler than I would have been able to muster.

"Wait, my clothes," she whined. Her hair stuck up in all different directions, the back looking completely matted.

"Don't worry, I got it," Fian said, bending down to grab them, stuffing them into the woman's hands.

"Goodbye, forget tonight ever happened." Fian dug her hand into the change purse attached to her hip. She deposited coins in her hand, shutting the door in her face. Fian stared at the door for a second before pivoting around, stalking toward me like an angry animal.

"Alieta, what the fuck? Does she know who you are?" Fian said as she crossed her arms. She stood in front of my bed, her legs a shoulder's length apart, making her look more imposing than I already knew she was.

I moaned, wiping the liquid crusted on my cheek from the night. My head was pounding. *I overdid it last night.*

"No, I don't think so. We never go to the exchanging of names part of the introduction."

"Gods, I've never seen you like this. Are you okay?" She grabbed the pitcher on my desk, pouring more water into my half-empty glass. I sipped it, not wanting my stomach to feel worse.

"Yeah, I'm great. Can't you tell?" I stood up out of bed, naked. Not caring if Fian saw any part of it. Even though Fian was one of my closest friends, the thought of revealing my worries about Uncle pained me. Worse yet, the loss of Elowen ate at me. So close, yet the space between us nagged at me like a missing limb, a phantom pain of what was once there.

"Look, I understand as the Queen of Ardour, you have responsibilities to your subjects. That doesn't mean you have to do it alone.

I'm your friend, your highness. Even if I don't fully understand, I can listen." She moved around the room, picking up the clothes with two fingers, her arm outstretched, trying to keep them far away from her.

Fian dropped them onto the bed. I sipped the water, peering outside the window, looking out onto the street. She busied herself behind me as I thought about what she said.

"Put these on. You'll scar anyone who looks up into this window." She stuffed clothes into my free hand.

I rolled my eyes again. "Anyone unfortunate enough to look up, It will be their fault for seeing me like this. Not mine."

"The men are ready to roll out. I made sure none of them hit the mead and beer too hard. Apparently, I should have been watching you too," Fian said, pouring herself a glass of wine from the decanter, taking a sip as her eyes lit up. "This is excellent."

"Of course it's good, it's from my cellar. I do not need to be babysat. I am a full-grown woman. It was supposed to be fun. The whore, however, was an accident." I grimaced as I bent down, putting on my trousers; my head was pounding.

"Ah, yes, the whore was the 'mistake' I see. I've never seen you get sloshed before we head out on something, either. Will you tell your friend what's going on, or am I going to keep picking up the pieces, your Highness?" She stressed the last two words, holding up her finger to silence me. Fian headed to the door, opening it. Two of my servants nearly fell in. Stumbling upright, they walked in, their faces red at being caught listening.

They mumbled apologies before moving around my room in a flurry. In less than ten minutes, the servants had cleared the room, my clothes packed away along with all the papers strewn across my desk.

The servants pulled out my chests as Fian and I exchanged looks. It was clear she was trying to read my expression. I had taken years to learn how not to reflect anything. I was unreadable. I crossed the room, clasping her arm, pulling her in. "Daveed is not all he seems. He has plans I do not know the full extent of, and most irritatingly, Queen Lilja is alive and with my beloved."

Her eyes widened as she listened. "Elowen? I thought she drugged you to escape. She's your beloved?" Fian whispered harshly, trying to keep her voice low.

I nodded, my face grim. "What about Daveed? What do you know?" She asked.

"Elowen said he is the means of the blight. He is the reason Valdis is failing. The reason all of those people are dying." I choked up toward the end of my explanation. Elowen's face replaying in my head as she told me of my uncle. The disgust that had flashed across her face before pity had shone through. She thought me a monster. *Perhaps I was one.*

"Elowen told you all this?" Fian asked.

I nodded mutely.

"Well, that solves it then. She was messing with your brain." Fian pulled an unlit cigarette to her mouth.

"No, she wouldn't. Lilja has planted herself too deeply in her brain. What does Elowen have to gain by telling me of my uncle? You didn't see him in Isold, the way his anger took hold of him. Sometimes when I see him, it is like he is a younger, angrier elf. Uncle has stories that do not line up," I said through gritted teeth. She didn't understand. *No one will.*

Each time Elowen seemed to appear on the map, a mysterious connection would appear between Uncle and the leaders. Or his meandering conversations about bygone eras.

She put her forehead to mine, a thing we did when we thought the other was getting out of hand. "Alieta, I will monitor Daveed. You have my word. This mission is getting out of hand. When you sent me word of Isold, I rushed here to meet you. If the reason is to stop Valdis from starting a war on our own land, so be it. But to do all of this for Elowen is a fool's errand. You cannot force a woman to love you. You must find someone who wants you as well. Now, clean your face and let us head out."

Fian pulled away as I fought the tears threatening to pour down my face.

"Let us get to Olken Ridge and see what Uncle dearest was talking about." I strode out the open door, *one step closer to you*, I thought as we started on our journey to the desert. Twelve able-bodied elves and my two servants made up my company.

Fian rode close to me as we departed the small village we had housed ourselves in for the last few nights. I made a mental note to send a thank you to the mayor, even though our stay was unknown. The inn had been enjoyable, even the whore had been adequate.

Link, Fian's right-hand man, rode close to us. His muscles rippled through his nearly too small shirt. His black horse was almost the size of my large white stallion.

"It'll take around a day and a half to reach Olken. From there, we'll disperse through the ruins, looking for Valdis' crew as well as the topic of conversation this morning," Fian said to me, her voice trying to drown out the sounds of the galloping horses. Link nodded, already in the loop about the Daveed suspicions.

As if speaking about him caused him to materialize next to me. Daveed rode up next to me, his horse significantly smaller than mine.

"What topic?" he asked. His eyes gleamed with darkness as he stared at me, trying to pry my thoughts from my head.

"Elowen, Sir Daveed. Queen Alieta would like her back where she belongs," Fian said, her back straight as she looked ahead, not even looking at Uncle. Her quick reply saved me as I still scrambled for a response.

"Ah, I see." He nodded slowly, as if mulling over the answer.

"Don't worry, your highness. Elowen shall be in your hands within the week. Lilja will be a speck in the history books as we push her off the throne and capture- I mean unify our two kingdoms," he said, mumbling toward the end, pushing his horse to go faster and leaving me with my thoughts.

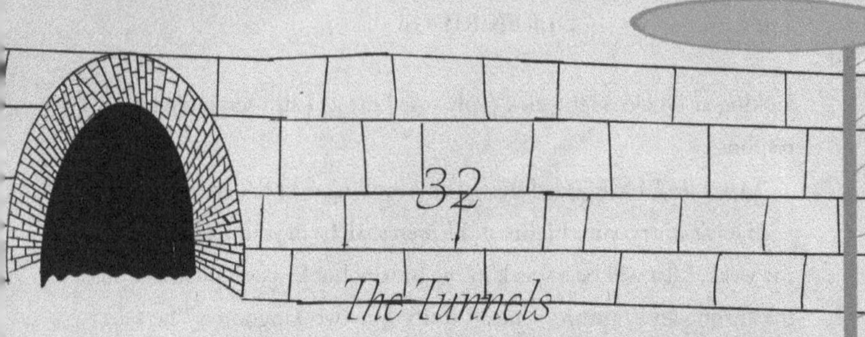

32

The Tunnels

Elowen POV

Lilja and Armand stared at Kallan, smirking. "Little bird, huh?" Armand teased as he made a bird shape with his hands.

Aidan stood behind Kallan, sending kissy faces in Kallan's direction.

His cheeks flushed with pink. "What are you guys talking about?"

"I've never seen you willingly stay in a cramped space before. Could it be because you like a certain little bird?" Lilja asked Kallan, her smirk grew into a full-blown smile, reaching ear to ear.

"What!? No, it's because I thought Armand would be the fastest. He has longer legs than I do. Look at his stocky form." He gestured to all of him.

"For God's sake, keep your minds out of the gutter. She's obviously a woman in trouble. You told me to help elves in need. That's precisely what I'm doing," Kallan grumbled before pushing past them. He grabbed his pack off the now clean floor, pulling out his blanket, and cocooning himself.

Lilja and Armand howled with laughter. I couldn't help but chuckle at their silliness, even though we faced danger and the unknown. These clowns always made it fun.

The sun lightly glowed on the horizon as we lay down to sleep. Bird songs filled the air along with the snores of Aidan and Keres. As darkness overcame me, I waited for the morrow.

"Rise and shine to the beautiful highnesses. Time to start the day, you know what they say. Early risers get the food." He stumbled over the words as he got confused about the wording.

I groaned, turning to Lilja's side, trying to avoid the booming voice yelling too early in the morning. We had fallen asleep as soon as we hit the floor, but my body protested as if I had half the amount of sleep. My joints ached, complaining of the feeling of the ground.

The traveling had caught up to me; perhaps the emotions I had tried so desperately to push away had finally emerged now that Lilja and I had reunited.

"Brother, let them sleep a bit more while we stock up. It won't delay us," Keres' voice piped up. Her response surprised me, and I was also grateful.

"Wake-y, wake-y." Kufo's voice called out, her voice annoyingly high. She sounded full of energy, no doubt ready to get paid. A black feather bobbed up and down as she pranced around the room.

"Armand, I swear to the Gods. It better be a decent time or I am going to wring your neck," Lilja grumbled as she sat up, untangling herself from me.

She stretched, yawning at the same time. "Come on, Elle, time to get up. Otherwise, this idiot will never shut up." Lilja smiled at me, her eyes roaming my disheveled body.

My cheeks reddened as I took her outstretched hand. "Can someone at least make coffee when they wake us up?" I half yawned, half talked. I finger-combed my hair, trying to get it to look somewhat clean.

"Already on it," Aidan said, holding out a glass to me with the black gold. The steam rolled off of it as I grabbed at it greedily, giving him a small smile. I blew on it before taking a large gulp right as Lilja grabbed it.

"Hey, that's mine," I whined, going to grab it from her. She held the glass up high to her mouth, holding out her arm to keep me far enough away as she gulped it down.

"What's yours is mine, sweetheart. We are engaged. Which means I am basically your problem forever." She grinned at me, handing my cup back to me, empty. I fought for my smile to remain as my heart ached.

Well, maybe not forever, I thought, turning away, blinking away tears. The sun had already warmed the air, and sweat stuck my hair to my forehead. I close my eyes, praying to Pavati, *please protect us when we come to find you. I need to get to you.* The dragon claw hung on my chest and seemed to burn into me as I turned to give my best award-winning smile back to the guys.

"Let's go find Pavati." I tried to keep my voice upbeat and confident as we readied to leave the abandoned house.

The outside was a different environment from the one we had left behind yesterday. People and carts crammed into the streets, their goods and services spread out through the crowd like chess pieces.

We layered Kufo in clothing with a scarf that covered her head, hiding any potential feathers. The Niphes book felt heavy in my bag as we traversed through the swarm of elves. Merchants shouted as they held up their products. Smells assaulted my nose as we passed the food stalls. My mouth watered as I diligently followed Kufo.

We kept walking, and people became fewer and fewer as we left the center of the city. Graffiti littered the walls. Buildings looked in disrepair, and the streets were quieter as we followed Kufo. She walked the streets with ease, her footsteps light and deliberate, following the shadows. My stomach grumbled as we rounded another street.

I'm hungry, I thought to Lilja. She smirked, turning her bag to the front and grabbing out a piece of dried meat. My cheeks reddened at her response as she continued talking. "Once we get our bearings, we will have a proper snack. Until then. This should hold you over."

I gnawed on it, savoring the seasonings and the saliva coating my mouth. As I took the last bite, the hairs on my neck stood at attention. My ears rang as if warning bells were inside them. I stiffened, my eyes slitting left to right.

"Lilja," I said through our bond.

"I feel it too, my darling," she replied, not needing me to finish the words that were weighing heavily on my heart. We were being watched.

Lilja tapped Kallan's shoulder, their years of friendship leaving them the ability to communicate nearly as well as us.

"Kufo, let's move a bit faster. I think someone is following us," Kallan said lowly, into Kufo's covered-up ear.

"FOLLOWED!?" She turned wildly, her eyes wide.

I looked up at the blue sky for a moment, trying to find the control to not raise my voice at her, but the moment was ruined by the shouts of our followers.

"Get her! Kufo, get back here!" A gruff man's voice yelled out.

My heart beat in my ears as we took off. "What do they want?" I asked, as I followed close to Lilja, who kept pace with me even though she could have been ahead of me in seconds.

"I'm not sure, but we are not staying to find out!" Our feet slapped the brick road as we rounded a dead end.

The sun was high in the sky as Kufo and Kallan pulled up a storm drain cover, their actions hurried.

"Who wants to go down first?" Lilja questioned as she peered down into the black hole. Armand stood at attention at the entrance to the street, his sword ready.

Everyone was silent before I spoke up. "I'll go," I shrugged, tightening the strap on my bag.

"Ha, no. Next volunteer." Lilja held up her finger. I rolled my eyes, making my way to the hole.

"We don't have time for this conversation. Someone has to go first. It might as well be me," I said as I sat on the ground, bracing my legs on the ladder. The metal was cool to the touch as I descended, creaking under my weight and clanking as I scaled down. Musty stale air filled my lungs as I coughed.

"Armand, come on. Move, soldier," Lilja barked out.

"I'm coming, Elle, don't die without me," Armand said as he jumped down, not bothering to use the ladder.

"Show off," I muttered, grinning as I turned away from him, crossing my arms.

He clapped me on my shoulder, his hand dwarfing it. "That's what happens when you have muscles."

"Who were they? Why were they following us? What's stopping them from coming down here and finishing what they were planning?" The questions spewed from my mouth as Lilja grunted, coming into contact with the sewer floor.

With a fist, she hit the curved brick wall, sending a collection of bricks where the entrance once was.

"Like that," Kallan said in a shaky voice as he tried to calm his breathing.

"This place is truly fascinating. Think about the time it took to create the tunnels underneath the town. What do you think came first? The tunnels or the town?" Aidan said with perfect timing to dispel the tension in the air. His hair was getting long, and the top part grew past his ears. His glasses sat at the tip of his nose, yet again.

"That feels like a chicken question," Kallan said as he traveled down next, Kufo right behind him. I coughed, attempting to cover a laugh.

"The tunnels here are big, many turns. Easy to get lost. No get separated," Kufo said, stumbling over the words as she talked, still not used to stringing together sentences. She wagged her finger at us. Armand grabbed at Kallan's bag.

"What are you doing? If you're going to manhandle me, at least buy me a drink first," Kallan said, trying to wiggle him off. "And if I'm not mistaken, this place is not a bar, so get off of me."

"Hold still, you scrawny elf. I'm trying to grab the glowing stone," Armand said as Kallan continued to try and wiggle away from him.

"No, no light. The light is a bad idea here." Kufo smacked Armand's hand away from the satchel.

"Alright, birdie, no light. Lead the way to the river." Armand held up his hands in mock surrender.

"No money first, then I will show you," Kufo said as she looked at Lilja, holding out her hand.

"You get one more coin. You can have the rest once we get to the river. Once you get the rest of us there safely, *alive*." She tossed Kufo the coin as she stressed the last word.

"Now, lead the way, birdie," Armand said as he cracked his neck. His other hand was on the hilt of his sword, and Aidan sketched in his journal behind me. Furiously, scribbling in notes and drawings.

The ground was dry as we began our trek; the walls were covered in random drawings. They started with cute flowers and made up animals with large ears that covered the smooth brick. As we ventured deeper into the tunnels, the tune changed, becoming less and less legible. Black swirls covered the walls; one large black dot covered a portion of the brick. Two white spots stood out on it, as if eyes were watching our every move.

"That's not terrifying at all," Keres said, moving closer to Cassia. I nodded mutely, not trusting my voice to sound brave.

"That's one of the monsters," Kufo said quietly as she pointed at it. "The monster bad." She spat at it, as if warding it off before continuing. Lilja snaked her hand into mine, pulling me along, as if she was worried the monster would run away with me.

33

The River

Water dripped somewhere. The smell of mold was more prevalent. I stood arm to arm with Lilja, my eyes barely seeing a step in front of me. It was almost like Kufo could see in the dark. She moved with ease in the tunnels. We could no longer hear the life happening on the top of the Ridge; only the rats, water, and our own footsteps.

A light illuminated on the wall, making me nearly jump out of my skin. I fought back the yelp of fear that threatened to ricochet across the bricks.

"Don't worry. This is my home." Kufo bounced excitedly. The eagerness in her voice was evident. Lilja and I exchanged looks as my own hand went to the small dagger that sat on my hip.

Then another light lit up further down the tunnel, as if it could sense our motions. We rounded the corner of one of the many tunnels we turned into. Crates and small wooden structures filled our view. Built as storage, anything that could be used was used. Paper hung on the outside of the walls, and blankets hung as a 'door'. A small fire was in a makeshift pit. An older elf stood next to it, his hands outstretched over it as if he were cold.

What once was long black hair was now streaked with gray and white with age. His face showed many seasons of life.

"Flotwihaw, twa twaru' dniwo," Kufo squealed as she launched herself toward him. He looked up, surprised, a grin growing on his face. His long mustache swayed as he held open his arms, and my heart sank a little. *I would never have that.*

"Flotwihaw, shwaw twi dyo fe. Twa proddage ru!" She shoved her hand in her purse, grabbed out the coins, and put them in his hand. He looked down at the coins, his face lighting up before confusion flashed over it.

His eyes went to slits as he looked up at us and then back to his daughter. "What have you asked my daughter to do?" He questioned us, his voice deep and rough.

"We need her to take us to the river." I stepped forward, Lilja matching my step.

"The river," he shouted, spitting to the side as if the word left a bad taste in his mouth. He threw the money back at us. Kufo stood behind him, her mouth agape.

Lilja caught the coins before they had the chance to pelt me. "Sir, with all due respect. Kufo is willing if we pay her. She's a full-fledged adult. She may do what she pleases." Liljas' vein popped in her neck, a red blush creeping up her neck.

"We're trying to find the Goddess. We need her help." I rummaged in my satchel, pulling out the book with the word *Pavati* on it. I tapped it, as if pleading for him to let Kufo take us.

"My daughter may be an adult, but she's never been one to interact with topsiders. Kufo cannot tell when someone like you are taking advantage of her. She's ignorant of the dangers of the world. The Acolytes will follow you here. You have exposed my family to danger." He pointed his knobby finger at us.

"Keep your money and go back up," he grumbled, turning away from us and limping to his hut.

"Taking advantage of her?! I will have you know we would never do something like that. We weren't followed, and we'll pay her for her assistance to the river. Pavati needs our help." I stomped my foot like a child, but I didn't care.

"I did not come this far, endure this much pain, just for some grumpy old man to tell me what his grown daughter can and cannot do. If you won't let her show us, then draw me a fucking map." I opened the book, grabbing a quill from my bag. He stood there, his mouth open with shock. I shoved the feather in his hand, holding the book open as if I were the table.

The people behind me said nothing as I stood there. I couldn't tell if I was shaking or if he was as he drew the outlines of the hallways with his arthritic hands. A tear ran down my face as I tried to contain the anger I felt simmering at the top.

"There, now get out of my camp. It should take you another day or two of travel to get to the river. Do not under any means necessary, go into the water. It's poison, it *will* kill you. Follow it. Another day of travel, maybe, and you'll reach what some think is the entrance to Pavati's true and last shrine. It's a nice fairy tale for the last of the Olken Fae that live down here. I've lived in Olken Ridge my whole life and never seen hide or hair of the Goddess, so I doubt you will either."

I mouthed a word of gratitude, not trusting my voice not to crack with emotion. "Let's get going, thank you for your help, sir," Lilja said. Her eyes were on me the whole time, concerned.

I ripped the page out of the book, shoving it into Aidan's hands. My heart ached from the crime of defiling a book. "Here, lead the way," I grumbled, allowing myself to fall behind the others, and Lilja followed.

Do you want to talk about it, she projected to me.

No, I shoved the wall down between us. A stray tear ran down my cheek, and it took a while for anyone to talk. Kallan spoke up first.

"So, Aidan, what kind of map did this old coward draw?" Kallan asked, holding out his hand toward him. Kallan's face was pale, and guilt tugged at my heartstrings as his fear dawned on me.

I wasn't the only one hurting. "This is barely decipherable at best. His hands must be extremely arthritic. He could hardly hold the quill. You saw him shake, as he drew it." Aidan's hand held the map, twisting it back and forth, as if it would suddenly make it easier to read.

Kallan walked behind him, peering over his shoulder. "Damn, you're right. We should have just taken Kufo with us. She was pretty to look at, too," he sighed, pulling back farther to walk next to Cassia.

"So you admit there was something!" Armand said, grinning. I rolled my eyes despite the anger I felt, I smiled.

"No, I just said she was pretty. That's it," Kallan scoffed, his face turning pink.

"I don't know, Kallan. Certainly sounds like you had a thing for your 'lil bird, '" Aidan said, still staring at the map.

"I can say a girl is pretty, and not want to have a thing with them. I think Elowen is pretty, but I don't want to get with her," he shouted indignantly, crossing his arms like he hit the nail on the head.

"You forget, Kallan, she wouldn't even want to be with you because she has me," Lilja said as she placed her arm around me, bringing me closer, wiggling her eyebrows at Kal.

I kissed her arm; it was clear by the topic of conversation they were trying to sway the mood that had blanketed us.

Cassia yawned, dark circles grew underneath her eyes since the last time I had looked at her.

The team seemed sluggish as we neared the end of one of the last turns. *We were so close to our goal. While they were exhausted, I was filled with newfound energy and anger.*

"Let us stop for the night," I announced, earning groans of acceptance.

"Finally," Keres said as she threw her pack to the closest dry spot, launching herself on top of it.

"Thanks the gods, I'm so tired," Armand said, pulling a thin blanket from his pack.

"Aw, my poor little Armand, want me to wrap it around you?" Kallan teased, pouting before breaking into a grin.

"Sure, want to snuggle with me, too?" Armand laughed, blowing him a kiss. "Do you think I'm pretty, too?" Aidan asked, batting his eyelashes in Kallan's direction.

I rolled my eyes at them. "Are you sure these clowns are not a couple?" I asked Lilja, laughing a little.

"You know, I would definitely not be surprised if they were one," she said, without even looking at her, I could hear the smile on her lips.

"Sorry, ladies, no entertainment for you. We have our eyes on the opposite sex." Armand pushed his hair out of his eyes, clearing it from his face. He stuck out his chin as if he was trying to smolder us to death.

"Speak for yourself," Kallan laughed, launching himself at Armand, his lips in an obnoxious pucker.

"Well, keep your eyes off my woman. She is already taken." She grabbed my hand as she spoke, as if trying to show off the ring she had proposed to me with. Her smile faltered. "As soon as we get back to Valdis, she is gonna be stuck to my hip and married to me." She grinned again, her eyes shining as she looked forward to the future.

What future was that? Pavati needed my blood to help with the spell. To release the curse on the land. What kind of life would Lilja run without me in the picture? I shook my head as if trying to push the thoughts out of my head.

It doesn't matter, I told myself. Her home and her life will be saved. She could find someone else to be with after I was gone.

I turned from the group, putting my blanket around my shoulders. The wall was cool to the touch as I settled my back on it, sending shivers up my spine. Lilja sat next to me, and she outstretched her hand to hold mine, but I pulled back. Her eyes searched mine for an answer.

Are you okay? She projected to me with concern etched all over her face. I looked away from her, forcing myself to nod, yes.

Was it right to do this? The attention we give each other. Should I just pull away from her completely to lessen the hurt of losing me?

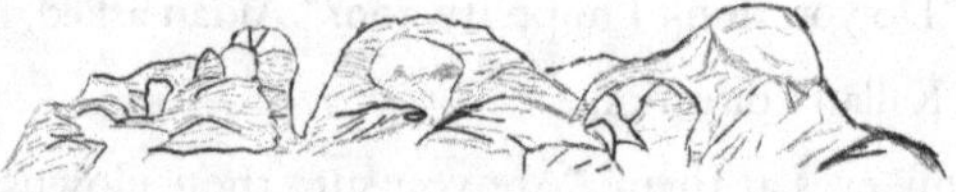

"Let's go, Elowen. We must move faster," Belle yelled at me. The trees and plants shielded the moonlight from reaching us. The dark was almost suffocating. Branches pulled at my skin and my clothes, nicking me as we rushed through the dense forest.

My heartbeat threatened to pop out of my chest. Somewhere, an owl called out. Shouts and dogs barking filled the air behind us. A sense of danger shot through me.

The scar on my arm ached, the memories of the past resurfacing as I forced myself to move in the darkness.

"Move, Elowen, you have to move faster," Belle shouted. Somehow, she had gotten ahead of me as the past plagued me. She stood on top of a large boulder. Belle was just like I remembered, tall and beautiful. Her brown hair cascading down her shoulders loose, as if she had snuck out at night again. We must have gotten caught, again.

I fell, my foot twisting at an unnatural angle as I snagged myself on a root. Pain shot up my leg. "I can't! Leave without me! I'll slow them down for you," I sobbed as I waved my hand in the air.

She had to move, she had to. She needed to survive this time. I can't be responsible twice.

Belle stood there for a moment, as if time had stood still. Her form shook as she morphed into Alieta. In an instant, she was in front of me, pulling me to my feet. "You left me! Me?" She said, like it was the most incredulous thing.

"You left me! I will come for you! I'm coming for you, darling."

I awoke with a start, sitting up. Sweat running down my face along with tears. Snore's filled the tunnel, as I tried to catch my breath. "Shh, it's okay, Elle. What's wrong? Did you have a bad dream?" Lilja sat up next to me, rubbing my back in little circle motions.

"I can't, I can't breathe," I gasped, standing, teetering as I stumbled down the hall away from the others. *They couldn't see how fragile I still was. I was strong; I didn't need anyone.* I repeated the mantra in my head as I gasped, willing for the air to reinflate my lungs.

I placed my hands on the wall, bracing myself. My stomach was rolling around last night's measly dinner. My heartbeat in my throat as my ears rang.

Calm down. Calm down. Just breathe, my inner voice chanted to me. Lilja was close behind, her eyes filled with worry and uncertainty as she stood close by. It was unusual to see her unsure of what to do. I knew she wanted to help, but she didn't know how.

My stomach lost the battle as my dinner clawed its way up my throat. I sobbed, nearly choking on the vomit as I spat off to the side.

Fear coursed through my body. Alieta was coming. There was a certainty to the thought as my breathing calmed. Maybe it was something in the air or even something in the tunnel systems underneath Olken. But someone was telling me, showing me. That Alieta was on the way. For me. She was coming for me. Maybe with whoever the Acolytes were?

I pushed my forehead onto the wall, allowing the bricks to cool me down. Sweat ran down the tip of my nose, falling onto the ground. With my head still against the wall, I turned to look at Lilja. She had inched herself closer. Barely an arm's length away. "She's coming," I said with such firmness it scared even me.

"Who is baby?" Lilja raised an eyebrow. Somewhere water dripped behind me, a rush of air following, sending a chill up my spine. It was as if the walls themselves listened for my answer.

"Alieta, she called to me. She called to me in my dream." I choked back the cry that wanted to come out. Tears trailed down my cheeks as I rushed into Lilja's arms.

"She won't let me go. I didn't mean for this to happen." I cried harder as she squeezed me. It's as if she were making sure I existed in the same space with her, next to her. Still hers.

"Don't worry, Elowen. Okay." She grabbed my face, forcing me to look her in the eye.

"I would let the world burn before I let anyone take you from me, as long as you'll have me and want me. The Gods couldn't separate us. So Queen Alieta could try, but she will fail." Her eyes hardened as she spoke to me, filled with a resolve that would make even the strongest falter.

34

Arrival of a Certain Guest

Alieta POV

The energy was high as we reached the steps of Olken Ridge, like the quiet excitement a child feels before the next great day. Fian and Link stood close to me as we climbed the steps. The horses seemed less excited than their Elven counterparts. They neighed nervously as we followed them up the stones.

"The story of Olken Ridge, taught to you young elves, is wrong. A few facts are indeed correct. As you can see, the land surrounding Olken is barren. Magic has sucked the life away from the land, it is true. However, the Olken Elves that lived here did not abandon or evacuate the site you see today. They adapted." Uncle spoke as he talked. His voice wasn't as shaky as it usually was, but strong.

Wrong? If my tutors purposely misled my understanding of Olken Ridge's history, what else did I not know? Warning bells rang in my ears, I made a mental note to have guards investigate Uncle's books when we arrived back in Ardour.

We reached the top of the steps, Fian and I exchanged looks. The front few streets were barren, the building dilapidated beyond repair. The roads were covered with sand as time absorbed them once again, as an offering to the land. A wall stood on the horizon, and two large doors marked the entrance to the beyond.

"Let's go," I said, motioning for my people to follow me.

"No, this way. I shall show you the most efficient way." Uncle held up his hand, wagging his finger, taunting me with my ignorance of the situation. Anger simmered in the pit of my chest, forcing myself to smile and nod. The heat from the sun only further encouraged it. My fire called to me, warming the tips of my fingertips. I pushed the feeling down, shaking my head. *Anger will not get the best of me*, I thought, following Uncle.

He hurried, his head down as he avoided the sun beating down on him. Streets of broken houses away, we stopped. Sand-crusted crates stood in front of a dead-end street. A land forgotten to be absorbed by the earth.

"You move these crates, and be quiet about it," Uncle said to Link. He leaned against the wall, watching as the three large crates were moved, revealing a large hole. The wall that separated the city was clean and well-kept. The top of the wall appeared to be unmanned; no guards patrolled. Not that I could see, anyway.

Dro stood next to Uncle. His hand was hovering over the handle of his sword. Dro was the manpower of Uncle's brain; his right-hand man. Older than me by twice my age, he's been in the company of my uncle since I was a child.

"Now, Dro, descend and ensure the coast is clear." Uncle flicked his hand, motioning for him to be quick about it. Dro's jaw clenched, and he tied up his hair.

"Yes, sir." Dro gave one last look at our surroundings before dropping into blackness.

"What's down there, Uncle? Can we not enter the front door?" I asked.

"All clear, sir." Dro's voice came out of the darkness. The whites of his eyes were barely visible.

"Your highness, we can't very well just go through the door and go unnoticed. If we did, Lilja and precious Elowen would be sure to hear of the newcomers to the Ridge. With the reputation they have, do you think they get visitors? The word of our arrival by the public is what we don't want."

Falling silent, I mulled over his reply. I couldn't help but agree with his logic. "I'll go down next." My hands cooled as I touched the metal ladder rusted with time. The rungs creaked but were still strong enough to hold as we descended into the blackness.

I needed to find out what else Uncle was keeping from me, tactfully.

Elowen POV

Lilja had believed me without question last night. We moved quicker than before. The team and I had woken up early to get closer to our goal.

No one noticed my disheveled appearance and dark circles, or at least they had the decency not to mention it. My hair felt like a nest, an inviting home to the rats running in these sewers.

Lilja held my hand as we walked, as if she let go, I would dissolve into a puddle of tears. The dragon claw sat heavily on my chest as we pushed forward.

"After this turn, the river should be right there," Aidan said. The sound of water solidified his map-reading capabilities.

As we turned the corner, a putrid smell permeated our noses. Keres gagged, covering her mouth. "What is that god's awful smell?"

"The poison," Lilja said. She inched toward the water in the canal, peering down into it.

"You can't even tell how deep it is." Kallan looked down.

"What do we do now?" Cassia looked at Lilja and then at me.

"Can you sense any clean water?" I asked Cassia, but she shook her head.

"Then I-I don't know." The words left my mouth anxiously, my blood pressure rising. *What did we do next? How do we find Pavati from here?*

A long pause filled the air before Lilja grabbed me gently by the arm, pulling me aside. Her eyes searched mine. I fought the instinct to squirm under her touch. She always had a way with me, her gaze unnerving. In a way, I couldn't understand why she loved me so much. Was it fate alone that attracted her to me? Or was she attracted to me before she realized? I pushed the thoughts down. *I'll spiral if I think about that for too long.*

"Did Pavati give you any indications about how to find her?" Her hand brushed my sides mindlessly. Aidan and Kallan argued about something by the river, and Kallan raised his eyebrow as he shook his head vehemently.

"No, she said, to acquire ingredients and come to Olken Ridge. Pavati never even warned me that the Olken people were alive." I said in a whisper-yell, not wanting to show weakness to the rest of the group. My hands were in fists at my sides, my nails almost cutting into my palms as a thought crossed my mind.

I scrambled to my satchel, grabbing the book. This is all I have in connection to her, the Niphes book. The cover frayed long before I got hold of it. With everything that had happened on our trip thus far, the book had gone through further wear and tear. A few pages had jumped from the stitches binding the book together.

The title shone proudly, as if taunting me with my ignorance. "Maybe I can reach her if I focus on the book. She can contact me. I should be able to talk to her." Hope flickered in my chest. *This was the way.* Lilja gave me a small smile, kissing my forehead before whipping her head around to glare at Aidan and Kallan.

"Gentlemen, if I can even call you that," she grumbled as she spoke. Her voice was light, even though her expression said otherwise.

"What in the Gods' names are you complaining about? I swear, little girls complain less." She pinched the bridge of her nose as I inched away from her. The river hurried by next to us in the canal channel. It was as if the water was being courteous not to splash, even though it rushed like a great rapid. No water sprayed the stones beside it.

I sat down, sitting on my pack to keep myself comfortable, clutching Pavati's book. I willed myself to quiet my mind, letting the sounds of water wash away the stray thoughts. *Pavati? Can you hear me?* I called out to her.

The inside of my mind was quiet, dark. The brick wall that I had built to protect myself stood around the sides. It was empty, consumed by fear and guilt as I followed through with the plan that would end with my demise. It seemed the closer I got to my goal, my happiness waned. The flowers and plants that once lived rent-free in my mind palace, gone, replaced with nothingness.

I walked up to the metaphysical brick wall that protected me, smacking against it. "Pavati? Please, I need to talk," I said again. A brick moved, shifting, causing the wall to crumble at my feet as my subconscious calmed.

"Alwyn, this is not how the Niphes book works. You know that," Leland said, his hands crossed in his lap, rocking in the chair by the fireplace. I looked around the room, and it was the same one from our last meeting. Books and trinkets piled to the ceiling, fire from the hearth, and shadows danced along the books like a puppet show.

"Hello, Leland," I gave a small curtsey. "I'm aware this wasn't the book's intended purpose. I need to find her. We found the poison river, but how do we find her? Cassia cannot sense the clean water." I crouched, outstretching my hands to the fireplace, letting the heat to sink into my bones. *Of course, Leland, the* Overseerer of Fate, *is stopping me. Can't anything be easy?*

He smiled at me, a hollow one. The one given when an argument is soon to be lost. "Alwyn, my dear. Pavati has already given you the clues to find her. You just have to listen."

"She didn't reveal how to get this far. I did, I mean my team, and I did." I crossed my arms, wanting to whine like a child.

"She has Alwyn. You just need to learn to listen." His old-time riddled body got up from the chair, shuffling toward me. His small form towered over my crouched body.

"Goodbye, Alwyn. Ardour is here. That is all I can tell you. Follow your gut." He held up his finger, poking right between my eyes. My eyes widened, my arms flayed as I lost the balance that kept me upright.

Leland laughed at my surprise as I fell into the fire.

I screamed, falling backward, and groaned as I met the hard stone floor of the canal room.

"What? What is it?!" Armand flung himself up from the floor, half asleep. His hair spiked up in every other position as he fumbled with his sword, dropping it.

Lilja was the first to reach me. "Are you okay? Did you speak with her?" Dark circles hung below her eyes.

She hugged me, her strong arms wrapping around me, making me feel small.

"Leland pushed me into his fire." I patted my body, checking for burns. Finding none, I continued. "He wouldn't let me talk to her. He lectured me, saying she already gave me the clues I needed to know."

"Gods are always so cryptic," Cassia said. She had cocooned herself in her bedding and cloak. Her face almost covered by blankets, she made no effort to move.

"So what do we do?" Keres asked. She sat up, untangling her hair with her fingers.

My stomach rolled around in my abdomen. *What clues had Pavati given me? The book!* Realization dawned on me.

All the water from the rivers comes from Pavati. Follow the water, my inner voice called to me, like it's the easiest answer.

Anxiety crept up my throat at the idea of following poison water. *I wish there were another way.* I pushed it back down as I looked at Lilja to answer. "We follow where the water is coming from. It has to hold some sort of answer to where Pavati's being held."

"Ooh! Then I can see how Olken people built their irrigation systems!" Aidan said, looking up from his notebook.

"Way to look at the bright side." Kallan clapped him on the shoulder.

"Owe, that hurt," Aidan said, grimacing.

"That's for suggesting we should throw a rat in the water," Kallan said. "We don't need a reputation around canals. One incident is enough." I raised an eyebrow at his comment, not saying anything. *What canal incident?*

"A rat? You'd throw a poor little rat in that poison water?" Keres asked, her hand flying to her heart.

"That's pretty terrible," Armand agreed, finally fixing his hair and righting himself. Clearly embarrassed by his wake-up call.

Aidan huffed, pushing his glasses up where they were supposed to be. "I said it was terrible, like I told Kallan, it's for science! We're the first of Valdis to travel this far in hundreds of years. The first to write about the blight in exquisite detail. This is history!" He exclaimed, snapping his journal closed, picking up his supplies off the ground, and stuffing them into his bag.

"We're history in the making," I whispered, standing up. *I'm closer to history than my friends. Who would live more years without me than with?* My eyes teared up at the thought before I pushed it down.

I looked up at the ceiling, summoning the courage to continue. "Let's go. Pavati is waiting."

35

Clearing Up

I couldn't put my finger on it. It was as if eyes followed me while we followed the water in the canal. *One wrong slip equals death*, is what Kufo's dad said. It seemed like words to abide by. Not wanting to test out the theory, we kept close to the wall.

"Is it me, or did the smell get significantly less worse?" Cassia said, taking a deep breath in, her hands on her hips.

I paused, taking a tentative, big breath in. "Maybe we got used to it?"

"No, I think Cassia is right. The water looks clearer here. I can even see more. I can almost see the bottom." Kallan inched toward the edge, looking down.

"Cassia, can you sense any clean water?" Lilja asked her.

"No-," she said. The words from her mouth were interrupted as warmth bloomed on my leg, where my satchel lay as if something inside was on fire. I gasped, pulling away from Lilja and the bag away from my body, dropping it on the ground.

I crouched down, pulling my bag open. Everything appeared visually normal. I reached my hand in for the book, biting back a yelp as I grabbed it. It felt red-hot, enough to leave blisters on my fingertips. With all eyes on me, I flipped open the book, and stars flew from it. With their help, Pavati's form grew whole.

Though not the first time watching, my mouth gaped with amazement. The beauty and the grace were astounding; her aura was addicting to stare at.

"Alwyn, the time grows near. Ardour is back on Olken soil. They disrupt the flow of my water once more. The Acolytes have begun moving once again. The scale is tipping; one wrong move and it will tip in the other's favor. You are close, my Alwyn. Move fast, and Valdis might yet be safe." Her small body, which materialized out of the book, disappeared. The stars forming her body dissipated, leaving the book in its place, vacant of her power.

What did she say? Lilja projected to me.

"It's like I suspected," I said, a shiver going down my spine.

"Ardour is here. Alieta and Daveed are here on Olken Ridge." Bile crept up my throat in disgust as I stared at the water rushing by us. *Maybe it's easier to jump in?*

Armand groaned, turning around to hide his facial expression. Anger radiated off of all of them.

"What do we do now?" Cassia asked us.

"The answer is clear, Cassia. We find Pavati, give these ingredients, and be on our way. She can finish the rest, and we can get off this hellhole of a rock and return home where we're needed," Keres said, awkwardly patting her brother on the shoulder as if petting him like a common pet was sufficient. Although Armand's and Keres' bond differed from most siblings, love was still present.

Aidan glared at the map Kufo's dad drew us intently, as if a hidden mark illuminated a way otherwise unseen. "Nothing on this map will help us!" He crumbled the paper up into a ball before chucking it into the river rushing by us.

"Aidan! We needed that!" I said, running to the edge. Lilja's hands grabbed onto my arms, yanking me back from the edge. Her grip was firm enough I would probably have a bruise.

"Elowen, NO! Don't be ridiculous. I can't lose you. It is a piece of paper." Her voice boomed, echoing along the tunnel. With the force of Lilja and me moving away from each other, she stumbled, losing her balance. We were tipping toward the water, to our death.

Everyone seemed to lunge for us. Kallan was the first to grab onto us. He was always close by Lilja, yanking us to safety. All three of us fell backward, away from the poisonous liquid.

"I want it on the record, I wasn't going into the water!" Tugging myself free from Kallan's and Lilja's grasp, I get up. With my eyes on the tunnel before me, I kept walking. Anger rolling off of me.

"Geez, Aidan. Did you really have to throw the map?" Armand piped in. *Thump.*

"OW! Lilja!" Aidan yelped. "That hurt. It was useless; the map was bringing us no closer to Pavati. The damn thing was barely legible; we made it thus far on luck alone."

"You know what hurts? My heart, you damn near gave me a heart attack." Lilja fumed.

"Yeah, why throw the only map of the tunnels we had into the water? I thought our little Elowen was going swimming for that shit," Kallan said.

"For the last-" I started to speak as a feathered hand reached out. I screamed, stumbling backward. The feathered form materialized in front of me, out of the darkness. A man, if you could even call him, stood before me. Unlike Kufo, who had a handful of feathers protrude over her face when excited. This elf had hundreds, if not thousands, of feathers of varying sizes coming out of his skin. It was almost painful looking, his skin pink and angry where they protruded.

A rustle of movement happened behind me, no doubt the rest of the team pulling their weapons.

"Well, hello-*caw*- my pretty,-*caw*-" he ticked his head back and forth, taking in a breath.

His eyes widened. "A human." His beak clapped shut and open, making a clicking sound. A sound off to signal the rest of his crew. Olken elves, once thought to be killed off in genocide, surrounded us. Their heads were ticking back and forth in unison, sending a shiver of fear down my spine as if the magic coursing through their bodies threatened to take over.

"A whole meal! *Caw.*" One clapped, with its feathered hands. The sound was almost inaudible.

"Fat chance," Lilja's voice sounded behind me. Her arm pulled me behind her, making me jump with the sudden touch.

"*Caw*, bold. A little fight will stimulate my digestive system," the man before us said.

"Why don't we talk about this? Can we come up with an agreement?" Aidan's voice sounded hopeful. I took a glance behind me to see him holding his journal to his chest, one hand hovering over the hilt of his sword.

"Talk? *Caw*- no. It will please Kayi when I bring him your bones, *caw*," he said.

It was clear whatever magic was used to transform them had ended badly; the line between elf and animal blurred. The unintentional sounds came out in between his words. *Maybe enough to turn animalistic, like the Ossory wolves,* I thought. My heart pounded as if in a cage, beating through the bars tightly.

Kayi?

"Eat, yes. *Caw*!" There were five of them. How they manifested from the shadows was a mystery.

"Fat chance of that chicken," I said, reaching forward as the man in front of me lunged for Lilja, his claws outstretched.

"Chicken?! *Caw*! No, Gee is not a chicken. *CAW*!" His voice became increasingly manic, jumping away from my blade.

"Kill them *-caw*!" He screamed, his voice strangled like he wanted to crow instead. They moved in and out of darkness like phantoms. With Liljas back against mine, we fought like synchronized dancers, twisting and swinging our blades with deadly accuracy.

The Olken elves pulled at our skin and clothes with their razor-sharp claws. Pain shot across my cheek as he swiped at me. I yelped, my stance faltering as I pulled my hand to my face.

Lilja pushed me further back, her eyes darkening with a deadly gleam. "Big mistake, bird-y. Nobody touches my queen," she snarled, striking forward, her blade seeming to hone into him like it willed itself to pierce his skin. The ground shifted underneath him as the blade found its home right between his ribs. The ground swallowed what used to be normal feet, now replaced with the feet of a bird.

"MAGIC!" He said, coughing, blood dribbling from his mouth. The two Olken elves, still alive, backed up, cawing in alarm. They saluted the last dying elf, Lilja, and I fought together. Joining hands, they muttered a few words. A glowing light emanated from them, shooting into the ground.

"Trouble comes and goes and meets the Acolytes," they chanted, their beaks turning up into a smile before melting into the shadows.

Heavy breathing filled the space as we caught our breath.

"Who the fuck were they?" Kallan asked, dropping the sword from his hand and leaning against the wall, clutching his side.

"Are you okay!?" Lilja grabbed my face, turning it side to side, checking me for injuries.

"Yes, yes. I'm okay, are you?" I asked Lilja as she dabbed the blood welling on my cheek on a handkerchief she pulled from her pocket.

"Yes, I'm good. Better now, I know you are okay. I lost my temper when I saw he landed a blow." She tilted her head to the wheezing Olken Elf before us. The earth captured him from the calves up.

Blood swelled onto his tunic, pooling at the wound site. He stared up at us angrily as he wheezed.

"The Acolytes will find you," he coughed weakly. "They have forbidden magic. If we cannot eat you, the Acolytes will finish you for us," he wheezed, his lungs filling with blood.

"Who are the Acolytes?" Lilja bent down, stray hairs escaped her hair tie, clinging to her face, glued with sweat. I fought the urge to push it behind her ear.

The man grinned, blood coating his teeth, shaking his head. "Not gonna *-caw-* answer."

"Answer me!" Lilja smacked his face, his head whipped to the side. He coughed again, spitting blood off to the side.

"What are you going to do? *Caw*, kill me?" He laughed maniacally. His breath was wrecked with liquid, and he wheezed with each inhale.

"I shall reach the afterlife, and the earth will find happiness in my absence. Blessed be the Gods." The light left his eyes as he finished.

Lilja pushed his body down, her jaw tense. She whipped around, staring at the rest of the crew. While they fought well, the Olken elves had inflicted minor damage. Cassia and Keres were the only ones completely unscathed. Kallan had a cut on his side. Armand had a cut on his forearm. Aidan had a busted lip. He clung to the pages in his book that had fallen out during the scuffle. His face was green with panic from the fight.

I helped him grab the remaining pages that had scattered further out. I dusted them off before handing them back to him.

"Pray tell me someone knows who the Acolytes are," Lilja demanded. She wiped the handkerchief she used earlier to wipe the blood from my cheek across her face. Her aura was angry as she waited for one of us to answer.

"Aidan? Any idea?" Without waiting for a reply, she said. "Report, soldier! I asked you a question!"

"No, your highness. I've never heard of them before. I didn't read a mention of them in the library either. No reports of them in the journals I read before arriving here, either. I'm sorry, your highness." He straightened his back as he gave his reply to the words she used, triggering a long-forgotten muscle memory in his brain.

"Anyone else?" She tapped her foot. "This is ridiculous!" She kicked the body of the elf the others had killed into the canal.

"Hey, Lilja. It's okay. We will-" Kallan pushed himself off the wall, going to reach for her, but she pulled away from his touch, fuming.

"No, it is not. We are this close." She held up her fingers to show a little. "We got a distressed goddess who doesn't give proper advice and no guide to show us the way. Plus, no map because someone threw it into the canal," she said as she walked a path into the ground.

Kallan and I shared a look, and he held up his hands in surrender.

"Lilja, let's take a breath. Find a nice place to sleep." I inched closer, like I was approaching a wounded animal that threatened to strike at any moment.

Bags hung under her eyes, and her chest heaved. She gave a small nod, the only indication she heard me.

"How are we going to sleep somewhere nice? I don't know if you noticed, we're currently in a tunnel with a poison river as a roommate," Keres said, pushing the other body into the river. She peered over the edge, throwing up in her mouth.

"Definitely don't touch the water yet. Aidan, look at this and add it to your book." She motioned him over, and I followed. Even though she'd given us fair warning about what we were about to witness, the scene flabbergasted me.

The body Lilja threw in moments ago caught on a broken stone pillar. Its body was riddled with black veins, as the water infected it.

"Interesting, though we appear to be in an area less infected with the poison. It's clearly still potent enough to infiltrate the body," Aidan said, making a quick sketch of the blackened lines growing on the body.

"Clearly," Kallan deadpanned.

One thing was clear: we were nowhere near where we needed to be. Pavati seems farther than ever.

36

Acolytes

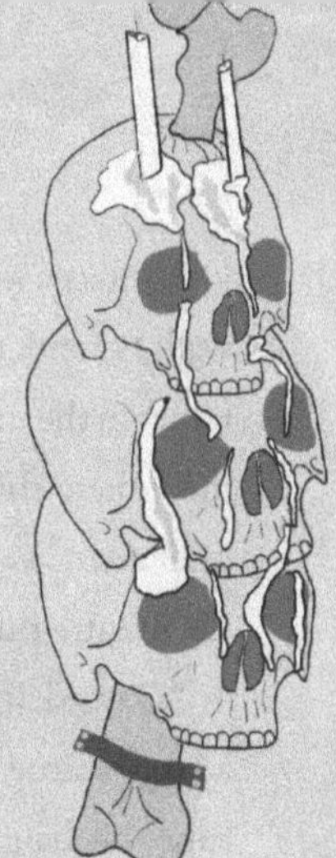

Alieta POV

T he air was dank. Fian followed close behind me, her hand on her sword hilt, ready for anything. "The Acolytes are farther up," Uncle said, his cane pounding into the ground.

"The Acolytes?" I asked, ducking my head under a large pipe.

"I have worked closely with the Acolytes for the last few hundred years. They are a small sector of non-magical elves responsible for creating the modern-day Olken Ridge," Uncle spouted off as we turned a corner. The aged brick once covering the walls was replaced with clean, tan tile; a stark difference from the earlier ambiance.

"Non-magical? I have the fire blessing, Uncle," I shot back at him. *What did Uncle know of this place?*

"Of course, I know. The elves here have a specific ecosystem in place. I have participated in the actions, and all things must have a means to an end. You will understand soon, your highness."

I bit my tongue at his ever-vague response. Uncle only ever gave me bits and pieces of information, as if it would satiate my hunger for control. I *was* queen. Although we might not be on Ardour soil, I was to be in control of this situation.

The strong survive and the unknown fail, my father's voice said in my head.

Lanterns were lit along the sides of the walls. Soot marks littered the walls behind, marking the use of time. Sunlight poured into a circular tablet in the middle of the hallway. I straightened my back. If I were to meet these elves, prepared and graceful was the goal. *I was the Queen of Ardour, and I deserved respect.* My thoughts ran through my head, the mantra pushing me forward.

"Daveed, it's been too long," an older elf said, coming from behind a large statue, blocking the hallway. He wore a white, loose-fitting robe, his hair speckled with gray. He held his arms open for a hug. *Not once had he hugged me, as if he'd give you one,* I thought, a small smirk growing on my face.

Uncle smiled, banging his cane on the tile. "Kayi, my old friend. My, have you gotten old." He met Kayi halfway, hugging him and patting him on the back.

"Me! Old? My friend, have you looked in the mirror? Dust itself is younger," Kayi said, his voice booming in the empty hallway. He was muscular for an old man. Even though his neck showed his age, Kayi held the energy of a younger elf. I decided he was easily likable. His voice was loud, yet welcoming.

However, his eyes were hollow. Whatever life once present was now gone from the monstrosities he helped create in their younger years.

"Humph, older the dust, aye?" Daveed put both hands on his cane, a smirk playing on his lips. Kayi's eyes slid to me and the rest of the elves standing behind me.

"Who are these strapping elves?" Kayi grinned, his teeth white.

"I am the Queen of Ardour, Alieta. It is nice to meet you. I'd love to learn about this place," I said, interjecting whatever my uncle was going to say. He snapped his mouth closed, his eyes narrowing.

"Ah, you didn't mention we were in the presence of royalty, Daveed. You should have sent word out earlier, my old friend. The space

I prepared is not fit for a Queen." Kayi peered at Uncle, pausing for a second longer than normal. He towered over him, nearly twice his height.

"Pavati remained silent for the last two centuries; however, her shrine has been lighting up. She's using her powers to contact someone," Kayi said, glancing around the room.

Pavati?

"Do not worry, Kayi, any space will be alright. We will not be here long," Daveed said. "Go on and show us to our space. Please explain the history of Olken Ridge. Perhaps it will put my niece, the Queen, at ease."

"Our problem will be over soon, Kayi. Ardour is at the height of wealth unseen by historians. Ardour shall be the strength of the south. Olken Ridge is prosperous in its own right. We send increasingly large amounts of food each time. Showing the growth of your population," Daveed spoke with such ease, enchanting anyone listening. Entranced by his words, a new, improved way for Ardour.

"Very well, my dear friend. I'll lead the way." He walked past the statue, revealing a large, open room. The space was free of everything, the stark cleanness unnerving. No sand or people littered the oversized hallway as we traveled through. Frescoes of forgotten times covered the walls as Kayi led the way.

"What is this place, sir?" Link asked as he stood next to Fian. The other people in my company, silent, their names unknown to me. I was constantly going through a rotation of new guards set by Daveed.

Ardourian elves were eager to serve their country and homeland. Daveed allowed them to work in my presence for a few mere weeks before rotating them. Although it was a curious thing, I usually never saw them again. I suppose it was because they moved to new positions as scouts or spies for my country.

Hundreds pass by me a day, wanting something. At this point in my reign, I didn't bother taking the mental capacity to learn names. After all, they ended up leaving anyway. Such is the way of being queen. The only constant companion was Fian, my closest confidant and Uncle. I snapped myself out of my thoughts as we descended the steps, moving farther underground.

Bones, thousands of them, appeared on the walls. No, they were the walls. I felt the urge to hold my breath as we passed the dead. I thought back to the myth my nursemaid used to tell me to scare me into behaving in funerals and churches. *Always keep your mouth closed as we pass the dead. If any of them are still roaming the earth, hiding from Runen, they will slip into your body to wear your skin!*

I shivered at the memory. Skulls stacked on top of each other, held together with a femur bone, served as candle holders. Wax dripped down the skulls like tears, as they cried for their lives cut too short, only to end up as a macabre decoration.

Olken turned the method of burial into art. A chandelier made of bone lit the floor we were descending to. The marble steps, well-worn, had small divots in each step that marked the location of past footsteps. Each one a unique shape, feeling like a step into the past.

A few people milled at the bottom. All of them wore similar clothes to Kayi. One held a stack of papers, short in stature. She shook as she walked, as if nervous. *Like Elowen.*

"This is what we call the hub, where we watch over Olken Ridge. Built by our forefathers and their supporters. To remind us of the past." Kayi had his arms out wide as he showed us the room, proudly.

"No disrespect, sir, but what do you mean, watch over? How can you observe underground?" Fian asked, she stood standoffish, like always. Poised for a fight, regardless of who was present.

He laughed his booming, yet irritating chuckle. "The magic users left on Olken work for me. As you might have gathered, we prohibit magic on the surface. Too much can go wrong with its usage. Greedy elves ruined the land for the rest of us. We have allowed Olken to heal from the magic abuse. Bevi, take it from here while I catch up with my old friend."

Kayi gestured to the anxious woman, who looked up from her task, surprised, dropping the papers she held onto the ground. Bevi immediately dropped, picking them up while profusely apologizing. I watched Uncle and Kayi walk farther down the skeleton-infested room and through a door.

Bevi straightened herself up, setting the papers on her desk. Fian and I shared a look, rolling our eyes. "With the use of the River Goddess shrines, we have the unique ability to oversee people." Her voice shook as she spoke.

A large basin of water sat between the bookshelves. "Please look." Bevi led us over. Next to the tub was an overflowing bookshelf. Herbs and jars jutted out of it, the smell of them wafting up and into my nose, and I resisted the urge to sneeze.

"The herbs are used to call on certain shrines. Different ones bring up a specific one." Bevi grabbed one, throwing in a few dried petals. The water glowed blue, rippling into an image.

Link whistled. "If I didn't see that myself, I wouldn't have believed it." The water revealed a courtyard, and people busied around. Carts floated behind them as they walked through the market.

"Can anyone see us through the water?" I asked, leaning over the bowl, being careful not to touch the reflection. My mind flashed back to the waterfall, where Father took me many times. Where Elowen ran away from me. My knuckles whitened on the rim as the memory played through my head.

A blue light surged through the ceiling, aiming for the pot. I jumped back as the water sloshed out of the bowl from the impact, creating tiny waves. "What in the gods' name was that?" I asked, peering into it.

"A message! They only come when scouts find something. The water will show the last few minutes before its transmission. Allow it a second as it loads the information."

I held my breath in anticipation as colors swirled on the water, merging into the image. I gasped, my emotions getting the best of me as Elowen's face filled the image. Blood welled from the side of her cheek. My jaw clenched, and the sword on my hip called to me to grab it and slay whoever laid their hand on her. *Who dares hit her?*

My mood only further worsened by the next person who graced the scene, Lilja. She pummeled the Olken Elf into the ground, his legs swallowed by the earth. He mouthed something, grinning, his teeth coated with blood.

"What, what's he saying?" I said, putting my ear to the water, praying to the gods to allow me super hearing.

"Unfortunately, the spell doesn't translate to sound, just image. These elves in the scene have used magic. The next step is to send out the retrieval team." She moved away from the water, grabbing a book from the shelf. Bevi muttered in a language I couldn't comprehend. The book shook before it flew toward Kayi and Uncle, shooting down the room with surprising speed.

"Where does that go?" Fian asked, our group not bothering to hide their surprise.

"That goes to our retrieval team. Chrim is their leader. Their job is probably the hardest of all. They go out in the field and apprehend the prisoner, and if they can't, we kill them. One less magic user on Olken is beneficial for the cause," Bevi spoke, gathering her papers.

"Kill them?" I said, fighting my instinct to kill her for the thought of killing Elowen. The fire licked under my skin, caressing me to explode.

"Well, yes," she said. She blinked as if it were the easiest information to comprehend. "Kayi orders the retrievers to kill the wanted Elves if they can't obtain them safely. Or they join the Acolytes. Not everyone sees the dire situation the plateau is in."

"Let us go with," I said, barely allowing her to get a breath in. "It will be a beneficial learning experience about the methods of Olken Ridge. A way to bridge the gap between our two kingdoms." I puffed out my chest, doing my best to appear diplomatic.

Bevi's eyes flitted back and forth between me and the door as Kayi entered. Her cheeks flushed red as she mulled over my request. "Uh, your highness. I'm unsure if it's the best idea. What if something happens to you? Olken, in its standing, cannot afford an all-out war between Ardour in this present moment. Any harm to your person would bring unwanted attention to Olken. We have done much to ensure our existence continues with secrecy." She squared her shoulders, pleased with her answer.

Pride filled my chest. I knew Ardour could crush Olken within seconds of a fight. One battlefield is all it would take. That much I knew.

"Perhaps instead of assisting the apprehension of the criminals," I grimaced at my word choice. Elowen was misguided. Influenced by Lilja, not beyond repair. I held the glue that could bring her back.

"I'm eager to observe the interaction. To understand the inner workings of the Acolytes."

Kayi approached from behind, his footsteps quiet. Bevi looked at him expectantly, her face passive. She wanted him to decide.

"I think it's a wonderful idea," Kayi said, clearing his throat.

They are treating us like children, I thought, making a fist at my sides. These days have felt dark, as if a hand shadowed the sun, like Goddess Niamh was playing a trick.

"A way to join our two kingdoms." He reached out his hand to me. Uncle stood behind him, barely visible from Kayi's tall form.

I clasped it, a shiver going down my spine. I studied his face, scrutinizing the darkness of his eyes, his stature, before concluding. *This man is evil. What side was I on? The good or the bad?*

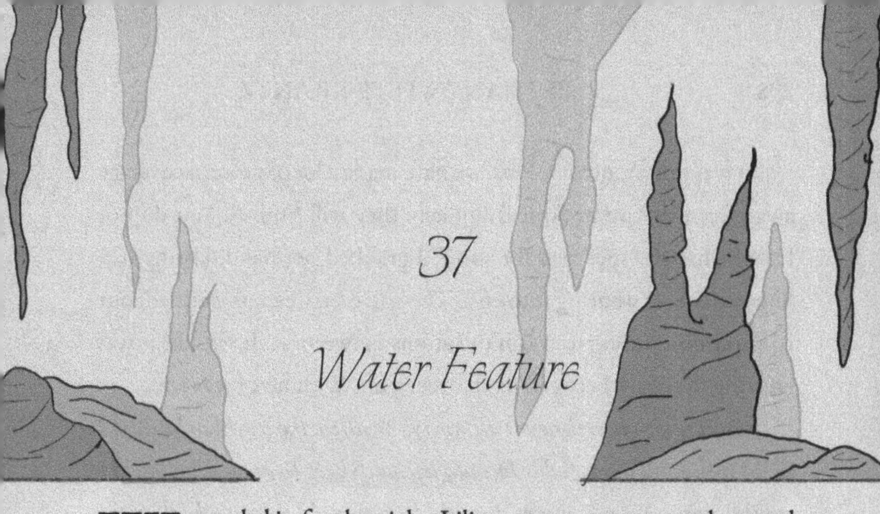

37

Water Feature

We settled in for the night. Lilja put up no protest as she paced the room, muttering to herself. I sat on my pack, the only cushion-like item I had available. My butt and body, sore from the constant moving around the tunnels. The fight didn't help. I grimaced as I applied salve to my cheek. The pain immediately lessened. With the leftover paste, I moistened my scar, sending tingles up my arm.

Aidan and I sat back-to-back, leaning on one another with his head leaning on my shoulder, his mouth agape, snoring. Keres slept soundly in one corner of the room. Her black hair covered her face, making her look like a monster crawling from a well. *Don't look her way when it's dark,* I thought, not wanting to spook myself.

Kallan spoke up first. "Lilja, come and lie down. This room isn't so bad. With the day we had, it's basically a palace."

"If this were the state of the palace, I'd need to redecorate," I mused.

She stopped walking mid-step, turning to look at us. "Kal, please understand. Valdis is at stake, and my little tantrum just sent a location spell to whoever the Acolytes are. Ardour is on Olken soil, and we are no closer to finding Pavati."

I got up, allowing Aidan's sleeping form to slump to the ground. He fell with a thump, his snoring stopping for a millisecond before rolling over, continuing. I rolled my eyes, *damn, I wish I could sleep like that.*

"It was not a tantrum. Plus, we have made a lot of ground coverage away from that spot. So it is unlikely they will find us. You do not know what the spell was for sure." I grabbed her hand, kissing it. I lingered, never wanting it to end. The space between us warmed, our connection seeming to warm the atoms between us. It felt like it was creating the spark between us all over again. With her, I was safe.

Was it worth it to throw it all away? To allow the world to burn so I could spend my short, feeble human life with her. To grow old while she stayed young. Yes, yes, it was. I would let the world burn and fall away into nothing if it meant I could spend one more moment safe between her arms.

I didn't want to die.

The thought passed through my head before I had time to reaffirm what I set out to the desert to do: die for the greater good.

I cupped her face. The rest of the team melted into the background as we held eye contact. The world would burn for her, and I would let it. I kissed her, a chaste kiss. Kallan cleared his throat, and I looked at him sheepishly.

"What?" I batted my eyes at him.

"You guys are making me uncomfortable with your love." He fake gagged, sticking his finger in his mouth. Kallan grinned at us, his acceptance of our love clear.

"Kallan, let's face it, bud. You want what I got," Lilja grinned, cupping my butt playfully.

"Get a room, you two." Armand shielded his eyes as he spoke, like a child covering his eyes when their parents kissed.

"When we finally get a room, no one is allowed to bother us. Unless they want to spend a week in a cell." Lilja puffed out her chest confidently. Cassia snorted, laughing.

"A week. Isn't a week a bit overkill? I don't believe anyone has asked me what I think."

"It is not overkill because I do intend to show you just how enthralled I am with you. Now, before we ruin Kallan's innocence. Let's go to bed to preserve our energy for tomorrow." Lilja kissed my forehead.

Water splashed as I ran through it. Black veins traveled up my calves, spreading to the rest of my body. The fighting was going strong around me. Shouts filled the cavern as I slid behind a stalagmite. Mud sloshing all over me as I tried to catch my breath. Swords clashed together, stray arrows hit the walls, thankfully missing the targets. The smell of iron filled my nose as I looked down.

Blood poured freely from the middle of my chest. "Alwyn?" Pavati sang out.

"Alwyn, where are you? I thought we had a deal? You were going to help me escape. Are you pulling out now? Are you a coward?" She continued, her voice ricocheting off the cave walls.

"Elowen!" Lilja said, her voice booming across the room. "Where are you? Don't leave me! Come back!"

I sobbed, wiping my tears off my cheek with the back of my hand, smudging dirt on my face.

"You came for me, Alwyn. You must keep your word. If you complete your task, I can guarantee Lilja and you shall have a long life together," Pavati said, as she rounded the rock formation, grabbing my arm, her hands cold to the touch, wet. Her braids swayed back and forth, almost hypnotically.

She pinned me against the rock with inhuman strength. I struggled as the words sank in.

"I will?" I coughed, blood spilling out of my mouth.

"The future is widely unknown to the Gods, but I can sense it with certainty. *You* shall not be the one to die on this quest," she said, lessening the grip she had on my arm.

"Okay," I breathed, my lungs clearer than before.

"I shall complete my end of the deal, Pavati, the River Goddess. You have my word."

The torches we lit the night before had long since fizzled out. Snores went off in intervals like a clock ticking. I was the first person awake. I got up, moving my items into my pack. My arms ached where Pavati had grabbed me.

My anxiety released as the resolve I had found yesterday was gone. I can be alive, and Valdis can be safe. Better yet, Lilja and I could coexist for a time. As I moved around, the rest of the team stirred. Before long, we were all up and ready. Keres pleated her hair to the side, pulling her bag across her shoulder. We desperately needed a bath. My hair was weighed down by the oil it created. Dirt seemed to cover every inch.

These days, we all carried light, almost nothing to weigh us down. I was almost disgustingly sure Armand didn't have a second pair of underwear. The number of times I've witnessed him stripping everything off to wash his own clothes with him as he bathed, before. Just to put everything back on, and that was before we got to Olken.

I wasn't sure if he needed a mom or a lady friend; in his case, probably both. I smirked at my own thoughts as we walked down the long, narrow tunnel. The air was damp and stale. I kept track of our movements, not from the lack of scenery, but from the marks Kallan kept making on the walls each time we turned.

"Why do you keep doing that?" I asked.

"It's to make sure if we need to run back. We just have to look, not think," Kallan said, sweat running down the side of his face. He rubbed his hand on his trousers, wiping the sweat on them.

Armand threw his arm around him, chuckling. "Yeah, he's always running away from a fight." He rubbed his knuckle on his hair, messing it up.

"Kallan, run away? Come on, Armand, that isn't believable. Maybe if we were talking about you. I don't know if you recall, but the rest of the group does. You running away from a fight because you thought the shadow on the wall was a lion?" Aidan wheezed, doubling over from the memory, slapping his leg.

"It turned out to be a kitten. A baby cat!" Lilja howled with laughter.

"Or the time you ran away from the Inn owner in Nyrim," Cassia said, her voice light.

"You would have run too if she were running after you with a ladle. She used to make bread; those types of people are ruthless and patient. Mama said, 'If you can wait for bread to rise, you can wait for anything.' Given the chance, she would have killed me in my sleep. She was roasting with anger when she found me with her daughter. Ah, Netel, I forgot about her. She was the one with the really nice-" His conversation cut short as the floor crumbled away. The fall was short yet hard. Rocks and pieces of flooring fell beside me. With the help of adrenaline, I jumped up, my dagger in hand as I searched the rubble for my friends.

"Lilja," I coughed, the dust from the collapse coating my nostrils. Rocks exploded from one spot. I scrambled over the debris just as Lilja was climbing out. Her face was painted with dirt and anger.

"Move back, Elle. This shit has to move. All we need to do is find one goddess. People keep fucking up our plans," she said, cracking her knuckles and forming them into fists. The pieces that had fallen shifted before projecting them into the air.

A vein popped in her forehead as she struggled to hold them in the air. Our friends scrambled out from underneath them. I gaped at her. The strength required to lift all of those and suspend them in the air was immense. It was as if the God Arlo yielded his earthly powers to her.

Lilja let the rocks fall again. She leaned against one of the larger slabs. Using magic sapped away at her energy.

"That was impressive," I said, running over to her. Blood trickled down her nose. *Magic always came at a price.*

"Move! Capture or kill!" A voice shouted.

I whipped my head around. Shadows moved around the edges of the room. Four men and two women emerged.

"In the name of Olken, we order you to cease and desist now! Or we will use force." They drummed their staffs on the ground. The tops of them changed from one point to three, becoming a trident. Strings of light thrummed through them, something powering them. Each of the Acolytes seeped evil. Their faces were down-turned in a vile sneer.

"Run!" I screamed as I bobbed and weaved through the haphazard path. I stumbled on rubble. Picking myself up, I made a beeline for the rest of the crew.

"This way!" Aidan waved his arm toward a tunnel. Shouts rang out behind me as one guard fell to his knees, shot with an arrow. The shaft of the arrow stuck out of his shoulder. He clutched it, screaming as he broke it, leaving the point of it embedded. *These elves were insane.*

Cassia stood toward the back of us, sending out arrows with deadly accuracy.

"Cassia, move. No one left behind!" Lilja shouted to her as we piled into the tunnel.

"Lilja! With me!" Aidan said. Elves closed in, nearly at the door. Lilja and Aidan exchanged looks before shifting the earth beneath us, closing us into the tunnel.

"We have to move now! If they have power to collapse a floor, they certainly have the power to break down our wall," Lilja said as Keres and Cassia led the way. Kallan and I, side by side. This tunnel was by far the smallest, only meant for a single-file line. Armand was right behind us, his broad shoulders making up most of the hallway.

Aidan and Lilja made the rear. Their hands on the walls, eyes closed.

"What are they doing?" I asked Kallan.

"They're searching for our way out," Keres said.

"They're feeling for any gaps behind the wall. Any space large enough to be a room." Armand clarified from behind me, his voice breathless from exertion.

I struggled to catch my breath, the walls feeling like they were closing in. Rocks crumbled down behind us as the Acolytes pushed their way in. I let out a scream.

"Elowen! Come back! Come back with me and be mine!" My blood ran cold as her voice rang through the air. I stumbled, my foot catching the uneven flooring. Kallan grabbed my arm, hauling me back up. There was going to be a bruise there tomorrow. *If you make it that far,* my inner voice sneered in my head.

"Elowen is not yours, Alieta! She is not a pet, you cannot own her!" Lilja said. Her hands skimmed the walls, dirt embedding itself under her fingernails.

A cackle filled the hall, an unnerving laugh sending a shiver down my spine. "Ownership?! That's rich coming from you. You kept her as a pet," Alieta roared, her voice echoing.

I glanced at Lilja, mouthing an apology. "She is mine. She gave me her body." Alieta's voice was painfully loud. A sharp ache went to my chest. The flash of a light flew past us. Only motivating us to quicken our pace. My heart pounded in my chest as I lost speed, my human body unable to keep up with my Elven friends.

Did I ever make Lilja understand what I had to do? I flashed through my memory, gasping for breath. "Here!" Aidan said.

"With me, Aidan." Lilja gripped his hand, the veins on her arm popping up. They both push with the other. Dust flew as they pounded into the wall. Rocks joined the chaos as the Acolytes gained on us.

"Get behind me, my queen to be. Lilja's going to kill me if anything happens to you." Kallan said as he and Armand's arms on either side wrapped around me, pulling me behind them.

Released from their sheaths, the swords sang, calling for blood. Runen's icy breath seemed to breathe down my neck as the opportunity of death grew.

"My darling, come home. You don't want me to hurt your friends, do you?" Alieta cooed. On my tiptoes, I peered over my protector's shoulders. Her body shrouded by the Acolytes in front of her.

"I am NOT your darling. You cannot have me, and you can't own me. I am not someone's pet!" Balling my fists at my sides as I pushed forward, pushing past Kallan and Armand. *Pavati said I would not die here.*

"You look ravishing, little mouse, as always." Alieta's towering form walked past the protesting Acolytes. She lit a flame in her hand, and it waved with life. Raw power came off of her as she stood in front of the guards. The flame shadowed her eyes black, the smile haunting.

"What are you doing here, Alieta? With your uncle, I presume. Is he here to ruin more lives? What have you done with Pavati? Where is she?!" I shouted. Aidan's hand grasped my forearm, attempting to pull me behind him.

"Pavati? The River Goddess? How is she involved?" Alieta's smile dropped, her hand falling away as she stared at me.

"WE'RE IN. Everybody go in now!" Lilja's voice boomed.

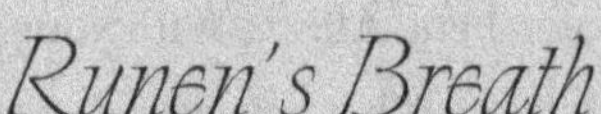

38

Runen's Breath

An Acolyte rushed forward, their spear going for the closest person, me. I stood there frozen. As Aidan's arm shot in front of me, the sound was sickening. It sliced through his arm like butter as it pulled away, and it sloshed, blood immediately pouring from the wound.

"Gods, that's not good," Aidan whimpered, clutching it. The words slipped out like second nature, as if responding to Armand's smart mouth.

I put my hand over it out of instinct, the liquid wet and sticky as it coated my fingers. Cassia's arrow shot between us, hitting the assailant in the eye. He didn't have time to scream. His hands were attempting to clutch it as he fell to his knees, dead.

"I said move," Lilja demanded, grabbing Aidan by the back of the neck, yanking him back. Her eyes softened as she saw the blood and the horror on my face.

My body followed suit. Once past the threshold, the wall slammed down, as if the doorway was never there.

"Aidan!" I said, clambering over to him. Cassia was already at his side with her satchel open, grabbing herbs and salves to stop the bleeding.

"I am so sorry," I grabbed his good arm.

His face was ashen. "Don't worry about it, Elle. I'm all good. Cassia is going to fix me up real quick. I'll be up and running in no time." Sweat clung to his skin, gluing his hair to his face.

"There's too much blood. I-I don't know what to do," Cassia shouted, her Havn accent showing through. Tears ran down her face. Aidan's arm was nearly severed, the bone peering up at us.

She held her hand down on the wound, looking around for Lilja, her movements frantic. "Let me see," I said, carefully getting up and stepping over him.

Blood pooled below Aidan's arm and side. *There was too much blood.* Wildly, I tried to remember everything I had read about blood loss in the books I traded for. My previous life had seemed like a lifetime ago.

"It must have hit an artery," I said. Deep down, I knew it was hopeless. Cassia released some of the pressure on his arm. Blood spurting out in response.

"Wait, what does that mean?" Kallan asked. He dropped to his knees, sword at his side.

"It means I am dying." Aidan coughed, his breath rattling in his chest. He closed his eyes, trying to find peace.

"No, no. You can't!" I leaned my head to his chest, the tears continuing to fall. Lilja, at some point, put his head in her lap; her hand stroked his cheek.

"We can cauterize the wound! Keres, you have to try! We have to do something." Tears ran freely down my cheeks as I stared at the blood on the ground.

"With the blood loss he's sustained, it's futile. He'll die of shock," Cassia said.

"You have done well, Aidan. A warrior's death awaits you. We will stay until you leave. Runen will lead you to the other side," Lilja said, kissing his gray skin.

"Thank you, my Queen. It has been an honor serving you." A cough wracked his bulky form.

"Aidan, you can't. It's all my fault. I should have stayed in the back." His eyes fazed in and out. His wire-rim glasses crooked, bent from the pandemonium.

"It isn't. It is my duty to protect and serve the Valdis crown. If not that, but because you're my friend." My eyes roamed his face, trying to capture all the details. His little smile lines, the blonde hair in desperate need of a trim.

"For my friend. May the air carry your spirit far, and may the earth find happiness with your absence. We shall miss you." Lilja's voice cracked as she spoke, her hand patting his shoulder. Keres and Armand held hands above her, their faces somber. Tears ran down Armand's face, leaving wet streaks.

Aidan gave a weak smile to the people surrounding him, his breathing becoming more ragged with each one. His eyes focused behind me. "Runen, you have come for me," he whispered, before letting out one last breath.

His body slackened. His hand that had held mine fell to his side. The remaining color seemed to drain from his face, his eyes open, unseeing.

"Aidan." I shook him a little, hoping it was all a trick or a cruel joke.

"Aidan! No! Come back! You can't leave," I wailed, choking on my spit, coughing as I swallowed the vomit that crawled up my throat. I pounded on his body, hoping my fists were enough to stop him from acting. *In just a few mere minutes, my friend was gone. Dead.*

"Elowen! Elle, stop. He's gone, baby. Listen to me." Lilja placed Aidan's head on the ground, getting up, clutching me to her.

I gasped, unable to capture enough air in my lungs. My vision hazing at the edges, the darkness creeping in, threatening to take me under.

"It's not your fault. Okay? Just breathe." Lilja pushed the hair that hung on my face behind my ears, kissing me on my forehead.

"What do we do now? We can't. We can't just-. We can't just leave him," I said, sobbing between my words. My tears stained Lilja's tunic.

She grabbed my face, so we were eye to eye. Tears welled in her eyes, her voice breaking as she spoke to me. "We have to. Aidan wouldn't want to slow us down. He would want us to survive. Now, let us leave this place. We will free Pavati and leave this hellhole and never return."

I gulped, swallowing the next sob that threatened to bubble up. "Hold on." I crouched down, cupping Aidan's face, his skin already cold. My lips brushed his forehead as I kissed him goodbye. I grabbed his glasses, gripping them in my hand. Lilja grabbed his satchel and the journal he always carried.

Lilja leaned down, placing her hand on his, staring down at his face. "I will publish this for you, my friend, I promise. This journal shall make its way far and wide. Not a single house will go unknowing of your knowledge." Tears flowed down her face, splattering on his tunic.

They would rue this day. Alieta would suffer, as would the Acolytes.

I took in my surroundings. Water covered most of the floor, and moss grew in the corners of the room, snaking its way to the exit. A rock fell from the wall as the Acolytes bashed in.

"Let's go," Keres said. A flame waved in her hand as she led the way. No lanterns hung on the wall, leaving only the flame as a light.

As we entered the next room over, clear, glowing blue water trickled up through the wet ground. The path it made was as if someone had stamped their mark on the earth. A well stood above us. The moon was high in the sky, almost centered in the opening as if greeting us. I sent it a mournful stare before walking under the rays.

"The water here is safe. Do not fear it. I sense purified water nearby," Cassia said, her voice quavering, as she took a tentative step into it

We moved silently, the six of us. No words spoken as we followed the glowing puddles of water. The Niphes book grew warm in my satchel as we walked, as if calling to me once more. Anger pulsed through my body as I yanked it out. She caused this. She was the reason Aidan was gone.

The book was almost burning the tips of my fingers as I cracked it open. Blue stars shot out like a firework, manifesting themselves into her.

"Alwyn," she said before I interrupted her.

"What do you want?" I said, speaking through my teeth.

She raised an eyebrow. "You are close."

"Tell me where you are, *now*."

"I cannot. It is against the rules for me to tell my location. It is up to fate to bring you to me," she said. My eyes narrowed, watching her glowing form above the words on the page. I took a deep breath, willing the words to grow from the page and choke her out.

"Aidan is dead because of you. Vague answers will no longer work." Lilja and the rest of the crew had long since paused, staring at me. Kallan held Cassia tightly, her shoulders shaking as she sobbed into him. "Insolent human. It is no more my fault than yours. You misplace the blame. The Acolytes are to blame here. I told you that you would not die. I did not say your friends would not die. No others are to blame. It is not my fault that I cannot tell you where I am. Niahm and Esmersey have long since decided that the gods cannot give concrete answers. The mothers long since decided the Elves must decide their day-to-day lives." Her form flickered, her face tired. Her hair was a mess, lifeless. The clothes that hung on her body were torn.

"How is this day-to-day if millions of Elves die if we fail?" My voice cracked, my emotions wanting to spill over the simmering pot I had pushed it in.

"'Tis' not my decision to make, Alwyn. You must understand. Your team is but a small picture in the grander scheme. Find me, hand me the ingredients I asked for. Let us save Valdis and the rest." Her form disappeared, leaving me to explain to the rest.

"Are you insane? Talking to a goddess like that? What if she kills you for your insolent tongue? We already have one friend dead. We don't need another," Keres said, the flame growing in her hand.

"We are failing our tasks. Aidan should be alive." I stomped my foot, water splashing up my leg. Its glow was sticking to my trousers.

"Let's go, Elowen. Feelings will accomplish nothing for the goal at hand. We must push down our own to succeed. You said she is close. Pavati is waiting." Lilja grabbed my arm, gently guiding me forward. She held me like a piece of fine china. Too hard a grip and I would just shatter into a million pieces.

"Regardless of how you feel, the task has to be finished," Armand said, his sword in hand. He led the way with Keres. Their years of training were evident as they moved in sync, one foot at a time.

His pain was barely discernible, his voice hard. Green moss grew on the sides of the wall, and the moon reflected off the water, causing waves of light across. *How can things be so calm after what happened?*

Alieta POV

We burst through the wall, and a body lay on the damp ground. My heart beat in my chest as I checked it for a pulse. His face was already gray, his skin cold.

"Is he dead?" Fian asked.

I nodded, wiping my hands together as I stood. Fresh air filled this room. It was no longer a damp smog.

"This must be an old well. The room extends up onto the ground level of Olken," Link said. He adjusted the large pack he carried on his back, looking up at the moon.

"I thought you would not engage, your highness?" The leader of the team asked. He stood before me. His jaw clenched, his hair slicked back, and mud streaked his face. The knuckles that gripped the staff he held were white.

"I wanted to talk to Elowen, as you may have heard. We have a personal connection." My hand hovered over my blade. *What they were doing here was wrong, killing magic users for just their blessing. But Uncle said it was a means to an end? What specifically was the goal?* The little voice in my head sang.

"The Acolytes allowed you on this run specifically if you didn't engage. Kayi won't be happy. He ordered us to put them in custody before they reached Pavati." Chrim spoke to me with such venom. His words were hard, as if frothing at the mouth. Like he'd bite– no better than a dog.

"That name again, Pavati. What does the River Goddess have to do with this?" I grabbed the edge of his tunic.

Chrim's eyes widened as his head hit the wall, his fellow guards pointing the spears at me. A silence stretched over us as they waited to see what I would do.

He held up his hand in their direction, telling them to wait.

"Your uncle really hasn't told you anything?" He barked a laugh.

"An Elven Queen, the sole person reigning over Ardour, yet you do not know what is going on. The ploys happening in your own kingdom. Kayi and Daveed are playing you like a puppet, and they are the puppeteer." I punched him in the mouth, anger fueling me. His head snapped back, hitting the wall, and blood coated his teeth as he smiled again.

"You insolent man, if you do not tell me what is happening right this instant, my team will kill you and leave you to rot with that one." I pointed my finger at the body that was once part of Lilja's team.

"Answer my Queen. Or may this be your last breath?" Fian's sword pointed into the soft skin of his neck, blood welling at the tip, making him wince.

Link had his dual swords pointed at the last two men. He grinned a crazy smile, like this was the highlight of his week.

Fian dug the tip of the sword in some more, the blood trickling down his neck. "Wait! Kayi and Daveed have the River Goddess pinned for the last couple of hundred years."

"Uncle managed to capture the River Goddess?" I gave Fian a look, my suspicions only proving to be more correct by the second.

"What are they doing with Pavati?" Fian asked, pulling the sword away, the threat clear. *Answer us or die.*

"Daveed wants to rule both kingdoms! He and Kayi are responsible for the blight! Kayi wants Olken and Daveed agreed." Chrim seemed to will his head through the rock wall I held him against as he attempted to shy away from my fist.

I loosened my grip as I held on to his throat. His eyes bulged as he regained oxygen to his brain. He hacked, dropping to his knees.

"What do you want me to do, your highness? Kill them?" Fian asked. She kicked the man's stomach, pushing him onto his back.

"No, I have a better idea." I grinned slowly, a picture forming in my head.

"Oh, I know that look. You have a plan, your highness." Fian's smile grew to match my own.

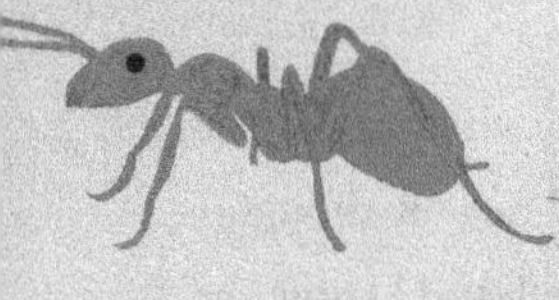

39

The Blood of a Goddess

Alieta POV

The Acolytes walked in between us as we made our way to the building where their station was being held. Chrim and I had reached an agreement. He does nothing dumb, and I don't kill him; a perfect relationship.

"Uncle, we have to talk." I grabbed his elbow, leading the older, frail man to a corner. I had never once touched my uncle in any capacity. No hugs, no gentle pat on the arm. His skin felt papery thin under my touch, and I withdrew my hand, grimacing.

"Where are they?" He asked, his voice shaking.

"What are you and Kayi planning? What are you up to? How is Pavati connected to this?" I fought the urge to grab his old man face and push it against the wall like I did with Chrim. Even though my body felt hot, seconds away from steaming, I concealed the emotions. To show feelings was to show weakness, and I was not weak.

Restraint would be the power I needed to rise above Daveed.

"Your highness, I don't know what you are referring to," he sputtered as he talked, the vein in his forehead bulging around his sun spots.

"Daveed, what are you planning with Pavati? I want to help. I have known for some time something had been happening. With you and me, we can rule the whole lower continent." *Then I could have Elowen.*

My mind flashed to the night with her, my body warming at the thought. The walk back to the stronghold had solidified my thoughts on the matter. There was a pull between Elowen and I, and I know she felt it as well.

She always shivered with delight, shying away from our connection. It was there. The love we shared was palpable. Even if she thought she loved Lilja, I could have her see reason. I would follow him to get my little mousse.

Daveed's eyes narrowed. He looked to Kayi, then back to me, trying to sense the lie coating my tongue.

"The blight, yes. It is our doing. The lower continent will be ours in the matter of years if everything goes according to plan. Pavati is stuck in a lower level, stuck for the last couple hundred years."

I took a step away from him, my emotions fighting each other, unsure of how to feel. "What do you hope to gain? What is the long run?" I crossed my arms, feeling the pressure of eyes on me. As the rest of the crew attempted to eavesdrop on our conversation.

"The long run? With Valdis off the map, their large wood exporting business is ours. Once the Valdisians are gone, Ardour will be free to conquer the other side of the mountain. The logging exports and farmland will be free from people and sickness. Ardour will be the strongest kingdom ready to take on the people to the east." He rested his hands on his cane, pleased with himself.

Chaikamen?

"Why have you waited to tell me? It is apparent this has been years in the planning. Longer than I and many others have been alive." I bit the inside of my cheek. *It was my duty to keep Ardour strong. To keep my people happy. Other countries were not my issue. I was not their keeper,* my inner voice chimed as I tried to reason, going along with him.

"With my plans long underway since before your conception, I saw no reason to keep you informed about the day-to-day operations of Ardour. I had planned to notify you once definite," Uncle spoke plainly, as if the answer to the question I had asked was clear.

"You plan to kill Pavati?" I tilted my head to the side. The answer this time was clear as day. I wanted to hear him say it, say the words I dreaded to hear. If the people found Ardour responsible for Pavati's death, the religious uproar would be instantaneous. My people would throw me off the throne, beheading me for the war crimes committed on Olken.

On the other side of the coin, it wouldn't be a bad thing to conquer Valdis. The popularity of the crown would be at an all-time high, and food would be on my people's plates.

He gave a nod, and my jaw clenched tighter. *That was not a good enough answer.* "Uncle, I need you to say it. Manifest it into the air."

"Yes, your highness, I mean to kill Pavati," Kayi and Daveed said at the same time. Their eyes appeared to be hollow of any emotion other than darkness. *With darkness came results. The results would lead the Ardour people, my people, to prosperity. The Valdisians pirates will cease attacking my ships and towns bordering the sea.*

"This is the right decision," Fian said as she spoke low in my ear.

"Give me a moment to discuss with my advisor." I nodded to Kayi and Uncle out of necessity, not respect. I led Fian to the other side of the room, away from prying ears.

"What do you think?" I looked to Fian for almost everything. Her friendship with me had been invaluable growing up, and now as queen. All the times I got into brawls when we were younger to getting us out of fights as adults. Fian has had my back.

"Think about it. With Valdis off the map, the people bordering the seas wouldn't have to worry about getting plundered. Ardourians wouldn't have to worry ever again," Fian said. She spoke confidently, her voice unwavering. She crossed her arms, glaring at Daveed and Kayi.

Fian leaned into me, whispering, covering her mouth as she spoke so no one could lip-read. "If we turn this into our idea, it could only go our way. Daveed can not become a problem. We can make him disappear if he proves to be a thorn."

The word assassination hung in the air, unspoken, but understood. Disappearing by any means necessary, and Fian meant it too. Death was something easily given by my friend. Those who disrespected me were gone by the end of the week, if Fian had a choice.

I nodded. It made sense. My heart ached at the idea of killing the goddess. My father always taught me to respect the gods and goddesses for all they did to aid our people. They play a big part in the ceremonies even today. *They were doing this for personal gain, no doubt about it. However, Pavati would only help my people if she were dead. There was no other reason to bring forth her demise.*

"Okay." I clasped her forearm, bringing her into a hug. Together, we would bring down a goddess and get to Elowen. I felt pulled to her by an indescribable link. When I first laid eyes on her, I was infatuated, drunk off the idea. She was mine. I took a deep breath, closing my eyes, and imagined my arms around her once more. She revealed the secret of Ardour. It was right under my nose the whole time. I was more than grateful.

I sauntered over to my uncle. "I will aid in the killing of the Goddess, but Elowen must come home with me. If anything happens to her, it is the end of our deal. Do you gentlemen understand?" I looked down at my uncle. He always acted like he was so big, as if larger than life, but he was nothing more than a small, unimportant man trying to make himself into something. Daveed's eyes looked up at me. *I wanted him to feel like he was small, a puny ant on a hill of sugar.*

It was my responsibility to make sure he didn't mess up anything of mine.

He held out his hand. "Together, your highness, we will rule the lower continent."

I grasped his arm, giving him a false smile, the grin not meeting my eyes. "The Valdisians are close to Pavati as we speak. I need you to show me a fast way to get there."

"I know exactly where she's hiding, your highness. We can be there in a matter of minutes." Kayi sent a hand signal to Chrim, who stalked over to the water basin. He pulled a vial out of his pocket, emptying the contents into it.

"What is that?" I asked as the water overflowed onto the ground. The water turned blue, glowing. It was clear, the purest water I had ever seen. The tile cracked, creating stairs instantly.

"It's Pavati's blood. We found through an accident, it can create portals to her. It's like it's trying to reconnect with her earthly form," Kayi said, close to my ear. Cold air whooshed up as the stairs stopped moving.

"Men, join Queen Alieta in killing the Goddess. Capture Elowen at all costs. She must not escape. We have to keep her alive and relatively unharmed. Tonight is the night we kill a goddess! The history books will write *we* are the saviors of our realm. No longer will we rely on the Gods to create our fate. It is a new age, without gods." He banged his staff on the ground, sending echoes into the ground. His men cheered as I cut in.

"Ardour shall reign over Valdis in as little as a fortnight! Tonight, we write our own fate."

Now it was my team's turn to cheer. Link clashed his knives together, and Fian gave me a wild grin. It was I who traipsed down the stairs first. Fian to my left, Daveed close behind. The walls were smooth at the start and progressively getting rougher as we descended, like the magic used to create it, ran out. Before long, I was jumping down large sections of missing steps.

I grunted as I contacted the floor at the bottom, rolling my body to distribute the impact. Years of training coming into use as muscle memory. We found ourselves in a once ornate room. Gilded wallpaper peeled off the walls. The stone tiles on the ground lay covered in dust.

"This is one of Pavatis' original rooms. Before we pushed her to the back of her enclosure, if you will," Uncle spoke, Dor picked him up to set him down on the main floor.

"Like a caged animal, with her gone, Olken and Ardour can thrive," Kayi spoke, jumping down. He was years younger than Uncle, it appeared; still having the capacity to move around with vigor. Venom seemed to coat his mouth as he droned on about killing the goddess. I drowned him out, plowing ahead and observing my surroundings. Three doorways connected the room to the further parts of Pavati's old home. I closed my eyes, allowing myself to listen.

Like my teachers used to say, *'A future queen should listen to the earth.'* Water trickled somewhere, a rock fell in another place, a splash and another. I flung my eyes open. Someone was nearby; holding up my hand, I signaled my crew, not bothering to turn around. I knew they were at attention, standing straight up, weapon in hand, silent.

I stalked into the other room, looking for our target. Elowen was nearby. I could feel it.

40

Death

Elowen POV

We sloshed in the water as we walked through the hall. It was once beautiful. Now, in such disrepair, it was disheartening. It appeared more like a ruin that an archaeologist would come to learn about past civilizations. *Aidan would have loved to see it*. Water was up to our ankles. The loss of Aidan hung heavy on my mind. Silent tears ran down my cheeks and onto my neck, soaking into my tunic. I wiped them away with the back of my hand, sniffling. Melancholy seemed to stretch over us like a heavy blanket.

"Wait, do you guys hear that?" Kallan paused, holding up his hand, telling us to stop. Stomping sounded in the hall, echoing from somewhere deeper. I had an inkling of who chased us. One thing was for sure: they were the wolves, and we were the prey.

Water splashed around us as we hauled it through the ruins. A previous battle had ravaged them, an explosion appeared to have torn through a wall, creating a rough tunnel that connected to a finished room. Shouts rang out as we entered the next room. The smell of the poison was back. Death hung in my nostrils. Water reflected on the walls. It was black with whatever created the blight.

Daveed's voice rang out. "Barricade them into the cave with Pavati. Let them die like the rats they are!"

"No, Uncle, we agreed. Let Elowen out! She is mine. I will break the sick hold Lilja has on her when I make her completely mine! She is to be unharmed." Alieta's voice ricocheted around the room, like the water's reflection.

"She's delusional," Kallan said as he nocked an arrow.

"We fight to the death," I said, my voice coming out stronger than I felt. The dragon claw felt like a weight on my chest. I fought the urge to yank it off.

"Death? Oh, my darling. Death will not come for you today. I can't say the same for Lilja," Alieta said as she and her thugs came into view, their faces concealed, only their eyes exposed. Masks to hide the faces of monsters.

"For the last time! I will never be with you! I got what I need from you. This thing you think we have between us is imaginary. A figment of your imagination. Touch my soon-to-be wife and I'll kill you with my bare hands." I swung my sword in my hand, cracking my neck.

"Attack them, you fool!" Daveed hit his cane on the ground, swinging it up, using the handle to scoop one of the thug's legs, pushing him forward.

They charged us, avoiding the streams that diverged into the river. Screams overtook the room. Dead greenery crunched under my feet as I moved around the chaos. I locked eyes with a man thrice my size, his face uncovered, an angry scar covered his milky-looking right eye. He grinned, rushing at me. I jabbed at him, reaching for my blade to slice into him. His large hands grabbed at me. I turned pointing my blade up, nicking him in his underarm.

"Aargh, you'll pay for that." With his other hand, he grabbed at my wrist, squeezing it, forcing me to drop the sword. *That will leave a bruise. If I lasted long enough.*

I screamed, "Let go of me, you monster." I kicked my leg up, I launched my foot at his crown jewels, and was rewarded by his face turning red.

An arrow whistled past me, embedding itself in the milky eyeball. For a second, he stood there, his hands dropping to his side. He reeled to the side and to his knees before falling forward. Dead.

I whipped my head to look behind me. Kallan stood against the wall, another arrow knocked and ready. I gave him a smile before turning forward, searching for my Lilja. She was fighting a woman. Their swords clashed together as they collided. Lilja had a split lip, her face stern.

I jumped over a body on the ground. Cassia and a man fought. He grinned at her as his sword cut a chunk of her hair off. Cassia's attacker stood directly behind the stream. I pulled at the back of his tunic, causing him to stumble, his foot twisting underneath him. His bulky form crumpled, falling into the water. He screamed as the water hit him, his skin bubbling. He seized before going still.

"No one touch the water!" Armand hollered into the crowd of fighting bodies. He and I made eye contact, breaking it to look at the body in the water as he grimaced. The body had turned black as the poison ran through it.

Still trying to reach Lilja, I looked around. Alieta grinned in my direction, her hair disheveled, her eyes wide as if she had thought of something. She surveyed the scene before her, before going to one of her fallen, snatching the arrow from their chest. Daveed smirked, handing her a bow he had grabbed from the massacre before him. Alieta's face was dark as she dipped the arrow into the water, pulling it back up to shoot.

My mind churned as my eyes landed on Lilja. They meant to shoot her. *Alieta can't.*

I ran toward her, not caring who I passed. *I had to reach her.*

"Lilja, move!" It was as if time had slowed. Alieta's arrow had already left the bow in her hand, flying forward. Lilja turned to look at me, without thinking, I grabbed her hand, pulling myself in front of her. *Thunk.*

The arrow had found its home, right between my breasts. "Elowen!" Lilja said. I stepped back, my body falling into hers. My eyes traveled up to Alieta's. *I can't believe you shot me,* I thought, meeting Alieta's wide eyes.

"Hold on. I got you. Just hold on!" Lilja's eyes were wild as they searched mine. The wall where the streams originated crumbled down.

"Alwyn, this way. You must hurry!" Pavati said, beckoning us to her. She stood in the new space created by the wall's collapse.

"Don't pull it out!" Lilja said as I ignored her, ripping the arrow out, the wound was black. *This was it,* my mind hazy. A whimper passed my lips, my veins turning darker as the poison crept up into the rest of my body, as if corrosive. My body clenched up, strung tight like a bowstring. I struggled to stand on my own, collapsing.

Lilja slung her arm under mine, and her other around my waist, practically dragging me toward the goddess. My vision darkened around the edges, my world hazy.

"RETREAT!" Lilja's voice boomed above the sounds of death. Kallan dropped the scrawny man he was strangling into the water.

Keres pulled her flames back in from the lady she was cooking alive. Cassia yanked the sword she'd sunk into the abdomen of a masked man. Armand kicked a man into another, his arm bloody.

We rushed to the broken wall, my eyes feeling heavy as Lilja pulled me over the rubble. As we passed the crumbled wall, it rebuilt itself like it had never been there.

My head lulled into Lilja's form. "She shot her. Please, Goddess, help her. I cannot lose her, too."

"Did you bring the ingredients, my young disciple?" She spoke only to me, ignoring the rest. Weakly, I nodded, fumbling for the blood vial in my bag.

"The ingredients! That's all you care about right now?! Elowen is dying, and you will heal her!" Kallan said as he staggered from shock.

"Alwyn knew what awaited her in this cave all along. Follow me. The rest can wait here." Protests filled the air as I handed over the vial. Lilja held up her hand, silencing them. She pulled me forward, following Pavati.

As we rounded the corner, crystal clear blue water glowed in a pond. It almost covered the entire room.

Pavati turned to us.

"This will work, young Alwyn. Are you willing to make the sacrifice?"

Pavati said I was to live; she promised. She has a plan. Fate is a fickle thing.

"Will it save Valdis?" I asked in a shaky breath, the pain almost becoming unbearable.

"No, Elle, don't! I can get Cassia to heal you enough so I can get Pelicia. We can figure something out! Please, don't leave me again! I can't be responsible for your death too, please," Lilja's voice cracked, unshed tears welled in her eyes.

"Yes, young Alwyn, it will, and more. It can be prosperous." Pavati reached out her slender fingers, smoothing my hair lovingly, almost like a mother would.

I coughed, black blood coming out with each hack. "You promise no special circumstances required?" My heart beat behind my eyes. I could feel it slowing. The blight was going to take me soon.

"Elle, no! We were supposed to have a lifetime together! A family! Little babies running around the castle! Late-night snuggles! Please, darling. Stay with me!" Lilja's tears ran freely down her face, her voice cracking as she spoke.

The ground rumbled. "They are breaking through the wall I created," Pavati grumbled.

"Sh-," I smiled weakly up at her, sweat running down into my eyes, making them burn even more. "Lilja, you'll find me in another lifetime, I know it. Valdis needs to succeed. I don't have exceptional abilities like everyone else. I'm dying. Let me do this, please. I want to do this." With all my strength, I squeezed her hand, pulling it up to my mouth, kissing it.

"I loved you from the moment I set eyes on you. Mabilia got this right. We were to be fated, together." My eyes rolled to the back of my head as I felt the world shift away, collapsing, Runen calling for me on the other side.

"Quick! While she is still alive! We have to do the spell! If she dies now, she will have died for nothing."

Lilja picked up my broken body, following Pavati into the water, the dragon claw she tied onto a string, set strung on her collarbone. The vial of Sylp's blood was tightly grasped in her hand. I gasped, the cool water coming into contact with my skin, my blackened blood swirling around us like the northern lights. The world faded away, the clashes of fighting quieting as if they moved farther away.

"Leave us, Queen of Valdis. She and I must finish the spell alone."

It's okay, I projected into her head, using the last of my strength. *I love you.*

Lilja's grip tightened, pulling my almost lifeless body into a kiss, before slipping me fully into the water.

Pavati murmured, her hands hovering over my floating body, the water glowing. Globs of water pulled up from the surface, becoming shining orbs of light. They hummed with life, like the souls Runen held when I first encountered him. Lilja stood silently, watching Pavati in silent sadness.

I love you too, Elle.

Pavati clasped onto the claw, yanking it off her neck, holding it up like a dagger. Before plunging it deep into my chest, I screamed as she plunged my body underneath the water. I watched as air bubbles flew out of my mouth and out to the surface. She pulled me up with a flick of her hand, without a touch. The water obeyed her will; her chants were louder now as she unscrewed the lid of the water nymph blood pouring it on top of the claw. *It has to be done; it has to be done. Valdis needs to survive; it needs to survive for her.*

My vision went in and out of focus as the green blood slid down the claw and into my wound. I coughed, blood splattering out of my mouth and into the water.

Goodbye, my sweet Lilja, let's meet again in my next life, I projected to her before slipping out of my body for the last time.

Goddess

I gave a small smile to the dark figure before me, Runen, the god of death. The mortal world seemed to melt away to blackness, stairs shone over us as if to mark the way to the afterlife. I took a deep breath, walking toward him, sadness still gripped my heart as if still alive. He held his hand out to me, motioning for me to turn around.

Confused, I slowly turned, the mortal world revealing itself to me. Rocks crumbled to dust around Lilja's crumpled form as her emotions overcame her control. I blinked, forcing myself to peek at my lifeless form in the water as Pavati chanted over it. The black blood that had flowed out of my body had turned bright blue in the water. It swirled before being separated by Pavati's magic. She stopped chanting, pulling the blood back to my wound, yanking the dragon claw out. She leaned down, kissing my body's forehead before exhaling into my mo uth.

Alarmed, I looked back at Runen. "It is not time for you to come with me, at least not yet, Elowen Alwyn. You still have much to accomplish. Next time we meet, it will be the last time." With a wave of his hand, darkness consumed me.

Pain. All I felt was pain. I sputtered, water dripping from my mouth. I coughed roughly, standing up in the waist-deep liquid. A blue finger went to my chest, their body invisible or nonexistent, I didn't know. *Pavati?* I closed my eyes tightly, half expecting more suffering. I felt a pull as I reopened them; the hand pulling away. Instead of blood coating its skin, only water dripped from its barely corporeal fingers.

Go, Miss. Alwyn. Listen to your instincts and save your friends and this world. Pavati's voice said in my head. Instinctually, my body moved to the first chamber. The fighting was still lively. Metal clashing against each other and the scent of blood filled the air. I looked around. Cassia held a piece of cloth over Keres's head. *She's dying.* Kallan stood off to the side, sending arrows into anyone close to Lilja. Armand clashed swords with an equally large man. Blood poured out of his side, and it soaked onto his trousers; he grunted as his strength had begun to leave him.

Leave him? How did I know?

Nobody had noticed my short form at the opening of the shrine.

Nobody had noticed as my hands moved as if on their own accord.

Nobody noticed the water until it was too late.

It forced itself from behind me, shoving itself to the Ardourians and Acolytes. The water encased itself around them, forcing itself down their throats, drowning them. The shouting stopped, and for a second, nobody registered what happened. Heads turned to me, their mouths agape. Lilja was the first to move.

"Elowen, is that you?" She grasped my face with her hands. Water rushed over her hands, splattering onto the ground.

She doesn't recognize me?

"How is this possible?" Lilja said, kissing my forehead.

"I have to— I have to get to the river. Please take me to the river." Confusion swept through me. *The river?* I felt a tug, my feet unwillingly walking toward the cave's opening. The dead grass marked the entrance to the cave as I stumbled to the water's edge. Liljas' tall form followed me, a barrage of questions flying from her mouth. Unable to answer, I stepped into the water. The dark water cleared almost immediately. My heart beat quicker and quicker with each step until I was in the middle of the river. The water was up to my breast. Instinctually, my hands hovered over it, like Pavati had taken over my body. Blue light shone from my palms, sending a cool ray to the water.

What was I doing? How was I doing this?

Once this water hits Valdis, the blight will be no more, Elowen. Once more, the water shall purify the land. Thank you for your sacrifice. Pavati's voice spoke in my head as the world swayed to darkness.

Lilja POV

My heart beat in my ears as I watched the form that was Elowen stumble out of the mouth of the cave. I went after her.

"What happened!?"

"I saw you die."

"Are you hurt?"

"What did Pavati do to you?"

The water from earlier dripped from my hands, the cuts sprinkling my skin, gone. The putrid smell of the poison wafted in the air as we neared the river flowing out toward my people, toward Valdis, my home.

She paused at the river for a breath, her blue body shimmering in and out of focus as if attempting to become translucent. Water dripped from her hair, the braid almost undone, wisps sticking out.

"Elowen, please, darling. Say something, and I'll help. I can help. Just tell me what's happening." The words flew from my mouth as she walked into the river.

I launched forward out of instinct, the urge to yank her back to the safety of the land. The poison will kill her.

My fingers all but brushed the side of her arm as she stepped in fully. The black water bloomed into a bright blue, and then to clear, clean liquid. Then she collapsed. I scrambled after her.

Elowen was translucent as she floated in the water.

Mud squelched under my shoes as I went after her. I pulled her to shore easily. She felt like my Elowen; she smelled like my Elowen, but she wasn't.

The earth seemed to stop turning as I gazed down at her. The sun rose for the new day, warming my skin. My cheeks were wet with water or tears or both, I didn't know.

Why was I so upset? The love of my life was alive.

"Hello, Queen of Valdis. I am happy to see you have made it through the endeavors alive. The Fates weren't sure if it would happen," Darach, the Goddess of the nymphs, said to me.

I refused to look up, to tear my eyes away from Elowen's beautiful face in my arms. The dead grass around us crunched as the person speaking approached. Their hand reached toward Elowen.

"Do. Not. Touch. Her," I warned, my voice sharp.

"Do not fear, Lilja, I couldn't hurt her now if I wanted to." She paused. "Well, not without great difficulty."

I turned my head up to stare at Darach. No longer did she don a green robe but a showy dress.

"What do you mean?" I asked, my eyes in slits.

She laughed, clapping her hands. Grass peaked out of the ground, and little buds popped up, begging to reveal the color of their petals.

"In time, all will be clear. The Fates have decided," Darach said as she blinked out of existence, a little tree in her place.

"What the fuck happened?" Kallan asked as he jogged to us.

"I don't know. Give me a report. Who remains? Where are Alieta and Daveed?" I said, returning my eyes to Elowen, memorizing the swirls on her face. The soft curve of her cheeks.

"All the Ardourians present are deceased, including Daveed. Alieta and her second are not among the dead. Armand is following her in the tunnels as we speak. I believe one other person is unaccounted for."

"And us?" I probed him again, my heart heavy as I thought of Aidan.

"We are all— the rest of us remain alive, your highness," Kallan said, his voice low, almost inaudible.

I winced at the title.

"Is Elowen?" The question hung in the air as if he was afraid to voice the fears harboring in his soul. A feeling I knew all too well.

I shook my head, finally looking up at my old friend. "It is time, Kal. Time to return home."

Elowen POV

Birds chirped somewhere in the distance, and leaves rustled together. Calmness washed through the room as I opened my eyes. The room was circular. A small window streamed in rays of the sunlight. The light seemed to bathe on an oversized chair by my bed, where Lilja sat asleep, and small snores came from her mouth. Her black hair was long again, brushing the top of her shoulders, and her hand was on her chin as she held up her face with her arm on the armrest.

I sat up, waiting for the pain of the last days to hit me. I ran my hand through my hair, gasping as I gazed at the hand moving closer to my face. It took me a moment to register that it was mine. My finger tips were blue, my skin paler than normal. The color streaked up my hand and onto my arm.

"Elle, it is so good to see you awake," Lilja's tired voice said from beside me. Dark circles bore themselves in her face.

"What happened to me?" I croaked, my voice hoarse.

"You sacrificed yourself. You wanted to leave me." Her voice cracked, her eyes brimming with tears as she clenched her hands. Her face hardened before getting up and walking out. The door slammed shut behind her as her footsteps retreated down the hall.

"This is my kingdom, my responsibility. MY mess, I shouldn't have let you do it." Her voice echoed as she got farther down the hallway.

I did this for us. I wanted Valdis to survive. I swung my legs off the bed, standing up, my body swaying as I did so. My hands were on the small bed frame as I teetered toward the large mirror. With my body in full view of the mirror, I gazed at someone I didn't recognize. My body had gone back to my beautiful, large self, as if I had never lost weight.

The rest of me was unrecognizable. My skin had paled. Blue swirls ran themselves up and down my exposed arms, my eyes were a milky white, hiding my original color. I pulled the nightgown covering me up and off, exposing myself to the mirror. All the blue lines connected to the space between my breasts, where Pavati stabbed me.

The vision passed over my eyes, as if I were omniscient. Everything that happened washed over me. I swayed with the energy, and tears ran down my cheeks as I sobbed. So much pain in the vision, so much death. *Aidan.* Water pooled beneath me in a puddle.

"Elowen," Cassia said as she entered the room. She ran toward me, instantly lifting me and putting me back on the bed.

"What happened? Did you fall? Did you get dizzy?" My friend's mouth moved a mile a minute, firing off questions faster than I could answer. The last thing I remember was her cool hands palming my face, searching for a temperature.

Voices sounded off in the room as I opened my eyes again. My chest ached as they fought around me.

"What do you mean, she is the Goddess of Rivers now? She's a human," Lilja said across the room, her shoulders tense, arms crossed as she stood next to the bed I lay in.

"She made the sacrifice. The Fates wrote about this time, long ago," Leland said, sitting on the other end of the room, rocking in the rocking chair.

"Elowen didn't know she would become the Goddess when she made the sacrifice," Cassia explained as she poured tea, her hands shaking.

"Regardless of whether Elowen knew what Pavati was asking, it has happened. The Fates knew since before she set foot in the Elven Realm. Why do you think Darach could speak to her even when she was in the human realm? The dreams? The Fates have decided. Elowen shall be and is the next Goddess of Rivers."

THE END